WRONG LOCKER

MALLORY GRANT

WRONG LOCKER

MALLORY GRANT

For those who feel like no one sees you. For those who feel like no one hears you. I see you. I hear you. You're not alone.

Content Warnings

This book contains scenes with child abuse, domestic violence, mild language, a parent with mental illness, mention of attempt of suicide scars, and homophobic slurs.

Playlist

Better- SYML
I'm sorry- Camylio
Blue (Feat. Alex Hope)- Troye Sivan
Who we love- Sam Smith & Ed
Sheeran
Song of the Sparrow- SayWeCanFly
If I have you- SayWeCanFly
Kissin' when we're mad- We Three
Sara- We Three
Dandelion Necklace- SayWeCanFly

Sometimes, it's the little things in life that mean the most to us. To feel the breeze against our hair, to breathe in the air, and to have the ability to breathe again... and again. To be the calm in the middle of the raging storm. I never thought I'd ever have the chance to find my calm. My storm had been nothing but the violent shakes of metal on rooftops, the slammed trash lid as it flapped back and forth in the wind. The loud ring of the wind chime bells as they slapped into each other violently during a loud storm.

Cars lifted and beeped as they rolled around in the sky, sucked into the vortex of wind as they tumbled around like a leaf in a breeze. The crash of metal against the ground, buildings shattered into rubble, and the countless cries of those who were unhappy. The storm inside me was dark and enveloped me like a blanket. It suffocated me, drowned me, pulled me under. Then you came. You held out your hand, like a lifeline, and when I touched you, everything faded away, the calm. Once I found you, I realized I was already lost, like a blind man who wanted to take one more breath, then one more. Until all I could do was touch you, cling to you, desperate for one last breath, one last quiet, one last calm.

And to think, all of this started because of a single letter... and the wrong locker.

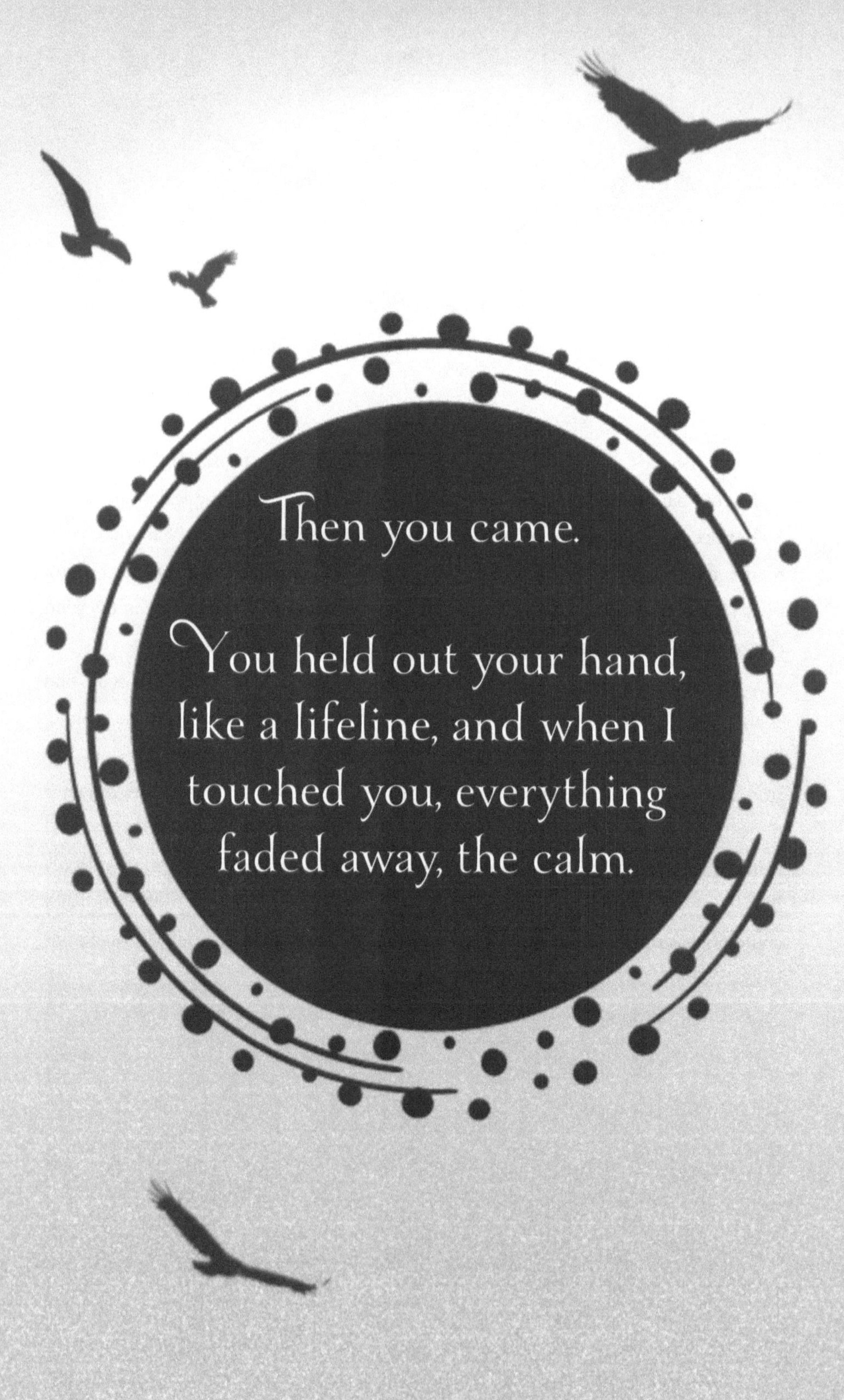
Then you came.

You held out your hand,
like a lifeline, and when I
touched you, everything
faded away, the calm.

Chapter 1
Kinsley

As I sat in the classroom, desperately trying to pay attention to the lecture, I couldn't help but wonder if my teacher's voice was secretly a lullaby designed to put us all to sleep. My teacher's name was Mr. Duckett, and he was one of those teachers who were way too young to be a teacher. Sure, he was old enough, of course. Had his degrees, whatever he needed, but his personality? Well, he had the personality of a teenager.

"Rebecca! This isn't a beauty parlor, put your makeup away and pay attention. Do you even know what class this is?" he asked as he walked over toward the girl and pressed his hand against her desk. I noticed with a chuckle that she had the wrong textbook out and it was upside down and covered in different variations of makeup vials and powders.

Rebecca was one of the cheerleaders and showed it proudly by being one of those girls to constantly wear their uniforms every day all day long. As if we would forget she's popular if she were to wear the same regular clothes as everyone else. "English class, of course," she said, splaying her hand out to indicate the textbook underneath her flood of products.

He snorted with a shake of his head at her as he pointed at the board, which held different mathematical equations. "Maybe all those products are getting to you. Let's leave the chemicals out of the classroom," he said as most of the class gave a halfhearted chuckle. She was popular, so they didn't try too hard to laugh at her misery, but if it was someone like me who was getting cracked on, they'd probably be rolling out of their seats and dying on the ground. Rebecca ignored Mr. Duckett and continued to paint her nails while he went to the board and resumed talking. I continued to stare at the clock, wishing it would go faster so I could be out of here. I never really was one for math class. It was easy enough that I could get about a C without really trying and that was good enough for me.

A little rectangle-shaped paper popped onto my desk, and I turned towards the sender, quirking my eyebrow at her in surprise. My best friend -my only friend actually- Isabella looked at me with an impatient glance, her brown eyes already growing frustrated as it took me longer than a second to pick up her note. I sighed, already knowing what it was about and dreading it, but still opened it anyway. Of course, it was covered in the recent picture she'd been messing with. Isabella was a tagger. Her artistic nature was what drew us together at the start of high school.

That, and the newness of it all. I had not been popular in middle school, but I had a few friends here and there. That was until I accidentally hurt Roan, and everyone turned on me. So, when high school started, I was sure I'd continue having no friends until Isabella transferred in. She was new, about three days after the school year started, but it was still noticeable. We lived in a fairly small town, and most if not all of us tended to go to the same schools from kindergarten through high school. Maybe even onto the same old community college, unless some were brave enough to try and go somewhere out of state or a few towns over to Oklahoma Baptist University.

Not only that, but the fact that Isabella stood out. Our town was pretty much nothing but white, overly religious country hicks. When a pretty Latina girl popped out of nowhere, everyone seemed to notice. Stupidly enough, instead of wanting to get to know her, everyone avoided her. She sat close to me during lunch, and no one wanted to sit next to me, leaving the table wide open. I was drawing, I remember that. I always drew when I had free time. She scooted next to me, shoved her sketchbook into my lap, and from the start of lunch to the end of it we were best friends.

Although I was that loser kid who got bullied by the basketball captain and his lackeys, no one ever messed with Isabella. There was just an aura around her that screamed *'Mess with me and I'll fuck you up,'* and no one even tried to deal with that. They might whisper rumors about us dating or something under their breath, but they mostly left her alone. Being bullied was strictly my thing, apparently.

Isabella made an annoyed sound with the back of her throat as she tapped her short nails on her desk, trying to get my attention. I chuckled under my breath, sitting up enough to look down at my desk, and slowly slid down my hood so I could see the note. I would have taken longer just to aggravate her, but I knew from experience she'd start throwing stuff at me and I didn't feel like getting detention again. The last time I pissed her off, she threw her textbook at me and I dodged it.

The textbook smacked into one of the wrestling team jocks, I couldn't care enough to try to remember's name, and he punched me. He had thought I was the one who threw it. All three of us ended up in detention. That resulted in me getting beat up even more, and it wasn't really something I strived to repeat. I smoothed down the sides of the paper and read the words I already knew were going to be sitting there. *'Tonight, at seven, meet me at our spot.'* The note read.

I frowned, slid my hand into my hood, and pulled it all the way down as I scratched the back of my neck. I shook out my hair, and my blond hair fell into my eyes as I pulled my hood back up and wrote out my reply. *'I can't. Mom and Dad want to talk to me.'* I said to her, before simply handing the piece of paper back without caring to fold it.

Mr. Duckett didn't really care about notes. He wasn't the type of teacher to flip out about it or make us stand and read it out loud. As long as we weren't getting an F in the class and we didn't start getting loud and giggling loudly over whatever was being talked about like some of the cheerleaders did, then he couldn't care less. For example, right now he was showing a math equation to Rebecca by using her makeup vials. Not giving two fucks that she never listened to him, he was instead moving them around on her desk to show her how items could help with math.

Absently she was painting his nails and he wasn't even flinching, mostly telling her she could have picked a different shade. While the girls in the class started to discuss which shade would match his eyes better, Isabella once more flicked the little triangle towards me. I gave her an annoyed look while I once more unfolded it gently, making sure I didn't rip it. So freaking dramatic for nothing. *'Is it about what I think it's about?'* She asked.

I looked up with a sigh at the front of the class and watched as the girls in the top row had sat Mr. Duckett down in a chair and stood around him, subjecting him to a makeup lesson. The guys in the class were getting up and forming their groups of friends. Clearly, the class was finished despite still having a good ten minutes or so left. Without a word, I scooted my desk up against hers since she sat next to me, and placed my elbow on my desk, pressing my cheek into the palm of my hand. She leaned close to me since neither of us was close to anyone in this school and didn't want them to know about our lives, and ignoring the stupid whistles of the guys closest to us, I nodded at her. "They kept pressuring me, bringing it up over and over again," I whispered to her, watching her face frown in annoyance.

"*Estúpido,*" She breathed out, rolling her eyes. I snorted, knowing enough of her Spanish from being her best friend for the past three years to know that meant stupid.

She knew I didn't care much for my parents, and honestly, she probably hated them more than I did. "Why are they so adamant?" she asked, her brown eyes staring into mine.

I moved some of her dark brown hair streaked with purple highlights out of her eyes, earning us another whistle. I wanted to throw something at them, but I was still recovering from Roan slamming me into the locker this morning. For people who didn't like me, they were always watching me. Though those two were friends with Roan, so it made sense, I suppose.

"Kennedy got a boyfriend," I said, talking about my little sister. She was in seventh grade this year, being quite a few years younger than me, and started her seventh-grade debut by getting a boyfriend right at the beginning. My parents, being the crazy people they are, started to give me crap about it. They wondered why I was sixteen, almost seventeen, and I'd never had a girlfriend before. I told Isabella this, and she snorted, throwing her hands up in the air and disturbing one of her recent sketches.

I grabbed it before it could fall to the ground, looking down at it with a cocked eyebrow, noticing she was trying something new. Still her same style, but this time it was of a little girl when before she'd been drawing older women. Isabella spent all her time drawing, and after school, she'd go home and make a stencil. It normally took her a few days to a week to make a stencil, and then she'd have me sneak out with her at night to find a new place to tag. I didn't do that stuff, I just drew to draw, but I still went with her.

It was kind of fun, and sometimes I did help her spray the background and stuff to make it go faster, but it never really was my type of thing. Isabella didn't even seem to care as I leaned over and slipped her paper into her sketchbook, making sure it wouldn't fall again, while she started to chant things in Spanish that sounded roughly like cuss words. Her hands were moving fast as they usually did when she was angry. A few people stared at her like she was crazy, but no one really knew Spanish, so it didn't matter to them.

Honestly, I probably should have known some by now, since we've been best friends for three years and her mother rarely spoke in English. It just didn't seem like an interest to me. It was already hard enough knowing two languages, since my mother's family is Italian and she spoke it quite often, so I never really had the overwhelming need to learn a third language.

Finally, Isabella settled down, though I could see by the anger burning in her eyes she was far from calm. Her eyes flickered over me, and I already knew what she was looking at. I had a lean, slightly muscular frame that I kept mostly hidden under the overly big black hoodie I wore constantly. I wasn't very tall, most likely because I was half Italian, and I was only about five foot eight, while most of the guys here were a lot taller, hitting over six feet tall easily.

My skin was permanently tanned with an olive tint, my mom's genes were strong, but my hair was light blond like my father's. I had a light scattering of freckles that dusted my cheeks and my nose, and it made me look younger than I really was. My wide light blue eyes didn't really help either. I was often called a freshman by those who didn't really know me, and I had gotten used to it by now.

I bit my lips, self-conscious of how full they were. One of those annoying things about me was that they were darker, making it look like I constantly wore lip gloss or something. A pretty boy. Isabella often called me Pretty Boy, or she'd call me her little pretty boy. "Are you even straight?" she asked, making me snort. I looked down at my hands. One was clenching the desk tightly, while the other was absently clicking the back of the mechanical pencil repeatedly, the dull click echoing loudly around me as my leg bounced up and down in agitation over her question.

It was a question I had been thinking about for a while now, back when Isabella first became my friend. She was gorgeous, and seriously smart, with one of the best grades in our year. Having a single mom, Isabella wanted to do her best constantly and always made sure to please her mom, even though she had an extracurricular activity her mother would never approve of if she found out. She had the right curves, and she wasn't dressed like a Barbie doll who wanted to show off every bit of her body in a cry for attention. She tended to wear skirts or shorts with tights underneath. I didn't think I had ever seen her wear less than two studded belts on her hips, no matter what outfit she had on.

Her shirts were always filled with band names, and she wore a camo jacket that was fraying at the sleeves, which belonged to her father. He had died during a camping trip when she was six years old. She and her parents were camping, and someone close by was hunting illegally. They were too close to the camping grounds and a bullet missed a deer and hit her father instead. Isabella was beautiful, confident, and amazing, and I had no idea why I wasn't attracted to her. But... I wasn't. "I don't know," I replied with a shrug. "Probably?"

"Well, it's an easy question. Do you like pee-pee's, or vaja-ja's?" she crudely asked, making me snort as I pressed my face against the palm of my hand to hide my face. She had no chill sometimes, I swear.

I turned back to look at her and shrugged again. "Not sure. Haven't found someone I've been attracted to yet. But I don't think gender matters to me. Girls are beautiful. Guys are beautiful. Whichever. I guess it really depends on who they are, probably." I said, sighing.

Isabella nodded in understanding. "Sounds pansexual to me, to be honest. Or maybe demisexual."

"I don't really care enough to figure it out. I don't want to feel pressured to label myself." I admitted. It had been hard for me the past three years, trying to figure it out. Finally, I just stopped caring. "It's less stressful to try and figure it out. Eventually, I'll love someone. And that's okay. Well, it's okay for me, that is. But my parents..." I trailed off with my hands splayed to show my predicament.

Well, it was more than them. I wasn't going to admit it out loud, but I was curious too. What did it feel like to fall in love? To be loved? I was romantic at heart. I read more love stories than I cared to admit when I wasn't drawing. "We have to figure out what to do. They know by now that you and I aren't going to get together, but, I don't know. Just look around. Stare at the girls and try to find someone you think your parents will like. Look, there are a few girls on the swim team over there, and there's one on the volleyball team." Isabella said, pointing at three girls.

I sighed, nodding. It wasn't hard to know the kind of girls my parents wanted me with. My parents were high school sweethearts. My dad was the champion of the football team, and if it hadn't been for his shoulder injury, he'd have gone pro. My mom was a cheerleader, and they met during the championships. She was from another state, but they fell in love despite that and when they got married, she moved here to be with him. Dad's family was always well-off, our family owned a few chain sports stores here and mom found a job in real estate, making us one of the richest families in town. They forced me to take up sports growing up, putting me in different ones constantly, trying to find one that I liked. That's how I ended up hurting Roan.

By the time I was in middle school, it was fairly known that I was unhappy with sports, uncoordinated, and clumsy. Basketball seemed to be easier for me for some reason and I took to it for a little bit. My parents were over the moon about it, and my little sister loved the sport too, so she loved me. Well, for a little while, that is. Roan's father was our coach in middle school and still is the coach over there. Roan hated me with a passion from the first day, probably because we both played point guard. His father gave me the position over him since he was better as a shooting guard than I was.

Roan was already picking on me, shoving me around, calling me shortie, and he made me anxious. During a big game, I tripped on air, literally. There was nothing there but air. I tripped at the last second and Roan fell over me, his knee slamming into the ground, and I swear everyone in the building could hear the loud crack of his bone. He was forced to sit out for the rest of middle school. So, he became my personal bully, even though he healed perfectly and is now the current captain of our high school team. This is the part where my sister hates me now. Roan's dad held a grudge and refused to let my sister on the middle school team because of me.

My parents were forced to drive her to the next town over for a different basketball team. They often stayed away for a weekend so she could play with the team. After middle school, I refused to play sports anymore and my parents fell away from me, not having anything in common with me. It was frustrating, and the tension was so thick whenever we were all together at home that I could barely breathe.

I stared at the three girls Isabella mentioned with a sigh. Well, they weren't attacking Mr. Duckett with makeup, so they weren't the same as the cheerleaders. Honestly, I would have rather been with someone in the art club. However, since it only consisted of: Isabella, me, and a couple of freshmen that mostly went to hang out in the back of the classroom and smoke, that wasn't going to happen. If it was my choice, there was no way in Hell I'd ever date a jock. The fact that my parents wanted it made me hate the idea of it even more. But... I sighed. If I could do something to get my parents off my back, I'd try it. I just had to figure out which one.

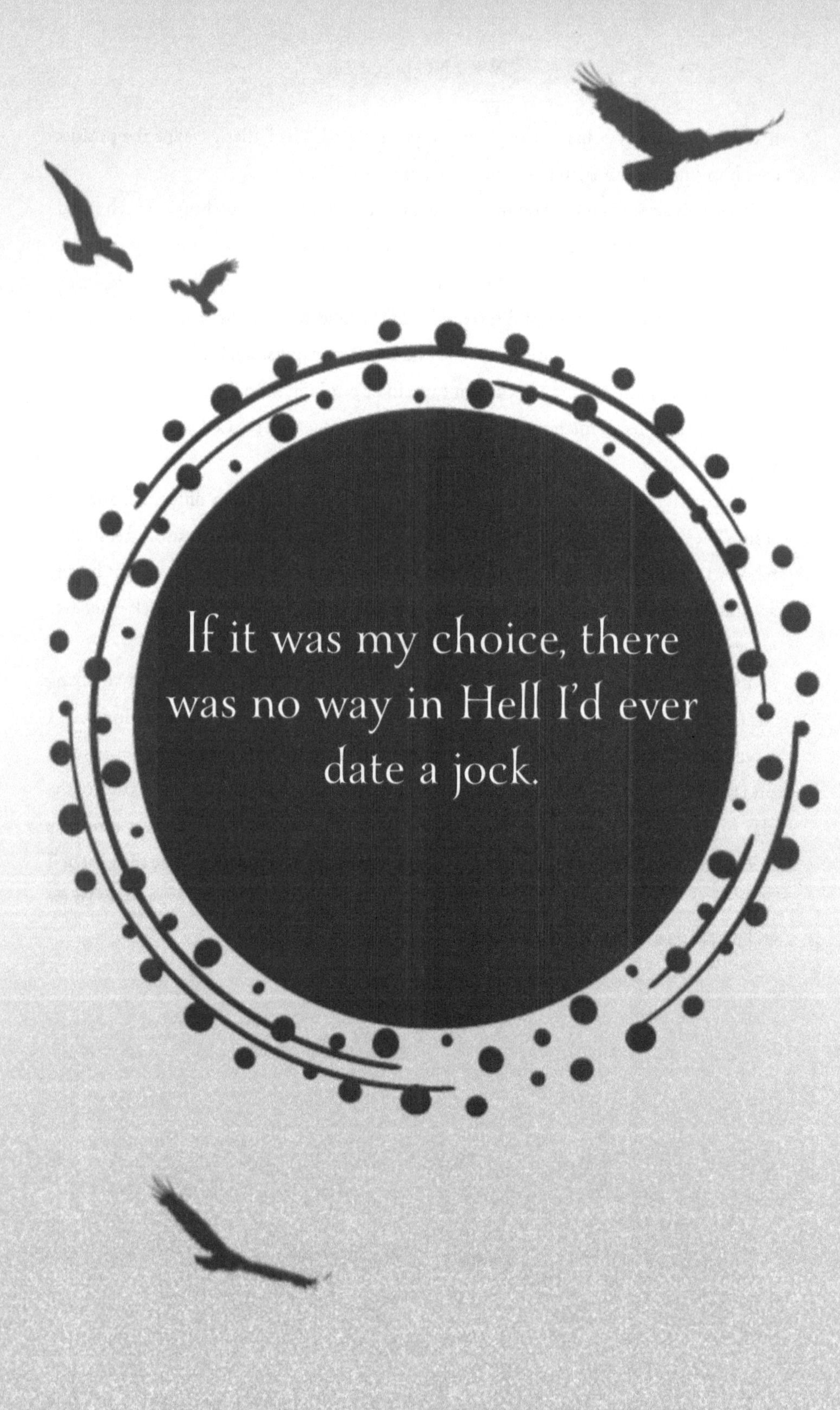
If it was my choice, there
was no way in Hell I'd ever
date a jock.

Chapter 2
Kinsley

"So?" Isabella asked. I didn't say anything, pretending I didn't hear her. We only had three classes together, but now that school was over, we were sitting in the art room. Every class I had with her she'd been posturing me, pointing out new sporty girls to ask out. A few of them she knew from classes she had with them, and a few she'd done group projects with. I was subjected all day to annoyingly being forced to open her tiny intricately folded little triangle papers, or listen to her constantly whispered facts about girls in my head.

Honestly, it was stressful. I didn't even remember which girl the facts went to, and by now they were all buzzing around my head, overlapping each other. I wanted a break from it all, so when the bell rang, I practically sprinted there. My haven, my favorite place in the school. The art club was placed inside a classroom that had been abandoned. When I was still in middle school, there was a lab accident that made horribly smelly green goo splatter all over the classroom. No matter how much they scrubbed at it, it wasn't possible to get it all out.

The kids complained about the smell constantly, and the teacher had asthma and was constantly coughing. They ended up leaving the classroom alone, saying they'd clean it again later, and then forgetting about it. It didn't smell bad to Isabella and me, and the random freshmen that floated in earlier this year and just ended up staying didn't seem to care either. Not that they seemed to care about anything. They were always high within a matter of minutes. Isabella had to stop one of them from trying to jump out the window once, announcing he wanted to see if he could fly.

It was on the third floor of the building, overlooking the football field. Even then, as I pretended like my music was on, I glanced out the window and watched the coach yell profanities at one of the players while the others stood there waiting for more commands. Isabella yanked one of my earphones out of my ear and stomped on my foot, making me wince. She was so dangerous sometimes. "I feel sorry for your future boyfriend or girlfriend," I muttered, rolling my eyes at her.

She snorted but moved her hands in a *'come on'* motion, which made me sigh. "I don't know, Izzy. Honestly, if I wanted to date any of them, wouldn't I have been interested in them before now? Maybe I just don't like high school girls. Maybe I need to go to the community college and find someone,"

The look she gave me was a mixture of horror and annoyance. "Like your strict, religious parents are going to be fine with their sixteen-year-old son dating a twenty-year-old or older woman?" She asked, throwing her hands up in the air. The group of freshmen in the back lifted their hands and cheered, their eyes already bloodshot as they cheered for me to get with my imaginary girlfriend.

After a chorus of: *'You the man, bro!'* and *'Damn, son, getting some older woman fun time,'* Isabella lifted her shoe, turning to look at them all and silencing every one of them with a glare. She huffed, sliding her shoe back onto her foot before flipping her hair over her shoulder and glaring at me. "Seriously, Kinsley. Don't make me throw you out the window."

I groaned, pressing my forehead onto the desk before lifting my head to look at her. She snorted, pointing out how I got the black lead on my forehead from my drawing. I didn't care, it was nothing new. I always had black smudges on my cheeks, and the bottom of my hands were always coated to the point I had to rub them with alcohol pads to get the lead off.

I looked up at the clock on the wall. It had a crack down the middle of it, and the time was three hours off, but it was still ticking away. Honestly, I was narrowing down my pick between the three girls she earlier pointed out in our math class. There was Peyton and Abby, the two on the swim team, and there was Allison from the volleyball team. I had seen Allison making out with a guy before the bell rang earlier so she was a no-go, but the other two were pretty calm. Actually, now that I remember, I think Peyton had a project with me when I was a freshman and she wasn't completely awful. "Maybe Peyton, I guess,"

I could remember how she always made a mess with her blond hair, pulling it up into a messy bun and complaining about how the strands hung in her eyes. I told her to cut it then and she stared at me like I was an alien. But she did participate, after all, so I guess that counts as her being a decent person. Usually, when I was paired up with someone, they tended to make me do everything so they didn't have to talk to me. "Oh! She's that pretty blond-haired one, right? I don't think she's seeing anyone. Why her? Are you attracted to her?" She asked, her brown eyes staring into mine.

I snorted, turning towards the window as the football players smacked into each other. I had no idea who was which number, but it didn't matter anyway. I never cared about football. I could see the basketball courts from here too and smirked as Roan missed the shot and kicked someone close by even though it wasn't their fault he missed. There were a few girls on the track team racing around the football field and I watched the coach pull off one of the players' helmets and fling it at another player, yelling at them to stop watching the girls run.

I shrugged, turning back to Isabella and her questioning gaze. "I guess she's pretty. I don't feel attracted to her or love or anything, but those things came when you got to know them, right? That's why people date first before anything else," I told her. It wasn't always true. As logical as it was, guys would walk up and down the halls as they talked about some party they had last weekend and the number of girls they banged in one night. It was like I was watching STDs walk down the hall. I was different from all of them, and honestly, I wasn't really bothered by it. Maybe other guys would be freaked out that they were almost seventeen and still a virgin but I didn't really care. It would happen eventually.

Isabella looked at me, lifting her finger and flicking me on the forehead. I groaned, rubbing my forehead and glaring at her as tears sprang unwillingly to my eyes from the sudden pain. "What are you, an old man? Were you my long-lost grandpa? Grandpa Kinsley," she said, earning a chorus of laughs from the group of freshmen behind us. One of them fell out of his chair and lay on his back looking up at his hand with wide eyes, informing his friends he had found all of his fingers. "You know people have sex nowadays without really caring who it's with, right? I mean, I don't. But I'm not a guy," she said with a half-hearted shrug.

I glared at her, shaking my head as I put both my headphones back in. "Not all guys are the same, Izzy," I told her. She didn't used to be so bad about guys. The reason she and her mother moved here was because of her mother's boyfriend. He was fairly nice, and respectable, but his son wasn't. Isabella had a pretty big crush on him, and when they slept together, he moved out, telling his father he wanted to live with his mother instead. Isabella was crushed, and then her mother ended up breaking up with the guy anyway so she never saw him again.

I saw him once when I was forced to go with my family to my sister's basketball tournament and he had two girls under each arm giggling and kissing his cheeks without a care. Once Isabella found out, she practically hated all guys. I think she only liked me because I was already her friend before all of this happened. Well, that, and the fact that I walked right up to the asshole and punched him in the face. I got my ass kicked but it was worth it to see how happy it made Izzy knowing I stood up for her. "What about your crush?" I asked her, making her roll her eyes.

"I don't have a crush on them," she said, knowing instantly who I was talking about. Over the past year, Isabella had a competition. Everywhere she tagged, within the week someone else either copied over her work or put something beside it. When Isabella drew a girl, the other tagger drew another girl kissing her girl, and it infuriated Izzy to have her work messed with like that. All taggers had a signature, and the person Izzy was currently fighting with used an S as their signature. Even Izzy's old things were getting attacked and Isabella was constantly trying to fix it. "Don't even talk about that asshole," she said in a clipped tone.

I snickered at her, but before I could say anything the window was opened wider than we normally opened it and we groaned as we grabbed at our papers that were scattered everywhere. "Aw, dammit guys!" I yelled as the drawing I was working on flew out the window. I groaned as it landed near the bench with the football guys' equipment on it, banging my head on the window. I mean, it's not like I couldn't redraw it, it just sucked because I was really liking that picture.

I had been drawing the football players lined up in position on the field, the goalpost in the back, and even the girls running in the distance. I was hoping if I gave it to the coach as a present, he'd stop trying to get me to play basketball during gym class. Every time I played, they tried to get me to join the team and I didn't want to be even more under Roan's radar than I already was. I turned my head in time to see one of the freshmen try to climb out the window. "Really? I thought we realized last week we couldn't fly?" I groaned as I hauled one of them back into the classroom.

He laughed as Isabella helped me pull him back inside. She was muttering something about hammering the windows closed when the guy flopped down on the ground and grinned at me. "I wanted to get some of that cotton candy," he said, pointing at the cloud. I snorted, shaking my head as I dug my hand into my pocket and pulled out a few twenties.

"Go get some food, normal food," I said to him, shoving the money in his hand. He looked at it with wide eyes before getting up and shoving one of his friends towards the door, whooping about how money flew out of the sky to land in his hand.

We stared in wonder as they raced out the door, both of us turning to look at each other before laughing. "I bet that *pendejo* thinks the money came from God," Isabella said, making me snort out another laugh. We cracked the windows but only a little bit, just enough to try and get rid of the smell the group left behind. Isabella and I had never really smoked. Her mother wasn't as religious as my parents but she would beat her ass if she found out she was smoking. Well, she'd probably beat my ass too if I was to be honest.

Her mother was as much hers as she was mine at this point, and more than once I'd felt the sting of her sandal on the back of my head. I looked out the window, watching with a frown as one of the football players grabbed my picture and stared at it, before looking up at the school. I couldn't see who it was through his helmet. They couldn't see me from up here, right? After a few minutes, the coach blew the whistle and the player folded my drawing and slid it into one of the bags, before running back out to the field. Strange, but whatever. He folded it, I didn't want it back now.

I groaned, walked back to the table, and started a new drawing. "You really think if I draw something for the coach, he'll stop hounding me?" I asked, staring at the field once more. The coach had a red face as he yelled at one of the players, throwing the football at him as he threw his hands up in the air. The one he was yelling at looked pretty short, so it was probably a freshman.

Isabella was humming, but she only had one of her headphones in, so I knew she heard me. It made me remember I hadn't pressed play yet. I pulled out one of my headphones and hit play. As the melody of *Song of the Sparrow* by SayWeCanFly, my favorite band, played softly over the headphones, she replied to me. "Of course. I drew him a picture of a uterus exploding with blood and told him this is how it feels like when he tries to make us play when we're on our periods. He hasn't given me or any of the other girls who sit out crap ever again."

I stared at her, my mouth hanging open as my pencil hovered over the paper, not sure if I should laugh or freak out. "Did you... I mean... how detailed was it?" I asked, choking out a laugh.

She looked at me as if she wasn't entirely sure why I was laughing. "Of course, it was the same type of model they put on the walls, but I did add skin. And hair, and lips. Well damn, I guess I drew a vagina, but maybe this way he'll know how to find one," she said with a shrug.

I pressed my head down on the paper once more, my shoulders shaking as I laughed out loud at her. I lifted my head as I laughed, wiping at the tears in my eyes and she had the audacity to stare at me like she had no idea why I was laughing.

"Did you," I stuttered out, taking a deep breath, my finger up in the air as if telling her to give me a second as I tried to calm myself. "Did you ask him if he found it?" I asked, snorting out another laugh as she smirked at me.

She threw her hands up in the air, and let out a sentence in Spanish that I couldn't even begin to translate, before shaking her head at me. "Of course not. Besides, he's terrified of me now. Won't look me in the eyes and will pretty much tell other people to tell me what to do instead of telling me himself," I could understand why. He was probably traumatized. We sat there drawing for a little while longer. I gave up on the notion of drawing a picture for the coach, I didn't think Isabella realized that it wasn't the act of giving the drawing that made the coach happy, but the fact that she scared the shit out of him instead.

He probably went home and cried after that, the poor man. This time I drew the scenery. From there I could just see the Quachita mountains in the distance and I chose that to focus on. The way the mountains rose and dipped, the trees scattered over them, and the stratus clouds sitting above the mountains. In a way, it was like the back of a camel lifting and dipping down, before lifting and dipping down once more. I was just putting in a few birds when Isabella tapped her finger three times on the corner of my paper to get my attention. She waited, knowing I wanted to finish the bird I was drawing.

We were both artists, and we understood how annoying it was to bother each other when we were drawing. So we simply tapped and waited, even if we had to wait for a few hours until we looked at the other. When you were making art, concentration was the key. Finally, after about five minutes, I lifted my eyes to hers, pulling one headphone out of my ear. I could still hear the drums going off in the song I was listening to, but it was muted as I placed it on the table. "Don't you have to be at your house today?" she asked, pointing to the broken clock.

I groaned, rubbing my face with my hand as I turned off my music. Normally, my parents didn't notice or even care when I didn't show up. They forced me to have family dinner with them every Sunday, but usually throughout the week, everyone was too busy to care. But of course, no work on Sunday, the holy day, so everyone was expected to be home and there for dinner. The rest of the week Kennedy was always out with friends after practice. Half of the time, since she had to go to another school's team, she ended up staying with the girl whose mother drove her back and forth for a few days.

I barely even saw Kennedy anymore, and I wasn't really all that upset about it. As for my parents, they never really came home either. Unless they were dealing with Kennedy, they were at the main office of Dad's shops. Mom has her own office there for her real estate and worked out of that, while Dad worked on his own company pretty much beside her. They said it was so they could stay close to each other despite always being so busy, and that was fine with me. It meant I could stay out as late as I wanted and do whatever I wanted, as long as it wasn't anything illegal. Well, as long as I wasn't caught doing anything illegal. Isabella and I were almost caught a few times, but we always seemed to run away in time.

She snorted at me as I put my drawing into my portfolio, put my pencils in their case, and slipped it all into my backpack. Isabella was the one who talked me into making a portfolio, even though it was pointless. Dad already had my future set for me. Go to college, get a business degree, and inherit his stupid sports shops. *It runs in the family, Kinsley,* 'he'd always say. "Unfortunately, you're right," I grumbled, standing up. She was already packed up as well, closing the windows. Our club had a teacher as all the clubs did, but our teacher didn't want to come into the room saying it smelled bad, so we were usually always by ourselves and cleaned up everything by ourselves when we were finished. Here and there, a new student came, but then they realized it was just us and no actual club activities and left. Unless they smoked, then they stayed with the freshmen. There were about five of them now. "Are you coming with me?" I asked hopefully.

She snorted as she shook her head no. "I'm not walking in there with your family all there again. The last time they called me the devil's daughter for my hair. Did I tell you they called Mami? She laughed at them and hung up." I smirked but didn't say anything. I knew about that. They gave me a lecture about hanging out with a bad influence. Then a few days later, they seemed to forget all about it and told me to have fun with my friend at school. They really had so little care for me. "But Mom is working a double shift again, so you can give me a ride," she said, blinking her eyes at me.

I nodded, not really caring. Our town wasn't the poorest town there was, but it wasn't the richest either. I was one of the few juniors to have a car. Honestly, I was just glad

Roan had one because he'd probably destroy my car in his jealousy if he didn't. Mostly the seniors had cars, and they tended to look like their parents' hand-me-downs that were all broken and rusted. My parents' having money was pretty common, and even though they couldn't bother to really care about me, they still wanted to make sure their image was intact. So of course, I had a car. The moment we walked out of the stairwell onto the first floor, I was shoved into a locker. I groaned, shaking my hair out of my eyes as Roan muttered, "Move it loser," at me.

I looked up at him, frowning. He was just as tall as always, and his giant muscular form didn't help me much either. I'd think of him as one of the beautiful people if he wasn't such an asshole. He had his head shaved though and that wasn't really attractive to me. Everyone has an acquired taste, after all. Isabella was mumbling curses at him in Spanish as I stood, wiping my hands down my pants to straighten them. I wrapped my arm over Isabella's shoulder and started to walk her out the door. "Come on, let's get out of here," I mumbled, stopping her rants. She nodded, her eyes dancing dangerously down the hall to burn into Roan's back before she allowed me to pull her out the door.

"Maybe Peyton, I guess,"

Chapter 3
Kinsley

I walked into my house, shut the door behind me, and sighed in frustration. I didn't want to do this. I didn't want to deal with them all two days a week. Once a week was more than enough for me. I could smell the exquisite smell of dinner being cooked and frowned. Yeah, that was weird. Why was I annoyed to smell home-cooked meals? But for someone like me, it wasn't ever a good sign. A home-cooked meal meant the cook was here. She only ever came once a week to make our Sunday meals, but they took the time to have her come an extra day just for tonight. Don't get me wrong, it's not that I hated her cooking, I loved it. I didn't love what it meant. It meant I was going to be forced to sit there with my family.

"Kinsley! Is that you?" Mom called out from the living room. I rolled my eyes, biting my tongue to hold back the retort I had poised and ready to go, and walked into the living room. She gave me a once over, a frown on her face as she stared at me. "Honestly, I wouldn't even be able to tell under that ridiculous black hoodie. The hood is up, you could be a gangster for all I know," She said, holding her hand to the front of her chest dramatically. I stared at her, studying her. She had her hair cut into a bob, and it was a light brown color.

Like Kennedy, they both had light brown hair. Although, Kennedy liked to wear her hair long, and sit in the middle of the living room constantly complaining about how tangled it was after a match. My mom had on a black pantsuit, and I wouldn't be surprised if she had been working up until this dinner. She probably planned on going back to work afterward. Isabella would be fine to hear that. Then I'd be able to sneak out to help her.

"Hello, Mother," I replied in a mono-toned voice as I pulled back my hood absently. She clicked her tongue at me as she stood, coming to stand in front of me. I cringed as she ran her fingers through my hair, tugging on the ends of it painfully.

She sighed, waving her hand at me as she sat back down. "Consider getting your hair done, it's been too long since the last haircut," I nodded, even though I had no plans on cutting my hair. I was starting to like how it looked. I had it styled to fall over my left eye, and the longer it got the less I could see. It was even with the bridge of my nose for now, but I was planning on growing it longer. The rest of my hair was just resting like a wavy mess around my ears. Maybe I'd cut that part and leave my bangs long. Isabella would love it; she'd try to dye it.

She was always trying to dye it but I hadn't agreed to it. I just didn't want to mess up the light blond hair color. Who knew what it would look like after she ruined it with dye? "Also, I got you something to wear for dinner. Try to consider being presentable," she said with her eyebrow raised. It was probably her way of telling me I wasn't allowed to argue with her, but I wasn't going to wear it. I never did.

Without another word, I turned around and nearly collided with my father. He grunted in surprise as he grabbed my shoulder while he steadied me. I tried not to flinch at the sudden pain as he let go. Despite his shoulder injury stopping him from going pro, he still worked out constantly when he wasn't working, and he had the body of a pro football player even now that he was older. Big and muscular, and about twice the size of me, if not more. Being close to him made me think about Roan and his friends and the flinch was pretty much automatic now.

"Hey, champ," He said with a grin. I frowned, already on the defense. Normally he ignored me or glared at me, never calling me names. Not unless it had to do with sports. He only called me things like champ when I was playing basketball. He rubbed his fingers through my hair and I grimaced, my legs bowing under his hand from the weight of it. He frowned, pulling his hand back as he looked at me. "You still have your muscles; I could feel it when I touched your arm. Working out again? Did you join the team?" He asked, hope in his voice. I tried to stifle my sigh; I knew it had to be about sports.

I knew what he was talking about. It was pretty obvious that the only sport I was good at was basketball. At night when I was home alone and bored, my fingers tired from the constant drawing, I would shoot hoops in the backyard since we had our own net back there. So, while I was keeping up with my lean muscular form, it was just for fun and to pass the time. There was no way in hell I could join the team again, not with Roan there. "No, Dad. I didn't join the team or any other sports," I told him sternly.

He glared down at me, annoyed. While my mother and Kennedy had brown eyes, Dad and I had blue eyes. It was the only thing about me that matched anyone since Dad had dark brown hair. Mom said my blond hair came from her mother. Sometimes when I felt really sorry for myself, I would lay there in my bed and wonder about how great it would be if some stranger came and claimed she was my real birth mom or these crazy people kidnapped me or something. Wishful thinking.

Taking a step back from me as if I had smacked him, he frowned, and instantly I was in the dark again. I knew that look, the look of disgust. Unwanted, disdain. They didn't have anything in common with me, they didn't understand me. They didn't want me. They probably counted down the days I graduated and moved out like I was. "Hurry up and get ready for dinner," he grumbled as he thundered past me into the living room. Almost like a light switch, he laughed as he pulled my mother into his arms. They said their hellos and kissed each other as if they hadn't been in the same building together all day.

Kennedy brushed past me, not even trying to talk to me as she gave me her familiar stink eye. She slammed her shoulder into mine and walked into the living room, adding to the nice and warm happy gathering. I turned to watch as Dad lifted her into his arms and called her his princess, and as she was placed back down on the ground, they watched her talk animatedly about her recent game and all I could do was sigh. It looked so warm over there. Where I was standing, all I could feel was the chill. I turned around and walked up the stairs, heading up to my room. I just wanted to get this all over with.

Our house had a fairly normal layout, but it was much bigger than we needed. All the houses in our neighborhood belonged to the richer crowd of our town, and Mom and Dad were friends with most of them. A lot of them used to know Dad from school, and they had parties at each other's houses a lot. Those nights I stayed with Isabella and gladly slept on her couch. We had five bedrooms, which was ridiculously stupid for having two kids and parents. We only needed three bedrooms if even. But Dad turned one of the bedrooms into a gym and the other into another office for Mom in case she wanted to work from home. We had a kitchen, a dining room, and two living rooms, and everyone had their own bathroom. The office was downstairs, and the gym was on the other side of my bathroom. In a sense, I'd probably have to share my bathroom if it was a bedroom, but I was lucky it was made into a gym, I guess.

Mom had one of those long narrow tables down the whole hallway upstairs filled with various decorations, along with a mirror above it. Sitting underneath the table were a couple of bags indicating she took time to shop or made someone else do it for her. I sighed, grabbed the bags, and went into my room, shutting the door behind me. My room was bigger than I needed it to be. I had one of those L-shaped desks in the corner.

It was the most important place to me, because on one side of the table sat my laptop computer, and on the other side sat my drawing supplies. I had cabinets filled with drawing supplies propped up against the side of the desk and as much as I could feel my fingers twitching to grab something and start drawing, I knew it would have to wait. Mom had two dressers in here, but I only used one. She seemed to think I should have more clothes than I have, but I didn't spend all of my allowance on clothes, I spent it on art supplies instead.

My bed was a queen-sized bed, perfectly made not by me ever. Mom had a housekeeper who did all the cleaning. I kicked off my shoes and left them in the middle of the room, pulling off my socks and sinking my toes into the soft carpet. Probably the best part of this house was the carpet. There was just something about the feel of your skin against the carpet. The other side of my room was filled with a few bookshelves and two doors. One led to my walk-in closet, which was only half full, and the other went to my bathroom. My bookshelves were filled with books on art, and my own portfolios. I had about ten now since Isabella made me start keeping my drawings.

Every time I filled one in, I just started another one. I sat down on the bed and looked into the bags, pulling out boxes. One had a shirt that was light purple and buttoned up, with long sleeves. I guess I could deal with that, but it was too big. The pants were black dress pants, also too big. Even the shoes were too big, and I threw everything crumpled up back into the bags and chucked it back into the hallway, before closing the door once more. You'd think my own parents would know what size clothes I wore, but nope, they could never figure it out. I pulled off my hoodie and the rest of my clothes, threw them in my laundry basket, knowing the housekeeper would have them washed and folded for tomorrow morning, and went to take a shower.

My bathroom was just as extravagant as you'd think. There was a giant shower that could fit more than one person, and glass doors that were made to possibly show the outline of your body through the glass but not really much else. Trays filled with various body washes, shampoos, and conditioners. I didn't take a long shower, knowing they were waiting, and stepped out pretty fast to dry myself off. I cringed, looking at my body in the mirror.

My side and my stomach had various healing bruises; my upper arms were covered with new bruises from Roan slamming me into the locker earlier. I had a tattoo on the inside of my arm that only Isabella knew about. It wasn't too big, a birdcage with a songbird trapped inside it. I frowned, running my finger over it, annoyed there was a bruise on it. With a sigh, I finished drying off and pulled on a long-sleeved black shirt, grabbed a pair of ripped jeans, and ran my fingers through my hair.

It was presentable enough to me, and they weren't going to pay more attention to me for five minutes anyway. If they tried, I'd just ask Kennedy about her latest match and they'd forget all about me. I didn't put any socks or shoes on. Something told me once the dinner was over, they'd all leave and I'd be alone again. Either I'd stay in and go to sleep or I'd go out and meet with Isabella.

The moment I walked into the dining room I was met with the delicious smell of ham, potatoes, and carrots. It made my mouth water and I couldn't help but smile to know there'd be plenty of leftovers for me to eat until Sunday. The cook only came for family dinners, after all, the rest of the week I either had to cook for myself or just heat up leftovers. "I think we should have another kid. Kennedy will be in high school soon, you know, and I've always wanted a boy," Dad was saying as I stepped into the room.

I sighed, very loudly, but none of them even cared enough to look up at me. "You have a son, did you forget? Or am I just a ghost?"

"Maybe he'll be a football player like you were," Mom said, patting Dad's hand with a soft smile. I rolled my eyes, mumbling under my breath as I sat down next to Kennedy and started to fill my plate. None of them waited for me of course. They had already started to eat as they talked about how they should add another child to their family. How lovely they were.

Finally, Dad looked up at me, his eyes pierced into me as he looked me up and down. I pretended like I didn't notice his strange creepy stare as I cut my ham and took a bite of it, quietly savoring the taste. Even when Dad looked under the table, probably cringing over my ripped jeans, before looking at me again. "Did you do the test?" he asked, making me sigh. I purposely took forever chewing my food, aggravating him. "Kinsley, did you pee in the damn cup?"

I rolled my eyes, swallowing my food. "Yeah, it's on the counter in my bathroom," I said, frustrated. "I'm not doing drugs though, so it's pointless. But have fun playing with my pee," I said, shrugging as I took a bite of my carrots. Every few weeks there was a new cup sitting there for me to pee in. At first, I fought it, saying it was stupid and they didn't trust me, but after a few years of that, I just accepted it and peed in the damn thing. It's not like I ever did drugs anyway, so it didn't really matter. Maybe a younger me cared that they didn't trust me but I was used to it at this point.

Dad gripped his fork tightly in his hand, annoyed with my words or my tone, probably both, and Mom cleared her throat to change the subject. "Why are you not wearing the new clothes?" She asked, a frown on her face. "Did you not like them?"

I wished tonight was already over with. "They were too big, mom. They're always too big. I keep telling you my size, it hasn't changed,"

She grimaced since I was still eating when I started to talk, but I was getting aggravated by all this scrutiny. Normally, they didn't pay this much attention to me. She quickly regained herself and straightened her spine, staring at me. "I do so much, Kinsley. I can't be expected to remember everything. It was the size your father wore when he was your age. Maybe you needed to start using the gym more, you always look so weak and skinny," she said with an exhausted sigh as if I made her life so hard for her. She could remember Dad's clothes size from high school, but not mine? Because that made so much sense.

"Did I tell you guys about my boyfriend?" Kennedy asked, batting her eyelashes at me. Of course, she wasn't even changing the subject much, just giving them something else to grill me about. The main topic of this stupid dinner after all.

For about twenty minutes, I was forgotten as Kennedy rambled on about some kid named Wyatt who was, of course, a football player. Dad told her to bring him over so he could give him some pointers and she was eating it up while mom joked about planning their wedding. Freaking seventh grade. If she stayed with him and married him when they were eighteen, I would be surprised. Eventually, everyone started to quiet down, and once again, all eyes were on me. I contemplated if I should grab the last four rolls and shove them in my mouth. Suffocate myself and knock myself out for the night, but I wasn't sure if they'd even attempt to save me.

I put my fork down and looked at them all. It was now or never, I guessed. At least I was somewhat prepared. Peyton. I was going to ask out Peyton tomorrow. "I'm actually asking out a girl tomorrow. A girl I've had a crush on for a while. I was waiting for her to be single; you know. Now that she is, I'm going to go for it," I said, shrugging like it wasn't that big of a deal. Half of that wasn't even true. Well... most of it. I had no idea if Peyton was recently single, I just knew she was currently single. And I never had a crush on her or even cared about talking to her if it wasn't for my stupid parents. They were quiet, just staring at me, and I knew what they were waiting for. "She's on the swim team," I added.

All of a sudden, everyone was excited. Dad even smiled and reached over the table, patting my back and nearly smashing my face into my plate in the process. "Way to go Kinsley! The swim team is really good! They had won for three years straight!" He said, grinning at me.

Honestly, I didn't even care enough to know that, but I gave him the fakest smile I could manage. "She's probably going to turn you down, you know," Kennedy added, and honestly, I wasn't going to argue with her. Peyton was probably going to look at me like I was a small bug and tell Roan to come to beat me up for bothering her. Oh God, I wasn't looking forward to this at all.

"Now, now, be nice. He's a Bryant, he'll do just fine. Who'd turn down a Bryant?" Mom said with a beaming laugh as she nudged her elbow into Dad's arm while they laughed at each other. I wasn't entirely sure if I could roll my eyes wide enough over how stupid that sounded, but I flashed her my fake smile and asked to be excused.

It was like me asking to be excused had unlocked the secret magic word, and everyone was instantly talking about how busy they were. Mom and Dad left to go back to the office, despite the fact that it was about seven o'clock now, and Kennedy went with them, wanting a ride to her best friend's house for the night. It was funny, how I was the one who asked to be excused, but I was the last one sitting at the table. The cook, Gloria, came into the room and I stood, smiling softly at her. "Thank you for the delicious meal," I said to her, grabbing the plates.

She smiled softly at me, pinching my cheek. "I made sure to pack up a lot of leftovers for you, and I baked a cake too. Don't tell the others," she said pressing her finger to her mouth as she winked at me.

I laughed, helping her clear the table. "Of course not. They're never home to go in the kitchen anyway," I replied. After the kitchen and the dining room were clean, she left and I went up to my room, putting away the laundry that had been cleaned and folded as we ate dinner. I considered going out with Isabella, but I was drained after that ordeal. Instead, I lay down on my bed with a deep sigh as I closed my eyes. I dreaded tomorrow. I couldn't help but wish there was a way out of it.

It looked so warm over there. Where I was standing, all I could feel was the chill.

Chapter 4
Kinsley

"Kinsley Bryant, you quit flopping over your desk like a fish, *cabrón*," Isabella said. I grumbled as I rolled back and forth over the desk. The moment the first period started earlier that day she had been hounding me.

She wanted to know when I would ask out Peyton, and why I hadn't asked her out yet. If she wanted her to be asked out so badly, she should just ask her out herself. "*Sei un pesce*," I mumbled in Italian.

My arms were draped over the top of the desk, my face pressed against the cold surface as my hood fell over my head, masking me in darkness. For a second I felt safe and warm in the dark cocoon I had created, until Isabella started to poke me with her finger. "What did you call me?" She asked with frustration in her voice. I lifted my head with a sigh.

"I said you're a fish," I mumbled, earning a smack on the back of my head with her shoe. The third period hadn't started yet and there was only half the class in the room, but the smack was loud enough to make everyone turn to look at us, even some of them calling out their stupid '*Oooohs*,' as if Isabella and I were about to fight each other. I merely rubbed the back of my head through my hood, cocking my eyebrow at her. "If you're going to talk to me in Spanish, I'm going to talk to you in Italian. It's only fair, you know," I reminded her. It was a fight we had since we first started to be friends in freshman year.

She threw her hands up in the air in exasperation, then slipped her shoe back on her foot. Seeming to realize we weren't actually fighting, the rest of the class went about their normal rumors, probably adding in a few more about how Isabella and I were having a lovers' spat. Then again, Roan had spray-painted the word '*fag*' on my locker that morning, so they might not think Isabella and I were dating anymore. It took me all of the second period to get the paint off my locker, but it had been there long enough for most of the school to gossip about it. "Just go ask her! It'll stop the rumors," she whispered with a frown.

"I don't care about the rumors," I reminded her with a shrug. I mean, I could end up with a boy or a girl. It was a mystery for me too. Kind of like those mystery grab bags in the dollar store; you grab one and you never know what you're going to pull out. "She's definitely not going to say yes. She was way out of my league, and now everyone thinks I'm gay. She's just going to laugh in my face. Can't I just tell my parents she said no and go on with my life?"

She shook her head sternly. "You know your parents aren't going to get over this. Look at their bright idea of you doing drugs. You've been forced to pee in a cup for years now. They stick to their strange commitments and you know it."

"If we can last until the end of this year and then senior year, we'll be out of here," I reminded her. "Both of us, getting an apartment together in New York."

Isabella looked down at her recent drawing. "You just want to go to New York because I want to go there. You can have dreams too, Kinsley. What do you want to do when high school is over?"

I traced the engraving on the side of my pencil as I thought. "My parents want me to-" I started to say before she cut me off.

"I don't give a flying rat's ass what those ingrates want! What do you want?" she nearly shouted as everyone turned to look at us once more. Whispers of Isabella being crazy were voiced throughout the room but one quick glare and the twitch of her fingers near her foot made them all shut up and turn away from us again.

I didn't reply to her question though, because thankfully the teacher came in just as the bell rang. I wasn't in the same class as Peyton for that period, and I was glad I wasn't being forced to stare at her in any way. It seemed like the moment I decided it was going to be her, I couldn't stop staring at her. She was pretty, had a slender athletic body, was well taken care of, and had messy hair that was always pulled up with just the most attractive messiness on top of her head. Her neck was nice and lean, which was mostly all I could see since the classes I had with her I sat behind her.

For some reason, I wasn't attracted to her. Of course, that didn't mean that we couldn't eventually be attracted to each other. I mean, sure Romeo and Juliet were instantly attracted to each other, but were all of the great romances of our lifeline?

There had to be some out there who chose to get to know each other first, and passion came second. The longer I dwelled on it, the more I didn't want to do this. I had no idea what I was scared of, it wasn't like I thought she'd say yes. I was absolutely sure she would say no. Probably threw Roan at me since the swim team had always been really friendly with the basketball team. Then, if it wasn't that, what was it? What was I afraid of?

"Mr. Bryant, do you know the answer to the question?"

"Obviously I don't, otherwise I wouldn't be sitting here dwelling on it," I replied without thinking. My cheeks heated up in embarrassment. Wait... class, teacher... good job me.

Mr. McCormick simply cocked his eyebrows at me from the front of the class, holding the ruler poised in between his fingers. He liked to slap it down on people's desks when they fell asleep, and one of those days I kind of hoped a piece of it would break off and cut someone so he could get fired; I hated this teacher. "Obviously, you have a lot on your mind, but would you mind pulling out your actual textbook and paying attention? It's page forty-three," he frowned. I swore he hated me because, despite everything, I still got the best grades in his class. English was so freaking easy for me.

I grumbled in annoyance as I pulled the hood further over my head and I opened my textbook to the right page, just as a perfectly folded little triangle slipped onto my desk. I nearly threw it back at her, as frustrated as I was. I hated how she folded these things. So tight and tiny, making me have to try to unfold them so I didn't break the note. Couldn't she just fold it like a freaking square? Was it that hard to do?

I took a minute to close my eyes and counted to ten, knowing I was being incredibly unreasonable and shouldn't take my frustrations out on a piece of paper. Once I was sure I wasn't going to burn the whole room down just to kill this perfectly folded little triangle, I opened my eyes and pulled it under the desk to slowly unfold so Mr. McCormrick didn't see. He was a really loud man, his country accent boomed so loudly sometimes that other teachers poked their heads in to ask him to keep it down.

I wasn't entirely worried about him hearing the paper rustling, but he'd notice me fumbling with it. Once it was finally unfolded, I smoothed it out over my desk and covered the top of the paper with my textbook as I read what she had written. To think it would take three exaggerated hours just to find one freaking sentence quickly pulled my frustration back out again but I ignored it. Of course, she was going to try and get me to ask her out during lunch. I quickly replied to her stupid message. *There's no way in Hell I'm asking her out in front of everyone,'* I wrote, before folding it like a freaking square and throwing it back at her.

Her reply was fast, and thankfully she folded it like a square so I didn't have to fight with it anymore. Either she was being nice or she realized I was about to blow a fuse. I wasn't normally a violent angry person, but there was so much pressure on me. With my parents I tried to appease them, to keep them off my back. On top of constantly getting picked on by Roan and his friends, I just wished more than anything high school was over and I could be out of there. It didn't matter if I wanted to go to New York or not. Anywhere was better than where I am now.

'Then what are you going to do? What about a note? Write her a note and hand it to her. That way she'll read it all, and maybe she'll write you a note back so it's less scary?' She asked.

I stared at her note for the longest time with a frown. A note. Just like this piece of innocent paper in front of me. Mr. McCormick started to walk down the aisles with last week's test results and I quickly scooted the textbook over the note. Honestly, I was glad about the need to hide it, because I started to have an idea and I wasn't sure how to word it. Mr. McCormick handed me my paper, an A, with a permanent scowl on his face. He took so long handing out the tests that the bell rang. I jotted down the homework he had on the board really fast as I started to pack everything away and followed the flow of children out the door.

It was lunchtime, and while most people headed down towards the cafeteria, Isabella and I headed to my car. Our high school didn't really have many rules for lunch, and I think that was mostly because most of the students didn't really have cars. It was only the seniors and a handful of the juniors, myself included. As long as we were back in time for our next class, they didn't really care if we left. A few students were walking down the road towards the closest place, fast food, while those of us with cars usually took our friends to other places farther away. Roan always had as many people as he could fit in his car, while I always just took Isabella.

She used to complain about it. She hated how I always took her to get food and paid for it. Then she realized I had an unlimited credit card, and the more that was spent the less my parents had. Her hatred for my parents allowed her to accept whatever I was willing to buy her. I tended to supply most of her art supplies as well when her mother didn't notice. Isabella might not have had a problem with using my parents' money, but her mother didn't like it. As far as her mother knew, Isabella went to the cafeteria every day to get free lunch, but usually, we went to a cozy little cafe that both of us liked.

It wasn't too far from the school, kind of like a seven-minute drive without traffic, and they had the best sandwiches. We weren't really coffee drinkers, but we loved hot chocolate. It was another shared passion of Isabella's and mine, but while she drank hers plain, I tended to put whipped cream, cinnamon, and sprinkles on mine. She thought it was disgusting and I thought it was Heaven. We ordered our food, and as the waiter walked away, I could tell almost instantly that Isabella wasn't going to wait any longer for this conversation. I held up one finger, noticing the waiter was coming back with our drinks, and fairly enjoyed watching Isabella squirm with annoyance as she ran her fingers through her purple-streaked hair.

The purple was starting to fade, which meant she'd either dye it something else or re-dye the purple fairly soon. "Kinsley," she whined. I merely gave her a look, waiting for the man to put down the hot chocolates and the sodas we ordered, before slowly walking away. The blast of hot air filled the cafe as the bell over the door chimed, and in walked some of the football team. I frowned, fairly annoyed. They never really came here. There were six of them, which meant they either all piled illegally into one car, or Bobby Fisher was the one who drove them. He was another junior who had a vehicle, he had a flatbed truck. It wasn't hard to know who had vehicles, they tended to belong to all of the kids who lived in the ritzy neighborhood and whose parents were friends with my stupid parents.

I took a deep breath of relief as they chose a table far away from ours, and the moment they started to get loud the manager came to kick them out. It didn't surprise me; his wife always came to work with him and she had constant headaches; she hated loud noises. I waited for the football players to grumble and complain as they left. The manager took a minute to apologize to everyone for the disturbance before I finally turned to Isabella. "I have an idea, but you're probably not going to like it,"

She narrowed her eyes at me, her fingers twitching towards her shoe, but she stopped herself as she moved her hands on top of the table and cupped her fingers around her hot chocolate. I could tell she didn't like how it sounded but she was going to give me the benefit of the doubt. "Well?" She asked when I had grown quiet.

I lowered my hood with a frown for a moment as I raked my fingers through my hair. Out the window, I could see the football players attacking a hotdog vendor. They shoved each other around and laughed. One of them trailed behind the others. He had a flat-bill cap over his head to shade his eyes from the sun, and a spring jacket with the hood over the top of the cap. For a moment, I wondered about him. I couldn't tell which one he was, not that I really ever cared to know who any of the football players were, but I was curious simply because while all of the others were loud and rowdy, he was quietly staring at a wind chime.

I wished I could see the expression on his face, but before I could really think more about it, Isabella snapped her fingers in front of my face to get my attention again. I pulled my eyes away from the random guy to stare at her. "Fine," I grumbled as the waiter came back and placed our sandwiches in front of us. We thanked him before I told Isabella my idea. "I'm going to write a note." She squealed quietly so she didn't disturb the owner or his wife. "Wait, there's more. The part you probably won't like," I added. Her squeal instantly died down and I smirked, already feeling the slap of her shoe on my head. Subconsciously, I pulled my hood back over my head to give it an extra cushion. "I'm not going to hand it to her. I'm going to put it in her locker."

She barely even blinked before telling me exactly how stupid that was. "What's the point of that? She's going to think you're a chicken! You have to be man enough to hand it to her, or else she might not even know who you are! Just writing your name on it isn't going to do anything. This isn't going to work, I swear,"

I tapped my finger against my chin with a frown. "No, wait. I don't think you understand me. I'm not going to put my name on it. Wait, let me explain. Obviously, she's going to reject me right away. Everyone thinks I'm gay apparently, or dating you. What if I sign it as a code name? It adds mystery to it all. She'll think it's romantic because a stranger is going out of their way to mysteriously tell her how much they're thinking about her. We'll get to know each other through secret letters back and forth through our lockers. That way, if we can't stand each other, we can tell them to stop talking to us and we'll never have to deal with a confrontation. But if we do end up falling for each other, then eventually we can see each other and go from there," I said with a smile.

She tilted her head to the side. "I mean, it might work. But it's not the kind of relationship your parents want. But then again, who knows, right? Tell them some lie or something. Everyone knows the swim team has a meet soon and they'll be gone for a few weeks before Christmas break. Just say it came early this year. Use it as an excuse to grow feelings, then after a few weeks, meet each other."

I didn't like that I only had a few weeks as a deadline, but nodded in agreement. If it was the best I had, maybe it'll work. I pushed my uneaten sandwich to the side and pulled out a notepad, turning it to the last page, the only blank page left, and pulled out a pencil. I didn't bring my school pencils with me and all I had was a drawing pencil. I was going to have to stop at the store to get another notepad after this. I wanted to write it down, while it was still fresh in my mind.

Hello,

How is your day going so far? That's probably a stupid question, pretty cliche, right? Obviously, that's the first question that gets asked. Though, when talking to someone who doesn't know you, that tends to be the go-to. Scratch that. Literally, scratch that. I don't have an eraser to get rid of it and I don't have any more paper.

I'm sorry, I'm going to start over. Ignore the ramble, I tend to do that when I'm nervous. I just wanted to tell you that I've been admiring you. I don't really know you, and I don't think you even realize I exist, but I'm hoping you'll give me a chance to get to know each other. Besides, what could it hurt? We might be complete opposites, or we might have a lot in common. Maybe it's better to do it this way? No pressure, no names, nothing. What's there to lose? Maybe we'll end up hating each other. It wouldn't matter anyway though, because no names, right? Or maybe...just maybe...we'll end up falling in love. Maybe we'll be the type of romance that's talked about, the type of romance that everyone envies and wishes they could have. If you want to get to know me, if you're interested, my locker number is 342.

Sincerely, Sparrow.

I smiled down at the letter, admiring it, before Isabella pulled it out from in front of me and read it. "Sparrow?" She wondered as she stared up at me with her eyebrows raised.

I shrugged. I felt slightly embarrassed as she stared at my letter. "All I could think of was my favorite song right now. You know, from the band SayWeCanFly," I mumbled.

She nodded, seeming to accept that as she reread the letter. "Are you sure you want to go with this? We can get more paper and rewrite it,"

I grabbed the paper from her and ripped it out of the notepad. I folded it into a square twice and shoved it into my pocket. "No. I'm scared if I try to rewrite it, I'll throw up all over it and she's definitely not going to like that. Come on, I have to run to the store to get a new notepad. I'm going to get some envelopes too," I replied as I stood.

She had already finished her lunch so she stood up and stretched as I pulled out a twenty and put it on the table next to the receipt. I grabbed my sandwich and together we walked out of the cafe. The good thing about this cafe was the fact that it was fairly close to a bunch of stores. My parents would probably be annoyed to see a simple little dollar store purchase on my card, but I didn't really care. They always wanted us to shop in rich places, to show how pristine we were.

I walked into the dollar store and within minutes the shopping cart was filled with things we hadn't even come in here to get. Isabella had raided the stencils, spray paint cans and tape, more hair dye, and accessories, while I simply grabbed the notepad and envelopes. At the last minute, I grabbed a new pack of pencils for school, but mostly there was only so much a dollar store had. We grabbed some boxes of cookie dough bites and threw those in the cart too before checking out. "Do you even know which locker is hers?" Isabella wondered.

I nodded as I handed the cashier my card while we grabbed the bags. We pretty much moved everything to the next register to get out of the way of those behind us so I could put the note in the envelope. "Yeah, I saw her stand next to it earlier when we left. She had been leaning against it and everything," She nodded, seeming to accept that answer as the cashier handed me back my card. Ignoring a grumbling old woman and her rowdy granddaughter, we searched through our bags to find the envelopes. I quickly slipped my note into it and tucked the top inside the envelope. I didn't really want to lick it and she probably would reuse the envelope if she replied back to me. It's not like people just randomly walked around with a box of envelopes to wait for someone to slip a letter into their locker.

We hurried back to school moments before the bell rang for the next class. Isabella went to her class on the third floor near our lockers. Mine was on the second floor, which was lucky for me because so was Peyton's locker. I had seen her at it when we were walking down the stairs earlier. Locker 213 was fairly close to the stairs. I passed my class and went to the locker and stared at it for a moment. No one was around since the bell had rung when I had walked up the stairs, and I creepily stared at it.

The cheerleaders tended to have stickers and magnets on their lockers, and I assumed most girls did, but it did not look like Peyton did. The locker next to this one was covered in pink and purple magnets, which was how I remembered without seeing the number. A strangely colorful locker like that stood out. I shrugged. I guess Peyton wasn't the type of girl to care about decorating her locker. I slipped the note through the three little holes at the top.

I started to freak out and regret it the moment I let go of the paper, but there was nothing I could do now. Taking calming breaths I told myself that she did not know my name or who I was. Once calmer, I clutched my notebook and pencil to my chest and went to class.

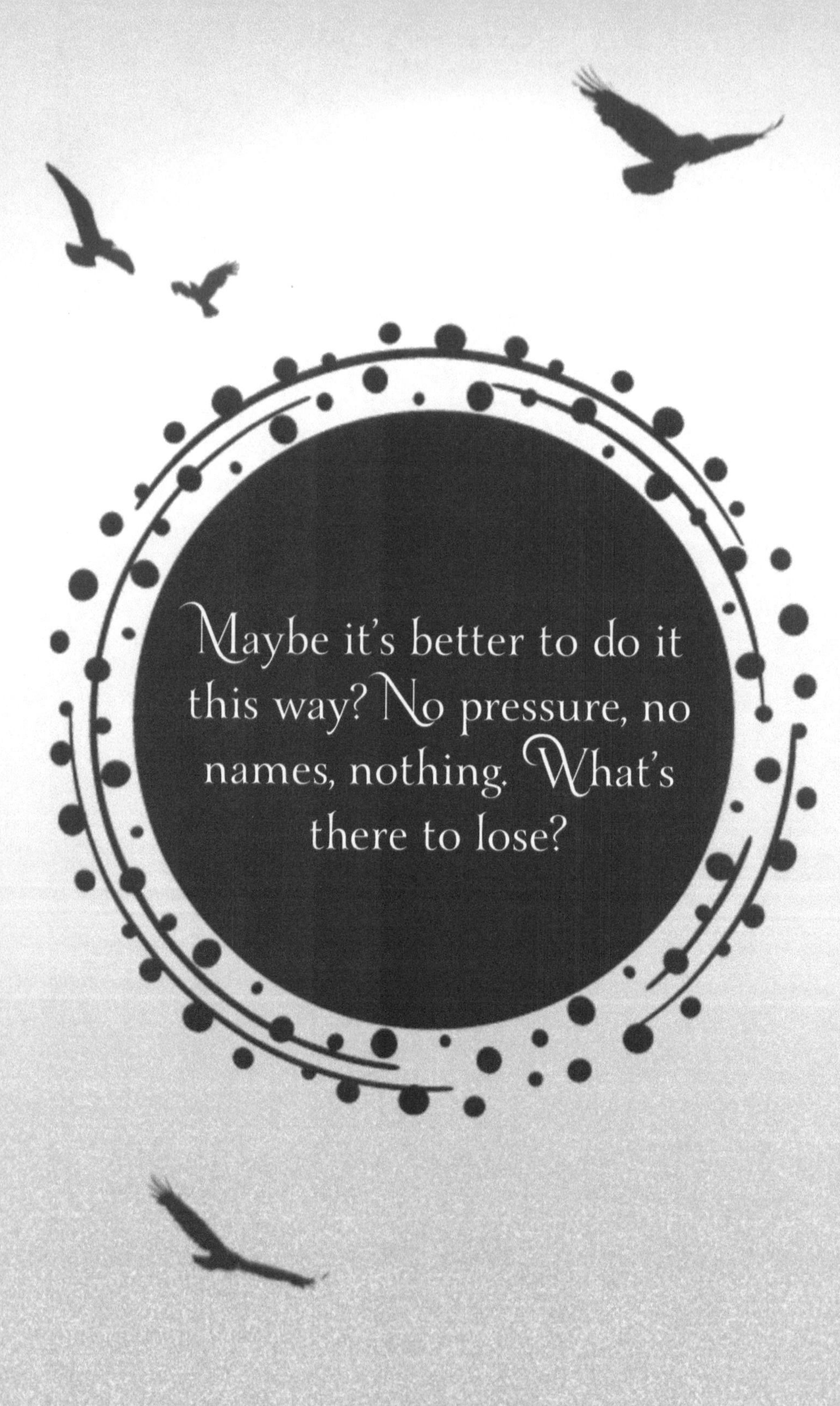

Maybe it's better to do it
this way? No pressure, no
names, nothing. What's
there to lose?

Chapter 5
Green

'Maybe I should try again.'

Those words echoed through my mind as I lazily laid my head against my right hand, my elbow propped on the desk. I kept remembering this morning, the screaming and the yelling, how my little brother ended up going to school with a cut on his cheek from a stray broken piece of plate my mother threw at my father. The plate broke against the wall, and none of them noticed he was bleeding. He didn't care, simply pressed a towel against the cut, and all I could do was stare.

Just the same morning, the same scene, over and over and over again. *'Maybe I should try again.'* The words echoed in my mind once more. Why not? What was the point? My left arm was lying lazily on the desk, the pencil perched in between the fingers of my right hand without care of the rambles of the teacher as they droned on and on in front of the room. I felt my left hand twitch and I stared at it with a frown. I wondered if it was remembering the memories of the past, or if it was anticipating the thoughts of what could happen in the future.

The bell rang and I got up and packed, moving like a robot going through the motions. Claps on the back, girls giggled hello, fake... all of it was fake. Would any of them really notice if I was gone? Sure, I was the captain. They'd notice, fake cry for the guy they pretended to know. But they'd move on. What would it feel like to have someone who actually cared? To have someone who actually loved me? Someone who didn't just cry when I died, but someone whose world shifted without me? Someone who couldn't breathe if I wasn't breathing. What would it feel like to have someone know me?

I wasn't sure I'd ever find out. Not me, not when I was only surrounded by fake smiles and pretenders. I swept my eyes through the halls, ignored the heys from the guys who saw me, and the shy giggles of the girls who thought I looked at them. In a sea filled with copies, was there actually someone out there who was genuine? *'Maybe I should try again,'* the voice echoed in my mind as the bell rang. I had taken too long, but I needed to get my books for the sixth and seventh periods so I lingered. No one cared if I was late anyway, not me. Not the star of the team. Just a big fake in a sea of fakes, hiding my scars under my sleeves and my sadness under smiles and nods.

I opened my locker and the first thing I noticed was a letter. I almost threw it away. It wasn't my first and it certainly wasn't going to be my last, but then I noticed something. It was simple, a simple plain envelope. No drawings, no heart stickers, no curly names, no reek of perfume. Just a simple envelope with the top folded inside. I sighed, curiosity getting the better of me, and I opened it. For the longest time, all I could do was stare at it. My eyes were wide as I reread it, over and over again. My hands shook as I took deep breaths, and looked around the halls- despite how empty it was- as reality crashed down around me.

Hurriedly, I smoothed out the letter and placed it inside my textbook. I pulled out a new piece of paper, sat down right there in the middle of the hallway, and replied to the letter. I felt the biggest grin tug on my face, and I realized as I slid an extra piece of paper and small little thin erasers inside the envelope, that it was a real smile. I sat there for who knows how long, but as the bell rang once more, I folded the note and slid it back into the envelope. I accidentally ripped the top of it in my haste as the hall quickly filled up once more.

My seventh period was on the third floor, so I didn't have a problem with the location of the locker. I stood up and stared at the hallway once more, my eyes scanned over everyone around me with a newfound light as I closed my locker and walked towards the stairs. Maybe, just maybe, there was someone here that would care if I died. Someone who would be destroyed without me. At least for now, the little voice wasn't echoing inside my mind anymore.

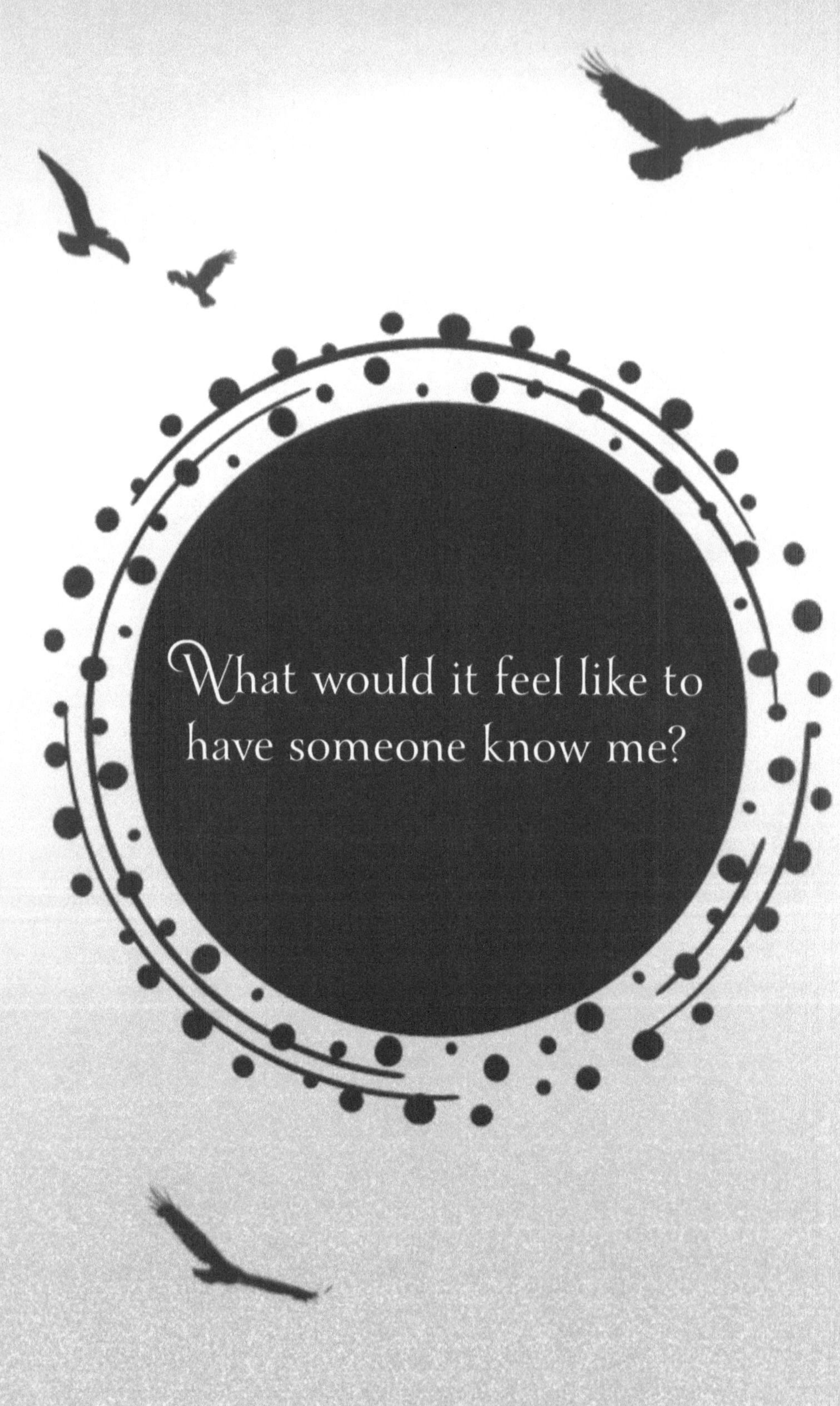
What would it feel like to
have someone know me?

Chapter 6
Kinsley

To say I was freaking out would have been an understatement. Peyton was in my fifth-period class, but she didn't look bothered by anything, so I assumed she hadn't gone to her locker. I should have waited until after school so I wouldn't have to look at her face for the rest of the day. No, that was a bad idea, because then I'd lie there all night long unable to sleep for fear of what would happen the next day. I should have just run away and joined a covenant. Wait, wasn't that for nuns? Fuck, I didn't know anymore, I just couldn't stop freaking out. "Chill your tits," Isabella said, flicking me on the forehead.

Mrs. Gee and I glared at her, Mrs. Gee's finger pressed tightly against her lips as she shushed us once more for probably the hundredth time since detention started. Yes, we had detention, but on the plus side, Roan did too, so that was fun. Well, besides the fact that he was glaring at me from across the library. Isabella had accidentally tripped Roan, I mean she said it was an accident, but it was Isabella after all, and instead of letting him shove her, I shoved him into a locker. Honestly, I think he was just as surprised as I was. I had never stood up to him before, but I guess I could have if I wanted to. Those few years of karate and the fact that I had at least attempted to stay in shape did something. Though, not much, since he lifted me by my collar and slammed me against the locker -his fist poised to punch me in the face- before Mr. McCormick found us.

Roan's friends all tried to say I started it but conveniently left out the part of him trying to hurt Isabella first. All in all, Mr. McCormick didn't care who did what and threw us all in detention. The basketball coach stormed into the library, making Mrs. Gee raise her eyebrow in annoyance over the noise, but nonetheless, she said nothing as he spat at her. Literally spat. He was a short angry man who spat when he yelled, and most of the time people did whatever he wanted just to stay clear of the shower of spit. While they were arguing, I turned to glare at Isabella, ignoring the way Roan was looking at me like he was going to throw me off the roof later. "I don't think that saying applies to men," I whispered, trying to sound tough but failing horribly.

She snorted, lazily pressing her hand against my chest. "Fine, chill your nipples," she muttered. "It's just a note, and you did the bare minimum. No names, remember? If anything, she won't even reply to it. She'll probably think it's a crazy stalker that goes off into the dark corners of the halls and fills up too many socks in between classes with unborn children." I wasn't sure if I should be more horrified over what she said or the calm way she said it.

I glared at her after the minute it took me to get over the shock. "You said it was romantic and mysterious!" I hissed quietly.

The coach seemed to get his way, either that or Mrs. Gee decided she needed a shower after talking to him because she was busy wiping her glasses with a disgusted look on her face while the coach started to motion Roan to follow him. I would say I hoped the coach would punish him somehow for getting detention and missing half of practice, but the way Roan turned towards me and flipped me off and the way the coach chuckled and pretended like he didn't see it made me know he wasn't going to do anything. Fucking jerks.

Mrs. Gee excused herself, glaring at us to make sure we behaved, before walking out of the room. I wouldn't be surprised if she came back with wet hair, I'd be scrubbing my face too after that conversation. The only ones left in the library were a few freshman boys crowding around a computer trying to get past the proxy to see porn, two sophomore girls who seemed to be working on a project together, and a handful of seniors with their noses shoved in books since college placement tests were coming up soon. Not bothering to whisper anymore, Isabella shrugged. "No, you said it was mysterious and romantic, I just agreed."

I simply laid my head down on the table, my arms spread out around me and sighed in defeat. I was so exhausted, and I didn't know what to do. "I wish I was sporty and straight and brainless like all the other jocks in this school," I mumbled. I mean, honestly, my life would be simpler if I could just fit into the perfect mold that made the Bryant family shine. Being one of the richest families in town made me stand out, but me being me... made everyone care less. I was ridiculed no matter where I went. The kids of the parents my own spent time with told their parents how ridiculous Kinsley Bryant was, and it just made my parents hate me even more. "I overheard my parents talking about having another baby.

They said hopefully they'd have a boy because they've always wanted one. *Maybe he'll be a football player like you!'* I said, mocking my mother's voice.

I felt Isabella pat my back gently, all of her normal sass gone as she sighed. "Good for them. I hope they do get another child. I hope that child comes out crapping rainbows like the freaking tiger off of Uncle Grandpa."

I snorted so hard I started to cough as I laughed, making Isabella crinkle her nose as she muttered an exaggerated ew at me. Mrs. Gee walked back into the library in time to see me trying to cover and contain my laugh, and the seniors glaring daggers at me, and sighed. "Go away, detention is finished early, I'm tired of you," she said with a frown. I didn't need to be told twice. Isabella and I bolted out of the library, ignoring her screaming at us not to run, and tore off down the halls. The moment we stood next to my locker, all I could do was pace. In our high school, we had seven classes a day, lasting about forty-five minutes each, two breaks, and a staggered lunch. And by staggered, I meant three lunch periods.

Mine and Isabella's was the first lunch after the third period. Some had a second lunch after the fourth period, and some had it after the fifth. I was never cursed with the third lunch; I wasn't sure if my stomach would last that long. I never checked my locker after the sixth or seventh period, mainly because I didn't need to after the sixth, and I couldn't after the seventh since I was shepherded into the library for detention. "Just open it Kins," Isabella said, throwing her hands up in the air. "I have to get to work."

Despite the fact that I had no problem throwing my parents' money at her, her mother still required her to work to help with bills around the house. Her mother had this thing about how everything should be split since she uses it too. Isabella has to pay for her own phone bill, and at the beginning of the month, her mom takes like twenty for each bill. After that, she'll put the rest aside in a bank account Isabella isn't allowed to touch, saying it's for her future, and gives her like twenty-five to live off of. Twenty-five dollars isn't nearly enough for her for two weeks, hence why I always pay for lunch and her illegal extracurricular activities.

"Hold up, I think I'm going to throw up," I said, holding my hand over my mouth. She crossed her arms over her chest, her foot tapping as she cocked her eyebrow at me. "Why is this school so weird anyway? I highly doubt she's going to walk all the way up to the third floor to put the reply into my locker. Why can't we have new lockers each year with our homeroom teachers?" I rambled, trying to stall. It was fucked up though.

When we started high school, we got lockers near our homeroom class. The only thing was, those lockers were our permanent lockers for the rest of high school unless we traded with someone else, which ended up happening a lot. So, no matter where our classes were each year, our locker always remained the same.

Isabella sighed, clearly tired of my crap, and opened my locker for me. Yes, we knew each other's combinations. Isabella's locker was on the first floor, and I tended to leave my second and third-period textbooks in her locker so it was easier for me instead of going up to the third floor and back down again within five minutes in between classes. Plus, our art club was on the third floor, and my locker was littered with all of my and Isabella's art supplies that we didn't trust the stoner freshman with. We were still working on begging the teacher in charge of the club to let us get a safe or something in there to keep our stuff safe. I squeaked and threw my hands over my eyes as I shrunk in on myself. "I don't want to know, I don't want to know, I don't want to know," I chanted, shaking my head back and forth.

"Um... Kinsley..." Isabella trailed, her voice breaking me out of my thoughts as I lowered my hands and stared at her. She was standing there with wide eyes, holding the envelope. It was the same one, with the top shoved inside the same way I had done it, but I could see it. There was a slight tear on the top as if Peyton had ripped it by accident trying to open it. It had been opened and reclosed. Either she had read it and put it back in and simply felt the need to return it... or she had replied to it.

Both of us were staring at it like Isabella was holding a stick of dynamite. "What if she replied with hate mail?" I asked, my eyes wide with panic.

"Then switch lockers with Kylee?" Isabella suggested. Kylee was one of the freshmen in our club who kept pestering me about switching with her so she could be closer to her classes. Her locker was on the second floor and most of her classes were on the third. I was starting to think maybe I should take her up on her offer. Suddenly, Isabella's phone went off, and she frowned in frustration. "I have to go, Mami's here," she said, glaring at the envelope with frustration. She was probably mad that I took so long to get to the envelope, and now she'd have to wait to see what it said. Of course, making her mother wait wasn't an option. Her mother was scarier than she was. Plus, they both worked together at the meat market her mother owned, so if Isabella made her mother late to open the store, she'd never hear the end of it. "I want to know what it says, take a picture," she said, pressing the envelope against my chest.

I watched her walk away, staring down at the envelope in horror, before finally forcing myself to move. I threw my textbooks into my locker and pulled out the few I needed for homework, throwing them in my backpack and slinging it over my shoulder. I closed my locker and frowned, staring at the empty hallway and stairs in the distance. Everyone besides those in clubs or sports had gone for the day since we had wasted time in the library for detention, so the halls were empty. I didn't really want to read this in the quiet loneliness of my house and found myself moving my feet toward the art club room.

We never tended to meet on the days Isabella had work, and the freshmen seemed to think it was a normal club routine to always be off on Thursdays and Fridays and never questioned it. The club room was empty, and absentmindedly I slung my bag down on the table and went to the windows, opening one. Even with no one in the room, the smell of weed and toxic goo still slightly clung to the air, and it was hard to be in this room without a window cracked or two. I wasn't even sure why I was here, but this was kind of my happy place and the only place I could think to be.

I wanted to be alone, and somewhere safe to open this. Maybe if it made me cry, at least no one would be around to see it. I had a sinking feeling in the pit of my stomach that even if the message was something stupid like *'I hate you'* or *'Let's get it on,'* I'd still cry simply because I got a reply. All of the stress of this was crashing down on me, this forced confession and these forced feelings and this forced life that I wanted no part of.

I sighed, closing my eyes for a moment as I sat down at the table, and listened to the steady sound of the whistle blowing on the football field. I wasn't entirely sure why that comforted me, but for some reason, it gave me the motivation to finally open the envelope and pull the letter out.

Hey, Sparrow.

I'm assuming Sparrow is your code name? I'm curious to know why. Is it because your favorite bird is a Sparrow? Love. You talk about love like it's the endgame. Maybe it is, but for now, love is the last thing on my mind. Romance talked about through letters? That's a funny one, but who knows? Someone who's been admiring me. There are probably a few, to be honest, I know my standing. Being on a sports team that does pretty well will draw a certain crowd so I'm not entirely surprised. Though if you're only interested in me because of my skills then you'll be surprised to find there's a lot more to me than the brainless jock label most of us have. So if you're searching for a brainless jock, I suggest you search elsewhere. As for love, I'm not sure what to tell you about that. How about friends? If you're fine with starting there, I'm fine with this charade. More than anything, it would be nice to have a friend. You seem to already know my locker, but in case you forget, locker 213.

Sincerely, Green.

P.S. I included extra paper and an eraser, in case you're still in need.

I stared at the letter, rereading it over and over again. After a few minutes, I pulled out my phone and took a picture of it. I sent it to Isabella for her to read as she had asked, before putting my phone on silent. I wanted to have a minute to just stare at it because everything felt...wrong. It felt wrong, but so right, all at the same time. I could barely remember Peyton's personality but I never would have expected her to write a reply like this. Honestly, I had expected her to freak out about me being a creep, especially after what Isabella had said. The more I read it, the bigger my smile got and all I could feel was butterflies fluttering around inside my chest. Green, she had labeled herself as Green. Strange, but maybe it was her favorite color.

I wasn't sure, but I was going to ask her. She had asked me about mine after all. After I had reread it at least three more times, I looked at my phone, knowing Isabella had said something about it. *I didn't know Peyton was that deep but dang, maybe you guys are a match made in heaven. Good pick, Kins! Write a reply! By the way, she gave you a piece of paper and an eraser. How cute is that?'* her text read.

I shook my head, feeling like if I smiled any bigger, my face would get stuck like that. Distantly, I was aware that the sports teams were heading inside to get changed, and I decided to linger to avoid Roan. Plus, if I was going to reply to her and put the reply back into her locker, I'd rather know I wasn't running into her. I took a deep breath, reached into the envelope, and pulled out the extra piece of paper and the erasers. There were two of them, thin and shaped like a smiley face, and for a moment all I could do was laugh. It really didn't seem like something Peyton would have but I couldn't stop laughing over it. How simple, how useful and cute the gesture was. To show just how much she wanted me to reply back. She had even gone so far as to supply a piece of paper, what was she going to do next, throw in a pencil?

That might have been pretty hard to slip through the holes of the locker. Suddenly, all of the panic I had been feeling earlier faded away. I was left with a giddy feeling, a wanting feeling, knowing more than anything I couldn't wait to see what she said next. I hadn't expected to be this excited over a simple letter, over a forced confession, over feelings that were starting to be less forced. Maybe everything would work out in the end. Maybe I would get the sporty girl my parents wanted me to get, we would get married and have sporty babies, and they would finally smile at me the way I had always wished they would. Maybe I would give basketball a try again. The future might be filled with all of these maybes, but right now all I wanted to do was think about the here and now. The letter, and the blank piece of paper, an envelope waiting for a reply. I pulled out the piece of paper she had supplied, smoothed it down, and smiled.

Hey, Green.

You asked about my code name first, so that's the first thing I'll answer. I chose it because of my favorite song. Well, my favorite song seems to change constantly, but right now it's Song of the Sparrow, by SayWeCanFly. So, I guess I get to ask why you chose Green? It's fairly simple, but there's nothing wrong with that. A favorite color maybe? I'm going to be honest with you. I have no idea anything about love besides what I read in the books. After I graduate, I plan on moving far away, anywhere, really, I don't care where, as long as it's far away from here. The idea of falling in love with someone in this town and being tied here for the rest of my life horrifies me. My parents wanted me to be in a relationship and this was honestly the best I could do.

To hand it to someone, to look them in the eye, to talk to them...the idea terrified me. But code names, the secrecy of the fact that we don't really know each other, it was appealing. So yes, Green. Simply friends is fine with me, more than fine. And I'll have you know, I never cared for the brainless jocks either. I couldn't care one way or another for the sport itself, or the skills required to play it. Knowing you're more than a brainless jock makes me want to keep talking to you. By the way, thanks for the paper and erasers, but I'm good now, I bought more. Looking forward to your letter, thanks again, Green.

Sincerely, Sparrow.

P.S. I'm not going to forget your locker number, I have a feeling it's going to be something I'll never be able to forget, even years from now. Hopefully, you won't forget mine either. 342, and sorry for it being so far away from yours. Maybe I'll switch with someone else to make it easier.

I smiled down at my note, rereading it over and over and over again. I was proud of myself for the depth of mystery and calm that radiated from my letter. It was filled with ease that sounded like I was sure of myself, despite the fact that I rarely was and that I was calm and confident in myself. I folded the paper and replaced the envelope with another one. Then I placed the letter I received from Peyton back into the slightly torn envelope and slipped it into a free sleeve in my current portfolio. I was sure Isabella was wondering what I said, but somehow... I didn't want to take a picture of it for her.

It felt too personal now that she had replied to me, and now that I couldn't stop smiling over her. I never would have expected Peyton to sound like this, to reply like this, but if the next letter and the next were just as personal as this one, I was sure it wouldn't take long for me to have feelings for her. It felt wrong that I knew who she was, but she didn't know who I was. But for now, she seemed fine with this, and if it was okay with her, then it was okay with me.

I put my portfolio back in my bag, placed the envelope with the new note in it in my pocket, and left the room. I walked to the end of the hall past the stairs to look out the window towards the parking lot. I almost sighed in relief to see almost everyone who was on the sports teams was filling the parking lot. Some were waiting for their parents to come to get them, some were standing at the corner near the bus stop, or some were piling into the seniors on their team or the rare few juniors who had vehicles. I could see Peyton standing with a few of the other girls on the swim team standing next to Roan and his friends on the basketball team and I frowned, wondering how she would feel to know someone she was friendly with was my bully. Maybe it was best she didn't know who I was right now, or anytime soon.

I could see some of the football players piling into a few of the trucks and the cheerleader girls trying to sit on their laps. I cringed, slightly worried, unsure if the truck could even handle that many people riding in the bed of it. Soon enough it sped off, and so did Roan and his group, and so did Peyton and hers. Once I was sure they were gone and I wouldn't have to deal with running into her or Roan, I walked down the stairs to the second floor, sliding my finger down the rows as I smiled.

I probably looked crazed, my hood pulled over my head, wearing all black, and an oversized hoodie to hide the bruises painted like a canvas over my skin, but I didn't care. I couldn't stop the smile from tugging at the corners of my lips as I found her locker, the big 213 standing there over the plain metal locker next to the overcolored one next to it. I tapped on the locker a few times, chuckling under my breath as I looked side to side, despite the fact that no one was around. I felt like I was the holder of a great big secret, the biggest secret, the secret that was mine and mine alone, and as I slipped the letter into the locker, all I could do was laugh and press my hands to my mouth to try and contain my crazy. It was hard to stop the happiness, despite the fact that this was venturing dangerously into the unknown.

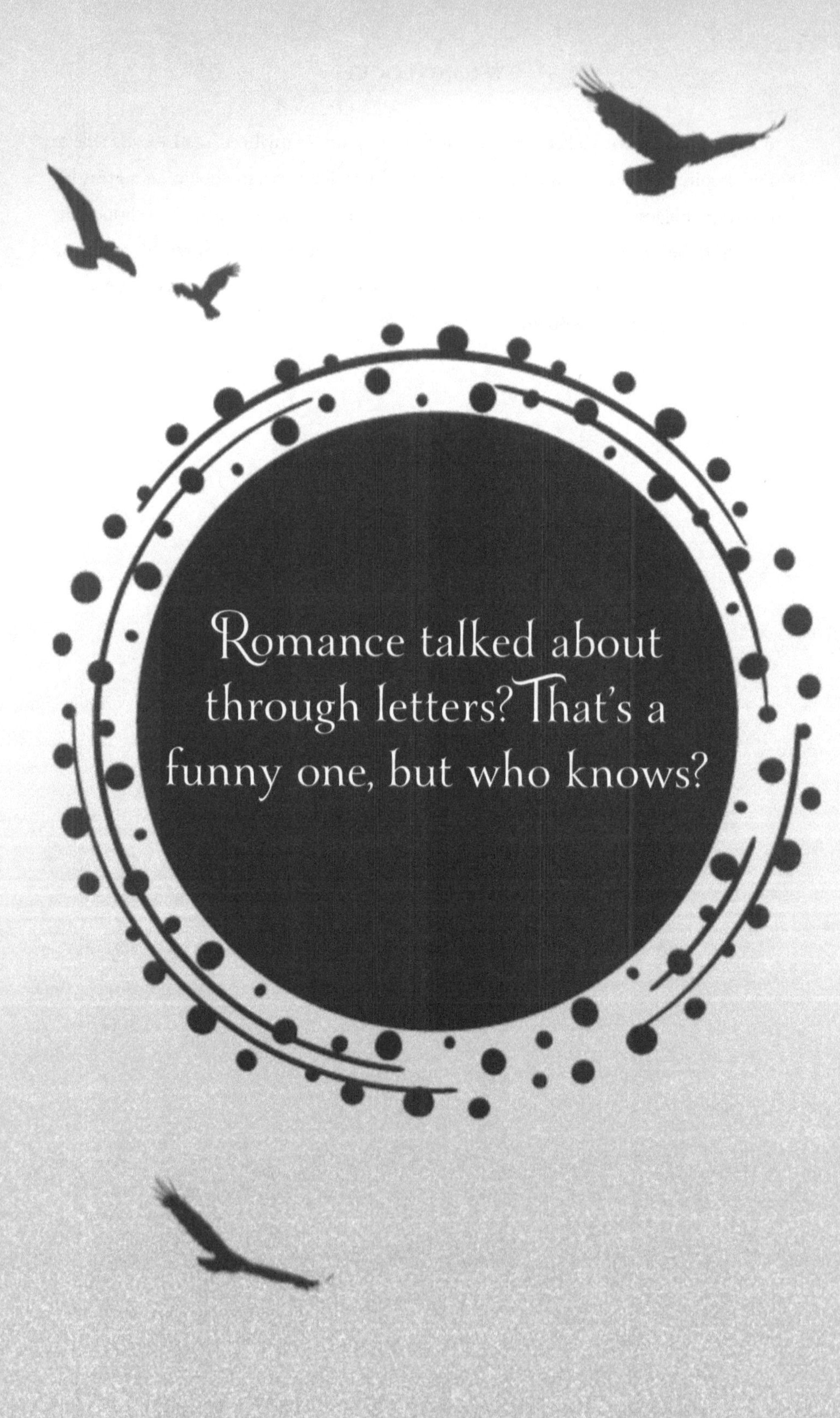Romance talked about through letters? That's a funny one, but who knows?

Chapter 7
Green

All throughout practice, I was impatient. I couldn't even count the number of times I got smacked with the ball. Guys and the few girls on the team crashed into me constantly every time I glanced at the doors. Normally during practice, all that mattered was the ball. The teamwork, the footwork, the stance, and the play. The rush of the wind in my hair as I ran, the feel of the ball in my hands, that's all that mattered to me. Now, all I could think about was the letter. Though this afternoon, I wanted the time to move forward, to make practice over, as ironic as that was. Normally, I wanted it to never end so I never had to go home. I wanted to just live here outside with the grass and the trees and the feel of the ball in between my hands. It was different now.

After practice, I took a shower, faster than usual. If anyone noticed, they said nothing, though I wouldn't be surprised if they had. Usually, I lingered outside and took the longest showers. My feet shuffled as I walked into the locker rooms and tried to make it last just a little bit longer. The feel of hands clapping against my back drew me in and out of my languid thoughts of the letter, and I wondered if it would be there or if all of it had just been a dream. I couldn't quite place my finger down as to why this letter was so different, why this girl was so different.

I hurried up the stairs to my locker, excited. My heart pounded in my chest, my hands shook, wet with nervous sweat. The moment I opened my locker, however, my smile fell. There was nothing there. I tried to tell myself nothing was wrong, but who didn't check their locker after school was over? I moved down the stairs and outside slowly, and if someone noticed how I went from happiness to sadness like the flick of a switch, they said nothing. More than once, I stood still and scanned the crowd of jocks. I wondered if any of them were missing or lingered inside for too long. No, as far as I could tell, everyone was here. The basketball team and the swim team were together near one car, while the football players were near another with the cheerleaders. There were others, the volleyball team and the swim team, who walked off in groups towards their few cars or the bus stop at the end of the road.

More fake heys, good throw, great pass, you're the man. Patted on the back, and people sucked up because I was the captain. None of them really mattered to me. It seemed like after I read that letter, all I could think about was how fake everything really was around me. I just wanted to play the sport, I didn't want the friends that came with it or the slutty girls draped over our laps that came with the title. We all piled into one car and as it pulled away, I stared up at the building with a frown. To say that I wasn't disappointed would be a lie. Hopefully, nothing was wrong. Hopefully, I hadn't angered her, whoever she was. Hopefully, it hadn't all just been a dream.

I checked my locker before practice the next morning. I never checked my locker before practice. What was the point of coming to school early and going to your locker? Despite the strange looks, I ran up the stairs to my locker. I ignored the stupid decoration Peyton had on her locker next to mine and opened it. I was surprised to see there was a letter there. Did the girl who wrote it play a sport after all?

Surely, I wasn't the last one out of the building yesterday. Maybe an athlete that came to school before the others tended to? Or maybe she was one of those kids who got dropped off early and had to wait for school? I frowned. I knew the coach would have a fit if I was late, but I wanted more than anything to read the letter, to see what she said. I put back the letter with a sigh. It would have to wait until after practice.

Practice sucked. I couldn't think of anything other than the letter that sat in my locker. One of the guys slammed into me because I hadn't paid attention. I knew the side of my body would be covered in bruises before the day was over. Despite this, I smiled as I walked into the classroom and slid into my desk before the bell rang. My homeroom teacher looked at me like I was crazy, but I couldn't blame him.

I was never on time, let alone early. Who fucking cared about English class? It was my worst subject, and the fact that I had it first thing in the morning did nothing to make me want to hurry to it. I tended to take long showers after practice, to drag it out as the hot water kneaded my muscles. The teachers disliked the jocks, especially the football, swim team, and basketball players because they were winning teams. The principal said more than once to be more lenient with the winning teams' students. Plus, not to mention detention wasn't on the principal's agenda either, not when it took us away from practice.

I smiled as I pulled out the letter and read it. I reread it, ignored the comments of my friends as they slapped my shoulder and asked me who the lucky girl was that gave me a letter. I ignored the teacher as the bell rang and we started into today's lesson. I pulled out a piece of paper and wrote a reply to the letter, placed the second one with the first inside the same textbook as before, folded up my letter, and slipped it into the envelope.

I couldn't help but turn around a few times shyly as I searched for eyes that lifted to meet mine, a soft feminine blush on a student that had apparently admired me. However, none of the girls really seemed to stand out in ways of a curious anxious gaze, nothing in the way the few looked back at me told me they anticipated a reply to a letter.

My second period was on the third floor, so it wouldn't be a problem for me. I pulled out my phone and pulled up my iTunes account, typed in the band and the song, and purchased it. I probably should have listened to it first to see if I liked it, but I had a feeling I would. There was something about this girl already that tugged me. The excitement I felt just to talk to her told me I'd probably like anything she suggested just because it was her.

Swiftly I pulled my headphones out of my pocket and slid them under my shirt, put them in my ears, and hit play. It was an emo band, and I had to lower the volume so I didn't get caught. I honestly didn't expect to like it, but I was glad I did. It wasn't something I usually listened to, but I would be now. Without care for the teacher or the class, I laid my arms on my desk and lowered my head on my arms, closed my eyes as the song repeated. I wondered if I put it loud enough, if it would drown out the storm at home.

I wondered if I put it loud
enough, if it would drown
out the storm at home.

Chapter 8
Kinsley

"Who crapped in your cereal this morning?" I lay on the desk, my cheek pressed against the cold surface, my hood covering my face as my arms were splayed over the side of it. This seemed to be my go-to position when I was frustrated. "Kinsleyyyy," Isabella sang. She poked her finger into my hood and tapped my cheek gently. I considered whether I should lick it or not, but she'd probably beat me. "What are you doing?" She asked, curious and slightly annoyed I hadn't answered her.

It was stupid. I knew it was stupid, but I was frustrated anyway. "I'm meditating," I mumbled. She snorted. Isabella seemed to realize I was in a mood and left me alone for a little bit. She mumbled something about crazy pretty Italian boys under her breath as she cussed me out in Spanish. I just knew without needing to look that those around us inched a little farther away from her, worried they were the cause of her angry Spanish rants. I didn't want to tell her why I felt the need to sulk because she'd laugh at me. There wasn't a letter in my locker this morning. Obviously, there wouldn't be one.

Logically, I told myself, I waited for her to leave school before I wrote my reply. She wasn't going to walk up the stairs to the second floor when she got to school in the morning, she would have gone to her swim team first. Even if she did go up the stairs to check for a reply, what was she supposed to do, reply while she was swimming in the freaking water? I was being ridiculous. Even though I knew all of this, I still pouted. Was I the only one happy about all of this? She sat there in front of the room with some girl who looked like an Olsen twin. They laughed over something on her phone, and all I could do was listen to her laugh. Shouldn't she look shy? Curious?

She walked into the homeroom and didn't even try to look around the room. Shouldn't she be curious enough to look around the classrooms each class and try to see if someone tried to secretly stare at her? I know I would be if I got a letter from a secret admirer in my locker. The bell rang for the first period, and since the homeroom was always the same as the first period, there was no point for any of us to move. I lifted myself off of my desk with a dramatic groan as I attempted to pay attention.

I wasn't surprised to get a note handed to me. I was, however, thankful that it was simply folded like a square. The way she looked at me with a worried expression made me know she knew I wasn't in the mood for her stupid triangles. I opened the note and wondered if she would actually be nice since she had a worried expression. A soft chuckle spilled out of my mouth at the audacity of that thought process. This was Isabella, when was she ever nice or subtle? *'Are you on your period? Do you use tampons or pads? I got you, girl,'*

I looked at her, and of course, she sat there with a tampon in one hand and a pad in the other, as if it was perfectly normal to sit in the middle of an English class and try to hand a boy sanitary products. Mr. Duckett stopped talking mid-sentence, and I turned to look at him. I felt a blush of embarrassment spread over my cheeks as his mouth moved without words coming out. His eyes were wide as he stared in horror at the products in her hand, and I couldn't exactly blame him. "Isabella! Put it away!" I whispered to her as she rolled her eyes at me.

Isabella did what I told her without a fuss. When Mr. Duckett started to talk again, a more scared and hesitant tone as he quietly stood there and questioned if I was secretly a girl or something. I wasn't surprised in the least when Isabella pointed at the note. I looked down at it with a frown, I knew she wouldn't quit until I explained my mood. *First, I'm not a girl. Second, I'm stupidly stressing out over the letter, okay? Maybe she didn't like what I said and decided to throw it away. Look! She doesn't care, she's over there painting Ashley Olsen's nails and hasn't looked around curiously or anything. Isn't that weird?'* I replied to her before handing her the note.

I wished we could just text, but Isabella hated to text in class when it wasn't necessary. She said the written word was more romantic as if that mattered for us. It wasn't like we were even together, so why did it need to be romantic? It wasn't long before her reply came, and I read over it with a snort. *'You're smitten,'* she had written. It was in big bold letters, curled and decorated like graffiti to make it stand out more. Even little swirls and dots scattered over it to indicate the word smitten as if I wouldn't have seen it unless she made it massive. Underneath it, she wrote: *'Chill. Don't get your panties in a twist, maybe she's just trying her best to think of a reply. Maybe she's not smart enough to write so deeply and needs help. Maybe Heather is helping her figure out what to write. That did seem pretty deep for her, but who am I to judge?'*

I looked at it, then at her in confusion. I mouthed the name Heather at her like a question, and she pointed at the Olsen twin. I never cared enough to figure out her name. Isabella snorted knowingly and shook her head at me like I was incorrigible. *'I don't think I want to talk to her if she has to have help from one of the Olsen twins to figure out what to say to me.'*

Isabella read the note and shrugged, a simple nod of her head. Since her WordArt of the word smitten took up most of the page there wasn't any more room left for notes. It didn't matter, the class was almost over and she had her next class with me. On the third floor near my locker. I gulped, as I scratched the back of my head. Then again, Peyton's next class was next to this one. I had seen her go in there enough times to remember that at least. Unless she replied to me earlier, there wouldn't be anything there, right? Maybe she was scared to drop the note in the locker. She didn't want names either, so I could understand her being worried about when I'd be there to notice. What if there wouldn't be anything there till after the end of the day?

I started to have a mini panic attack and forced myself to calm down. I tried to understand why this bothered me so much. Friends, we were just going to be friends. She knew I was fine with it and it's what she wanted too. I was honest with her; I wasn't interested in love in this small town. I needed to stop acting like a middle schooler with a crush. I pressed my hand to my forehead with a sigh as the bell went off. Because there was a pull. It was just one letter, but I couldn't get the words she had written out of my mind. The way she had written them, the meanings behind them. I felt connected to her on a level I wasn't entirely sure I was going to feel, and it startled me. I just wanted more.

Honestly, if I was brave enough, I'd walk up to her now and talk to her face to face. I was scared she'd back down when she saw who I was. No, I needed to calm down. Keep going the way I had been, and if there was a letter at some point in my locker, then great. But if there wasn't, then that was fine too. I'd get past it, it wasn't like we were instantly bonded to each other, right?

"Can we stop by your locker? I left my science textbook in your locker," I said as the bell rang. Isabella shrugged as she popped a piece of gum into her mouth and slid her things into her bag. I copied her as I followed her out of the room. Mostly it was the girls who wore giant purses so they didn't have to carry their books all the time, but Isabella and I carried messenger bags filled with mostly our art supplies and a few books. I still carried most of my textbooks in my arms so I didn't mess up my art supplies, but Isabella refused to carry her books. Either she didn't bring them with her or she stuck them in her bag, despite how heavy that made it. She had designed a cool design on my black bag at the beginning of the year and it's been the same bag I've been using since.

Isabella started to tell me about a fight that happened between two customers at her job last night as we walked up the stairs. Honestly, I only half-listened, one of my headphones in my ear as I listened to my current favorite band. As we headed towards her locker, I only nodded. It was fairly close to Peyton's locker and I couldn't help but feel nervous, but I watched her duck into her next class on the first floor so I knew she wasn't up here. There was no point to look, no point to care.

Isabella pulled out her phone to show me the spot she wanted to go tag next and I glanced at it as I opened her locker and pulled out my book. I couldn't help but peer at Peyton's locker, the bright 213 in bold numbers, but I figured it wasn't touched. She was already in class, so why did it matter? I shut Isabella's locker as she moved on to another picture. She had started to talk about which one would be easier to do and which one was watched by the police when I was shoved into a locker. I gasped as his hand cupped the side of my head through my hood, and he turned my face at just the right angle that when he slammed my face into it, the lock cracked into my cheekbone.

The pain shot through my body as I was thrown towards the lockers on the other side of the hall, straight into a group of football players. "Damn, Roan, what'd he do to you?" A boy with a thick country accent asked as I apologized for falling on him. I mean, it wasn't his fault he became my landing site.

I looked up at him as Roan growled, annoyed to be interrupted while he tormented me. Another boy on the football team stepped in between Roan and me, his head down as he shuffled his feet, and I realized it was the quarterback. The number one was big and bold on the back of his jersey, his hood over his head. I was confused, while all of the others started to joke around with Roan and the few basketball players that were with him, this guy was planted firmly in front of me. He waited in a patient position as he quietly hid me from view. Why? Why was he different? "He's a faggot, why should it matter what he did?" Roan spat as the bell rang.

I wanted to correct him, but it didn't matter. It didn't matter what he thought, what any of these assholes thought. Roan muttered something about how I needed to stay out of his way and I sighed, absentmindedly poked the aching knot under my eye as Isabella screamed at Roan in Spanish. One of the football players held her back as they laughed and called her a spitfire.

Roan turned to face me, his expression morphed with anger as the quarterback took a step back and to the side. He covered me completely from Roan's view. I stared up at his back in wonder, confused, unsure of what he was playing at. Maybe he didn't realize I was here. Yeah, that was it, probably. He searched inside his bag for something, a black plain backpack as he whistled a soft tune I didn't recognize under his breath. Finally, Roan seemed to give up when the teachers started to shout at us all to go to class. The basketball players left and Isabella promptly flipped them off even though in their strange way they helped me.

One of them asked her for her phone number and she kicked him in the balls as the others oohed and laughed at him. "Come on, bro, what are you doing?" One of the guys asked. The quarterback jolted in surprise. He pulled something out of his bag and without turning around he handed it back to me. I studied it and he shook it impatiently, and when I took it, he walked away.

"What's that?" Isabella asked as I unwrapped it and stared at it.

I lifted my head to thank him, but all of them were gone. All that was left was us and a few stragglers. I looked down at it again and shook the pack back and forth. I pressed the icy coldness to my cheek with a content sigh. "It's an ice pack. He's an athlete, they probably all have them,"

She stared at me under my hood and I lowered it as she stared at my cheek. "I'm going to kick his ass one of these days," she threatened as we walked together up to the third floor. We should have gone to the nurse and got a pass, but Mrs. Masters would understand once she saw my cheek. "Locker?" She asked with a tilt of her head toward it.

Isabella knew I didn't need to go to my locker. I already had my science book, but then I remembered the note and a blush spread over my cheeks as I nodded. I was glad for my hood, the overly large hoodie to hide my body, and my blush. It saved me the trouble of explaining to her why my cheeks suddenly decided to turn a deep red. I wasn't even sure why I started to blush. Friends, Peyton had said. We were just friends. These were just letters, nothing big.

Despite that, when I opened my locker and saw an envelope, I felt a grin spread over my cheeks. It sent a jolt of pain through me as my cheekbone throbbed. She must have dropped it off before homeroom started, or maybe she had a friend drop it off. Was that weird? Was it weird if she told people about her secret letters? I wasn't sure if I was happy with that, I wanted these to just be between us. Especially since I didn't show the contents to Isabella anymore.

Isabella and I didn't sit near each other in science class, Mrs. Masters was strict. We had to all sit in alphabetical order by our last name, and I was thankful I got to sit in the back of the room. I didn't like to sit back there because I was one of the troubled kids, I got a fairly steady B in her class, but I liked to be in the back if I was going to be all alone. Mrs. Masters started to grumble when we walked in late until she saw my eye.

She was big about the health of the students. Her daughter had a disease that she didn't talk about, but it was something that we all picked up from rushed conversations here and there during the school year. She was absent a lot and sometimes needed to rush out of the classroom because of it. After a few minutes of her fingers jabbing against my cheek to make sure my cheekbone wasn't broken, she allowed me to sit down. Isabella had slid in without notice when I was being babied, and as I walked past her to get to my seat, she gave me a thumbs-up and a wink.

Almost immediately, I sat down and piled my books at the top of my desk. I pretended to be a good student as I turned it to the right page. I pulled out the envelope and slipped my headphones back in my ears when she turned her back and started to write on the board. I always concentrated better with music. The taps of pencils, the scratch of the lead on paper, the bounce of feet, and the scuffle of chairs were distracting. While we normally got in trouble for headphones, mine were never really noticed, black headphones hidden under a black hoodie. I turned it up just loud enough to erase the annoying noises but not enough to block her voice out in case she called me. I pulled out the note, and my heart raced as I read it.

Sparrow,

I have to admit my reasoning is really simple and lazy in comparison to yours, and I feel slightly discouraged to tell you. However, if you must know, I chose green simply because my eyes are green, and I couldn't think of anything else on the spot. Though talking about your code name, I have to admit something. Do you know how they say when you like someone you start to like what they like? I'm not saying I have immense feelings or anything for you. But, I listened to the song you mentioned before and now I can't stop listening to it. Maybe it means nothing, maybe it means something. But when I close my eyes and listen to it, I think of you. Silly, right? Thinking of a person I've never met.

When I hear this song, I think of you, and everything looks a little bit brighter. Anyway, what you said about your life, I can't relate to that very much. Your parents want you to date so they're forcing you to ask someone out? It's funny, I wonder what it would feel like to have parents that cared enough to notice I'm not dating anyone. Anyway, I understand what you mean. I would be horrified to be stuck here forever.

Oh, you don't have to worry about switching lockers. I know my locker is on the second floor, but most of my classes are on the third floor this year, with only a few on the other floors. Plus, I don't mind running up the stairs to deliver the letter. If it's something worth it, I don't mind the extra effort. Anyway, talk to you later, Sparrow.

P.S. Cause what's a letter without a PS? How are you planning on telling your parents about this? They're wanting you to be in a relationship, right? This isn't really a relationship.

I stared at the letter, my heart beating faster and faster, as I read her words. It was so different from what I'd expected from Peyton. I frowned, feeling like something was off. Were her eyes green? I couldn't remember, but they were, right? She wouldn't have said that if they weren't. I took the letter she had written and put it back into the envelope, slipping it into my portfolio with the other one. I thought about her question and how best to answer it. I wanted to be honest with her, but at the same time, I didn't want to push her away.

This had all been so new, and despite how new it had been, I had been scared of it ending so soon. She had said this wasn't a relationship, and I knew it wasn't, but at the same time, I had to wonder if this really was what one felt like. Besides the fact that she didn't know who I was and I can't exactly go talk to her. I pulled out a new piece of paper and a new envelope from the box I still had in my bag, and took a second to study Mrs. Masters. I turned the page in my textbook to a new page she had written on the board, then leaned down and started my reply to Peyton.

Dear Green,

I'm sorry that your parents don't care enough about you to notice your lifestyle, but at the same time, I'm going to have to say I'm kind of jealous. I wish my parents paid less attention to me, or tried to pay the right attention to me, honestly. They barely talked to me, but they always seemed to know everything about me from what they heard from their friends. They only seem to care about what I'm not, instead of what I am, if that makes sense. But I'll never be the person they want me to be, as much as I wish I could be, so in order to keep as much peace as I can, I'm trying my best. As for your question, that's a hard one. I don't know what I'm going to do. You're right, this isn't really a relationship, and they are expecting one.

I don't know what I'll tell them, but whatever it'll be will be a lie, obviously. Whether I make something up like the person I asked out has a lot of practice and I can't bring them by until after the season is over, I don't know really. I guess by the time they start giving me crap about it I can say I got dumped. Sure, it'll lead to them wanting me to try again, but...for now, I'm not too concerned. They only really talk to me once a week anyway, and I'm sure I can escape their scrutiny with some sort of lie for at least a few weeks, if not a month.

Ps. I don't want you to have to worry about it, because then you'll probably feel bad in a way, but none of it is your fault my parents are crazy. I like things like this, I like this just the way it is, and I don't want to stop talking to you. I hope you feel the same. I really like being your friend, Green, and who knows, maybe something more, one day. But for now, I'm very much content with the way things are.

I smiled down at the letter. I folded it and slipped it into the envelope, then into my pocket. With a raised hand, I asked to go to the bathroom, trying to hide my excitement. This was so new, but it felt so good at the same time. It was nice to have another friend and a secret hope that one day maybe something more. I went down to the second floor, looked around to make sure the coast was clear, and slipped the letter into the locker. I gave it a soft tap of my knuckles against the metal, grinned, and walked back to class.

When I hear this song, I think of you, and everything seems a little bit brighter.

Chapter 9
Green

My mom had manic depression. I wasn't sure if it was my father's fault, or if he just made it worse. She was fine sometimes, and other times she faded away. Her new job loved her so they understood as long as she went to a therapist and proved she took her medicine. I was the reason she lost her last job, though strangely no one really blamed me for it. Or, if they did, they didn't mention it. They didn't really talk about it, despite what happened for her to lose her job.

I knew by the way Dad banged on the bedroom door and yelled for her to unlock the door and come make dinner that she was in a bad state. My little brother barely stayed at home anymore. He went to his best friend's house most of the time, so it was only me. I could have done it too, but I didn't have best friends. I didn't have a friend's house to go to, or someone to talk to, I just... existed.

I went to school early every morning, all of us piled into one vehicle as we hurried to get to practice before Coach got angry. I was the captain, I had to be there early anyway, to set the example for the others. After practice, I would float through the haze of fake smiles and heys, an easy fake grin plastered to my face to hide the fact that on the inside all I did was scream. Then there was work, long hours in the garage while I worked on cars. I enjoyed it. The feel of the grease and the smell of the oil, the way the engine purred when I put it together just right. It was messy, but I loved it. If I didn't go pro, I considered going to college to be a mechanic so I could own my own garage one day.

When my shift was over, I went home. Always home, to the house that wasn't entirely a home. To the storm that raged around and around inside pretty walls covered with a layer of white paint and soft flower arrangements to hide the fear that was trapped inside. I hated going home, but I had nowhere else to go. I couldn't make close friends, they would want to come over. I couldn't invite anyone over here.

After my shower, I locked my bedroom door. Always lock the doors in this house. I was hungry, but if mom was having a bad day, then it looked like another day of no food. Father didn't let the guys in the house cook, he said it was a woman's job. From the way he yelled, I knew he wasn't going to leave anytime soon for me to go downstairs and make something. It wasn't the first night I went without dinner, and it wasn't going to be the last, either.

I pulled the letters out of my textbook and read them over and over again. I wondered what the next one would say. I grinned as I lay down on my bed and closed my eyes. Even as the screams echoed through the house, the sound of something glass being broken, and the tremor of hunger that gripped my stomach, I smiled. I scooted under the blankets as I stuck the letters back in the textbook and put them in my bag. With my headphones in my ears and the song Sparrow had talked about full blast through the speakers, I was glad to see that it was loud enough to block everything out. I chuckled quietly under my breath as I pressed my hands to my eyes and sighed. I actually had something to look forward to now.

I chuckled quietly under my breath as I pressed my hands to my eyes and sighed. I actually had something to look forward to now.

Chapter 10
Kinsley

When the first-period bell rang, I was already packed up and ready to run out the door. It had been a little while now since I had started mystery letters with Peyton, and I had started to feel torn by everything. We had gone a good two weeks of writing back and forth before Christmas break came. Those few weeks without being able to talk had been torture, but the first thing we did when we came back was flood each other with letters from the time we'd missed talking to each other, and it made up for it once it was all said and done. Fortunately, my parents hadn't had another dinner with me since the last one, since both of them had been really busy with work for the holidays. I didn't have to try and give some crappy explanation as to what I had started with Peyton or how my dating life had been. Honestly, I wished they'd stay away forever but I knew it was a matter of time before they came back to bug me.

They'd remember, of course they would, because I was the eldest. While they were disappointed in who I was, they weren't going to forget about something that would make them look better. I wouldn't be surprised if they wanted me to get with a sporty girl in hopes she'd motivate me to go back on the basketball team. They were obsessed with the idea of it since it was the only sport I had ever been any good at. It didn't matter though, because as long as Roan was there, I doubted I'd ever be able to. I hadn't been as focused as much as I should have been on what my parents wanted, or on much of anything lately. I'd only really been focused on the letters.

I still found it strange how Peyton acted in school. She never looked around, never cared about the others around her. No matter what we had talked about in the letters, she never looked unconcerned or curious. She just came and went the same as she would have been before. I started to feel like the letters were probably the most important thing to me, and it scared me. They could just stop or fade away and I didn't want them to. Maybe this was all a joke to her. Maybe it had started off as something simple and unconcerned for me, but the more we talked to each other, the harder it was to stop. I didn't want it to stop.

As strange as Peyton had acted during school hours, the letters still came as fast as ever. It wasn't really on a regular schedule, and at first, it was simple questions about things. Like our favorite colors and how our day had been so far, the way two strangers tend to talk until they get comfortable with each other. However as a week passed, and then another, I started to want more. I started to linger at Peyton's desk when I'd stand to go to the bathroom. I'd stare at the top of her head as I passed her, her eyes lowered over her phone or her textbook as she bluntly ignored me. I wanted to write her a note and slide it onto her desk when she wasn't looking, saying something mysterious, or even something from the letters to see how she'd react.

I had written in the letters that I knew who she was, but she didn't know who I was. The more I wanted to talk to her face-to-face, the harder it was to stop myself from the need to approach her. She didn't want that now, not yet, she had said. As hard as it was, I was patient. This would have been easier if she showed even some remote amount of interest in it outside of the letters, but she never seemed to care about anything except herself and the Olsen twin who hung around her constantly. Hilda, or whatever the heck her name was.

It was Friday now, and I already dreaded it. I was pretty sure my parents would come home this weekend, but I hoped they wouldn't. I wished they'd just stay away. I knew sooner or later they'd show up again now that it was January, and the holidays were over. As silly as it was that my mother couldn't even remember my clothing size, they'd remember that they wanted me to ask out a girl no matter how long it had been. A little while ago, Peyton had asked me in the letters what I'd tell them, and despite the few weeks I had to think about it, I still didn't know what to say. Maybe I could tell them it was still new and she was shy. Or maybe she had another person who was interested in her and approached her at the last second.

From what Isabella had told me, this was the first time she had seen Peyton single for so long and I had to wonder if that was because of me. Maybe the letters had affected her in some way. I had to hold on to the hope that even though we weren't really together, maybe I had made some impact. I tried to remember what I had written in my last letter to Peyton, but honestly, they had started to blur together now. What she had written to me I remembered clearly, the words she had written were memorized in my mind. Even when I was at home I'd take them out and reread them constantly. I felt enamored with a stranger I barely knew face to face, but I had started to know soul to soul. We had begun to talk about songs again, our favorite bands, and our favorite songs. So far, she hadn't really said much about hers, but she had started to ask about mine. She had told me she wanted something loud and deep to listen to when she needed to be surrounded by something else.

I wondered what that meant, to be honest, and what her life must have been like at home. She had said once her parents barely cared about her existence and I wondered if she realized just how similar we were even if our parents had a different way of showing how little they cared about us. If someone had told me even a month ago I'd see similarities between myself and a jock I would have laughed in their face. The more she wrote to me, the deeper we got, the more I compared our lives. Not the same, but similar, in a way. "Locker time?" Isabella asked me as she pulled me out of my thoughts.

I realized I had followed her to her locker and then back up to the third floor for our second-period class without noticing. Both of our textbooks were balanced in my hands as if she had handed me hers to see if I'd notice. I grinned at her as I looked down at the textbook in my hands. "Of course, always locker time," I used to never give a shit about my locker but now in between every class I checked it, and even during class sometimes if I could get away.

My teachers probably thought I had bladder problems, and even Mrs. Masters asked me once if I needed to go to the nurse to get checked out, but I didn't care. I couldn't stop the excitement I felt when I saw that little letter in there waiting. As much as human Peyton bugged me because she didn't really seem to care much, the letter version of Peyton seemed to be just as invested in our letters as I was. She'd complained about how long the weekend was on Monday and admitted to how much she missed the letters despite it only having been two days of a break. "I noticed your textbook was with mine. You know, in my hands. I wonder how that happened?" I said sarcastically as I opened my locker.

She hummed under her breath as she looked around the crowded hallway. "I don't know, I think it was lonely. It wanted to be with its best friend. It was sad, it had been lonely." She said with a fake sigh. I grinned as I gently picked up the letter from where it sat and slipped it into my textbook. The last letter I gave her was a list of songs, bands I liked, and songs I was currently obsessed with. Like a current band called SYML that had a softer and calmer sound to it.

I added that one to the list too but made sure to tell her it was calmer since she had specifically asked for something loud enough to drown out the sounds around her. She had also asked for my current favorite song since it changed so often, and since it changed to Better by SYML, I had no choice but to add it to the list.

I shook my head at her as the bell rang, my large hood hiding my grin as I shut the locker. "Of course! You are so kind to think about your textbook's feelings like that," I said with a soft laugh.

Isabella stopped me before we went into the classroom, a soft smile on her face as she lifted her hand into my hood and pressed her hand against my cheek. A chorus of oohs and awes flooded the hallway from those who slid past us into the classroom, but we ignored them. "I like how happy you've been lately, Kins. I have to admit I was really worried about this plan. It really pissed me off that your parents were forcing you into a relationship you weren't ready for, but you're happy, Kins. I'm glad you're happy,"

I was also worried. I was worried I had fallen too fast too hard for someone who didn't know who I was. The moment Peyton and I decided it was time to see each other face to face was the moment I knew all of this was going to crash to the ground, and I was scared of the inevitable. For now, Isabella was right; I was happy. "I know, but if that happens, I'll be here for you Kins. I'm always here for you," she said as if she could read my mind. I grinned down at her until the teacher started to talk, and we were forced to split apart and head to our different seats.

As always in this class, hers was in the front while mine was in the back, and I handed her the textbook that was hers as I headed to the back. I slipped into my seat and slid my book onto the desk. The windows were cracked open, and I could smell the scent of rain in the air, a smell I had always loved, and couldn't help but smile over it despite how dreary the darkened clouds were in the sky. As Mrs. Masters started the lesson, I opened my textbook. I slid the letter out of the envelope quietly and set it down on the desk. For two weeks now, this had been the tradition, and honestly, I was surprised I still made fairly decent grades. I needed to try harder; I knew my parents would find out if I made anything less than a C on any subject. However, when I had a letter in my hand, it was hard for me to concentrate on anything else.

Hey Sparrow,

The list is awesome, I bought all of the albums, even the one you said was calmer than the others. It's a really good band, to be honest, it's probably more of what I listen to, or at least before I met you. Now I've kind of gotten attached to the Screamo songs, mainly because of how loud they are and how they block everything out. I like the rhythm of them and the lyrics too. But SYML is a really good band as well, and the song you said is your favorite? I love it. I've probably listened to it on repeat this whole class period. I'm going to have to work a few extra hours to make up for the amount of money I spent on all of those albums but it's worth it, don't worry.

Maybe this would have been easier if I had the confidence to meet up with you in person, to go over to your house and get the songs from your computer like you suggested, but I know neither of us is ready for that yet. Two weeks seems like such a long time but it's really not, at least, not for me. Maybe that makes me a coward, but I can't help it. I've never told anyone the things I've told you, not really, and while I haven't really told you much, it's still more than anyone else. I really enjoy talking to you Sparrow, and I know this can't last forever but I hope to hold onto it for a little while longer, even if that does make me a coward.

P.s. Because a letter must always have a P.S. I know you keep making fun of me for it, but I can't help it. Letters without a P.S. are boring. I'm curious to know what you are, like… label-wise. You have no care for sports and you're different from all of the people around me. Honestly, judging from your favorite song I'd assume you're a quieter kid, more to yourself. You can learn a lot about someone by their favorite song, even someone like you who changes their favorite song constantly. My favorite song is Sara, by We Three. What does that tell you about me?

I shook my head with a smile as I stared at the letter. A quieter kid, huh? That was a nice way to say she thought I was an emo kid. I had to admit that while black was probably my favorite color, I wasn't really sure what else besides that made someone emo. Maybe I was, I don't know, it didn't really matter to me. I never was one to fit into a single stereotype, I was just me. As I thought of the letter, I pulled out my phone and typed in the song she wrote in the letter. I wanted to hear it before I replied back to her. I had plenty of time since class had started not too long ago. She said she had spent a lot of money to buy all of that, and I kind of felt bad. I didn't even know she had a job, and I hoped she didn't need to pay for rent or something like that.

It would probably be creepy for me to offer to pay for it for her. We barely knew each other after all. She'd probably think it was weird if I slipped a few hundred dollars into an envelope and slipped it into her locker. The least I could do was listen to her song since she had listened to all of mine. I purchased the song and listened as I stuck the letter back into the envelope. I'd never heard this song before, but the band was slightly familiar. It didn't take long for me to realize this was a type of song I needed to pay immense attention to.

It was fast, and I never was one for faster songs, but these lyrics... My hands shook as I put the envelope with the others in the portfolio, pulled out a new sheet of paper, and stared down at it. I tapped my pencil on top of my desk as I listened. I was surprised when I felt tears start to gather in my eyes. This was a song about someone who had tried to kill themselves. For it to be her favorite song meant she resonated with it. It meant she had tried as well, at some point, or she felt like she was going to someday. I felt my head jerk up so fast that I stared at the back of Isabella's head in the front row. I wondered distantly if she could somehow feel my sadness, the tears brimmed in my eyes as I took deep breaths.

I was quiet, and if anyone noticed my sudden tears, they didn't say anything. Then again, I was blessed to be in the back. No one behind me could see my shoulders shake, and those in the back row with me looked to be mostly asleep, so that was a plus. To cry for a song, I never thought I would. All I could see in my mind was a pair of sad, scared green eyes, wrists cut open as the song played. I looked down at the paper and noticed a few drops of tears had ruined it already, and I closed my eyes as I listened. I put it on repeat and sent Isabella a quick text to tell her I was going to skip my third-period class as I crumpled the ruined paper and pulled out a new one. I tried my best to steady my hands as I replied to Peyton.

Green,

I don't know what to say. I'm not going to lie, you shook me. I didn't expect that, and you're right, you really can learn a lot about someone by their favorite song. I have questions, but I understand if you don't want to tell me, or if you want to tell me when you get to know me more. You're right, two weeks is a long time, but it's not long enough and I don't want to pressure you. If you want me to tell you what that song tells me about you, then I think the best way I could, is if I showed you. I don't know your classes, I barely keep up with remembering mine, but I have history with Mrs. Yank on the second floor for the fourth period.

I'm not telling you this to make you feel uncomfortable or to try and figure out anything but, underneath the chair in the last row, there will be an envelope taped to the bottom of the chair. I think that'll show you how the song makes me feel about you. Also, funny thing, it'll answer your question about what kind of person I am.

P.S. Because what's a letter without a P.S.? What happens if we can't think of a P.S.? Does it not count as a letter? Also, don't think you scared me away just because of your song. It just makes me want to know more, so much more.

I went through the familiar motions. Folded the letter, pulled out a new envelope, and placed the letter inside it. It was tricky, my idea. Anyone could find it, and she might think it was stupid but it didn't matter. I'd skipped the third period and ate lunch in the art room. Then when the fourth period started, I would put the envelope under the seat. I wrote a quick note to beg Isabella to get lunch and take it to the art room, raised my hand, and asked the teacher to go to the bathroom. Mrs. Masters gave me that look again like she was five minutes away from writing down the name of her daughter's doctor to have me checked out for bladder problems, but she simply nodded and waved her hand at me to go ahead.

As I walked past Isabella's desk I slid her the note, my car keys, and my wallet, then went down the stairs to locker 213 and slid the envelope inside it before I could change my mind and rewrite everything. After all, what was the point of doing this, if I wasn't going to be entirely myself? I didn't want to hide any part of me from her. I was going to show her every part of my soul, and when she was ready, I'd show her who I was as well. Hopefully, by then it wouldn't matter, but for now, I wasn't going to back down.

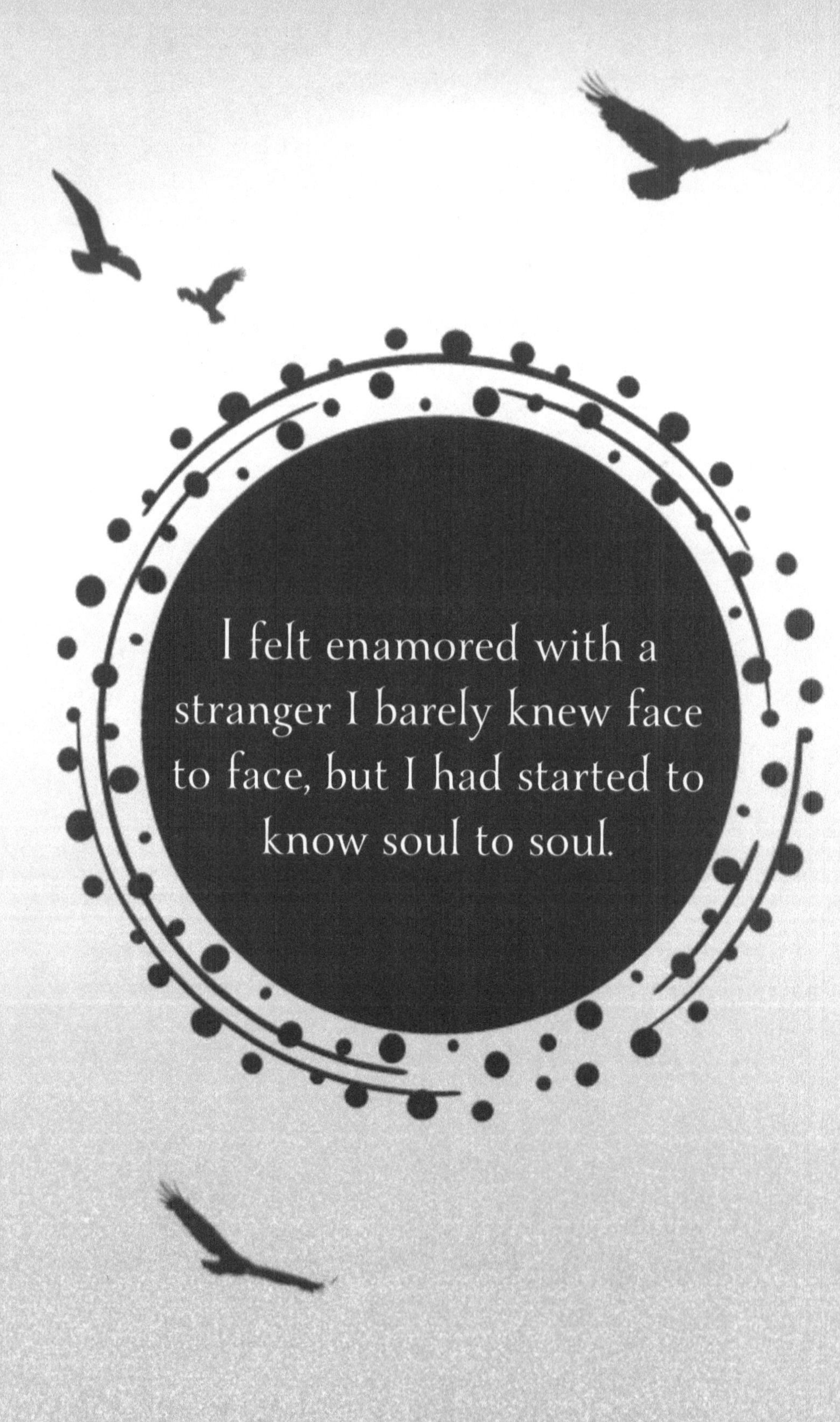
I felt enamored with a stranger I barely knew face to face, but I had started to know soul to soul.

Chapter 11
Kinsley

When the bell rang, I was already packed up and out the door. I knew Isabella would ask questions, but unfortunately for her, I wasn't going to wait to answer them. For our third period, we had Mr. McCormick together for English class. It was on the same floor, so I assumed when I hightailed it out the door she'd have followed me to the art club. However, she went to the other end of the hall to our third-period class, and when my phone went off it was a text to let me know she'd cover me in English class.

Mr. McCormick wasn't like the other teachers. He had a sign-in sheet at the front of the class, and we were supposed to be old enough to sign ourselves in at the beginning of class instead of him taking time to do a roll call. If we forgot, we were marked as absent that day. It was simple, just stop and put a check next to our name, then go to our seat. It was risky though, if he decided to call me based on the check being on the sheet, he'd automatically know she did it but it seemed she was okay with the risk. No questions, not yet, but I was sure she'd ask a bunch once lunch started.

I didn't mind her questions or her being there, she was my best friend after all. I just didn't know I'd feel like this or that I'd get so invested. I didn't know that there could possibly be someone in this town for me. Someone that could make me feel like everything was worth it. I had been going through the motions. To wake up, go to school, with the notion that one day high school would be over and I'd go to college with Isabella and we'd finally be able to live. I never thought that I'd find someone who made me feel like this before I had a chance to leave.

It was scary, this feeling, but I couldn't ignore it. Not when I sat there, the windows cracked to let out the smell and let in the soft sound the rain made when it sprinkled against the windows, not when I had her song in a loop in my ears. Not when I had this paper in front of me, ready for my art. I couldn't change the song, even though I went ahead and purchased the rest of the songs from this band. I didn't explore them, not yet, but I would. If she liked this song, she probably liked some of the others as well. I could still feel my cheeks heat up as I remembered she had liked my songs.

Peyton had purchased all of them just because I mentioned them. *'When I closed my eyes and listened to it, I thought of you,'* one of her first letters had said. *'When I heard this song, I thought of you, and everything looked a little bit brighter,'* she had written. Because of me. Did I really make her feel the same way she made me feel? Not love, surely not, not yet anyway. But the possibility of it one day?

It was like there was an ache in my chest and I wanted to do nothing else but sit on one side of the door, her seated on the other, and slip our letters back and forth over and over all day long. To forever talk, not even needing to see our faces, just to bare our souls to each other. Her soul was beautiful and I could understand why Isabella said demisexual before when she tried to label me. The soul that was attached to these letters was beautiful, and I wanted nothing more than to lose myself in their written words.

I hummed along to the song then as I bobbed my head up and down, my left hand held the paper as my right hand slid around it. The feel of the lead as it brushed against the paper, the strokes of the marks as the lines started to intertwine. The picture in my head became part of the paper, and all I could do was think as I worked. I put every part of myself into that drawing, for Green. Maybe I wanted to show off, or maybe I wanted to make sure she understood. I needed her to understand what I felt, how her song made me feel, and that I wasn't scared of her.

Did she try to kill herself? Or had she just thought about it? I had a feeling she had already tried, but as I drew that picture, I hoped she could see just how much someone cared about her. I was a stranger in a sea of strangers but I hoped when she saw that, she'd know that although she didn't know what I looked like, that at least I looked at her. I didn't want her to feel alone, I didn't want the letters to stop, and I didn't want her to die. I brushed my finger against my cheek and ignored the throb of my bruised eye from Roan as he shoved me down the stairs yesterday. I wiped the tear away so it didn't fall on the paper. I didn't want to ruin it, and I didn't want to scare her away with my tears.

She said I helped make her world a little bit brighter. I hoped I'd be able to make it brighter and brighter until it shone so brightly that all she could see was the light. I wanted to be her light, her strength. I shook my head as a soft chuckle slipped from my lips; I felt slightly crazy. It was strange because I looked at Peyton and I didn't feel like this near her. I didn't feel the same that I felt when I looked at the letters. I didn't hear her voice when

I lay there at night and stared at the ceiling as the words of the letters rang over and over again in my mind. It was surreal to know they came from her. It was almost like it was someone else.

I shook my head, a frown on my lips as I put down my pencil and traded it for a blue one. It was probably just because she hadn't ever talked like this to my face. Maybe she was just shy to show the true her. When we wrote back and forth, she could be anything and everything she wanted to be. As bold or as shy as she wanted, because she didn't have to hide anything from me. I tried to associate her with the letters. Her hair fell in her eyes as she sat across from me a year ago for the project we worked on. I could still hear her voice when she constantly complained about her hair being in the way and I remembered that when I had told her to cut it if it bothered her, she had looked at me like I was an alien.

I could see it now. Her blond hair in her brown eyes... Wait, what? Brown? No, that wasn't right. She said green in the letter. I took a deep frustrated breath and replaced the brown in my mind with green, but it was off, not right, off-kilter. Something was wrong, but I couldn't quite put my finger on it. Before I could dwell on it further, I saw a wrapper gently slide toward me. It was slow to give me time to notice it so I wouldn't get scared and mess up. The best thing about being friends with another artist was we understood how to get each other's attention. There was nothing worse than being startled when you were in the middle of something amazing, and your hand slipped.

Even a small little slip is enough to piss off an artist. To erase was unacceptable, and I'd be angry if I had to start this over. Especially this because as I slid my blue down the page, I couldn't quite stop myself from being in awe of the picture. It was by far one of my best pieces, and I wondered if that had something to do with who it was for. Smitten, Isabella had written on the note. I started to think she was right. I was smitten with the letters. Not with Peyton, because I still couldn't quite place her with them. But with the letters, I felt drawn to them on a level I couldn't even understand.

I finished the blue and placed the pencil down as she slid a drink to my left to make sure it was nowhere near my picture. I wasn't finished, but I was close. I was surprised she was being quiet. I had my music turned down enough that I could hear her if she tried to talk. She knew I knew she was there, but she had kept quiet, waited patiently, and watched me unabashed. I wondered if she could see what I saw, just how amazing this picture turned out to be.

I didn't want to stop even though I asked her to bring me lunch. However, I sensed that Isabella was going to wait for me to look at her before she started to talk, and I took a second to push the drawing softly to my right, far away from the food and the drink, and grabbed the burger. It was fast food, something close and easy. "Aren't you going to ask me anything?" I wondered as I took a bite out of the cheeseburger.

I lifted my eyes to look at her, tilted my head to the side, and noticed she didn't look at me. Her eyes were wide as she stared down at my drawing, a slight sparkle to them as she took a deep breath and turned to look at me. "Kinsley, I know Roan always messes with you and your eye looks like fucking death right now, but you've dealt with his bullshit for years now without a blink of an eye. This isn't Roan. Kinsley, who hurt you?" She was worried; I could hear it in her voice as she reached her hand out to me and touched the back of my hand. I realized she had thought I drew this for myself.

I chuckled softly as I felt all of the feelings of the song slide through me over and over again. Without a word, I handed her a headphone and she walked around to sit next to me. She pulled her food closer as she listened to the song. I restarted it for her, and for a few minutes of the length of the song, I ate my burger while she sat there with her hands over her mouth and listened. Her eyes closed as she listened with her heart.

Another thing about Isabella and me was our similar taste in music. She had more interest in others than me and tended to branch out to other bands, but I rarely listened to much more than the same ones over and over again. I usually only added a few once a new song from a band I already knew was made. Once the song was finished, I pulled her headphones away and I could feel her eyes on me. "Peyton said this was her favorite song," I tried to explain. I couldn't look at her as I sucked my bottom lip into my mouth.

"She told me a few things. She said she chose the code name green because her eyes were green. She said she listened to my song and it made her world a little bit brighter. Then she told me her favorite song and asked me what it told me about her. So, I told her I'd show her, and I have been here, drawing this ever since." I gave her a short breakthrough of the letters I had received.

It was the best I could do. I didn't need to tell Isabella I wouldn't show her the letters anymore; she seemed to understand that I wanted to keep them private. Her lips were pursed in a frown as she stared down at her drink. I wiped my hand on my pants, pushed my wrapper out of the way, and pulled my picture back. I still had one headphone in as I picked up a red pencil. She was quiet and watchful as she slowly ate her food next to me. There was a loud current of chatter from outside. Girls squealed as they walked back from their cars and complained about the rain.

Isabella seemed to sense it was a distraction. She lifted the headphone she had used and placed it in my ear, and I couldn't be more grateful to have someone like her as my best friend. She scooted over to pull out her own art stuff so she didn't bump me. We had about five minutes left by the time I finished, and it was enough for me. I searched the room for a larger envelope. I wanted to make sure the picture was perfect. I had started to softly sing the song now, I had pretty much memorized it by then. I took out a piece of paper and started to write a small little note on it. It wasn't a letter, but it was enough to explain.

'Angels harm themselves because they don't feel right in the world they're living in. This world destroys them, so they harm themselves to try and return to Heaven again. You're an angel, Green. But I hope you know that no matter how dark the world is, there's a light waiting to shine down on you,' I wrote. I wondered if it was enough. I bit my lip as I slipped the letter inside the envelope with the picture, and I wondered if I should have written more. I wanted to be your light, Green. Should I have written that? Surely it would have freaked her out. It was better to wait, wait until she was ready. Wait until we were ready.

"Are you ready?" Isabella asked as the bell rang, signaling the end of lunch. I felt a knot in my chest as I placed the envelope in my textbook and grabbed some tape from one of the drawers. We cleaned up our mess and threw it in the trash, closed the windows since today was Friday and we didn't have club on Thursdays and Fridays. I realized if I completely freaked Green out, I might not have a letter on Monday. What if she didn't write anything for the rest of the day? What if she didn't see the letter until after school let out? Maybe I should wait until after practice.

It started raining pretty hard, a cold rain since it was January, so outdoor sports like football, basketball, and track were usually canceled. However, the swim team still had practice at the indoor pool because there was a meet coming up soon, and it would be strange for them to cancel it. I wondered how I could survive the weekend without getting a reply. I never thought it would continue like this, especially for this long, but now it was all I could think about.

We walked out into the hall and went our separate ways. We only had the first three classes together; the rest of them I had by myself. I was nervous, and as I walked past my locker, I stupidly wondered if Peyton had already replied to it. It wouldn't have been possible, right? Was it too fast? It's not like she would reply after every class. Maybe she would wait to see what I would place under the seat for her. Sure enough, I opened my locker and replaced my books for the next few classes, but there wasn't anything there. I searched the halls for a sign of her, but she wasn't anywhere around. Honestly, I should probably start searching for her before I opened my locker.

She didn't want to know who I was, not yet anyway, and I didn't want to push her to find out early if she wasn't ready. My head was lowered as I walked down the stairs to the second floor, in the opposite direction of Peyton's locker, and went into the classroom. It was now or never, it seemed. Even though I had to walk down a floor to get to class, I was earlier than most of the kids.

Once again, I was thankful for a seat so far away from everyone else. I was thankful for Mrs. Yank, who didn't care where we sat on the first day of school and just made us stay there to make it easier on herself. Those who sat around me weren't there yet, so when I casually went to my knees beside my desk and gently taped the envelope to the bottom of the chair, no one seemed to notice. I started freaking out, worried it would fall or someone else would find it, but I didn't know what else to do. I told her it would be here, now all I could do was wait and hope it would be.

There was nothing in my locker after the fifth period, and I went to the sixth period cranky. My sixth period was just a free period, so the teacher was just Mrs. Gee, the librarian. The Library was located on the third floor, and every period, a class filled the tables to quietly work on whatever they were behind on. I tried to tell myself that there was a chance she already had history class today and would have to wait until after school to investigate. None of the normal logic worked for me, and I couldn't stop the frustration. What was wrong with me? Why did I feel like this?

Isabella texted me pictures of something she drew during class, and I tried to give her nice replies, but my mind was on a letter and the anticipation that it might be there after class. After my free period, I went to my locker. It was stupid, I didn't need to. My last class was on the first floor. I had taken an Italian class as my language elective. Isabella wanted me to take Spanish so I'd understand her better, but Italian was my second language and an easy A for me. Even though I knew I didn't need to, I stopped at my locker without much care that I'd be late for my last class because, at this point in my life, I was obsessed. I had accepted my obsession, and I knew there wasn't anything that could ever stop it. There was a letter in my locker.

I started hyperventilating as the bell rang, and as everyone started leaving the halls to their classes, I sat down in the middle of the hallway and opened the letter.

Hey, Sparrow.

I'm not going to lie, your picture did something to me. In a good way, definitely in a good way. Did you draw that? Can I keep it? I feel like it should be in an art gallery. Is this what you meant when you said the best way to tell me what you are is to show me? So you're an art student. It really sucks being an art student in this school, since there's no art teacher right now. I have so many questions, and I wish I could talk to you more than this but not yet, not quite yet. I don't think I'm ready to go past the letters.

There's something about the fact that you know me but I don't know you that makes me want to get to know you first before actually talking to you face to face. I hope you don't mind, even though I'm going to be lonely over the weekend now. I don't think I could find the words to explain how I feel right now. If you have questions, I bet I can figure out what they are. I don't know how to explain my life to you. I've hidden it from everyone for so long, how could I start to explain it? I hide behind smiles. I hide behind my sport. No one really knows me. How could I just tell you? I'm not sure you'll like what I have to say.

More later, Green.

P.S. If we can't think of a P.S., then it still counts. I'm sure there will always be something. I don't know about you, but no matter what I write, I keep wanting to write more, and I hate writing. But for you, I would write ten pages if I could.

I felt my face burn as I pulled out a piece of paper, laid down on my stomach in the middle of the empty hallway, and started to reply to her letter.

Hey, Green.

An art gallery? I'm flattered. I have to admit, I skipped the third period to draw it. I guess that makes me a bad influence, but it was worth it to know you enjoyed it. Yes, of course you can keep it, I drew it for you. Yes, it's annoying that there's no art teacher but I'm in the art club. Well, I guess I probably shouldn't have told you that, since you don't want to know who I am yet. But I'm not the only one in the club, there are a lot of other kids in there as well. Okay, exaggeration, but there's a handful. I understand what you mean. I've taken to checking my locker after each class now, and I'm sorry to say there will probably be a time we end up running into each other at some point, but I don't know what to do about that.

I'm just really excited to receive your letters. I can't explain why, I'm not sure how to put it into words. I just know when I see a letter, I smile, and when I open my locker and there's nothing there, I get sulky. You make me smile, Green, and I hope it's the same for you.

P.S. I'm pretty sure even if I can't think of a P.S., I'll still write it, even if it's simply to make a smiley face, or to say goodbye, something, anything is better than nothing. You're right, I don't want to stop writing either. Hopefully one day, maybe we can sit next to each other and talk back and forth like normal people, and remember the time we used to write letters back and forth. Oh, and I forgot to say something. I understand what it feels like, hiding. I only have one friend, but I hide from everyone, so trust me when I say I understand. But I have a feeling nothing you say will ever bother me, or scare me away. You don't have to hide anything, not from me. I promise, Green. I'm not going anywhere.

I folded the letter and slipped it into the envelope, walked slowly down the stairs, and slipped it into her locker. I felt like I was as light as a cloud as I floated into my last class, and nothing could touch me, not even the teacher as she yelled at me for being late. I couldn't stop the smile on my face as I stared at the back of Peyton's head. I watched her brush her fingers through her blond hair as she lazily leaned back in her chair. It felt weird to look at her and feel like this. It felt off, so I simply looked out the window, watched the rain as it poured against the glass, and smiled.

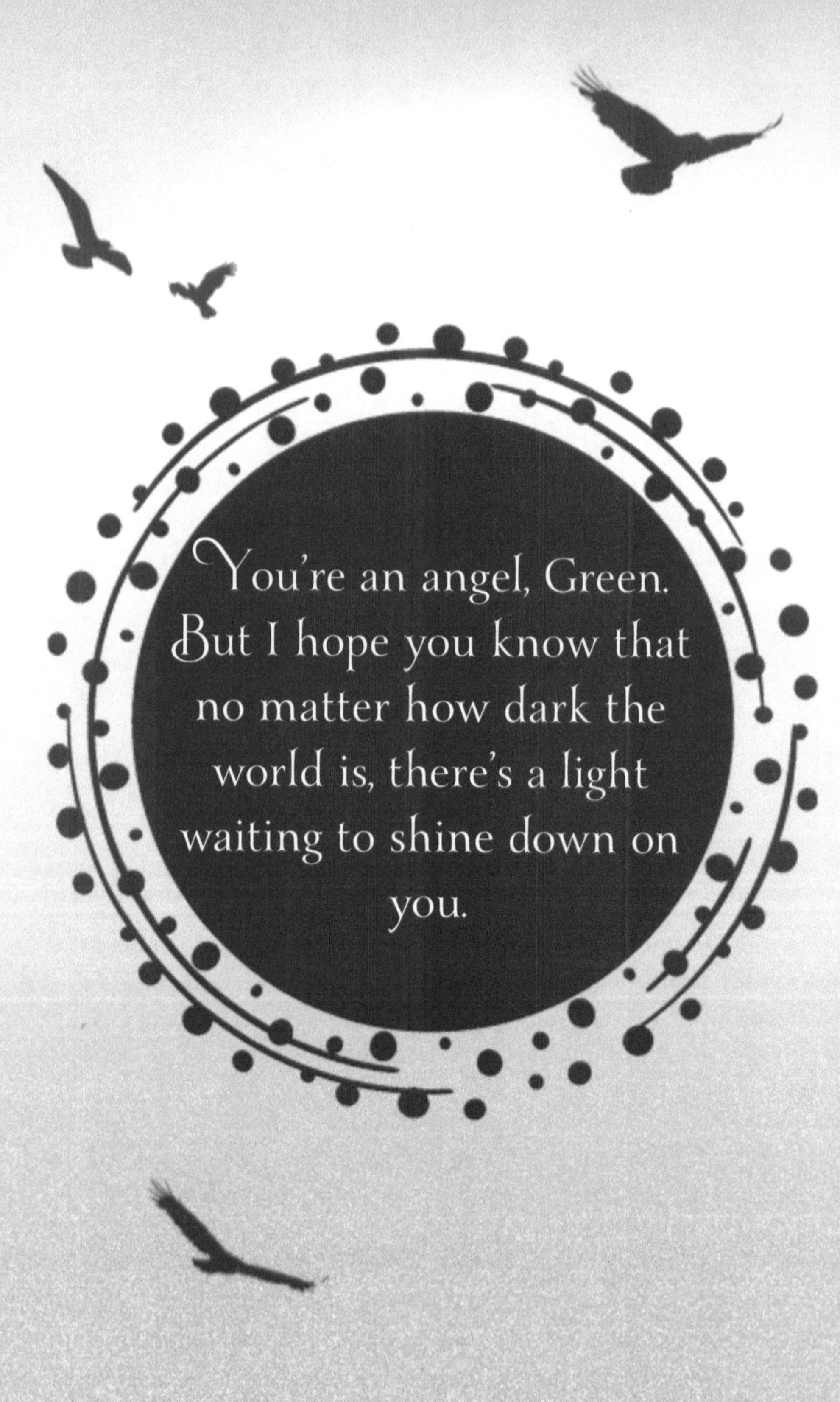
You're an angel, Green. But I hope you know that no matter how dark the world is, there's a light waiting to shine down on you.

Chapter 12
Green

I had been fairly scared about what the reply would be. To tell her about my favorite song, it was private. Sure, we'd talked back and forth for a while now with letters, and while I felt close to her, I was still scared to open up. I'd never opened up to anyone before, but there was something different about her. My brother didn't know about my favorite song, none of my so-called friends knew, no one knew. But to a mysterious person, a simple envelope, I revealed a secret. I felt exposed like I had opened a small part of my heart and waited for it to be stabbed.

My hands shook as I read the note. I hadn't expected it to be there when I opened my locker after the second period, and I sat there in third with wide eyes, and all I could do was grin. She didn't care about the song. No, it wasn't that she didn't care, it was more like she had felt it on a whole new level. Like she had felt me on a whole new level. Could she feel what I was feeling?

I could feel a little bit of hope spread throughout my body and I had to force myself not to laugh out loud and pressed my fist against my lips to hold in my laughter. *'Also, don't think you scared me away just because of your song. It just makes me want to know more, so much more,'* the letter said. I folded it back and placed it in my textbook with the envelope. I could have replied to it now, but I was curious to see what it was that waited for me.

Her fourth period was my sixth period. It worked out perfectly, to be honest. I'd get her thing, I'd reply to her, then slip the letter into her locker before seventh. This killed me; how slow these replies were. I considered if I should give her my number to text me instead but I was worried it would make her feel rushed. No names, she said.

She didn't even really admire me like she originally said, just picked me because her parents were assholes. I wondered if she liked me now because I had problems trying to stop the butterflies that spread throughout my chest whenever I received a letter. I sat down at the desk at the back of the class. It wasn't my normal seat but no one said anything. I was popular, all I had to do was high-five the guy next to me and say I wanted a change of scenery and no one cared. Not me, I was untouchable in their eyes.

When class started and I was sure no one would notice, I leaned over and slid my fingers under the seat. It sounded horrifying. What if there was dried gum under here? But I felt a crumple of paper and traced it, found a corner and some tape, and worked at it. It wasn't long before I could pull the long white envelope out from under the seat. Curiosity made me stare at it as I placed it on top of my desk.

It was one of those envelopes you mailed an important document in or maybe took to school if you had an important project and couldn't hand in a wrinkled paper. What kind of person just had this lying around? Was she organized? Did she have OCD or something? I told her she made me think of her as a quiet person, but I guess that was my way of telling her I thought she was an emo kid. There were a lot of them. They walked around in all black and acted like the world was going to end. Maybe instead of an emo kid, she was a nerd, studious and quiet. Whatever she was, it honestly didn't matter to me. Because she was Sparrow, and that was good enough for me.

I opened the envelope, gently pulled the paper out, and stared as my breath was trapped in my throat. *Breathe*, I tried to tell myself. *Inhale, exhale.* It was an angel. The wings were big and white, perfectly shaded like they were real. I brushed my fingers over them, convinced for a moment that they were. The Angel was a girl and she was naked and wrapped in a blue scarf. Despite how naked she was, I didn't think of it as sexual. It was beautiful, every part of it was beautiful.

Her arms bled, her hands covered her face, fingers splayed to show hints of green eyes as the blood dripped down her arms. A bright wide smile lit up her face, like the type of smile you wore if you were so happy you laughed without restrictions. I stared at the picture and sniffled, pressed the sleeve of my shirt to my nose as I tried to pretend I had allergies. I slid the picture back and I realized there was a note wedged in there as well. I felt like it was my birthday. Another note, and this freaking masterpiece? Was I even allowed to keep this? It was perfection, it needed to go to a gallery. I took a deep breath and read the small little note, and my fingers started to shake.

I slid everything into the envelope and pressed it inside my jacket up against my heart. I grabbed the envelope from earlier and a new piece of paper zipped up my letterman jacket and raised my hand. Allergies, I told her, need to go to the bathroom. My eyes shone, my nose red, she didn't need much more than that to believe me.

I went to the bathroom and went into the last stall. I stepped on top of the toilet and sat down on top of the tank, pulled the note out once more, and reread it. An angel, she called me. *'You're an Angel, Green. But I hope you know that no matter how dark the world is, there's a light waiting to shine down on you.'* I placed the note back into the envelope, placed the envelope back in my jacket, and dug the fingers of my right hand into the material of my sleeve on my left wrist. I squeezed it tight, as tight as I could.

I pressed my forehead against my knees and wrapped my arms around my legs, arched my body in a way that the envelope wouldn't get crinkled. With my face pressed against my knees, I let out a shaky breath. "If I'm an Angel, then you're my light," I whispered as a tear slid down my cheek. Once I calmed down, I went out to my locker and pulled out a piece of paper and a pencil. With another sniffle, I replied to her, folded the note carefully into the small envelope, and stuck it in my pocket.

I was too scared to carry around this masterpiece, what if I crumpled it after the sixth? Plus I knew it was raining, even if the coach wanted us in the gym for practice. I placed the picture in my locker in between two textbooks, shut my locker, and ran up the stairs to her locker. I slid the envelope inside it and went back down to my class. I walked in slowly, sat back down in my seat, and drummed my fingers on the desk in anticipation.

"If I'm an Angel, then you're my light."

Chapter 13
Kinsley

I wasn't really surprised to not see a letter in my locker after the seventh period. What did I expect? She replied after sixth, and I had dropped my reply off on my way to seventh since I had already been late anyway. Peyton literally had the same seventh period as me, but I was still disappointed. I wanted to stay after school and draw in the art club room, but I knew it was stupid. I would be all alone since Isabella worked today and the freshmen thought it was supposed to be a no-club day. The thing about the art club room was the rain always seemed to pour into the windows. If it was windy, like it was today, the rain sprayed everywhere and soaked everything. It wasn't worth it to try to go in there and shield my paper from the rain just so I could draw, especially if I was going to be alone. If I was going to be all alone, I might as well be alone at my house where it was warm and I could draw in peace.

I knew I only stayed to see if I was going to get a letter, but after the last bell rang, I watched Peyton walk out the front doors with a couple of her friends. They tried to brave the rain, and I guess they didn't care to go to their lockers before they left. It kind of made me feel strange to know she just left without even a glance toward her locker. From what she said in the letters, she made it sound like she had been eager to read them, eager to get to them, eager to talk to me.

So why didn't she race to open her locker to see if there was a reply? Maybe she thought I wouldn't have time to reply before the last class and figured to just wait until Monday to check. I shrugged, walked down the stairs to the second floor, and waited in the stairwell for Isabella. Normally I went to Isabella's locker to wait for her, but I just didn't feel up to it today. "Look at you, I don't think I've ever seen you smile like that, bro. How's the lucky lady doing? Do I get to meet her?" I looked up in surprise and moved to the side for a group of football players to walk past.

"What? Do you have a girlfriend? No way! Who is she? I thought you were going to take me out on a date!" I rolled my eyes at how needy that sounded. I never did understand the strange groupings of this school. The football players always had the cheerleader girls attached to their hips, while the basketball team always had the swim team and the volleyball team girls with them. It was like they thought they couldn't date outside of their group or something weird like that. It made me wonder what would have happened if I had stayed on the basketball team despite Roan's bullshit. Maybe Peyton would have naturally got with me, or maybe one of the other girls. I have no idea why that made me cringe so much but I shuddered as I felt a cold chill race up my spine.

One of the guys chuckled as I lowered my hood to hide away from them all. "She's not my girlfriend, not yet anyway. We've just talked so far. I don't know how to explain it, she was really special," the guy replied. He had a deep voice, but it was soft, like a melody. I lifted my eyes, I wanted to see who had said that. Unfortunately, the group was already out of sight, and I couldn't even hear their conversation anymore. I wasn't really sure why I wanted to see who said it. It just sounded so real. It was different, the way he had spoken of her, and the sincerity in his voice touched me. Normally when I overheard the football players talk about girls, they made crude jokes about how easy a girl was, and how they were all the same. This was a guy called her special, and it touched me.

"Let me guess, no letter to go home with over the weekend?" I snapped my head up as Isabella slipped her hand through my arm and pulled me with her down the stairs. She walked faster than usual, but I knew her mother waited outside for her. There was no way she could keep that woman waiting, she was relentless.

I chuckled softly with a small shrug. "Actually, there was a letter there and I replied to it, it made me late for the seventh period. But then Peyton ran out the doors after the bell rang without going to her locker so yeah, no reply I guess." She looked at me with a strange look on her face and I knew I didn't really need her to speak to know she figured out my mood. "The letters make it seem like she's really interested. Like she's eager to get them and to read them, and maybe it's just me, but her running out the door without even stopping to think to check her locker kind of annoys me. I don't know, it's probably nothing. She probably just thought I wouldn't have had enough time to reply and decided to wait until Monday to check. I'm probably making too much out of this," I said to her, shaking my head back and forth.

She reached her hand into my hood and she gently pressed her thumb against my cheekbone. I hissed quietly from the soft pain on my face and she frowned as a group of people walked past us whistling for us to get a room. "I don't know, something doesn't seem right. Maybe it's true and she didn't think you'd get enough time to write a reply but I don't know. I think I need to investigate something." she declared. I must have looked at her in a way she knew I was terrified at the sound of that because she shook her head at me with a laugh. "No, *Dios mío*. I won't go anywhere near her or talk to her. I want to look at pictures, that's it. I promise. I can do that in the safety of my home. After work, of course, because Mami will kill me if I try anything now."

I glared at her as we walked out the door. We instantly pulled away from each other as we slipped our bags under our coats. Others ran into the rain using their backpacks as umbrellas, as if that would protect them when all it did was soak through them and their school supplies. We wouldn't risk it ourselves, not with our drawings and art supplies in our bags. "Fine, just pictures. And tell me tomorrow what you find?"

"Tomorrow?" she asked as her mother's car pulled up. "Oh! Right. Because we were meeting up to tag that clean wall on the side of the post office. See you tomorrow, Kins," she leaned over and kissed me on the cheek.

I waved goodbye to her and blew a kiss to her mother through the window as they sped off, then made a run for my car. I knew it was going to rain that day, so I parked closer than usual. I instantly slipped my bag out from under my hoodie and pulled out the letters to make sure they were still good and dry. I sighed in relief, looked at the school once more, and frowned. It really was going to be a long weekend without hearing from Green. I realized I had taken to calling her Green instead of Peyton lately. The letters just didn't feel like her.

What if something bad happened? What if I messed everything up? I was known to do that, so I really wouldn't be surprised. I shook out my hair as I ran my fingers down my face and stared at the school. I could see the gym lights from there, the tell-tale sign that it was filled with jocks for after-school practice. I knew the swim team didn't practice today, but that was because they were going to a meet tomorrow and the coach wanted them to rest for it. Though I couldn't help but wonder, couldn't she have considered staying to check her locker? I groaned as I banged my face on the steering wheel. I couldn't get over how strange her actions were in comparison to the letters, but I was acting stupid. "Where was the Kinsley that didn't give a crap about anyone or anything besides Isabella?" I scolded myself in my rearview mirror. "Here you are, moping around like some love-struck middle schooler over the loss of a letter."

I nodded as I tried to ignore the nagging feeling in the back of my mind that something was wrong and drove away from the school. It was annoying trying to drive out of the school in the rain. Since so few students had vehicles, most either rode the bus or their parents picked them up. There were a few who braved the rain by running as they clutched onto their umbrellas or piled in as many people as they could into the few cars in the parking lot. Because of this, rainy days sucked. Those who walked hated every bit of it, and more than once I've had people stop me for rides.

I was nice sometimes, but I really didn't feel like it that day. I just wanted to get home and mope around doing nothing I always did in the large house that was nothing more than a cage. I blasted the new song from SayWeCanFly and locked my doors so no one could jump in. It was always so much of a hassle to drive in this because everyone blended in when it rained, like beautiful shades of grays and blues. As I moved slowly through them, I watched the students as they ran, laughed, screamed, and danced in the rain. I wondered sometimes what it felt like to just not give a fuck like that.

To stare into the eyes of someone I loved, throw my head back, and laugh in the rain. To not care about being soaked through or wet, or that I'd probably get sick the next day. Just me and them, at that moment. Would time stand still? Would I think about how wet and gross I felt, or would I think about nothing but those eyes, that smile, that face as it stared into mine? Those green eyes. I blinked, and the car behind me beeped at me to keep going as I frowned. Why was it whenever I thought of Peyton I saw her with brown eyes? The letter clearly said green. I sighed as I drove out of the parking lot and tried to ignore the kids who decided to run on the road instead of the perfectly good sidewalk as I went around them.

I considered fast food but remembered that Gloria, the cook, had actually stopped by a few days ago with some already-made food in containers for me. She knew that I knew nothing about cooking and that I was home alone for weeks without home-cooked meals. I swear, the number of times I begged that amazing woman to take me home with her was countless. She still made sure to remember me and bring me food when my family forgot about me, which was constant. I still had some containers left I could heat up and decided against fast food. Something about the rain made me want to have a home-cooked meal, even if it was something heated up from a container.

I lived in one of those gated communities with all the other rich families in town. They seemed to like to keep the bigger fancier houses inside a large gated area. As if they had to separate them from the poorer houses so they could feel even more special than they already did. It made me feel like I lived in the Zoo like each house held a different breed of animal. I waved at the guard, unsure if he even saw me with all the rain but the sleek sticker that we all had rested on our windshields was too hard to miss, and he lifted the barricade for me to drive in.

Our house was further near the back, where we had a large private backyard. It was filled with all kinds of unnecessary things. A pool, basketball court, and a garden that my parents had probably never walked in to save their lives but were meticulously taken care of by our gardener. There was a gazebo, a light brown gazebo, probably my favorite part of the garden. I liked to sit in the swing on the gazebo and draw the flowers, especially when my family was home. The farther away from them I could get the better.

I pulled into the driveway and opened the garage with the button in my car and parked where I normally did. Mom and Dad's cars were gone, as usual, which left just mine to sit near the few cars my parents collected over the years that they barely drove. There was room for more cars, of course, but for now, we didn't have any others. The next one would probably be the bright pink convertible Kennedy wanted, and I didn't look forward to the day that horrifying bright hot pink color thing lit up like a neon light inside the dark garage. I got out of my car, grabbed my things, walked through the door, and kicked my shoes off.

Our family liked to wear slippers in the house and even had extra slippers for guests, but I never bothered. I either walked around in my socks or bare feet, since I liked the feel of the carpet. As always, the house was empty. Well, not entirely. I knew the housekeeper was around somewhere cleaning something, but she was mostly silent and ignored me. She also didn't speak English or Italian, and I had no way of communicating with her even if I wanted to. She did like Isabella, however, and the two of them would talk constantly whenever Isabella came over.

I heated up some leftovers and took the plate up to my room, sat down at my desk, and sighed. "Fuck," I groaned as I placed my face in my hands. I just couldn't understand why I couldn't get past it, and the intoxicating smell of baked potatoes and roast beef with carrots wasn't enough to pull me out of my sour mood. She never tried to look in her locker. Nothing added up and it bothered me.

I grabbed some paper and a pencil with a sigh as I blasted music on my stereo system. Sometimes the music made me feel even more alone. Inside this large cage where I could open all of the doors and run up and down the halls and scream along to the lyrics and hear nothing but the echoes of my voice and the choked sobs of my tears. Despite this, most times I craved the music because the silence itself was just so freaking loud.

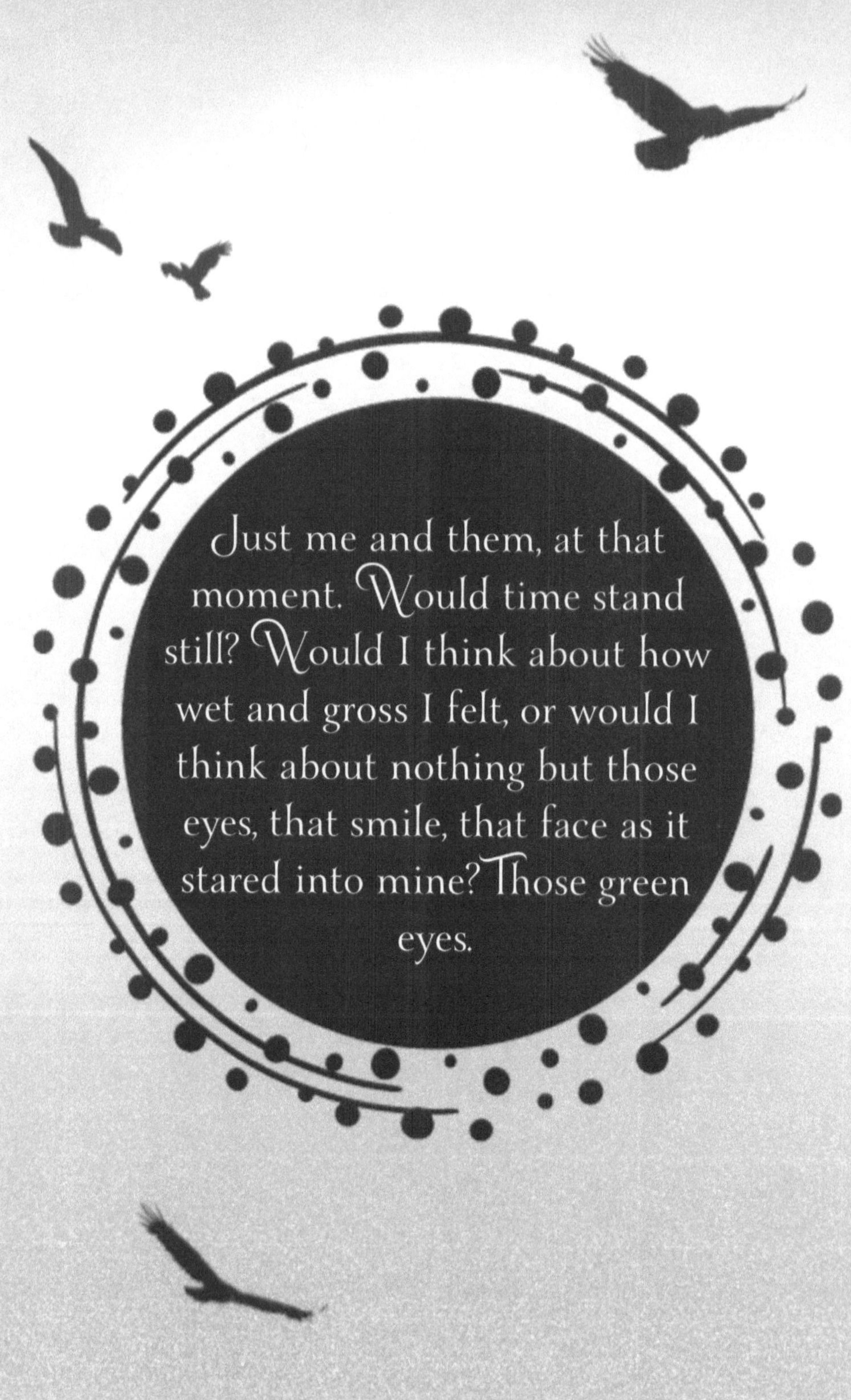
Just me and them, at that moment. Would time stand still? Would I think about how wet and gross I felt, or would I think about nothing but those eyes, that smile, that face as it stared into mine? Those green eyes.

Chapter 14
Green

I don't know why I did it. Maybe it was because of the way the rain hit just right against the building. The howl of the wind as it slapped the trees into the glass windows, or the fact that everyone else ran to the cars and tried to brave the storm. I didn't join them; I didn't want to. Sure, I could have hurried and slipped the letter into Sparrow's locker and then ran back down to get into the truck. The guys would still be there for a little while. They thought it was funny to get the girl's uniforms wet so they could tease them. I just wanted to see. Maybe I was scared she'd be there, that she'd be in the room. Maybe I wanted her to be there.

What would someone who was real look like, compared to the fakes that surrounded me all my life? Would she be surrounded by others? Or would she be by herself? I found myself in front of the art club room and frowned, unsure of what to do. Would she notice me? She knew who I was, even if I didn't know her. She'd definitely notice me, but would I notice her? I felt like I would. I felt like I knew her soul enough by now that she'd be obvious to me. Sure, I told myself that, but whenever I scanned the hallways to search for whoever she could be, none of the girls ever seemed to stand out.

I felt the envelope in my pocket, waiting for me to reply to it. I didn't have enough time before school ended, I only had enough time to read it. I should have written something fast, or maybe waited until I got home to write something down and dropped it off before school started Monday morning. I should have done anything other than stand in front of this solid oak door with the broken nameplate that should say *'Art Club'* but said *'A lub'* instead. Some of the letters had fallen down and broken, long since swept up by the after-school janitors. I should have taken a step back and run into an empty classroom to reply to the letter where she wouldn't accidentally see me. I should have done something else, anything else. No matter how many times I tried to convince myself to run in the opposite direction, I couldn't stop my hand as it gripped the doorknob.

Brave, I told myself. Sparrow is brave, going out of her way to write a letter to a stranger, she was brave. I needed to be brave like her. I took a deep breath, my hands shook as I turned the doorknob and pushed the door open. I wasn't sure if it was because of the fumes from the leftover goo smell that lingered in the air, but I let out a breath of relief that it was empty. I had mixed feelings because as much as I was glad it was empty, I was sad at the same time. Another weekend without her letters.

I could just give her my number. I don't know why I hadn't. Texting would be better than how slow letters are. It would go faster, and we wouldn't have to stop the secrecy either. Unless, of course, we already had each other saved on our phones, but I highly doubted that. Besides a few of the players on the team, my brother, and my parents, I didn't have anyone else saved. I shook my head and walked into the room, over to the window, and sighed.

I stared out at the football field, and all I could do was laugh. The drawing. Sparrow had to have drawn it. The styles were similar, but they didn't have as much detail or love in them as the one Sparrow had drawn for me specifically. I wondered if that was when she started to look at me, to see me, and think... *'Maybe I should write him a letter?'* I knew she wrote down in the letters that she didn't really know me, she was just interested.

She was so uncaringly honest about that, whereas most girls who liked me threw themselves at me. They would tell me they were in love with me even though they didn't really know me. Sparrow was different. In a sea of fake words and loose lies, her honesty was refreshing. I tapped my fingers on the windowsill in the rhythm of the water pitter-pattering on the glass. The rain had let up some and I was glad, I had been worried I wouldn't be able to take the drawing Sparrow gave me home since I didn't want to risk it getting wet. I never really liked art or saw the point of it, until Sparrow.

Now all I saw was art. Like the rain that was painted against the windows and how it ran in spider-webbed lines down the glass. Intricate designs of different shades of blue and clear, shadowed by the heavy clouds that wiped away the sunlight and left everything dark and murky. I loved the rain, a little secret of mine. I would sit on my porch if everyone was gone. Or I'd stay in my room curled up under the open window and breathe in the smell as I listened to the boom and the crackle of the storm and wonder which one was louder. The booms of nature or the screams of my parents. Sometimes I wondered if they were competing. Each one grew louder and louder until they were so loud that I wanted nothing more than to make the noise fade away.

But then it faded away, and the silence came. I wanted nothing more than to hear something, anything. The silence was lonely, but the screams were deafening. Then it got to the point where I couldn't breathe without hearing anything but the screams as they echoed through my mind, through my soul. Sometimes I wished I didn't have to pick between the two options. Either I could have the screaming or the silence, but I wished there was a third option, a normal option. *'Maybe I should try again,'* a little voice whispered in my mind, the little voice that tried once again to remind me of my failures. I stared down at my left hand, my body always covered with my jacket. I always wore long sleeves, no matter what season it was. I stared and stared at the loose material that floated over the lines and wondered if I should.

'You don't have to hide anything, not from me. I promise, Green. I'm not going anywhere.' The voice of Sparrow was louder than the one in my mind, so much louder. It blocked out all of the pain, all of the darkness, as the light shined through and showed me there was another way. I let out a deep shaky breath, my hand wrapped around my left wrist tightly. I let go and turned around slowly. Without Sparrow, there was no light, and without light, there was nothing but darkness. Sparrow was a lifeline, and as scary as that was, I couldn't do anything else but let it shine on me.

I lifted my gaze to look around the room. The classroom was mostly dark, but it was bright enough to see the artwork that was hung around the room. The corner of the room that had a heavy weed smell was filled with drawings that looked like a child would draw, a group of kids that messed around, most likely, and I turned away from it. There were a lot of really well-done drawings that hung around the room, but as my eyes caught this one, I couldn't see anything else. My breath caught in my throat as I took a shaky step toward the drawing. My fingers trembled as I lifted my hand, inches away from the marks. A face shadowed in darkness, a black hood, or a black blanket covered most of the face. Unrecognizable, as if the face was no one important. The details were perfect.

Eyelashes, freckles, lines, and the soft tendrils of bangs poked from under the top of the blanket or the hood that was over their face. But the eyes, they were what drew me. The artist had rendered the model beautiful and alluring in its mysteriousness. The picture was drawn with charcoal. The dusty charcoal lines and shading were angry, harsh, long, and jagged, back and forth like the person who drew it was screaming. Swirls laid down on top of the long lines, swirls of lazy contentment, a smile, happiness, and I wondered as I looked at this picture if it was about me.

A picture drawn from unhappiness, but touched over time and made softer and happier. A picture that had been drawn in a span of time where the person who started it was sad and angry but became happier. To think that I had the power to make someone happy was such a foreign concept that I brushed it aside almost immediately. I knew the way I didn't matter.

It made me remember white halls filled with the sharp antiseptic smell and a bandage wrapped around me. No matter how deep I went and no matter how hard I screamed. No matter how much I bled, no one could see me. The screams were just echoes, the violence of a storm wrapped around me. A reminder that no matter how happy I was now, it was only a matter of time before I wasn't in the eye of the storm. Until the wind swept over me once more and carried me away with the destruction. I had never seen this picture before, but I felt it deep in my soul. With every swift line, every sharp angle, and every curled swirl, I was a part of every bit of it.

While I didn't draw this picture, my soul recognized it anyway, as the other half. I could smell how thick the charcoal was, pitch black, layer on top of layer. Amidst all of the blackness, there was something bright, something light, something beautiful. The eyes were bright blue, cerulean blue. When I say eyes, I don't mean the drawing was just a slit with a white orb and a blue around a black pupil. These eyes had every dark line drawn through the white for veins, the eyelashes swirled expertly over the lip of the lower eyelid. The eyes hooded and looked down, and every part of this picture tore at me. *Hidden*, Sparrow had said. *Similar*, She had written. In a sea of fakes, it seemed that all along, there was someone who was just as real, and just as hidden as I was.

I took a deep breath and took a step back, pulled out my phone, and took a picture of this masterpiece. As much as I wanted to send her a letter to beg her to let me take this home, I felt like it wasn't finished. I sat down at the table, pulled out a piece of paper, and smiled.

Amidst all of the blackness, there was something bright, something light, something beautiful.

Chapter 15
Kinsley

I woke up in an empty house and did my normal routines. I swam a few laps in the pool, shot some hoops, and drew, as I usually did in the mornings when there was no school. My weekends and breaks tended to always be me just trying to find something to do to keep out the silence. Even if it meant I blasted music on my stereo so loud it could be heard throughout the house. Finally, it was time to meet up with Isabella. By the time I pulled up in front of her house, I was a bundle of nerves. She had stayed at work late last night and didn't have a chance to look at the thing she wanted to look at until today. I was torn between the need to wait, and the need to just flat out ask her what she needed to investigate. My compromise was to wait until she got into the car, and then I'd beg her to explain. "Damn, Kins, did you drink too much coffee today?" She asked as she slipped into the passenger seat. I pulled out of the driveway and headed to the location she had marked earlier.

I tried to give her a few minutes, so she wouldn't call me obsessed, but when I started to drum my fingers rapidly on the steering wheel, I realized I couldn't hold back anymore. "What were the results of your investigation?"

She chuckled at me as I reached over and turned down the music. "Look, Kinsley, it could mean nothing. A trick of the light, or something, okay? But the more I thought about it, the few things you'd told me about the letters just didn't really sound like her. You have to agree with that. You've said more than once that she never sounded that deep when you were lab partners together. Then there was the fact that she didn't even seem curious. I'm just going to say this, if someone started to write letters to me, I'd definitely freak out trying to figure out who they were from. I'd look everywhere to try and see if someone was looking back. So, there's that strike. Plus you said she never tried to go to the locker and just ran out the door. Then I thought about something you said on Friday in the art room, and I realized something. I wasn't entirely sure, I don't stare at her, so I didn't want to say anything until I looked at the pictures first. So I stalked her Facebook," she held up her hands to hide her face from my reaction.

I parked the car and cut the lights before I turned to look at her. The soft hum of my engine was the only noise as I watched her. "Okay? I mean, damn, that's a good idea. Why hadn't I thought of that?" I asked as I mentally kicked myself. "So what did you find?" I had to physically stop myself from grabbing my phone and searching for her myself. I never really did bother with my Facebook. I mean, I had it, but I barely used it.

Isabella waited while I turned off the car and I turned to look at her. "Look, Kinsley. It might be nothing, but her profile was filled with statuses that said things like, this guy I've had a crush on forever just looked at me, and things like that. It made it sound like she's had her eye on someone for a while. I highly doubt that someone is you, since why didn't she mention the letters or anything? Maybe she had just tried to keep up appearances so I ignored that, until I looked at her pictures," she paused. I watched her bite her lower lip and frowned. "Look, Kinsley. It could be the lighting in the pictures, but really, all of the pictures? It wouldn't make sense, you know? I'm just going to say it, alright? Peyton has brown eyes, not green. The letter said the person you've been talking to has green eyes. I don't think you've been talking to Peyton. I think you put the letter in the wrong locker,"

I felt my heart race as I looked down at my hands. Absently, I wiped my sweaty palms against my black jeans. "There's no way. It's her locker, I know it is. Look, maybe something's off. What if her real eye color is green and she just wears colored contacts? She could just hide herself from those around her. There's got to be a different explanation for it all. There's no way I've been talking to a stranger this whole time," she opened her mouth, closed it, opened it again, and all I could do was sigh. I leaned back, grabbed a spray can, and shook it at her.

"Come on, let's not talk about this anymore. We have a wall to tag, remember?" I pulled my hood up and jumped out of the car. I could hear her curse me out in Spanish under her breath, but I remained quiet. Both of us had our headphones on turned down low to hear the cops just in case. Our hoods were up, and we dressed in all-out black apparel as we took to our spots and started to paint. We had on a pair of disposable respirator masks, so we didn't breathe in the fumes, so it was easy to not have a reason to not talk. She went all out as she always did. She put up the stencils she had made ahead of time and blended the colors on them, while I just painted a random image to try and distract myself.

All day long I had wanted to know what her investigation was, but now that I knew, I wished she hadn't told me. What if she was right? What if it hadn't been Peyton this whole time, I'd been talking to? What if it's been someone else? But then who was she? Who was the girl I wrote to?

"I Think you put the letter in the wrong locker."

Chapter 16
Green

The weekend was terrible. My mother had another episode all weekend, and my brother was nowhere to be found. My mother accused Dad of hiding him, and I stayed upstairs in my room wondering if she'd ask where I was. If she'd notice if I was there or not. She never asked for me, never wondered about me, and sometimes I wondered if either of them remembered if I existed or not. Dad threatened to bring a woman home just to cook, and I ended up cooking instead just to try and keep the peace. Dad refused to eat it. Said men shouldn't cook, threw his plate against the wall, and left. Mom didn't eat it; she was too depressed and wondered if he really was going to another woman. I didn't have the heart to tell her he probably was. It's not like this would be the first time he cheated on her.

She sat there at the table in tears as she stared off into space at the wall covered in crimson-colored sauce. Noodles were scattered all over the ground and little lumps of meatballs splattered over the carpet and tile. I left my father's mess, I left my untouched plate, and my mother's untouched plate on the table. I felt exhausted as I trudged up the stairs. My feet dragged as I slowly walked to my room, locked the door, and buried myself under my blankets. It was a habit, one I picked up long ago when my parents were always screaming or when my father was gone and my mother would just stare into the unknown. I hated when they yelled and fought, but I hated silence even more.

I grabbed my phone and put in my headphones. I held the newest letter tight to my chest as I reread it over and over again. *'You don't have to hide anything, not from me. I promise, Green. I'm not going anywhere,'* she had written. I wasn't sure if she even understood how much those words resonated with me. I imagined lips, soft full pink lips. A soft voice moved through my mind as those words echoed repeatedly. I couldn't help but wonder what her voice sounded like, what she looked like, and what her name was. All I could do was curl further and further into a ball as the sounds of my mother breaking furniture crashed through the house.

Why did it matter what she looked like or what her name was? I couldn't ever meet her; I couldn't ever let her come here. I couldn't let her in, otherwise, she'd just leave. I wasn't sure if I could survive that kind of loss. I wasn't sure when the letters became my lifeline. I curled up tighter into a ball and squeezed my eyes shut, letting the music drown out the crashes downstairs. The letters were my everything, and I never wanted them to end.

I lay in bed as my body ached from the pain. All weekend long I worked. After school I worked, and I picked up as many shifts as I could. Trying to save money, trying to pay for lunch, trying to get out of here the first chance I got. I remembered what Sparrow said in her first letter, about wanting to get out of this town, and I was half tempted to ask her to take me with her. Maybe because it was her, maybe because I was connected to her, but I felt like if we could keep this going until we graduated, I might have the courage to meet her then. What if she didn't want to wait that long? It wasn't like I didn't want to meet her; I did.

I had two girlfriends before, but they were never really much of anything. I went to their house, always to their house. We kissed, and we fooled around. I was too scared with the first one, she dumped me because I wouldn't have sex with her. The second one was recent, earlier this year, even. For the second one, I worked up the confidence to do it, but only in the dark. How to explain to them that I didn't want to show off my scars? I was ashamed of my failed attempt, ashamed that sometimes I wanted to try again just to silence the storm. I didn't really like it. Maybe because it was the first time?

She got clingy and wanted to come over to my house but I couldn't bring her here, I couldn't bring anyone here. She left me and I felt relieved. Should I have felt relieved? I was worried I was just as screwed up as my parents were. Maybe I shouldn't date anyone if it meant I'd have to make girls cry. Maybe with every crash of glass and every pound of the doors I was broken right along with the objects. Little by little, pieces of me were broken off until there was nothing left.

I curled up in a ball under my blankets and tried to ignore the screams as I felt the traitorous tears stream down my cheeks. The crystalline path was woven again and again to the point where sometimes I wondered if people could see it. Could they see the tears stained on my cheeks, the pain that echoed in my heart? Could anyone even see me? They'd smile, they'd clap my hand and call me bro. They'd bat their eyes and they'd giggle, but did anyone even see me?

Even through my tears, I felt my cheeks warm slightly. I remembered what I wrote in my letter to Sparrow. *'What if I was simply a nobody, someone who went home each night and curls up in a ball under my blankets to block out the noises, someone who pressed my hands against my ears wishing I had someone to talk to, someone to call when I can't stop crying? Would that terrify you?'* I wanted to scream into the blankets. I wanted to scream out loud, to join in with the sounds of my mother's broken heart and my father's rants. I wondered if Sparrow would ever break my heart like my mother's broke day after day. I wondered if I'd turn into my father, just an angry man who spouted out everything without care for how others felt. We were told from a young age to aspire to be like our parents, but what was there for me to aspire for?

It reminded me of elementary school when my teacher had us draw our parents. Everyone stood up in front of the class to show off a mother with soft hair and pretty dresses, or a father with a mustache and a briefcase, successful and happy. I remembered that day, even now after so long. I had been so nervous to stand in front of the class. My hands shook, my palms were sweaty as everyone shifted their eyes at me. We were just kids, we had to stand on a stool she had in front of the room to show off our pictures. While other kids stood there and explained their mom and their dad, I stood there and thrust my little hands up in the air, and silently showed off my picture.

When I stood up in front of the class I had a different type of picture, but I had worked hard on it and I was proud of it. The room had been silent as I lifted my paper in the air for everyone to see. A piece of paper filled with black paint and yellow beams of lightning. My teacher scolded me, her face red as she told me I didn't listen and the kids laughed at my crimson cheeks. I couldn't help but sit down at my desk and cry in embarrassment because I did listen. She had told us to draw our parents, and my parents were nothing more than a storm.

I did listen. She had told us to draw our parents, and my parents were nothing more than a storm.

Chapter 17
Kinsley

I knew in about five minutes that Isabella was right. Sunday morning I was woken up with a note from the housekeeper that said my parents were going to Italy for a little bit. My grandmother was sick. My grandfather died around Thanksgiving last year and she was all alone, unable to take care of herself. A crap load of other information about how they were still going to be running their businesses, just from Italy for a little while. I was just glad that meant I didn't have to deal with the Sunday family dinner or be forced to go to church. Kennedy would stay at one of her friends' houses until they got back, so she could keep going to school since she was too young to watch herself. That meant I'd have the house to myself for a while.

Hopefully for the rest of my junior year and all of my senior year, but I doubted I'd be that lucky. I woke up Monday morning and swung by Isabella's house as I always did, only to see a perplexed look on her face as she stared at me. She didn't want to tell me what she knew, though, because she said she wasn't sure if it was true or not. I was confused but I went with it. After all half the time Isabella didn't really make sense especially when she first woke up. I drove both of us to school and went to my locker. I grinned because there was a letter there. However, the trek up to the third floor and then back down to the first was long, and by the time I slipped into the classroom, the bell was about to ring. Five minutes, barely five minutes since I got to school, but what Isabella was frowning about was right there, smack in my face.

I just stood in the doorway, Isabella next to me, and watched her. Watched them, Isabella's eyes wide with worry as she looked at me. "I wasn't sure, so I didn't say anything. She posted something about this on her Facebook, but I didn't know for sure. I'm sorry, Kinsley. It looks like it started yesterday," Isabella whispered in my ear as I watched Peyton sit on top of her desk. Seated in her seat was a guy named Tyler, Roan's best friend, and another one of the basketball players. This wasn't even his class. He had his large hand wrapped around her leg as he held her in place and pressed his lips against hers.

I wasn't even sure what to think about this. The letter in my hand, the letter I hadn't even read yet. It felt like it burned me, and all I could do was stare. Someone behind us started to complain that they couldn't get into the classroom and Isabella pulled me toward our desks. I sat down mechanically and stared down at the letter on top of the desk. My hands felt sweaty, my heart beat too fast, and all I could do was stare at it. "Either she's the one writing these and she's pranking me or teasing me, or you're right Isabella, and I've been talking to a stranger this whole time,"

Isabella tapped her nails on her desk as she eyeballed the letter with a sigh. It was almost like she was going to burn a hole in the middle of my desk. The bell rang and Mr. Duckett came in. He yelled at Tyler to get out of the classroom so he could start teaching. All the while, I slouched down on my desk, and my eyes never left the letter. "This is dangerous, Kins. You don't know who it is you've been talking to; it could be anyone. You should stop, it's not the same now. Stop writing to this person, tell your family she dumped you or something. Tell them to get out of your business and to get a life of their own," she snapped. Her eyes were filled with rage as she moved a strand of dark blue hair out of her eyes. She must have dyed it again on Sunday, it still looked new and shiny.

Mr. Duckett was busy telling Peyton she couldn't make out on top of her desk, which earned him a group of boos from other students as they yelled stupid things at him. I leaned closer so I could whisper and she could hear me. "I don't care, Izzy." She looked at me like I had grown three heads overnight. "I don't care if I don't know who they are. All I know is I don't want to stop,"

It wasn't entirely a lie, but it wasn't entirely the truth either. I was terrified to know that I had been pouring pieces of myself out onto these letters for someone I didn't know. This person knew more about me than anyone except for Isabella. However as the letters came, the deeper they were, and I knew it was a matter of time before we started to talk about heavier things. Things we were too scared to tell anyone else, even those closest to us. However, I had to remember that this person, whoever they were, had never known who I was from the start. I had the upper hand, to begin with. I had been calm and collected over it all because I thought I knew who Green was. But this is what Green had felt from the start. The terror of talking to a stranger.

They risked so much to reply back to me. To trust me to keep their name and their letters secret. It could have been a prank on them from the start. I could have been awful and manipulative, just pretended to care. I could have taken their letters and put them up somewhere with their name and picture, told everyone their secret words. They trusted me, and they were brave. Green kept going, and I didn't want to stop. I wanted to know this person, to keep learning about them. As I clutched my hand tightly against my chest and looked down at the letter; I realized something.

Love, I had talked to them about love. Love through letters, how preposterous that would be. Love with a stranger, someone I had never seen. To never see their face, hear their voice, or feel their touch against mine. Despite all of what I lacked, the feeling was there, building steadily like a soft pang in my chest. Like a soft drum in a large quiet room that tapped softly at first, then faster. With every letter, it got louder, like a symphony.

Mr. Duckett had started to actually teach by then and I tried to listen. I really did, but all I could do was stare at the letter that lay there on my desk and look at it in a new light. Did it look brighter? I kind of felt relieved that it wasn't Peyton. The more weeks that went by, the more I slightly despised her. Sure, during our lab assignment, she was mildly nice, albeit uncaring. However, over the past few weeks of actually studying her, I came to realize she was just as loud and snotty as the other girls around her. I had tried to ignore that because of the letters, but all I felt as I stared at this letter was relief. Relief that this stranger, whoever Green was, wasn't her.

Honestly, I didn't care who they were or what they looked like. I didn't care what they sounded like, they were beautiful to me all the same. I wasn't surprised that Isabella was quiet for most of the class period. I expected her to sulk after what I had said and how dangerous this was. I felt sweat forming on my forehead and realized this would be the first time I had gotten a letter and I didn't respond immediately. I was scared, to be honest. Scared I'd read the words inside of it and see Green as a completely different person. I didn't want to view her any other way than how I had been this whole time. I wanted to talk to her, to keep going, but I was scared.

As the bell rang, I tucked the envelope into my book and slipped it into my bag with a frustrated sigh. I followed behind Isabella like a zombie to the third floor, our science class with Mrs. Masters. I looked forward to it only because I wasn't going to sit next to Isabella. She was sulking now, but I knew once she got over it she'd want to talk to me. I just wasn't sure right now what to say to her. I needed a second to breathe, a second to think. Isabella started to look at me with a wounded animal look and I kept my eyes trained on my locker as we walked past it. As we slipped into our classroom I settled in my desk with my chest aching painfully, and the blood pumping in my ears. I felt guilt settle in my stomach because I didn't reply to Green's letter. Because I didn't even read it.

Love, I had talked to them about love. Love through letters, how preposterous that would be.

Chapter 18
Green

Everything about today sucked. I had a black eye because I stood in the way before my father could hit my little brother. Honestly, I didn't even think my father realized it was my brother. He swayed back and forth more than a lopsided table, his white eyes lined with angry red lines that snaked back and forth like the bark on an oak tree. Then he grabbed my shoulders, stared me right in the eyes, and spat that word out at me. *'Faggot,'* I hated that word with a passion. It was all he ever said when he was home, or when he paid any attention to me or my brother.

Both of us grew up hearing it. He'd spit it at us when we were in the sandbox and drew shapes in the sand. He'd spit it at us as we looked at ourselves in the mirror for a little too long. He'd scream it at us if we walked down the aisle at the store and stopped to look at a stuffed animal. I tried my best as I grew up to be anything but that word. No matter how far I ran it was still there. Screamed in my face, yelled at the top of its lungs. I tried out for a sports team to run from the word and found out I enjoyed the sport. I worked out, and it wasn't enough for him. I worked at a car garage on cars when I wasn't home, but nothing I did was enough to run away from his words. They were just words and meant nothing, but all the same, it burned me from the inside out. A fire that I wanted more than anything to extinguish.

I never checked my locker when I got to school anymore because what was the point? I'd be late to practice and I couldn't bring the letter to practice. During school people just smacked me on the back and whistled at me. They called me the man and high-fived me. It wasn't unusual for someone like me to get a letter, it was just unusual for me to read them. But I'd read Sparrow's letters over and over again. They were like oxygen to me, as if I couldn't breathe unless I had an envelope in my hand and Sparrow's words to drown in. In the locker room, it was different. Everyone was still pumped from the adrenaline from practice. They were sillier than usual, and wanted to get out all of the pent-up energy they had accumulated before the adrenaline faded away. They'd grab letters out of people's hands and read them out loud, so everyone else could ooh and awe at them. I didn't want anyone to touch Sparrow's letters, they were for my hands only.

When I checked my locker before the first period, I was surprised there was nothing there. I knew by now that Sparrow wasn't a jock. She had made it very known how she felt about sports, but she did seem the type to get to school early enough to slip a letter into my locker before class started. I felt worry tear through me as I sat there through half of the class. What if I freaked her out with what I said? I had written things that would make her think I was a murderer. Obviously, I was kidding, but the part about me being a bad person? Plus in my letter to her, I had told her I had gone to the club room. Maybe she thought I was a stalker now?

Maybe I had scared her. I went into her personal place without permission. Maybe she was terrified now. She probably didn't like the idea of writing to a scared boy, a boy who hid under the blankets late at night to hide out the sounds. I was scared, I rocked back and forth in my first class. Mr. McCormick stared at me occasionally as if he didn't know what to do with me. I think he was just as relieved to let me go out to the hall as I was to be allowed to when I told him I had forgotten my English book.

I shrugged off my jersey, I felt too warm with my long-sleeved shirt and my jersey on at the same time. It was a hot day, despite the fact that it bordered winter and spring. The moment I closed the classroom door behind me I nearly ran to my locker. When I opened it, there was nothing there. I was so stressed out that I slammed the door. I had ruined everything, absolutely everything, and what did I have left? I had nothing more than a storm to live for. When did I start letting myself be so reliant on nothing more than letters? Was this even healthy? I took a deep breath and tried to center myself as I went to the water fountain and leaned down to take a sip.

'*Calm down,*' I tried to tell myself. '*Maybe I should try again,*' the little voice in my head said.

'*I promise, Green. I'm not going anywhere.*' As the different voices echoed through my mind they battled against each other. I cupped a handful of water and ran it down my face, spreading it through my hair. I felt the water trickle down my wrist and against my scar and shuddered.

'I need to be brave, brave like Sparrow,' I said to myself. I found the little voice and choked it deep down inside me. I grabbed my books and went back to class. I hoped desperately that I didn't just ruin everything.

'I need to be brave, brave like Sparrow,'

Chapter 19
Kinsley

I shuffled past Isabella to my seat in the back and nearly collapsed against the desk like a fish, as Isabella would say. My books and my bag still hung from my shoulder, burned against my side as if to remind me the letter was still there, untouched, waiting. I wasn't surprised when about ten minutes later my phone vibrated in my pocket. Where I sat, I could get away with texting because the girl in front of me had hair that was thick and curly. Most of my seat was hidden behind her luscious curls.

As for Isabella, however, I never could understand how she was never caught texting when she was sitting in the front row. She seemed to master so many things I'd never understand, and I gave up trying to question it a long time ago. I pulled my phone out of my pocket with a dramatic sigh and put my bag down on the ground as I studied the text message. *'If you're going to keep writing letters, I think you should be honest,'* she sent me.

I shook my head no with a frown even though she couldn't exactly see me. *'I'm not going to tell her who I am, we're not ready for that. She said she wasn't ready yet,'* I replied.

Even from this angle, I couldn't quite figure out how she ever saw the text or even typed a reply. Her eyes were straight and her arms unmoved, but not even a few minutes later a reply came through. *'I don't mean your name, Pretty Boy,'* her text said as I rolled my eyes. *'I mean you should tell them that you have discovered the person you thought you were talking to isn't who you thought they were. Tell them the truth, that you don't actually know who it is you're talking to. They might not want to keep talking like this, knowing neither of you knows who the other is. Maybe they won't care.'*

Not even a second later another text flickered onto my screen. *'If you two end up deciding to meet and fall in love or something and this comes up later on, she will be very upset and think you lied about liking her from the beginning. Or she'll think you always liked someone else and just accept her now that you know she's different. She'll feel like she's second best, and you need to tell her before she catches feelings. It's only fair to her,'*

I studied the texts, my eyebrows furrowed together, and realized she was right. I already said earlier I didn't want to lie to Green. I wanted to give every part of myself to her, to make sure I was completely honest. She would understand, I'm sure. I had to hope she would understand. *'You're right, Izzy. I'll tell her. It's only fair,'* I texted back. Her reply was simply a thumbs up, and I shook my head at her. I felt slightly lighter as I pulled the envelope out of my textbook and studied it. My heart pounded as I slipped it open. It felt like I was opening the first letter for the first time all over again now that I realized this wasn't Peyton. Now that I didn't actually know who Green was.

Sparrow,

An art club, to be honest, I didn't know our school even had one. You might get more club applicants if you considered putting up fliers, you know. I had to ask around, I probably shouldn't have, but I know the location of the art room now. I have to admit, I went into the club room. After practice, it was all very empty. So many different teams shoved into the gym. The volleyball team, the basketball team, the football team, and the softball team. It was interesting to try to practice with all these teams shoved into such a small area for so many people. I went up to the third floor to see if I could... well. It was a bad idea, to be honest.

What if I ran into you? I don't even know the club hours, and I don't know who you are. But I figured if you saw me, since you know me, you'd jump or stare at me with wide eyes, and I feel like... I don't know how to say this without sounding stupid. I feel like I'll know you with one glance, despite never actually seeing you. How to know someone based on their soul, even if you have never met them? I have to admit there were a lot of different artworks inside the club room, but there was one that I felt drawn to. It felt like yours. it wasn't signed, I don't think it was even finished, but that charcoal picture on that canvas was probably the most beautiful thing I've ever seen, besides from the other drawing, of course.

I'm not stupid. I'm sure we'll run into each other at some point, because I'm no different from you. My teammates all make fun of me for constantly running up to the third floor even when I don't need to, but I can't stop myself from checking my locker. From putting a letter into your locker, over and over again. You said no matter what I told you, that you'd never go anywhere, right? No matter what? Nothing will scare you away? I have to admit, that meant so much to me. These letters are like a lifeline to me, and I never, never want them to stop. Unless of course, I work up the courage to see you, face to face. Then I guess we won't need the letters anymore.

P.S. As to my life, to your questions about who I am, who I really am. I'm slightly terrified to show you. What if I'm a murderer? What if I have done horrible things in my life? Or what if, I...What if I'm simply a nobody, someone who goes home each night and curls up in a ball under my blankets to block out the noises, someone who presses my hands against my ears, wishing I had someone to talk to, someone to call when I can't stop crying? Would that terrify you?

I read the letter, reread it, and reread it again, horrified by how hauntingly beautiful that was. She narrowed it down for me though, but not by much. In all of the teams in the gym, there were two girls on the basketball team, and there was one girl on the football team that I knew of. Volleyball was mostly for girls, and softball was an only-girl sport. It wasn't narrowed down by much, but it was something. I felt my cheeks lighten up at her words about the club. She had gone to search for me, to search for the club. I felt my breath quicken, my heart pounded in my chest. I had almost stayed after school on Friday, and she would have seen me.

I wondered if she would have recognized me if she had known me. What if she wasn't even a junior? I didn't think I really cared even if she was a freshman, at this point. I just cared about her. About her words, even if I had no idea who she was. As for the charcoal drawing, it was mine. It sat there abandoned, I hadn't finished it in over a week because I wasn't sure how to finish it. I never left a project unfinished, but sometimes I needed to step back and pause before I could finish it. Her P.S. pulled at me, drawing my eyes back to it over and over again as I chewed on my lip. I hoped she wasn't worried I hadn't replied to her after the first period like I normally did. I pulled out a fresh piece of paper and started to write back to her.

Green,

Before I say anything else, I have something to confess. I had told you from the very beginning that I had only started to write the letters because of my parents, and that I knew who you were but barely knew you, just someone I had noticed in passing mostly. However, I started to wonder over the past few weeks if you were who I thought you were. The things you write in the letters are so deep and beautiful, and I feel so connected to you in a way I'd never feel with the person I thought you were. Then I kept thinking about what you said about your eyes being green, and that tugged on me. My friend looked up the person I thought you were online, and realized your eyes are a different color.

Not only that, but I found out this morning that the person I thought you were, is now in a relationship. Not that, you and I are in a relationship or anything I just... wow. I feel embarrassed right now. I'm just going to say it. I just assumed with how we talk back and forth, how connected we are, that despite not being together, we kind of are at the same time? Um anyway, so yeah. I just wanted to tell you that whilst I thought you were someone else, I now know you're not. I have no idea who you are, just like you have no idea who I am. If that scares you and you don't want to talk anymore, I understand, but I hope you still do, because when you said these letters are like a lifeline to you, I feel that, Green, I really do. It's no different for me.

P.S. That was my charcoal picture, and you're right, it's not finished yet. I haven't figured out how to finish it yet, but I'm working on it. If you want to come by when I'm there, or if you want to come by when I'm not, the club days are Monday through Wednesday, we don't meet on Thursday or Friday. Honestly, I might be slightly hesitant if you're secretly a murderer, but at the same time I might also slip you a list of names to add to your murder count, so I still think I'd be game, to be honest. Even if you have done horrible things in your life, you're not a bad person, Green. From my soul to yours, I really don't think you're a bad person. As to the last thing you said, if that's true then I wish I could be the one you call at night when you can't stop crying.

I ran my fingers through my hair with a sigh as I stared down at the letter. I wanted to crumple it up and throw it in the trash can, to keep up the pretense that I knew who she was for a little bit longer. I was scared she wouldn't reply back to me now. Instead, I slowly folded the letter up and got out a new envelope. I shoved it gently in my pocket and raised my hand, stood up, and clutched my stomach as I pretended to have stomach pains.

"One more time, Kinsley, and I'm going to need you to go get checked out. You know what I said about my daughter having medical problems, you children are always so sickly looking. I didn't recognize the signs with her at first either, you need to take better care of yourselves," she snapped at me. I nodded my head at her as I walked down the rows of desks and out the door, letting out a breath of relief as I shook my head with a soft chuckle. As I walked down the stairs to the second floor, I heard the slam of a locker and a heavy sigh, the sound of books dropped onto the ground, and frowned as I walked slower. With the hope that they'd finish what they were doing fast, I rounded the corner and spotted him. I watched as he lowered his face into the water fountain down the hall from Green's locker and took a deep sip with a sigh.

He wasn't close enough that he'd be able to see me, but if he turned his head to look in this direction he might. I didn't want to risk it until I knew he was gone. I watched as he got a handful of water and splashed it onto his face, the water droplets dripped down his nose and chin as he shook his face.

He hadn't seen me as he leaned down and gathered his books back into his hands, and I watched him walk in the opposite direction toward English class. It wasn't strange, people forgot their books constantly and went to get them. Maybe he came to school late, but I couldn't help the boom in my chest as I walked to the locker and slid the letter in. My eyes never left the English room's door.

I shook my head no, turned around, and walked back to the third floor, ignoring it. It was nothing, just fear of almost getting caught, and nothing more.

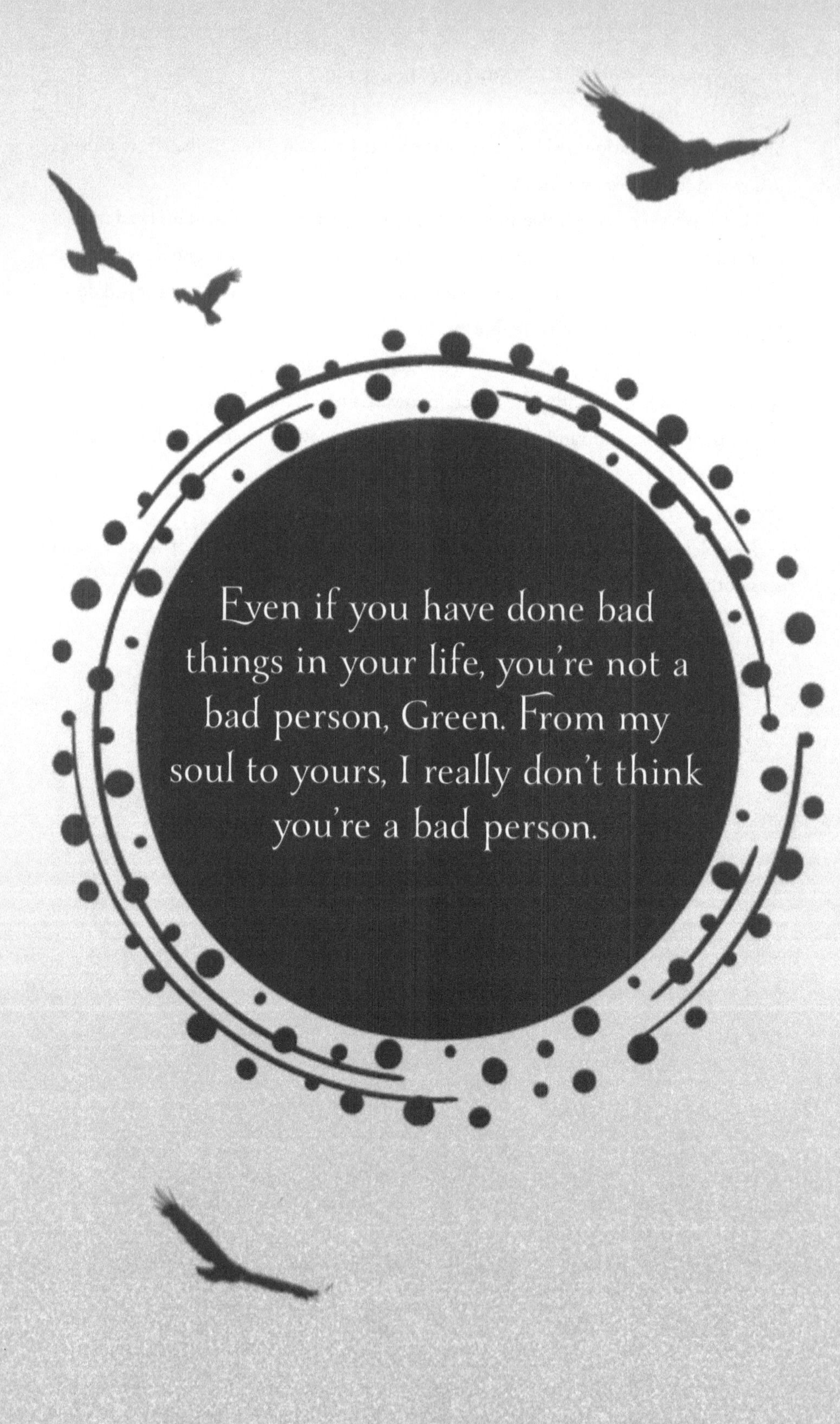

Even if you have done bad things in your life, you're not a bad person, Green. From my soul to yours, I really don't think you're a bad person.

Chapter 20
Green

I was happy when I opened my locker after my first period and confused at the same time. How did she reply after I had just checked it barely ten minutes ago? I felt a blush rise to my cheeks and wondered if she had watched me out here. Waited for me to walk away and slipped the letter into my locker after I went back to class. It started to get to me, the fact that she knew who I was but I didn't know who she was. I wanted to know. I wasn't sure if I was ready to meet her yet or not, though. To subject her to my home? To my life?

I hurried to my next class and sat down fast. I felt excitement spread through me, but fear at the same time. Was she late because she freaked out from what I had written? Maybe it was something silly like she felt sick this morning and ran late, and I was just worried for nothing? However, I couldn't help the bad thoughts as they swirled around inside me. What if she didn't even want to write to me anymore? What would I do if she had written down that she couldn't do this anymore, or that she had switched lockers so I couldn't talk to her? I shuddered but forced myself to open the letter and tried to make myself relax.

I scanned the letter with a mixture of fear and confusion as I read it and reread it before I could understand exactly what she had meant. She said she had put it in the wrong locker, she didn't know who I was. Before I could fear much of anything there she was, saying the things that I felt myself, deep in my soul. Soul mates, she had said. I felt a blush rise across my cheeks at her words, how important I was to her, just as important as she was to me. I realized it was better this way, the fact that she didn't know me. I didn't know her either. At least this way we were both the same in every way possible.

Though I couldn't help but wonder, as I slipped the letter into Sparrow's locker, just who was Sparrow? I scanned the halls, looked past the boys, and went straight to the girls, an automatic reaction that I've been doing for a while now. *Faggot,* I cringed as I tried to shove my father's words out of my mind. His voice, his screams. No matter how many girls looked up and giggled at me, none of them were my Sparrow. I didn't know how I knew, but I knew all the same.

I skimmed over all of the girls and walked around the guys. My eyes trained on every delicate face, every curve of every lip, every slope of every feminine nose, every crease of every soft neck, and all I could do was sigh. None of these girls were my Sparrow, none of them. I wasn't entirely sure what that even meant, but it didn't mean I was going to stop. I couldn't stop, not just yet. Not when these letters were my lifeline.

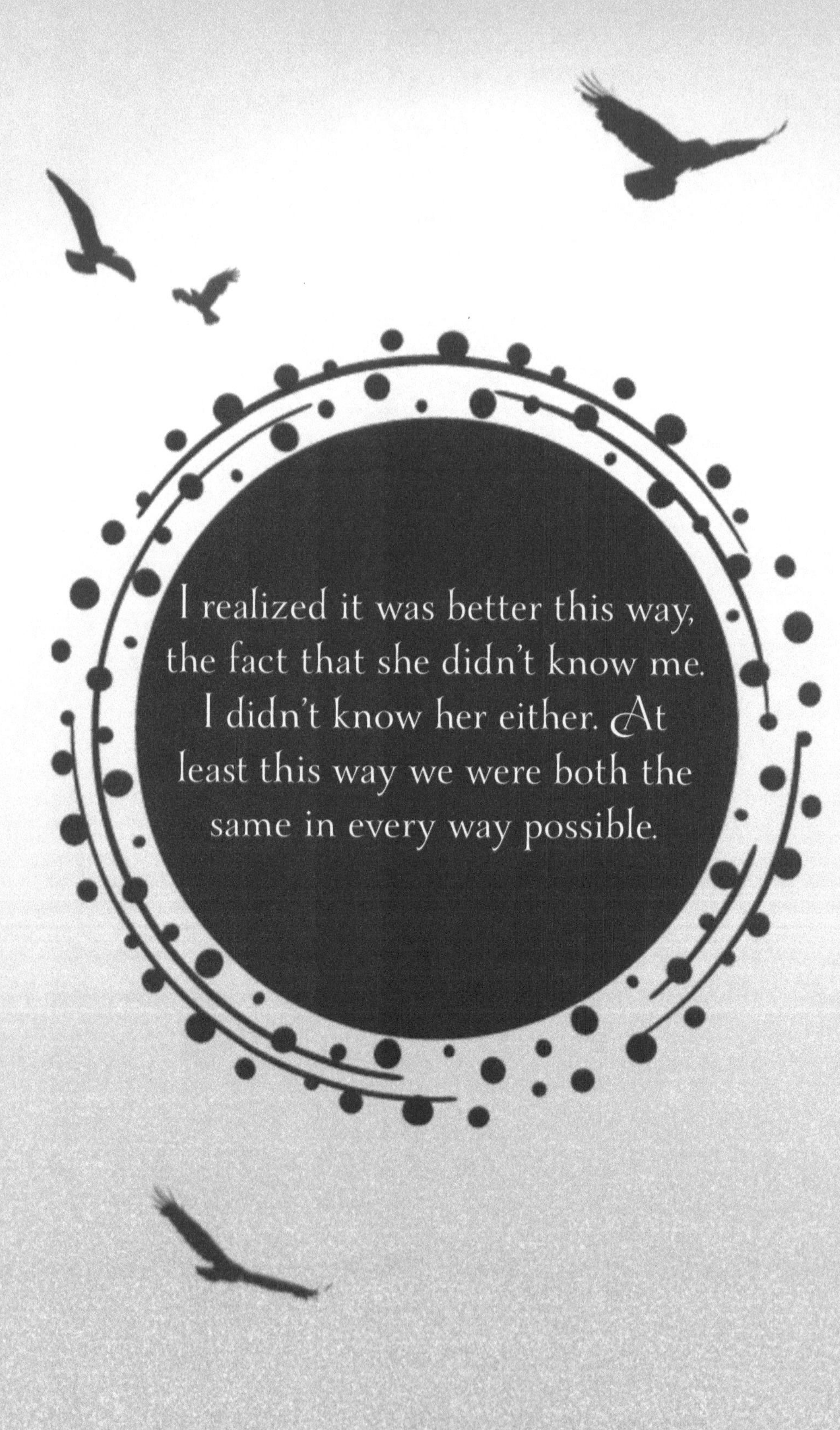
I realized it was better this way,
the fact that she didn't know me.
I didn't know her either. At
least this way we were both the
same in every way possible.

Chapter 21
Kinsley

Even though I was fairly sure it wasn't going to be there after the second period, I was still slightly grumpy that there wasn't a reply. It was stupid and unfair, to be honest. Green was probably worried that I hadn't replied after the first, like I usually do anyway, but here I was grumpy that there was no reply from her, when she wouldn't have even had enough time to reply. Isabella and I sat next to each other in the third period, in our English class.

Most of the classes were made up where the desks were separated, nice and neat vertical rows where someone always sat in front or behind someone else. English class was different. The seats were linked together, two to a group, much like Psychology class. In English class, we had stayed in the same seats all year long, and of course, Isabella sat next to me, but in Psychology class, we tended to move around more depending on whatever assignment we were given. I hated Psychology class because Roan was in it with me. I was yet to be forced to be paired with him, and I was hoping I'd get out of it for the rest of the year.

Isabella had already gotten yelled at for chewing gum, but as she leaned over to whisper into my ear, I could smell the sweet smell of her cotton candy gum in her mouth, making me half-tempted to grab a piece from her. I really wasn't someone who liked gum that much, but maybe the repetitive motion of chewing on something would get the fear out of my mind. Isabella, however, always knew exactly what was going through my mind. "You're worried about what she'll say? You told her, right? The truth?"

I nodded, frowning as I looked down at the picture Isabella had been drawing. She was always drawing for her next stencil, and while I normally never messed with anyone else's drawings, I knew this was just a rough draft that she'd end up redrawing at least three more times before she made it into a bigger picture to turn into a stencil. I leaned over, drawing a few lines that she'd missed a moment ago, hearing her mutter a thank you before replying to her. The best thing about Mr. McCormick, our English teacher, was the fact that he was partially deaf in one ear. That sounded awful, but for kids like us who liked to whisper to each other in class, it was the best thing for us. He never seemed to notice the crumple of papers or the occasional whisper of students talking, as long as it didn't get too loud and when he turned to look at us, he didn't see us doing anything we shouldn't be doing.

So as Isabella and I whispered back and forth, our eyes were mostly trained on him, watching him writing on the board a sentence he wanted us to correct from a Shakespeare play we were working on in class. "Yes, and yes. I told her the truth. I told her it wasn't on purpose, that we had done some investigating and noticed the eye color was off. I hope she still wants to talk though because I was really starting to like her." *A lifeline,* I had told Green. I was too scared to tell Isabella exactly how deep I was getting here, too scared to really tell myself, to be honest.

I didn't mention the fact that I had word vomited onto the paper to Green that I thought we were together. I still regretted writing that because she was clearly going to be freaked out by that alone, not to mention everything else that I wrote on the paper. She said from the beginning friends were all she was looking for, and here I was, telling her she was pretty much my girlfriend. I wanted to slam my face into the desk repeatedly but was scared I'd end up getting laughed at or sent home. The last thing I wanted was for the school to call my parents and make them come back from Italy. I hoped they stayed there forever.

"That's good," Isabella whispered, nodding. *No, it wasn't,* I wanted to tell her. *I told Green she was my girlfriend,* I wanted to say. I was too scared of Isabella's reply though, I just knew she'd tell me I was being a dumbass for even saying that. I felt like a dumbass. "Hopefully she'll still want to talk to you. After all, she's been talking to you this whole time without knowing who you are, so why would she be any different knowing you didn't know who she was?" We were quiet for a while before the bell rang. As always, Mr. McCormick waited until after the bell to put the homework on the board. I wasn't sure if it was because he liked to make us exercise or if he liked making us squirm. He knew we all had lunch after this but liked to prolong our hour of freedom by five minutes.

After we had written down our homework, all of us grabbed the piece of paper filled with the few paragraphs of the play we were supposed to be translating into nowadays speech, and we all moved into the hallway towards our lockers. "To the locker?" Isabella asked as if that wasn't obvious at this point. "Geez, you don't have to look like you're about to crap your pants," she mumbled under her breath. I took a deep breath, feeling terrified. What if she hated me now?

We walked through the masses toward my locker, and as I opened it, I took a deep breath, feeling all of the air in my lungs rush out of me. I tried desperately to remember exactly what it was I had written in my letter to her. I told her the truth, that I didn't know who she was. What if she admitted to me her eyes weren't really green but brown? What if all of this was some fucked up prank from Peyton after all?

I told her I wanted to be the person she called late at night when she was crying. Who said something like that to a stranger? But they weren't a stranger, not really. Why did their name need to matter? Their skin color, their hair length, the shape of their face, or the color of their eyes? Why did any of that need to matter for me to know who they were? I knew their soul, their beautiful soul, and as I lifted the letter into my hand, I realized that was the most important part, after all.

Isabella and I both shoved our books into my locker since that was a third-floor class and we tended to keep our third-floor classroom books in my locker anyway. "Are we going to the cafe?" I wondered, slipping the letter into my messenger bag. She nodded at me, giving a shrug indicating she didn't really care about the matter. It was our go-to place, however, and we rarely ever went anywhere else unless we were craving something new. I wanted to just go home and curl up somewhere. I was scared of the letter, scared of what it said, but at the same time, I was just relieved it was there. If I had really pissed her off, she could have just stopped writing to me. Then again knowing her the way I did by now; I didn't think she'd be that petty.

She seemed nice, and I had a feeling that even if she didn't want to do this anymore, even if she didn't want to talk to me anymore, she'd have taken the time to tell me why. I wondered if eventually, that would be what would happen when she found out truly who I was. She'd reject me, face to face, but she'd be gentle about it all the same. Maybe it was a good thing that I placed the letter in the wrong locker because at least I was given a kind person to talk to, instead of someone cruel. "Could you drive? I want to read the letter," I said softly.

She nodded, her deep brown eyes studying my face for a moment, before pulling my hood further over my head and patting the top of it. I wasn't the tallest boy in the world, shorter than most of the boys, to be honest, but I was taller than the girls at least. However, Isabella was really tall for a girl, like a supermodel with tall long legs, and she was just about the same height as I was. She didn't really get picked on for it, not that I knew of, mostly because she was scary. I did catch the basketball coach trying to recruit her more than once, however, before she decided to draw a detailed picture of a vagina and give it to the football coach. I had a feeling none of the coaches were going to bug her anymore after that and to be honest, I couldn't really blame them.

Everyone who had first lunch was pushing and shoving to get outside, to run to the few cars that were there and swarm them. Even if someone who owned a car didn't have the first lunch, usually their friends got to borrow their car, so from what I could tell most of the cars were usually leaving the lot as soon as possible, filled with as many kids as they could fit. That's the good part of being a loser, no one really tried to bug me and Isabella even though I always had an empty backseat that could fit at least three people safely, and around six if people sat on someone's lap like everyone else seemed to do around here. No one really ever wanted to eat the cafeteria food, it was rumored to have kids running to the toilets for the rest of the day and it was mostly avoided by everyone who had the money to eat out or the friends to pay for them to eat out.

As Isabella sat down in the driver's seat, a shout from Roan and about half of his group called out towards us, teasing us. "Look at that! He's so much of a faggy girl, he has to get the Latina to drive him around! She's more of a man than he is!" Roan howled out, earning a large amount of laughter from most of the group around him.

I rolled my eyes and pulled Isabella back into the car before she could jump out and expertly smack him upside the head with her shoe. I had no doubt she'd be able to hit him from this distance. I have seen the way Mami can throw her sandal down the stairwell and land it expertly against the back of Isabella's head, and Isabella's aim wasn't any different. I ignored her loud stream of Spanish cuss words as I put on my seat belt, cracking open the window as she started to drive. I could still smell the wetness lingering in the air from the storm that had been on and off since last Friday, wondering if it was finally finished or if it was going to rain yet again today. It was making me feel sleepy, and I wanted to just lie down in the art room and take a nap. I considered it, but I was worried the toxic goo fumes would go to my brain and I might not wake up again afterward. Maybe if I started taking out small amounts of money from my card from the ATM and stuck them to the side, I might be able to talk the housekeeper into sneaking into the school and scrubbing the inside of the art room once and for all.

I had to get Isabella to do all the talking, and I was sure I had to pay her a small fortune for braving that smell, but that woman was a miracle worker who could clean just about anything from what I noticed, and I was sure if she went in there, the fumes would be gone once and for all. I shook my head, trying to pull myself out of my sleepy thoughts, and opened the letter. I could feel Isabella turning to look at me, but she was quiet now, letting me concentrate as I opened the letter with shaky fingers and read Green's reply.

Hey, Sparrow.

I just… wow. I was worried when there wasn't a reply from you after the first period, but I guess this is why. You were scared, right? I thought I had scared you away with what I wrote, but I didn't expect that. I can get why you're scared. To be talking to someone, and having no idea who they are? Yeah, trust me, it's scary. But at the same time, we really are the same, you and I. A lifeline, it really is, and as long as you're fine with continuing this, so am I. Yeah, the eye color, I guess that's a pretty big indication if they're different. My eyes are a light green, if that matters. I don't feel like that tells you too much so you'd be able to figure out who I am, nearly half of the school probably has light green eyes. I guess I should probably wonder about your age though?

If you're over eighteen, like a lot of the seniors are right now, I should legally inform you that I'm only sixteen, I'm a junior. But you're right, after all. No, I'm not seeing anyone right now, and while this isn't really dating, it's not…not dating either, in a way. I wouldn't be with someone else and do this as well, because honestly, I've been in a relationship twice in my life, but none of them were as serious as this. I couldn't be with someone else while doing this. So as long as you're okay with this, so am I. Who knows, maybe letters can lead to romance after all. Maybe this'll be something people talk about for ages, one day.

P.S. No matter what? …Even if it's four in the morning?

I felt like I couldn't breathe. The way I felt right then, the way my heart was beating so profoundly in my chest. The spread of crimson touched every corner of my cheeks, it shouldn't have been allowed. Was this what love even felt like? I felt like this was love, or was that word even allowed for something this deep? To be almost seventeen and to be able to feel this feeling spreading throughout my body. I couldn't help but think about how much I wished everyone would be able to feel like this, at least once in their life. Would I regret this, when they found out who I was?

The boy who was rumored to be gay, was shoved around by Roan and his gang. The boy that the teachers mostly turned a blind eye to because the basketball team had won a trophy last season and they were still considered celebrities around school. As Isabella pulled into the parking lot next to the little cafe I didn't speak, and I was grateful she didn't try to talk to me.

She knew me better than I knew myself most of the time. She could see the wheels turning at the back of my mind and she knew I was thinking about what to reply, about what Green had said in the letter that was being tightly folded back into the envelope and gently slid inside my portfolio with the rest. Isabella excused herself to go to the bathroom, and I had a feeling she only did so because she knew I wanted space for a few minutes to reply to the letter. I knew she'd ask me about it afterward and I was fine with that, but I needed to concentrate first.

I ignored the tables filled with people, couples who were having their lunch break from work together, older people who had on sweaters for the community college we had in this town, and a handful of students who went to our high school. There was a small giggle coming from a group of softball girls and I did a double take, wondering if Green was among them. I had been doing that lately, looking at all of the girls that walked the halls, all of the cheerleaders that wore their uniforms knowing very well that it was still considered a sport as well. Most of our jocks on whatever team they were on would wear either their uniforms around the halls or jackets from their sport, or the girlfriends would wear their boyfriend's jerseys. It was pretty easy to spot the jocks, and I found myself studying all of them.

Looking for a hint of light green, and even when I found a few, I still didn't know if they were right or not. I walked past them all and went to the table in the back, watching Isabella disappear around the corner towards the bathrooms. She had stopped to talk to the owner, who was so used to us by now that I wouldn't be surprised if she asked him to wait to send someone to our table until she got back, making sure I wasn't disturbed by a waiter either. I don't think I'd ever be able to find a better friend than Isabella, she really was one of a kind. I pulled out a new piece of paper from my messenger bag, tapped on the end of my mechanical pencil, and smiled.

To Green,

You're absolutely right. I was scared, but I realized I didn't need to be. Because who I thought you were was never really even someone I cared much for, to begin with. To be honest, I'm glad you're not that person, because the more I learned from you in these letters, and the more I learned about them from watching them from afar, they really aren't a very good person anyway. But you, Green. You're a good person, and even if we go the rest of our lives simply talking back and forth through letters, you're probably going to be one of the best people I know. I'm glad to be your friend, or your 'more than a friend', whatever this would be called.

Soulmates? It's way too soon to call whatever this is soulmates, and as you said your sixteen, a junior, and so am I on both accounts. We're way too young to use the word soulmates, but honestly, it's the best word I can think of for this situation. I'm really glad you're okay with continuing, because honestly, that was what I was scared of the most. The fear that you'd want nothing to do with me if you knew that both of us had no idea who we were. Besides, at the end of the day, why does what we look like or what our names are matter? At the end of the day, you're Green and I'm Sparrow, and that's all that really matters.

P.S. Even if it's four in the morning, Green.

I folded the letter nicely and neatly, slipping it into a new envelope when Isabella came back from the bathroom. Behind her was a waiter carrying a tray of what we usually ordered, and I smiled, slipping the letter into my pocket when the door opened, and in came a small group of football players. It was only around four of them, three of them had cheerleaders hanging on their arms, but I noticed one of the football players trailing behind the others, almost like he was part of the group, but away from them all at the same time. They all had sunglasses on, and Isabella tugged on my arm as the waiter finished placing our drinks and sandwiches down on the table. I could already see the owner moving to yell at them as the cheerleaders started to squeal loudly over something they were talking about.

It seemed like they were only there to get to-go orders anyway though, so the owner hastily led them towards the counter to pick up their orders. Softly, I explained to Isabella a brief summary of what Green and I had talked about. I didn't want to show her, it was so personal to me, but at the same time I didn't mind telling her and I knew she was worried about me. I was still too scared to tell her what we had said, however, about what Green and I were. It was such dangerous territory, and I knew Isabella would be really worried if she understood just how much I had gotten wrapped up in these letters. For a boy who had never fallen in love before, I was swimming in these words that were wrapped around the soul of Green, and I found myself willing to drown if it meant one more letter, one more conversation, one more peek at who Green really was, on the inside.

To be more than letters, more than friends. To be together, but not at the same time. It was more than we had started off with. I could feel the strain Green felt through the letters, because I felt the strain too, especially now that I realized I didn't know who Green was. The strain of wonder, wondering who she was, who she could be.

We were late going back to school from lunch. Both of us rushed up the stairs toward the second floor. The bell was going to ring soon for class to start, and while Isabella had her fourth period on the third floor, mine was on the second.

A group of kids ran past us towards class and Roan was with them. He shoved me into the locker that was decorated with so many useless decorations, the one next to locker 213. Although Isabella's next class was on the next floor, she kept me company as I slid the letter into locker 213, her lower lip caught in her teeth as she looked at me. "You know, this decorated locker right here is probably Peyton's. That's probably why I saw her against this one, that day. I'm glad I got it wrong," I said with a laugh as I slid my finger against one of the massive number of decorations.

"Kinsley, I couldn't help but wonder about something," Isabella said softly, so softly I had to lean closer to her to hear her. We had moved towards the stairs now; my Psychology class was near the stairs anyway and she needed to go up them to her next class. "What if Green is a boy?" She had moved so close to me that her lips were close to my ear so no one could hear. The few kids that moved past us snickered and started to whisper about us kissing. I could see why they'd think that since her face was inside my hood. It didn't help when she pulled away I started to blush.

I shook my head but then nodded, unable to stop my slight panicked sputter. "There's no way, right? I mean... what?" I asked, clearly thrown.

She laughed as she shook her head at me with a small shrug. "I mean, you never know, right? Either way, whether she's a girl, or he's a boy, I ship it," she snapped her fingers and blew me a kiss with a wide grin. I watched with a shake of my head as she walked up the stairs, and couldn't help but let out a slightly panicked laugh as the bell rang. A group of jocks ran up the stairs as I walked into my Psychology class.

However, my surprised mood changed when I walked past Roan and realized that Roan was a jock. A captain. If I remember right, the letters at one point talked about Green being a captain. I shook my head no slowly as I sat down and ignored the way the girl who was forced to sit next to me cringed and scooted as far away as she could with our desks being connected. I didn't really care if Green was a boy or not, to be honest. As long as he wasn't Roan, or she wasn't Peyton, then I was fine with that.

143

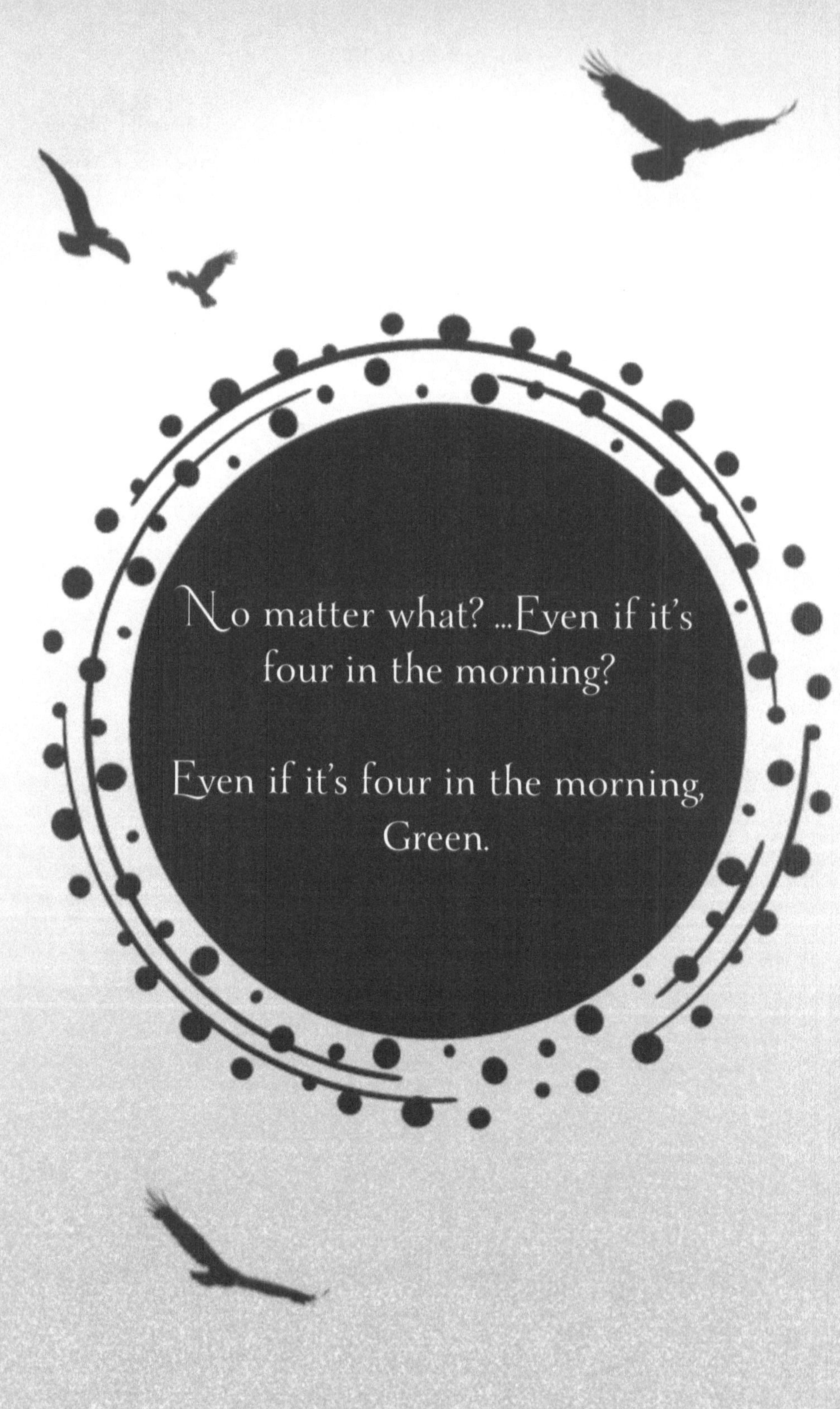
No matter what? ...Even if it's four in the morning?

Even if it's four in the morning, Green.

For the rest of the week, Green and I continued to talk back and forth. Our letters became continuously deeper and closer, to the point where I couldn't help but look at everyone who walked by me and wonder if it was them. I wanted to know more, and I could tell Green was hesitant about it. Whenever we talked about what they had said about crying at night, Green would change the subject. It frustrated me. I knew I didn't have a right to demand to know their life, but I couldn't help but feel protective of the person who I'd been talking to for so long now. Who was I to be protective of someone else when I got beat up daily? However, I knew I'd stand up for Green, no matter what. I might not have been the strongest guy in the world but I'd do anything for them. When Isabella mentioned Green could be a boy, I felt scared and curious at the same time. Sure, I had no problem with having feelings for a boy, but it was considered standard for me to have feelings for girls.

Everyone grew up expected to love the opposite gender. Their family expected it, and their friends, teachers, and strangers expected it. If two guys went out on a date and a hot girl was the waitress, she would flirt with the guys because she would just assume they were friends. The standard was opposite-gender couples, and while I had no problem with being with a guy, if Green was indeed a guy, I was scared all the same. Scared of what would happen if we were seen together. If I wanted to hold his hand or kiss him. Scared to try to figure out what came with a deep healthy relationship. I would research it, of course, but it didn't make it any less scary.

Fear of the difference, something that I wasn't prepared for. Even parents, when their kids got older, sat them down and explained to them what sex was. What the guy did, how to use a condom, and how to be with a woman. But our parents didn't look at our little nine to twelve-year-old selves and think: *He might be gay, I should prepare him for sex with a man instead,*' they just assumed their children were straight. They expected their children to be straight. It was terrifying to be something different from what was expected of you, terrifying that I could disappoint them more than I already had by being something they didn't expect or want me to be.

If I were to come out to my parents, they would probably throw me out. Or they would take me to church and try to *'heal me'*. They would tell me I had to beg God for forgiveness, but why should I beg him to forgive me for being how he made me? To think being different would be something I chose. Why would I choose to be anything that was different from the standard? To choose to have things thrown at me, to choose to have Roan spray paint my locker or shove me down the stairs. Why would I choose to live my life dealing with whispers, rumors, glares, and laughter? We never chose to be different from the standard, it's society's fault for how they expected the standard was the correct way, to begin with. So, because of society, those around me, and because of my parents, I was terrified that Green could be a boy. Terrified, but curious, all the same.

By the end of the week, I was a ball of nerves. The letters were all I held on to. The fear suffocated me, Isabella's words wrapped around and around me like a snake. She didn't do it on purpose, of course, but they were there now and I couldn't make them go away no matter how hard I tried. They suffocated me like smoke from a cigarette. Trapped inside my lungs and burned me, devoured me from the inside out. "Kinsley," Isabella said. It was the kind of tone someone would have if they'd tried to get your attention for a while but you ignored them. I felt a small pinch against my cheek. I instantly recoiled backward as I glared at her and rubbed the palm of my hand back and forth against my cheek, the normal hue turned a soft reddish color as the shock of the pinch settled into the skin.

She rolled her eyes at me, her fingers fiddled with the pair of sunglasses she had perched on top of her head. It was pretty sunny today now that it was spring, and I was both glad it was spring now and terrified at the same time. Spring meant spring break was coming soon, which meant a break from Roan, but it also meant a break from the letters, too. Christmas break had sucked, but I lived, and I guess I could live this time too. Spring break was shorter, after all. It also meant I would turn seventeen soon since my birthday was always during spring break or right before it was over, and in about four more months the school year would be over. At least my parents were still gone, but I wouldn't be surprised if they decided to come back just to torture me with their presence since they knew I couldn't escape them and go to school during the break. "Don't glare at me like that, I've been calling you forever," she said with a deep sigh.

"Dramatic," I muttered.

She snapped her fingers at me, flicked her hair off her shoulder like a diva and I giggled at her. "There's your smile, Pretty Boy. I have tried to get you to smile all day. What crawled up your ass and died there?" she wondered as she grabbed her drink and wrapped her lips around the straw. Mr. McCormick kept us all after class to finish the test he had given us, and Isabella and I decided to go somewhere closer to school. We were worried if we went all the way to our favorite cafe that we wouldn't have time to eat before we had to get back. It was the kind of sunny day that made me want to just skip the rest of the day and take Isabella to my place to swim. However, now that I had the letters, I didn't want to miss even a single second of school. I didn't want to do anything that would cause the school to call my parents either, not now that I was given some freedom from them.

"I can't shake the letters, Izzy. Now that I know that I don't know who Green is, I can't help but stress about who they are. Do you think this is what they felt like at first? Do you think this feeling will ever go away? I stared at everyone, girl or boy, and I was scared of who it could be. What if it's Roan? What if it's one of his goons on the basketball team? What if they are secretly a nice person but when they find out I'm me, they try to kill me or something? I wanted to ask Green to just meet up with me and get this over with, but they said they weren't ready yet. I'm freaking out, and I just want to throw up. Why did I ever even start this?" I wondered. I felt like I had aged ten years since Isabella said Green could be a boy.

Isabella stared at me with wide eyes as I realized I pretty much spat that all out at her so fast I didn't even breathe in between words. She made me repeat it all slower this time, and for some reason the second time I said it, I felt guilty. Guilty for the fact that, despite what I said earlier, the letters weren't enough for me. My soul was happy enough to get the letters and read the words, but my fingers ached to have a hand to hold. My arms ached to have a body to hug; my lips craved the touch of another, but not just anyone: Green.

I didn't care what they looked like, and honestly, I was fairly sure that no matter what they looked like, I'd be attracted to them just because they were Green. I just wanted to know who they were. Even if I did find out who they were, they wouldn't want me anymore. Not someone like me. "Tell them you want to see them then. Tell them you're going crazy and you need to see them, or you're going to burst," Isabella said with a shrug as if it could even be that easy.

I shook my head no before she even finished talking. "Green said they're not ready," I said simply. I had started to refer to Green as they or them because I was so unsure of who they were, that I didn't even try to assume anymore. It's funny all of this started with a simple letter of an unconcerned possible romance just to make my parents happy. A simple letter that was meant for a girl but slipped into the wrong locker. To think such a small act became something that was so monumental to me. It felt like my world was coated in a thin layer of gasoline and I could either wash it off or let it ignite, to burn everything around me. I wasn't sure which one would be better at this point.

Isabella had that look on her face, the one where I knew she was about to suggest we do something we shouldn't. It was the same look she got when she wanted us to go tag a building that wasn't abandoned and we would have to go fast and hope we didn't get caught. She was an adrenaline junkie but I wasn't. While she would run and scream with laughter from the cops when they chased us, I would just run terrified. I would question why I was best friends with such a psychopath, but then I'd remember she was amazing and worth every bit of it. After all, when you were best friends with someone and they called you up and asked you to help them with a dead body you do it, right? That's just as illegal, so at least this way she was happy and we didn't kill anyone.

"Come on, Kins! We can hide and just see them, that way they won't see us! Right across from the locker is a bench, right? Those benches are so big, and there's a trash can on one side and a plant on the other, we'll be hidden from view," I mean, we could probably get away with it. No one ever sat on the benches in the school. The janitor went off once on the kids because he was tired of having to scrape off the gum and wipe the sticky surfaces from them whenever they skipped class and made out on the benches. Now no one wanted to sit on them for fear of what diseases they could get from them.

"How would we even skip our last period?" I crumpled up my wrapper on my tray and entertained myself as I blotted the wrapper with the ketchup and pressed it into the tray liner to make a strange version of ketchup art.

Isabella rolled her eyes as she lifted her fingers to my forehead and poked at the large knot I had sitting there. It was still throbbing from when Roan tripped me on my way out to lunch earlier, and my forehead had collided with the concrete step when I fell. "It's still bleeding. To be honest, you should probably get it checked out anyway, and some ice. We should skip the rest of the school day together so you can rest in the nurse's office. I'll just say I have cramps."

I mean, I could do that. I gave the school nurse my home phone and if she felt the need to call my parents, they'd either get the answering machine or my housekeeper and she didn't speak English so that didn't matter. I kind of hated this plan, but Isabella was so sure it would work that by the time we had driven back to school, she shoved me up to the second floor to the nurse's office before I could complain. I pulled down my hood and the nurse gasped in surprise. She shoved me to a bed and had me lay down in it. Clumsy, I had told her. I wasn't sure if she believed me or not, but she never argued with me, so that was something.

It didn't matter if she knew the truth or not, Roan was the principal's nephew anyway, and with the basketball team being so successful lately, there wasn't much the school was going to do to him. Isabella got away with her cramps story. She was shown to a bed across from mine, and the nurse gave us both some ibuprofen while she cleaned my forehead and bandaged it. She gave me an ice pack for the bruise and told us both to try and rest. There were six beds in the nurse's office. All had a cloth that could be pulled over them to hide us for privacy reasons, and the nurse pulled both mine and Isabella's closed so we could get rest. When the nurse turned her back on us, Isabella ran into my curtain and slid next to me on the bed, her head pressed against my shoulder as we both stared up at the ceiling. "I don't know if I want to do this," I admitted as I moved to pull some of her hair out of my mouth.

She lifted both of her hands straight up into the air, her fingers spread wide as if she had tried to touch the ceiling, and then let them fall above her head. One went over my neck and next to my ear, while the other fell on the other side of her head. I shifted around so my arm was underneath her back and rolled over to press my chin against the top of her head as I draped my arm across her waist. She grumbled as she rolled over so her back was against my chest and I moved her hair out of my mouth once more before we settled down comfortably against each other.

"You don't have to if you're not ready, Kins," she said softly. When the nurse had taken care of me earlier Isabella ran out to my locker to check it for me, but told me there wasn't a letter in there. I didn't think there would be, since Mr. McCormick let us out late. I had to slip the letter into Green's locker later than usual and they probably didn't get it until after lunch was over. I could see the small circular clock hanging from the wall through the tiny slit in the curtain from where I lay and felt slightly calmer from Isabella's heartbeat against my chest.

"It's not that I'm not ready. More than once I was the one who hinted in the letters to Green that I wanted to see them, which I knew was stupid because I'm me and Green said they were a junior, they must know about me. They would take one look at me and laugh in my face," I said with a sigh.

She lifted my sleeve and pinched my skin. I yelped and buried my face into her hair to try and keep quiet as I cursed her out in Italian under my breath. "Or they will be a decent and kind person who will take one look at you and say: Oh, I know that boy! He's so pretty, he's quiet and misunderstood. Now that I know who he is, I can't help but see how perfect and wonderful he is!"

I grumbled as I closed my eyes and settled down against the pillow. "I think I'm going to throw up," I muttered before I drifted off to sleep.

Isabella didn't let me sleep for long. She had left the bed when she heard the nurse come to check on us and tell her she needed to go to the bathroom. She woke me to give me a letter. After I replied to it, I held it close to me. My heart beat wildly in my chest as the blush rose on my cheeks. The hardest thing I ever did was reply to Green's letter as I normally did, but I made sure not to give away what I planned to do. I was so scared as I watched the clock. When the bell rang for the start of the last class, Isabella and I both grabbed our bags and told the nurse we would try and push through our last class before school ended. She didn't suspect anything, but we knew she had already called the teachers to tell them we were sleeping there so the teachers wouldn't expect us.

She gave us both passes that we threw away the moment we were out in the hallway. As we walked down the second floor, we weren't very surprised that it was already empty. The class had started not too long ago by the time we were finally let out, and I slipped the letter into locker 213 as Isabella pulled at the bench to get it away from the wall. She grumbled over how gross it was and all of the diseases she would catch by touching it. "We could still just go to class if you want, Kins, or we could just leave. I know it's Friday but I don't work today," Isabella said as we stared in disdain at the hole she had made behind the nasty bench. "It's inventory day. Mami doesn't like me to help with inventory, she said I mess up her figures. Pilar is much better at helping than I am." Because her mother owned the meat market, she was forced to help out with it. Pilar was another employee who worked there with Isabella and her mother, usually on opposite shifts to help out when Isabella was in school and during the week so she had time to study.

I nodded my head as I tried my best to listen, but I couldn't stop the nerves that coursed through me. I could leave, go home. No one would notice, no one expected us now. Crank the music and beg Isabella to cook for me, and have a two-person pool party. But the more I thought about what I could do, the more I realized what it was that I wanted to do. I wanted to see who Green was, I needed to know. I knew it made me a coward, but I couldn't go forward without knowing. So, without a reply, I climbed over the bench and slid into the hole. I scooted over so she would have room too because I didn't want to do this alone. By now seventh period was almost over, and Isabella sighed deeply as she climbed over the bench with a chorus of ewes and gross, before she quieted down.

She pulled out her phone and texted her mother she would go home with me for the afternoon so she wouldn't come to pick her up, and for the rest of the period, we played games on our phones. We had our bags tucked beside us in the small hole we made, our bodies shoved practically on top of each other as we waited. The bell rang and we cowered even closer to each other, worried we'd get seen as the halls were filled with screams and laughter. I was on edge because no matter how much I looked, no one came to the locker. The halls were soon empty and we stayed because Green was in a sport. Sometimes there wasn't a letter after seventh, and Green told me sometimes their coach liked to come to get them during their last class to make sure they had extra practice time. So, we continued to wait.

We waited for another hour or two before the sound of laughter and screams was heard once more. Different kids ran up the stairs with their groups as they laughed with their teammates. We watched as they stopped at each other's lockers. I could see different groups of girls in various sports all huddled together. They giggled with each other as they went to different lockers in the hall. A fairly large group of basketball players surrounded Roan as he walked down the hall toward us and my breath caught in my chest. My hands trembled when the group stopped in front of the locker.

I let out a breath of relief when a few of the lockers on the row were opened but none of them were Green's locker. Isabella slipped her fingers against mine and laced our fingers together as she brought my hand to her chest, cupped it with her other hand, and rested her chin against it. I wanted to curl up in a ball and close my eyes against her, to let her do this for me on her own, but I couldn't close my eyes.

My heart pounded in my ears as the basketball players left the area and were replaced by a group of wrestlers who went on about how they were screwed now that one of the best players had gotten hurt for the rest of the season. "What if Green went home early? What if they never come?" I whispered under my breath as the wrestlers left. A few cheerleaders twirled and jumped towards the lockers, and then I saw Peyton with two other girls on the swim team, all of them so close to Green's locker, so dangerously close, but not close enough.

"Shhh," Isabella whispered under her breath into my ear. I curled closer to her. I wanted to bury my face in her neck but was unable to turn my face away from the locker. Then I saw them, a small group of five football players walking down the hall. They all looked like they were fresh out of the showers, hair still wet as they talked and laughed over some joke about the coach. One of them slapped another one on the back and the others left, leaving one of the football players alone. I couldn't see who he was or what number he was. His back turned to me and his jersey hung on his left arm, a few books shoved against the jacket and his side.

I realized I held Isabella's hand so tightly she would probably complain if we could talk right now, as I watched the guy open the locker with wide eyes. Green's locker, my Green. The locker was messy, a few books and papers fell out, and he cursed under his breath as he dropped my letter on the ground. The way he flung everything in his hands to the ground without care just to gently pick up my letter humbled me. For a moment I wondered if this was simply his girlfriend's locker, but then again, Green said they weren't with anyone. Plus, why would a boyfriend be that happy about his girlfriend receiving a letter? That would be really freaking weird.

I knew without a doubt that this was Green. No matter how scared I was, I was excited too. At least he wasn't Roan, at least he wasn't a basketball player. He gathered all of his books and papers and threw them messily into his locker, pulled two of them out, and shoved them into his bag before he slid his jacket back onto his body. I couldn't see the number how he was angled, but I realized as he closed the locker and turned to face the bench, I didn't need to. He didn't look at the bench but at the letter in his hand. The look on his face was filled with excitement and happiness as he smiled warmly down at the letter.

The guy pulled out his phone and checked the time, a frown on his face as he rocked back and forth and groaned. "I'll be late, crap. No time to reply to this now. It'll have to wait until Monday," he said with an annoyed sigh. He looked put out at the thought and my heart ached as I nearly vibrated beside Isabella. *He is just as excited about my letters as*

I am about his. I couldn't help but think in awe. Finally, he slid the letter gently into his bag and yanked one of the straps over his shoulder.

I stood up. I ignored Isabella as she tried to pull me back. I climbed over the bench and watched him walk down the hallway, turn, and walk down the stairs. He never once looked back at me. He didn't need to, because I had seen him all the same. Those soft light green eyes, that bright smile on his face, and the number one that was so large and so wide on his back. "That was Luke, the captain of the football team," I said softly, my eyes never once left the place where he disappeared down the stairs.

"The very straight, captain of the football team," Isabella said hesitantly from behind me, apprehension on her face as she held both of our bags in her hands.

I frowned at her, then looked at the locker and walked over to it. I banged my face on it softly. "Fuck," I muttered under my breath. My voice shook as my forehead throbbed from the wound. I felt hot tears brim in my eyes, and I couldn't stop the soft whimper that spilled out from my lips. Just one smile, one look at those beautiful green eyes, at the way he had so carefully taken care of my letter, was enough for me. Enough for me to see him. To remember every single word he had written in his letters. It was enough for me to feel the words wrap around his image, to become one with them, until all I could hear was his voice, see his eyes, and envision his touch in my mind.

"What are you going to do, Kinsley?" Isabella asked as she rubbed soft circles on my back. I couldn't reply to her, couldn't look at her, all I could do was try to force myself to breathe. I tried to force my heart to stop breaking because I already knew I had no chance; I already knew I was inescapably in love with him.

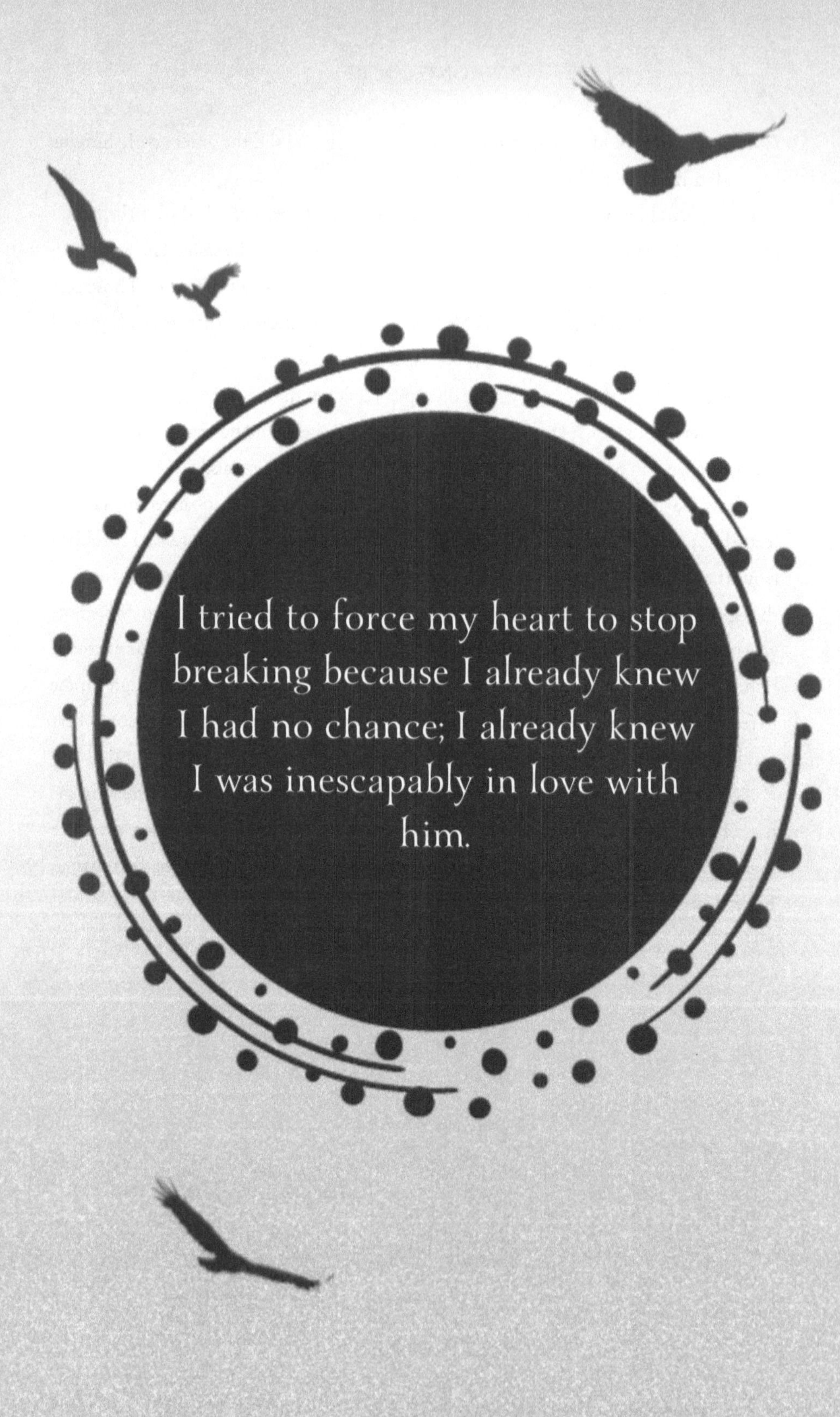

I tried to force my heart to stop
breaking because I already knew
I had no chance; I already knew
I was inescapably in love with
him.

Chapter 23
Kinsley

I stared at the letter in my locker as if it were on fire. If I reached in and touched it, or even attempted to pull it out, I would ignite the hallways, the plants, and the students around me, until the whole world was on fire. As dramatic as that sounded, it was how I had felt. I closed my locker, left the letter inside, and walked down the steps to my first class. I never even grabbed my books for my first period, just sat down absently in my seat next to Isabella. She had waited for me in the classroom because she thought I needed some space, but that's all I'd had all weekend long. I wasn't sure how much more space I needed before I started to suffocate from silence and lack of human contact. My parents were still in Italy, my mother texted me every once in a while to make sure I behaved and my dad texted me once to remind me for the millionth time that he didn't mind if I used the home gym.

He had told me he didn't mind for years now. He only told me because he thought if he brought it up more, I would suddenly want to be athletic and be the son he could be proud of. I didn't hear anything from Kennedy, but that didn't surprise me. It's not like I tried to reach out to her either. Izzy tried to get her mom to let her sleep over, but she was strict about things like that, even though she knew nothing would ever happen between Izzy and me. So I had been left alone in a house with a housekeeper who didn't speak any language I knew, and an unlimited balance on a credit card to keep myself busy. Maybe it was the type of lifestyle most kids wanted. Not me, though. Someone to talk to, someone to come home to that would smile at me and ask me how my day had been, that was the only type of lifestyle I wanted.

Sometimes I could remember them, back when I was on the basketball team. They used to smile at me. My father would smack my shoulder and pat my head, he would tell everyone who was close by that he was proud of me. My mother would come to lay down next to me in bed when I had nightmares and she would hug me and ask me how my day was. I used to love the smell of her, that warm motherly smell that instantly made you feel safe and calm. Sometimes when I was a freshman and I had a nightmare I would go to her walk-in closet and lay there and just breathe in her scent, to try and make everything better again. Not anymore, though. I had long since forgotten what she smelled like.

I almost wished my parents did have another kid just so they would be home more. A baby that screamed would be something instead of the silence. Even if they all ignored me, at least they would ignore me while they were in the same house as me. Isabella chewed on her lower lip as she leaned over and pulled my hood down. She ran her fingers through my messy blond hair and tried to tame what I had never bothered to brush that morning. I let her do whatever to me as I stared down at my desk, my empty desk, and felt guilty.

I should have grabbed the letter. I felt like I cheated, in a way, when I left it in there. Is that how girls felt when they saw that little read pop up under their text and knew their boyfriend had read the text, but they never got a reply back? I couldn't help but wonder, what if Luke was nearby when I opened the locker? What if he saw me open the locker and shut it? What if he got curious about who I was too? "It's not right, I need to tell him," I mumbled under my breath.

Isabella put a few bobby pins on my bangs as she tried to pin them to the side so they stayed down. She pulled my hood back up for me once she was finished. Normally she teased me about how I wore it constantly, how I used it to hide from everyone underneath it, but not this time. She knew my anxiety and knew I was already freaked out. She knew I needed the warm and dark comfort that came from hiding. She let out a soft gasp as a few people started to gossip about us.

They wondered if I was indeed gay or if I was dating Isabella. Some mumbled a rumor of Isabella being secretly trans, probably because Roan yelled out the other day about her being manly, but we ignored all of it as she scooted her desk closer to mine and showed Mr. Duckett that she was doing it to share her textbook with me. "You're talking about Green, right?" she asked softly. Her eyes darted around the room to make sure no one could hear us.

Mr. Duckett let out a gross cough and spat into his trash can, as he had done all morning. He didn't feel well and gave us all a list of one hundred problems we needed to get done by the end of class. He assigned each row opposite the one next to them which ones to do. So my row had to do all of the even-numbered problems of the hundred, while Isabella's row had to do all of the odd. We pushed the textbook to the top of the desks and pulled out paper to do the classwork while we talked. We weren't the only ones who did this, and Mr. Duckett didn't seem to care as long as the whispers stayed quiet and we continued our work.

It's not like we could cheat off of who was next to us, so he didn't seem to care right now. "Who was I kidding, thinking I could be with a guy in this school? There are only two gay guys out in this school and they're picked on worse than I am. If Green was any of those guys and we started to go out, we'd get killed. But none of it matters because it's Luke, and you're right Izzy. He's straight, he's always been straight. He just was in a relationship with one of the cheerleaders earlier this year," I whispered to her but kept my eyes down as I slowly wrote out the equation.

She let out a clicking sound, her tongue smacked against the roof of her mouth as she doodled a flower around her name before she started her work. I thought, at this point, all of her teachers were used to her doodles on all of her papers, it was just expected. If she ever turned in a paper that wasn't covered in doodles, they'd probably pull her aside and make sure she was okay at this point.

"I know, Kins. I can't stand her. She started those rumors about him being a horrible person and bad in bed and such, but nobody believed them. All of the girls who broke up with the popular guys tended to spread rumors when they were pissed off. Like, they can't just be mature enough to break up on a nice and friendly note. But no, they all had to be little *pendejas* that hated themselves so much, they suck the life out of everyone else around them," she said angrily with a shake of her head back and forth as she worked through her equations.

I was quiet for a while as I thought about what I said, about what I should do, as I slowly worked on the classwork. I probably got all of it wrong. I mean, math wasn't too bad, I passed with a low B or a high C, whichever... but my eyes stung from unshed tears and I just wanted to go lay down somewhere. It's what I did all weekend long. Just hid under my blankets frustrated as I tried to figure out what to do and where to go from there. I hated being depressed, I hated being frustrated because I was the kind of kid that when I got angry or frustrated I cried and I hated how weak that made me. I was already shorter than most of the other guys my age, and then I'd stand there crying when I got yelled at or frustrated.

If I hadn't hurt Roan in middle school he'd probably still find a reason to pick on me anyway just because of how freaking emotional I was. Sensitive, my mom had called me once when I was younger. I remember that was when I was around five or six. She hugged me against her, cooed in my ear, and told my father to calm down because I was her sensitive little boy. I remember they fought over that. My dad told her she would make me a wuss and then they started me on baseball the very next day. "How are you going to tell him then? When? Why?" She wondered as she snapped me out of my thoughts.

I clicked the end of my mechanical pencil absently as I watched the lead grow, then held down the back of it and pushed the lead back inside, just to make it come out again. I was so freaking stressed out my hands shook. "It's not right, none of it is. If I found out he was one of the gay guys in school, it would be different. But Luke isn't gay and Green's not a girl, and the longer this goes on, the worse it will be. He'll know that I know, I won't be able to hide it. I don't hide anything from Green, he knows me better than you do, in a way. He'll know I'm hiding something, and when he finally does come to want to talk to me face to face, he'll see the guilt all over me. If I tell him now then at least there are no hard feelings."

Soulmates, I had said. *A lifeline,* he had said. How could we go from that... to nothing? I felt dizzy, my palms sweaty, and my pencil fell from my grip and to the ground with a soft clatter that made Mr. Duckett's head lift from the desk where he laid it on his arms. Isabella leaned over to get the pencil and he turned his head to spit in the trashcan once more while the girls in the front row squealed over how gross he was. "I guess, I could see how it would be good. I don't know Luke very well, I don't think I've ever had a class with him. I've heard he's quiet and thoughtful, and doesn't say much," she said absently as I remembered.

I remembered the guy with the baseball cap who stared at the wind chime outside of the cafe. He always walked slower than the others around him, always off to the side, as if he belonged with them but didn't at the same time. It was strange how everything I learned in the letters was suddenly pressed against him, like pieces in a puzzle that never fit with Peyton. Now that I knew they were Luke, they fit one after another, made everything whole at last. I used to wonder if I'd ever see every single piece of his puzzle. If I'd ever get another piece of Green to put down and press lightly against the others, to watch with a satisfying smile on my face as it slowly and steadily became a picture of something good, something whole.

I wondered before if, maybe, I was a piece of Green's puzzle. If they were lonely because somewhere deep down inside them, they were missing me, missing the piece that linked both of us together. But while I sat there and thought about Green being Luke, I realized none of the pieces were of me, and most likely, none of them ever would be, especially when he found out who I was.

"He stood in front of you before, I remember that. Handed you the ice pack." He didn't even look at me, and I had been behind him the whole time. I wondered if he would have, would he have known me? Would I have known him? Like a cheesy romance movie where we both lifted our eyes to each other and suddenly recognized the other half of our souls and rode off into the sunset? "He'd understand, I'm sure, given you are telling him like this," she said slowly. "Because you're letting him know that you found out on a whim, and you wanted to make sure he knew, right? So are you going to write him a letter? Letting him know who you are?"

I shrugged, unsure if that was even the best way. If I wrote Luke a letter and gave it to him in person, he'd throw it in the trash. Luke knew me, even if he didn't look at me. He might not have known me personally, but he was in my psychology class, and we had been in and out of the same classes all our life. We were people who knew of each other but were never friends. Who'd want to be friends with me, after all? "I should write him a letter telling him the truth," I said slowly as I wrote *'IDK'* as my answer for one of them, then moved on to the next.

"I mean, he probably won't even reply to it, but, I don't know. I don't want the letters to stop, but I can't lie to him either. A part of me wishes I'd never written the letters, to begin with, but then where would I be? Asking out random girls and getting beat up trying to appease my parents? A part of me wishes I'd never snuck around and saw him, that I'd waited until we were both ready to meet each other. But then what? Because we'd see each other and what would come from that? This is over before anything even started. I feel like I've already been dumped,"

"See him face to face. You should write in the letter for him to meet you after school in the art room after his club lets out. Tell him you found out who he was and that you feel like he needs to know who you are as well. I don't know him very well, but I don't think he'll hurt you. And you never know. So he dated two girls, but that doesn't make him straight. What if he's secretly bisexual? What if it all works out in the end? I'll take the freshmen down to get ice cream or something, I'll tell them it's a field trip, and they'll be so excited. That way you're alone. Either you can pick me up afterward and we can go to your house and talk it out, or I'll have Mami come get me, whatever you need, Kins. I'll always have your back," She spoke so calmly, so reassuringly as she pushed her hand into my hood and pressed the palm of her hand against my cheek.

I lowered my face against her hand, a soft tear slid down my cheek and against her hand. I let out a sigh as someone threw an eraser at the back of my head, a soft whistle as they made kissy noises. Why was it so hard to believe two people of the opposite gender could just be best friends without romantic feelings? It was beyond me. I hated that I cried when I was frustrated, I hated that I cried when I was sad, and I knew that no matter what happened in the art club after school, I'd end up crying. But she said to have hope. What if he was bisexual? No one truly knew how I felt, they just assumed I was gay and teased me. I refused to believe that in a whole school full of people, those two gay guys and I were the only ones who were open to same-gender relationships.

Heck, even Isabella had made out with a girl before. I felt my cheeks redden as I imagined a whole new type of hope. The hope that maybe, just maybe, everything would work out in the end. The bell rang and Mr. Duckett assigned the rest of the work for homework, which was probably for the best since I had only answered three equations and written *'IDK'* on two of them. I walked up to the second floor slowly, my eyes lingered on locker 213. I watched as Luke opened it and frowned.

Why hadn't I ever noticed before that it was his locker? Probably because I had always just looked at Peyton at first, and then after that I mostly looked at the girls around it, my eyes always skimmed over him. Even from here, I could see his light green eyes as he sighed, his shoulders lowered in disappointment. He lifted his hat off of his head and ran his fingers through his soft dark brown curls, put his hat back on, and grabbed his books.

Isabella wrapped her arm around my shoulder and tugged on me, pulling me away. I couldn't help but think about him as I grabbed his letter out of my locker and walked into the next class in a daze. I sat down at the desk in the back and could feel Isabella's eyes on me from the front of the room as she nervously watched me to make sure I didn't break down. Did I even deserve to open this letter now? But then again, I didn't do anything wrong, right? This wasn't fully my fault, right? I opened the top of the letter as the bell rang and Mrs. Masters started to teach, but I couldn't slip the letter out.

My head rested against my arms as hot tears slid down my cheeks because I was scared. That's what it was, the biggest part of all of it, the thing that tugged at me since I saw his resplendent green eyes and his bright and smiling face on Friday. I was scared that this was all going to end. I was scared he'd call me a homophobic slur like everyone else and walk away from me. Maybe he'd hit me, though I doubted it. I almost hoped he would. I hoped he'd pummel me over and over again, instead of walking away. Because I was almost absolutely sure the moment he found out who I was, he would call me disgusting and never want to talk to me again.

My body shook through my tears and I quietly sniffled. I felt like a loser for crying during class and I was glad no one ever paid attention to me. Why would they? Why would anyone ever notice me? Sometimes I wondered if I died, would anyone besides Isabella and her mother notice? I sat up slowly, wiped my face on my sleeves, and tried to be brave. Brave like Green, brave like Luke. He had been braver than me, from the beginning. He got a stranger's letter in his locker and still talked to them. I wasn't brave, no matter how hard I tried to pretend I was, but for Luke, I'd be brave. One last letter, one last time. I'd be brave, since I knew with every part of me, that this was the end.

Hey, Sparrow,

So, I have a confession to make. I really, really suck at drawing, but I tried to draw you something. I know it's stupid, right? I just wanted to make you smile. You can laugh at it if you want, crap this was probably a stupid idea. To give an artist a crappy drawing? Yeah, I guess this isn't going to be scoring me any points here, I'm sure. It's just, you draw things for me, and I swear I've never even cared about art until I met you. I'd walk down the halls or I'd walk home if I don't get a ride home from someone, and I never really cared enough to look. But now, all I see is color. I can see the different hues, and then I think of you, and all I can do is smile. You know, before I met you, everything was just dark. Like a storm. But then you came. Your letters came like a lifeline, and everything faded away; the calm. You're the calm to my storm, Sparrow. You make me strive to be better. To be brave like Sparrow, to be bright like Sparrow, to see the good in people like Sparrow. You're the light in this dark desolate wasteland, and without you, the darkness is suffocating.

P.S. Because what's a letter without a P.S.? I'm glad I met you, Sparrow.

I felt my breath getting shallow as I folded the letter back into the envelope, put it gently in my bag, and stood. Mrs. Masters didn't even have a chance to say anything as I ran out of the room, my breath stuck in my throat. I could hear Isabella's voice with Mrs. Masters and knew she was probably giving a long intricate story of me eating something bad for breakfast so I wouldn't get in trouble. I was glad Mrs. Masters' room was on the third floor since it was so close to the art room. I practically ran into the art room, ignored the suffocating stench of the goo, and sat down in the corner on the ground. I pulled Luke's letter out of my bag and made sure it wasn't crumpled because I knew it was going to be my last one.

Inside it was a small index card-sized piece of paper that I hadn't noticed before and I couldn't help but let out a soft strained laugh as I stared down at what I assumed to be a tree with rain pouring down on it. It was the most beautiful imperfect drawing I'd ever seen. It was perfect simply because it was from him to me. I turned it over and saw a small little note, just a few words, but it was enough. *'Maybe one day, we can sit outside together, hand in hand, and watch the rain falling around us.'* With trembling lips and wet eyes, I pulled out a new envelope and paper and replied to him.

Green,

I'm sorry I didn't reply right away. I don't know how to say this, exactly. You tell me that I'm brave, that I help you be brave, but it's a lie, Green. I'm not brave, not like you. From the start, you were brave enough to talk to someone without knowing who they were, but I wasn't. Then when I found out you weren't who I thought you were, I wasn't able to handle it. I was scared. I'm still scared, so entirely scared. I don't know how to say this without pissing you off, but I'm not going to lie to you. Not to you, Green.

Friday, after school. I waited, and I watched. I couldn't help myself. I just needed to know who you were. So no, Luke. I'm not brave, I'm a coward. If anyone is brave, it's you. I didn't reply to your letter after first because I was scared. Scared to open it, scared to reply to it, scared to tell you what I did. But here I am, laying it all out there for you, because you and I have always been Green and Sparrow, and even if this is the end, at least It's ending in the truth. I'm sorry I ruined us, Luke. I'm sorry I looked, because now that I did, I know you're not going to want to keep talking to me.

P.S. One last P.S., right? After you get out of football practice, I'll be in the art club room, all alone, waiting. Waiting for the inevitable end.

I took a deep breath, folded the letter, and put it in a new envelope. My tears slid softly down my cheeks as I looked up and stared at the picture I had drawn with charcoal a few weeks ago. Isabella said a self-portrait was always required for art schools. I stood up, frustrated with myself, with everything. I flipped my picture off, then walked out of the room and towards Luke's locker.

One last letter, one last time.

Chapter 24
Luke

I woke up with a sense of dread. The house was empty, and while it wasn't entirely unusual, it happened so rarely that I felt a sense of panic reside inside me. Days like this, when my mother was gone earlier than usual, scared me and made me wonder what was going on. With her depression, she would be fine one minute and screaming the next. The idea that she could be out getting groceries or driving a car scared me. Mostly because she was the parent I could stand. When she didn't stare at the walls and scream, she would smile sometimes.

Sometimes, if I let myself think about it, I could remember small things. Times my mother would hug me close to her, how she used to smell like cookies. She used to bake us cookies and other sweets. Mom wasn't this bad when I was younger, which is why I wasn't sure if she'd always been depressed or if it was my father's fault. Maybe it had always been there, resting under the surface, but like a hawk, he had poked and poked at her. He broke through her hard shell and released all of her demons, leaving her there to sweep up the mess that he created.

I didn't know why, but I couldn't shake the feeling that something bad was going to happen that day. Even when I found a note from her. The note spoke about Shawn, a therapy appointment with the school guidance counselor before school, and that was why they were gone. If Dad wasn't here, that probably meant he never came home last night or he had snuck out early. So it was all just normal, after all.

Shawn was a good student, with the best grades in his class. However, he had drawn something bad in art class, and when the guidance counselor pulled him out to ask about it, he told them enough to worry them. Dad had been pissed when child services came but managed to convince them that it had all been a dream. He blamed it on my mom and said she scared him when she was off her meds. Because of that, the school seemed to think they needed to have meetings with her and Shawn together sometimes, school-enforced therapy sessions for both of them. It bugged me because I already knew what they'd see.

Mom would sit there with her best dress and her makeup meticulously done, a warm smile on her face as she told the teachers she didn't know what was wrong with him for him to act out like that. She'd say that everything was fine, that everything was always fine. I wondered how many people heard the words: *I'm fine* and simply nodded and smiled. I wondered how many of them stopped and looked again, narrowed their eyes, and examined them. Wondered if they actually told the truth or if they hid underneath a mask. The most depressed people out there smiled the brightest smiles if only to hide away their sadness. Embarrassed to feel it, to begin with.

I grabbed a pop-tart and pulled out my phone to look at the time. I had to ignore the stains on the wall from the last plate thrown, the crunch of glass that had not fully been swept away as it crunched underneath the soles of my shoes. If I didn't hurry up and get to the corner of the street, Bobby would leave me behind. I had a car at the shop and paid five hundred for it. My boss would have sold it for parts, but I was determined to fix it up with spares, determined to get it ready. I hoped by the time I turned eighteen, I would be gone, out of here.

I didn't have a letter for Sparrow that morning since I had given one last Friday and had to wait for a reply. I grabbed the letter last Friday and went all the way down to the truck, only to find that Bobby had left. Instead of immediately leaving, I went around the side of the school to the bleachers, read the letter, and replied. It didn't matter that I was probably the last one in the school by then, besides the janitor. I ran up the stairs to the third floor and slipped the letter into Sparrow's locker before I walked to work. My thoughts always rested back with Sparrow, especially when I started to think about sad things or the after.

After high school, I always assumed I'd grab Shawn and split with him. The thing about Shawn was the fact that he was so much more than our Dad realized. Dad gave him crap because some guys are bigger built like me, and some are skinnier, like him. Shawn was always a pretty boy, he took after my mother in that regard, and no matter how many times I tried to get him to throw a football around with me or work out, he just never really got any bigger. Not that I thought there was anything wrong with that, but it was my responsibility to make sure he was safe.

No matter how hard I tried, he just never felt safe. He started to stay out more when he met Brett, and in a way, I was glad for it. I'd find him in various places curled up and asleep. Like at the shop or at Brett's, in his shed, or in a random old abandoned tree house. It was sad, but it was better than here. I wasn't sure if Dad would even care if Shawn wasn't here anymore. Mom was never really all there, he'd be better off with me.

Sometimes it made me feel overwhelmed in a way, the fact that I was all he really had. Mom was there, but she wasn't at the same time, and it was only me. I stepped up at a young age to be everything Shawn needed. I wasn't sure how well I succeeded in that, but I tried, at least. No one could say I didn't. I did worry about my mom. The stress of it all, I felt like maybe that was why she stopped trying so hard to take her meds all the time.

Maybe once Shawn and I were gone she could finally go get the help she needed. She pretended now. Pretended the smiles were real, pretended the meds weren't still in the bottle on the top of the bathroom shelf. She went to the therapist every other week as required by her job, but she was a liar. I knew how much of a liar she was. She lied every time she held me close and told me it was the last time she'd let him hurt me. Her lies weren't enough. She didn't try hard enough, and it felt like no matter how hard I tried, everything would always endlessly tear apart at the seams.

In a way, I didn't blame her. How easy could it be to tell a stranger she wasn't happy, no matter what they tried? But at the same time, I wished she'd try a little harder, for Shawn's sake, if not my own. No, not mine. I gave up wondering if I was good enough for my parents a while ago, back when they didn't seem to notice how much I had almost died. I wish someone would tell me what I had to do to be enough. All I knew was that I wasn't.

'From my soul to yours, I really didn't think you were a bad person.' I clenched the strap of my messenger bag tighter around my body and let out a shaky breath as I looked up at the sky. It showed a soft light pink strip that melted into the light blue, a dark orange glow as the sun lifted over the horizon lazily, taking its time to light up the world that gravitated around it. Sparrow was everything. Her words were what kept me going. I realized at this point that despite how unhealthy that was, I couldn't do anything about it.

I wondered sometimes over the past weeks where I would've been right now if I had never opened that letter if I had thrown it to the side like all of the others. I wondered sometimes if I would even have been alive right now if it wasn't for that letter. What would happen after? After school, after graduation. I always thought my plan would be to grab Shawn and get him out of there. But now that I knew Sparrow, what would happen after?

'Maybe we'd be the type of romance that's talked about, the type of romance that everyone envies and wishes they could have.' I wondered sometimes, how I could hear Sparrow's words but not exactly hear a voice to match her. No matter how hard I tried, I couldn't hear it. The high-pitched lithe to a feminine voice, the soft giggle, and the gentle curve of female lips that slid into a smile. I imagined Sparrow with a more alto-type voice. Not deep, not high, but chill and soft, like a feather.

I felt slightly lighter as I walked to the end of the curve, moments before Bobby arrived with half a truck full of guys from the team and a bunch of girls jammed onto their laps. As always the front seat was clear for me. No one complained anymore, not about me, not about the captain. I saw one of the cheerleaders bat her eyelashes at me and I shook my head firmly with a frown because she wasn't my Sparrow. She wasn't the one I was in a relationship with, but not at the same time. She wasn't my soulmate.

I didn't know who Sparrow was, but I knew with one look into the eyes of every girl near me right now that none of them was her. I felt like with her, I had searched for her longer than I knew I was. Searched and searched, and maybe one day I would see her, really see her. I wondered if it would happen fast, or gradually. Would I know her the moment I saw her? Or the moment I heard her voice? Would I wrap my arms around her and instantly feel like I was home? Or would I stand there dumbstruck, unable to say a word? As scared as I was to take her home, to have her see every part of me, I found it harder and harder to stop myself from wondering.

I thought this would be the best way for me. Letters back and forth until the end of the school year. Every once in a while, Sparrow would hint at our meeting, and while she had never pressured about it, I couldn't help but feel a small pain settle in my stomach just at the thought of it. I wanted to meet her, but I was scared she'd see me. I was scared she'd see through me, and she'd run away from who I truly was, deep down inside. I wanted to touch her, to hold her, to stare into her eyes and hear her voice speak the things she wrote in the letters. I wanted more than anything to know her, but I was scared of what she'd see when she finally did. Scared she'd see what I'd always known all along, that I simply wasn't good enough.

I couldn't pull through my mood no matter how hard I tried. The feeling that something was wrong settled deep down under my skin like a splinter, shoved so far down inside me that I wasn't entirely sure if I could pull it out. Maybe because it was Monday, or maybe because that morning started off quiet and that usually meant it would end in a storm. I was scared of just how strong that storm would be. I forced myself to practice without going to my locker. She didn't go to the art club after school on Fridays, so she wouldn't have replied and left it in my locker over the weekend.

As the long practice wore on, I pushed myself as I watched the sun slowly lift higher in the sky, if only for the promise that there would be a letter in my locker once I was done. Like a lifeline, the letters pulled at me. They gave me air to breathe, a reason to keep going, sanity to push through. I was the first in the locker room, the first to shower, the first out. It wasn't unusual for me, not anymore.

Before the letters, I was the slowest, wanting everything to drag on for a little longer, the day to keep going and going so I didn't have to go home. Now, however, I was eager to race up those stairs. I just barely held myself back to pretend there was nothing going on. The guys already suspected I had a girlfriend and wanted to know more; I didn't want to give them more to question. They didn't know me, they wouldn't understand me.

All they wanted was simple, and that was all I would give them. I opened my locker, and I could internally feel myself deflate like a balloon. It felt like a child had held onto the end of a balloon and slowly let it go, the loud squeal as the air leaked from the balloon's opened seal hissed in my ears as everyone around me chattered without care. I wondered sometimes how they could all be so happy, so carefree as if the world around them wasn't on fire. I guess some people simply didn't notice the flames.

My spirits were broken as I trudged to Mr. McCormick's class. Fake high-fives nudged shoulders, and claps on the back were exchanged as I struggled to breathe through the claustrophobic wave of expectations. *'Smile, Luke,'* I told myself. I pictured my mother as she did the exact same thing while she sat in front of the guidance counselor with Shawn at her side. *'Smile and pretend like everything is okay.'* I felt my face falter, my body shook as I noticed the similarities between me and my mother. I took a deep breath and closed my eyes. *'Be brave, brave like Sparrow.'*

I tried to pretend, I tried to do the best I could. My headphones slipped inside my jacket as I listened to Sparrow's songs. I was the only kid in the classroom who wore long sleeves as I ignored the heat that settled inside the poorly insulated room. There was no letter after the first period. I felt myself tear apart at the seams and wondered if this was it.

It was stupid and illogical, and I wondered what would happen if it really was the end. Maybe she had grown tired of talking to me, or maybe it was something simple like she was at home sick. It would make sense. The rain was constant and everyone sniffled, red cheeks and noses decorated every other student, but until I knew the truth, I wouldn't be able to calm down. She wouldn't do that, I told myself with a sigh as I closed the locker and made my way to my third-period class. She wouldn't do that to me. I was absolutely certain that if she felt like she was done talking to me, she'd at least tell me.

Third was slow, and I barely tried to contain how panicked I was as I forced myself to walk to my locker after class. Everyone ran around excited for lunch and I missed it. Bobby probably already left by now as I lingered in front of my locker for a moment before I opened it. Within an instant, the smile tugged at my lips as I looked at my open locker. It was like all of the panic was gone, all of the worries washed away, and all I felt was happiness. Maybe she had been late today, I told myself as I slipped the letter into my pocket and made my way outside and to the bleachers.

I already knew Bobby was gone, and this wouldn't be the first time I missed a meal, but at least this was the first time it was worth it. As the wind whipped through the air around me, I sat down on the bleachers with red cheeks. I was unsure if they were from the happiness I felt as I held one of Sparrow's letters, or if it was from the wind. I could smell the rain, and it made me feel even happier. I realized I would never have felt this happiness if it wasn't for Sparrow.

I wondered, as I started to open the letter if this was what love felt like. That alone was enough to scare the crap out of me, but it was just a beat of my heart before the real terror set in. One moment I had wondered if this was love, and the next I shook in terror. My eyes were wide as I pressed my hand against my mouth and tried to stifle the scream that slowly built inside me. I read the letter, and reread the letter. My eyes noticed every single time she wrote my name, *my name*, like an affirmation of the inevitability.

Twice, that four-letter name was spilled on the paper. Her meticulous handwriting was slightly slanted as if she had written in cursive most of her life and struggled to print instead. I had thought it was cute, and I even wondered once before what my name would look like with her handwriting, but now all I could feel was the bile rising in my stomach. It burned as I leaned over and threw up.

The rest of the day was a blur to me. I didn't reply, how could I reply to that? It was different the first time when I thought she already knew me. Then she didn't, and now

I couldn't really fault her for wanting to find out. After all, I struggled with it myself. I wanted to see her and hear her voice, to know her. But it was what she wrote, how she wrote it, that really tore me into pieces. *'I'm sorry I ruined us, Luke. I'm sorry I looked.'* I felt like I was going to throw up again and again as I left class early. I ignored the looks of the others as I ended up staying in the nurse's office until the end of the school day.

I went to practice, because what else could I do? Her words sent me into overdrive. My body shook, my throws fumbled, and the slam of the other players as they rammed into me over and over again during my distraction was barely enough to stop the words as they slid around inside me. *'I'll be in the art club room, all alone, waiting. Waiting for the inevitable end.'*

I looked up at the art room window and wondered if she was watching me. From up there she could see me clearly, but from down here with the angle of the windows and the way the sunlight hit it, I couldn't see anything. After practice, I considered just leaving.

She was unhappy with who I was, she didn't want to talk to me anymore. Waiting for the inevitable end. How could this just end? Romance written from letters indeed, and all I could think about was Romeo and Juliet as I climbed the stairs. All of the great romances started with happiness. The flutter of smiles, and the throb of what would come next. Then came a challenge, and as Sparrow said, the inevitable end. She must have seen me, she must have known me with a glance. Spread the skin apart, and saw who I truly was deep down inside. Not enough, simply not enough. I wished I knew what to do to be enough, but I realized as I walked up the stairs to the third floor, that it wasn't possible. Not for me.

My hair was still wet, barely dried as the chatter of laughter surrounded me. People hurried to their lockers as I climbed the stairs in a daze and ignored everyone else. Why was I still walking? I should leave, just go, and never come back. *The end.* I wondered if this was what Romeo felt when he stared down at his supposed dead beloved when he pierced the dagger into his chest and fell by her side. My heart pounded in my chest as I walked slower and slower to the far door, the one with the missing letters, missing like the pieces of me.

I stood in front of the door, my heart roaring in my ears as I smelled the breeze from the window sliding from under the door. It was thicker with rain, telling me it had probably started to drizzle. How fitting, one of the last things I loved, coming down on the day everything would end. Sparrow's words flashed in my mind: *'Maybe we'll end up hating each other.'* A wince slid through my body, causing me to shiver. My hand hovered over the doorknob as fear roared through every part of me.

I had to close my eyes, willing myself to turn the knob. I told myself to be brave, brave like Sparrow. Even though she said she wasn't, she really was. She thought I was brave simply because I had no qualms about talking to a stranger. That wasn't brave; there was nothing brave about it. I just wanted to see if there could be someone who saw me and still wanted to be by my side.

But she had seen me, she knew me, and all it did was confirm what I already knew. I was nothing, absolutely nothing. Like a storm, my emotions were a whirlwind in my mind as I pushed the door open. My heart pounded as I took a step inside, and then another. I shook as I spotted the black figure in the middle of the room. Their body pressed against the window, fingers slipping daintily out from the sleeves as they clutched the opened window.

They breathed in the fresh air, the air thick with rain, and I wasn't even surprised that we had that in common as well. Sparrow's words fluttered through my mind: *'Maybe... just maybe... we'll end up falling in love.'* It was enough to force me to take a step forward, and another.

I took a minute to study Sparrow from behind. I wondered why their figure was so familiar. It took me a second to remember Sparrow was a junior too, and we most likely knew each other, at least in passing. The large black hoodie swallowed them, making it almost impossible to tell if they were skinny or fat. All I could see from her was the olive-colored skin poking out from the sleeves of their hoodie, black jeans that nearly swallowed Converse shoes.

An emo kid, as I expected, but I wasn't entirely surprised. "Sparrow?" What surprised me, however, was what happened next. I didn't know, as I watched them flinch, their fingers gripping the window tighter and tighter, shaken in fear as they straightened up. I didn't know why I never suspected. Maybe it was because of my father, the words I hated most of all that pounded through me in time with the beat of my heart, keeping me from considering it.

Even when Sparrow told me they didn't know who I was and that it was the wrong locker, I never suspected it. Why? The writing wasn't girly, but it wasn't harsh like a guy's either. The envelope wasn't covered in perfume or cologne of any kind, just the soft scent of sandalwood every once in a while. Everything had been so gender-neutral, now that I think about it, but for some reason I never suspected.

When Sparrow turned around, their hood pulled tightly over their face, they peered up at me with blue eyes, bright cerulean blue eyes. I was shocked, my eyes instantly meeting theirs. At first, I saw the gentle curve of their face, the soft creamy olive skin only imperfect from the dark streak of charcoal that was smeared on their cheek. The eyes were what drew me in, the first thing I could see, and for a moment all I could think was, *'Oh... I found you.'*

Then they moved, and as they pulled their hood down slowly with shaky hands, I felt a shock race through my body. Because I never suspected anything. I never expected in any of the past few weeks, not even for a minute... that Sparrow could be a boy.

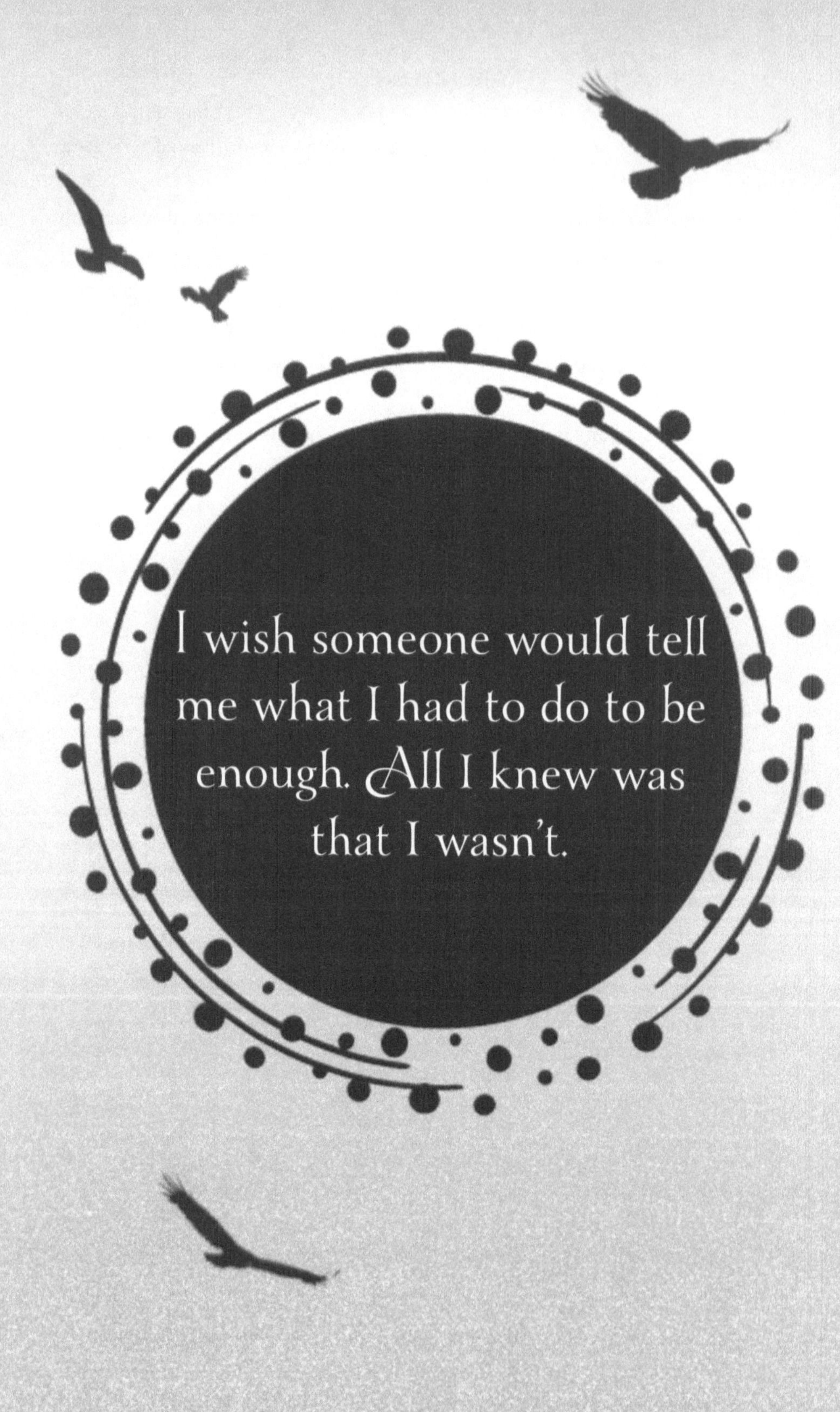
I wish someone would tell me what I had to do to be enough. All I knew was that I wasn't.

Chapter 25
Kinsley

I felt numb. I stood there as I stared out the window and watched the football players pummel each other. I didn't know enough about the sport to tell if that was normal or not, but from the way the coach blew his whistle and threw things at them, I didn't think it was normal. Some were off, I could tell that by how the coach kicked over the bench and made a giant container of what looked like fruit punch spill everywhere. Then the Coach shoved a smaller kid over and grabbed their helmet, threw it at the one who was apparently the cause of the problems. The one who stared up at the window, staring right at me. I knew it was Luke without knowing at the same time. From my soul to his, I recognized him.

I couldn't see through the helmet, and I knew for a fact that he couldn't see me at all, but the way we stared at each other was enough to know we felt each other. He was probably confused because of what I had said. I didn't realize it until after I had sent the message. He might have thought I didn't want to talk to him anymore because I found out who he was. It was the opposite of that though. I still wanted to talk to him. I wanted to touch him, I wanted to hug him. To hold his hand and to tell him everything would be okay.

It was strange how I started all of this with the expectation to meet a girl and protect her. While some would see me and Luke and consider him the stronger one, I knew differently from the letters. He was strong physically, but mentally? It hurt me to know he was curled up night after night crying with no one to talk to, thinking no one cared. I wanted to be the person to sit next to him and run my fingers through his curls, I wanted to be the one he called. I just wanted to be his. I was scared of that, to be honest. I was fine with the idea of being with him, but to actually stand there and touch him and kiss him would be two different things entirely. Then again, he was probably straight, so what's the point, right? God, I was terrified.

I took a deep shaky breath as the football players ran off the field and I started to pace. My hands felt slick with sweat and I kept constantly wiping them on my pants, and my heart raced in time with every step I took. I felt my heart pound with every step. I stopped, shook my hands and arms out, tried to do something, anything to get out of my head. I was going to go crazy. My heart pounded, I was afraid I was going to have a heart attack at this point. That wouldn't go over well, I was sure.

He'd come up here with the expectation to meet some girl, only to find a half-dead guy on the ground. Would he even care? I mean, he's kind. He'd probably call the hospital I guess, but I'd most likely never see him after that to explain. I decided I needed to do something, anything to calm down while I waited.

I turned to the window once more, my eyes closed as I breathed in the wind. It was thick, with a slight wet feel to it. Small little drops dripped against my fingers as I clutched the window tightly. Rain, it was starting to rain. I loved the smell of the air when it was thick with rain, and I wondered if this was a sign. A sign that everything was going to be okay because something I loved was starting. Or maybe this was simply a sign that everything was going to crash and burn, and the world was getting ready for the inevitable flames by providing the rain ahead of time.

'Maybe one day, we can sit outside together, hand in hand, and watch the rain falling around us,' Luke's note had said. Of course he had the same feeling I did, it was why I knew we worked so well together. If only I was a girl, or he was a girl, then maybe all of this would be okay. But I wasn't, and he wasn't. No matter how long I stood there and hoped and prayed that everything was going to go alright, I knew it wouldn't. I could almost feel the sting of Isabella's shoe on my head, I knew if she was here she'd tell me to behave and think positively. She'd call me names in Spanish and tell me I was only allowed to think about myself as wonderful and amazing. But no matter how hard she tried, when I was alone I couldn't help but feel those feelings. To know that I was just not good enough.

I lifted my head slightly and felt the rain mist my face as I tried to calm myself. He probably wouldn't even come. He didn't want to meet me face to face anyway from the start, and I was probably just never going to hear from him again. Well, at least like that. I still see him every day in the halls, and we have psychology class together. Not to mention next year, we might have a few classes together. Maybe it was better this way.

The school year would be over in a few months. I'd be seventeen soon, and I was sure he would be too. We were so close to the end of high school. If he didn't show, if there were no more letters, maybe it was better this way. Everything would be gone, but we had managed beforehand, right? I wasn't sure how I could go on without his letters, but maybe everything would be okay. "Sparrow?" I flinched, every part of me instantly on high alert at the sound of his voice.

I hadn't even heard him come in, my body shook and I was instantly covered in a cold chill as I tried to force myself to move. His voice, my name, I had never expected to hear his voice this directly before. Then again, I had never loved him before either.

Before the letters, he had been nothing more than a hot guy who roamed the halls with all the other hot guys and girls. He was just a jock and I was just an art kid, and we were nothing to each other. Two beings, one beat after the other, like a heartbeat. Luke for one beat, Kinsley for another, always separate, never caring. Then the letters came and we became so much more than that. Sparrow and Green, as if we were one heartbeat, together. What now? What would come of us now? I turned around slowly.

I had expected before I knew it was Luke that I'd look down at Green, but here I was peering up at him through my eyelashes. His light green eyes were so close to me, close enough that I could see gold flecks littered through them as if someone had spilled some glitter into his eyes and it decided to rest there instead of fade away.

What are we now? I wanted to ask him as he stared at me with wide eyes. Luke and Kinsley, two separate beings without care for each other? Sparrow and Green, one heartbeat, together? Or were we Luke and Kinsley once more, except this time more? I lifted my trembling hands to my hood. I tried to decipher what he thought, what he felt, as I slowly lowered my hood. His eyes widened and I realized he hadn't known before. It might have been too dark, and he didn't recognize me with the hood.

'Yours,' I whispered in my mind as I stared at him. I wondered if he could hear it. My words echoed through my mind, through my soul, to him. *'Your Sparrow, your Kinsley, yours,'*

'Be brave', I told myself, *'Brave like the Sparrow he expected you to be.'* "Hi, Luke. I'm um... My name is Kinsley Bryant. I'm not sure if you know who I am," I ran my fingers through my hair nervously. I felt naked without my hood, naked under his deep gaze as his light green eyes peered through me. I wanted to know what he saw when he stared at me. Did he simply just see my gender? Or did he see me?

Luke was hesitant for a moment, and I could see he was in shock. He stood so close to me. He took a step back, then another one. His eyes searched around the room and

I noticed a light sheen on them, as if he held back tears. I felt everything around me fall apart as I saw his eyes. I wanted nothing more than to grab his hand and reassure him, but I didn't. How could I reassure someone who was going through something like this? I could tell by how his chest rose and fell, his hands clenched at his side as he took yet another step back, his eyes searched everything he could see but determined not to look at me, anything but me.

I could tell just by that, that Luke Wilson was absolutely straight. Why else would he have tried to stop himself from shattering from the knowledge that I was a guy? I knew it from the moment I saw him. I ruined everything, absolutely everything. "I know who you are, Kinsley," he finally spoke. His eyes were fixated on my charcoal picture as if he was unable to look at me, but at my drawing instead.

A shudder raced through my body at his deep voice, and how he said my name. Dammit, I wanted to punch myself. I wanted to jump out the window and get all of this over with. Why did I have to write those letters? Why did I have to search for him? Why did I have to fall in love with him? "You're in my Psychology class, right?" Every word he spoke was a strained whisper.

I wanted to move closer to him, to hear him better, but the way he stood and the way his hands clenched and unclenched over and over again reminded me of a cornered animal ready to flee at a moment's notice. My phone vibrated in my pocket and I ignored it, I knew it was probably Isabella. She wanted to know if he had shown up and if I was okay. If I needed her to run back to the school and save me. I wanted to tell her yes, come save me, come take me away, come end this all for me, but at the same time, I hesitated.

He hadn't yelled at me, he hadn't tried to kick my ass, and he hadn't done anything except stand there and try not to cry. I was glad he didn't let the tears come. I was fairly sure if he started to cry I'd break into a million pieces. Because I knew every single one of his tears was my fault for starting this. Then I realized, that for him to be this affected, this wound up, meant something. It meant he had feelings for me too, or at least for Sparrow.

"Yeah, I'm paired up with Krissy," I said awkwardly as he gave a tight nod. He knew who she was, I was sure. She was one of the cheerleaders in our class. Pretty sure she was best friends with his ex, who was also in our class. Today just all around sucked.

He finally looked at me. His body was still poised, but his eyes were less shiny. As if he had managed to shove down his initial panic and despair. "I'm um, I'm sorry, Kinsley. This is weird. I didn't expect this. How do I know you're Sparrow? Just how?" He stammered as he nervously ran his fingers through his hair.

I blinked a few times as I tried to stop myself from thinking about how soft his hair was and how nice it might feel to run my fingers through his dark brown curls. I let out a soft sigh as I pulled out a chair to the table closest to me, the table that had my bag on it. I grabbed my sketchbook and some pencils and started to draw. It felt strange to draw without music, but I didn't want to tune him out.

Besides, as he pulled out the chair on the other side of the table, I focused on him. His breath, how slow and steady it was, and I started to imagine his heartbeat in the same way. I drew something simple, a butterfly since there was one perched on the branch that poked into the screen of the opened window. It was enough for him to see my style of drawing, for him to see that it was me. Every time he breathed in calmed me. To know that he was still there and that he watched me.

I felt my cheeks heat up under his gaze, but after a while of his silence and my steady hand, my blush fell away. I couldn't help but think as I drew intricate swirls for the butterfly wings, my pinky finger slid against the edges to shadow it. Maybe it was possible for us to remain in one heartbeat, as Sparrow and Green did, even now that we were Luke and Kinsley. Maybe it was possible for us to remain as one.

I took a deep breath and lifted my eyes to his as I slowly pushed the paper toward him. Luke gently grazed his finger against mine as he pulled the picture from me. He jumped slightly with wide eyes as he let out a shaky breath. He chewed on his lower lip as his eyes lowered to the paper, and I was given a moment to study Luke up close. *'I found you,'* I whispered in my mind as my eyes roamed over his features.

Luke's dark brown curls had a few dirty blond strands that poked through. It made me think his hair was the kind that lightened during the summer and darkened during the winter. Delicate lines formed his jaw, his cheeks, and the top of his nose had a few light brown freckles that dotted against his tanned skin. I wanted more than anything to reach out and run my fingers through his curls.

This was the first time we had ever really spoken to each other, ever looked at each other for longer than a few seconds in passing, but I knew him, all the same. I studied him as he stared transfixed on the lines of my drawing, and tried not to make any sudden movements to disturb him. I slowly slipped a piece of paper out of my bag, twirled my pencil until the lead was against the paper, and I wrote him a small note. *'Maybe now that it's raining, we can sit outside, and watch it fall around us,'*

I lifted my eyes and noticed his burned into mine as he watched me. Slowly, I turned the letter around and pushed it to him, my sleeves swallowed my hands except for a small hint of my fingers as I pushed it closer and closer to him, before I backed away. He leaned down, studied the letter, and let out a shuddered breath as he closed his eyes.

I had a feeling he was counting. It was what Isabella did when she was flustered or angry. She would close her eyes and count to ten, trying to calm herself down before she did or said something stupid. Not that it ever really stopped her, but at least she attempted it. When Luke opened his eyes, I was transfixed by the small blush that rose across his cheeks. I felt my heart race as I stared at him, unsure what this meant. Was he happy? Was he shy? Or was he simply embarrassed?

"I'm not gay, Kinsley. I heard the rumors about you, not entirely sure if they're true or not since Roan's an asshole, but I'm not." I flinched. In an instant, I felt everything inside me crash down around me. "I mean, if you're gay, I don't have a problem with it. I know most of the kids here would, it's a small town and they're pretty religious. I'm not going to beat you up or anything,"

I let out a shaky breath as I felt my tears start to clog my throat. I coughed and tried to put on a small smile as I shrugged my shoulders. "I'm not gay," He blinked at me, his head tilted to the side, and for a moment I wondered if he was going to feel relief. I almost expected him to lower his shoulders in relief. Before he could, I felt like I owed it to him, at least to him, to my Green that I'd never lie to. "I'm not straight either though," I blurted out.

He stared at me, and for the longest time, I just sat there and waited for it. Waited for him to punch me, to climb over the table, and just beat the shit out of me. I was half tempted to ask him to just get it over with. I felt so tired. I wanted to just go home and curl up in my bed, and never wake up again. "Well, cool, I guess?" He stammered. I closed my eyes, because what else was I supposed to do? This was exactly what I thought it would be in the end. Exactly as I had said, the inevitable end. "Kinsley, I'm not good at this. I'm sorry if I offended you. Look, I don't know what to say," he let out a frustrated breath. I opened my eyes and watched him struggle to think of what to say.

"It's so fucking weird to know that you're Sparrow. I keep replaying all of the words I've been reading for weeks but they're coming back in my head with your voice and your image and it's just, I don't know how to handle this. I thought you were a girl. I thought I was falling in lo-, I thought… I thought you were a girl," his words gradually softened as he spoke, his eyes lowered to stare at his hands in despair. For a moment he flinched, and I wasn't sure why. It was like he heard something else, something loud that had startled him. "I'm not gay," he said again. His voice filled with a wave of soft anger, his hands clenched into fists as he looked up at me.

This is it. This is when he's going to punch me. I put my pencil back in my bag and moved it to the ground as I put my hands to my side, ready for it. He blinked, then let out a frustrated sigh as he ran his fingers through his hair. A nervous habit, it seemed. "I'm not going to beat you up, damn," he muttered as he shook his head at me.

"Look, I get it, okay? You thought I was someone else. You were honest with me from the start. You told me when you realized I wasn't who you thought I was, and you gave me plenty of opportunities to back down. You never lied to me, you didn't play me, we were both blindsided here. I got it, okay? I'm not mad at you, and I'm not going to beat you up. It was all an accident." He tried to be reasonable, but honestly, I wished he'd just beat me up at this point.

Despite everything, I felt a small bit of hope spread through me. I didn't know why, to be honest, because he had said more than once that he was straight but maybe we could still be friends. It would be hard as fuck to be friends with someone I was in love with, but at least if I could talk to him if I could be by his side, maybe that would be good enough. The knowledge that he'd get up and walk away and I'd never talk to him again horrified me. If friendship was the best I could get, I'd take it. "Can we still be friends? Can we still write letters to each other? Or maybe text, something?"

He closed his eyes and I realized almost as soon as I said it out loud that he was going to say no. As he opened his eyes and stared down at my small little note I took a deep breath. I almost hoped he'd change his mind and beat me up so badly I wouldn't be able to wake up. Maybe if I was in a coma I wouldn't have to feel this tear of my heart, this pain that spread through me.

Luke lifted his eyes to mine as a soft breeze filled with the sweet smell of the rain wafted through the room. I watched as his hair moved around his face and tried to study him. I tried to memorize every line, every curve, every freckle, because surely this would be the last time I would be allowed to see the guy I was in love with up close. "I'm sorry, Kinsley.

I can't keep doing it. Not after knowing you're a guy. But thank you for talking to me. Even for a little while, it was nice having someone to talk to."

I watched, unable to speak a word as he slid his chair back and stood. I wondered if he even realized he had the picture and the letter in his hand as he clutched the strap of his bag tightly and turned his back on me. The door had been open this whole time, and he walked through it. I stared down at the table, refusing to watch him leave.

I closed my eyes, my hands clenched tightly on top of the table as I willed them to stay still, not to shake, not to show just how much I was breaking. *'Don't cry, don't make a sound, don't show them they've hurt you.'* I let out a shaky breath as Isabella's words flooded my mind, something she used to say to me back when we were freshmen. I had played basketball in middle school, but because of Roan, I didn't attempt it in high school. My parents didn't understand, they didn't care, and they pressured me more than ever when I was a freshman. If it hadn't been for Izzy, I wasn't sure how I would have survived it. I never knew her advice would apply to this as well.

I lifted my head, turned to look at the door, and knew he wasn't there. Why would he stay behind to stare at me? In the end, I still looked and felt disappointed that I was right. The doorway was empty, nothing but the empty hallway with the soft whirl of the machine the janitor used to clean the floors.

I stood up. I wanted nothing more than to get in my car and drive to Isabella, to hug her close and cry and let her comfort me as she cussed Luke out in Spanish, but at the same time, I didn't want that either. He hadn't done anything wrong. It wasn't his fault he was straight and I wasn't. It wasn't his fault he didn't feel comfortable talking to someone who wasn't straight. It wasn't his fault I had started all of this, to begin with.

I pulled out my phone and sent Isabella a quick text. I told her to ask her mother to come to get her because I wanted to be alone for the rest of the day. She didn't ask questions, simply sent back a heart emoji and told me she'd be near her phone in case I wanted to talk to her. It was then that I felt them. The tears and the despair as they bubbled up inside me, threatening to burst at the seams. I couldn't stop my lips from quivering as I looked at my self-portrait, my hands shook as I glared at it. Suddenly all I could feel was embarrassment and anger, white-hot anger that burned inside me.

"Why can't you just be normal!?" I yelled at my picture as a choked sob caught in my throat. I couldn't stop the sobs as they burst through me, and before I knew it, I had the piece of charcoal in my hand. I pressed it down against the picture as hard as I could and destroyed it. Long angry strokes slid rapidly over and over it, covering every ounce of my picture in the darkness I felt inside me. The black hole that had slowly grown bigger and bigger, and threatened to swallow me alive.

I fell to my knees, my hand ached from how tightly I had clasped the charcoal, and my breathing was shaky and pained. I pressed my forehead against the middle of my ruined picture, ignoring the black that most likely stained my skin and my bangs. My tears slowly slid down the length of it, slid down in a dark gray smear, and rested on the easel it sat on.

"Why can't you just see me?" I choked out as I gripped the edge of the easel as hard as I could. But as I sat there on my knees, I had no answers to any of my questions, no solutions. Nothing but the jagged pieces of my soul as they fell piece by piece inside me, shattered one by one.

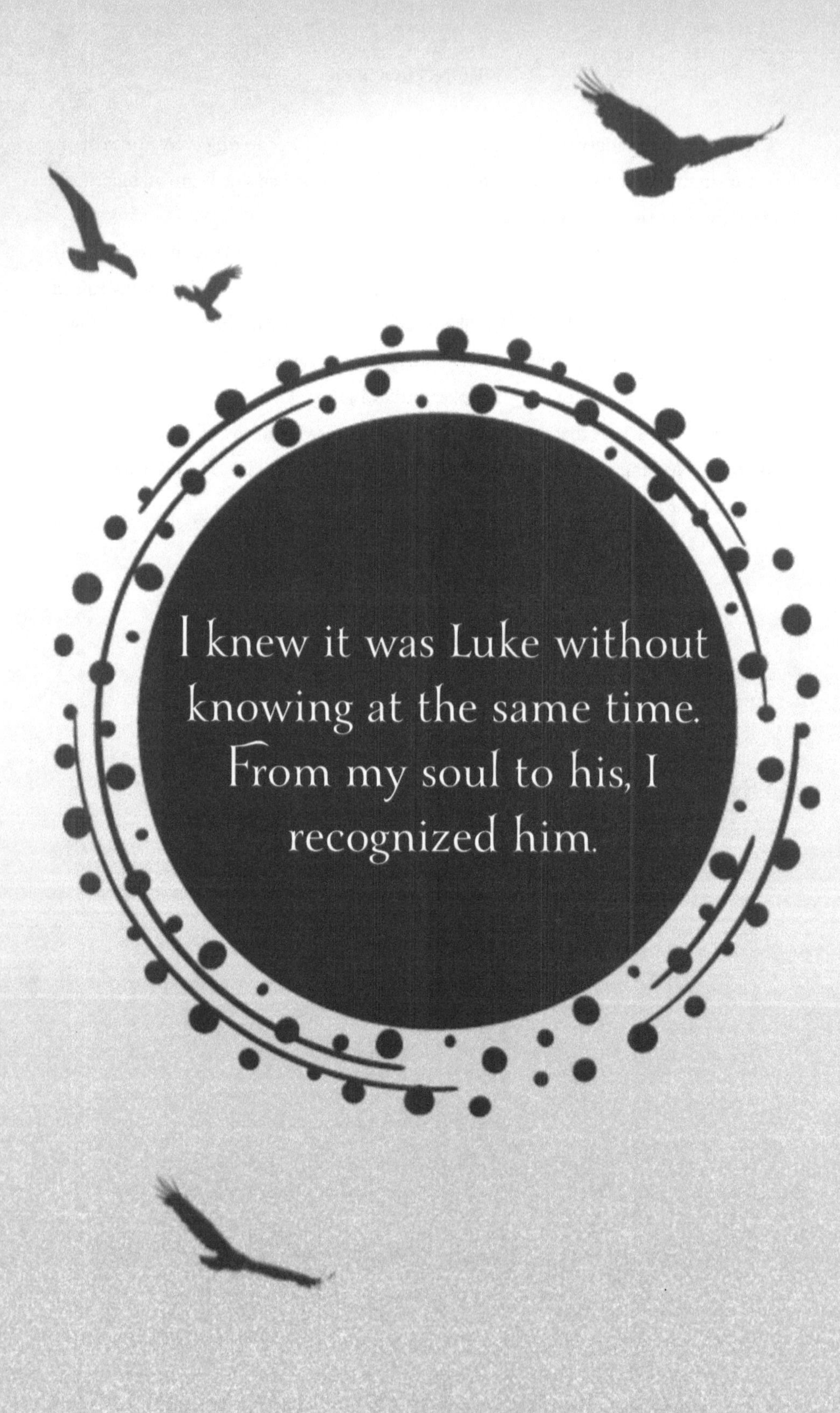
I knew it was Luke without
knowing at the same time.
From my soul to his, I
recognized him.

Chapter 26
Luke

I walked out of the door, and all I could feel was the storm. It was like being in that room with him was the last of it, the last of the calm before the storm. The whirl of the janitor's machine was loud, and the breeze from the open window was strong enough to float into the hall. I closed my eyes and pressed my forehead against the nearest locker as I let out a shaky breath, hearing nothing but the inevitable. I couldn't stop seeing him. HIM. Why was Kinsley a guy? Why was Sparrow a guy? I took a deep breath, then turned my head towards the art room door.

I could still see the hinges, a dark musty gold color, in desperate need of replacement as the paint around it chipped away. The part of the door I could see had a splinter that ran diagonally up the side of the door, and I realized it was so entirely imperfect with its chipped paint and its broken door, the words that fell away from the sign, that it was perfect just the way it was. Perfectly broken, like me.

I didn't know how long I stood there and stared at the door or what it was exactly I waited for before I realized I still had Kinsley's drawing and his note in my hand. Did I wait for him? Wait for him to come to chase after me? What would I even do if he did?

I heard the crackle of thunder in the distance as a soft sob echoed from the room, and for a moment, I wasn't sure if it was Kinsley crying or if I had imagined it. The thought of him crying tore through me. My heart felt like it was ripped out of my chest, and I wondered if this was all my fault, to begin with. I should have thrown away that letter from the start.

I turned my back on the club room and convinced myself it was nothing. Kinsley wasn't crying, everything was fine, and he didn't care. I had looked back at him when I had walked away, but he never looked at me. This was all a shock to him too, I had to imagine. Sure, he said he wasn't straight. I wasn't vain enough like most of those ridiculous guys to think every guy who wasn't straight was attracted to them. Just because Kinsley said he wasn't straight didn't mean he was interested in me.

He wanted to be friends, just friends, but I couldn't do it. How could I be near him when all I could hear was my father's voice in my mind? The whole time I sat there, all I could hear was my father. His voice boomed louder and louder, that awful sneer on his face, his features contorted in anger, and his spit as it flew around the room. *'Faggot,'* he'd spit. The word I hated the most, the word I couldn't escape from no matter how hard I tried.

I could just feel my father behind me as he told me in that loud voice that everything was my fault. He'd tell me I had caused this, I started this, I should have known from the start. *The smell,* he'd say. I should have been able to smell the gay on the letter as if gay people had a different scent from straight people. He never made rational sense, but when you grew up being terrified, it didn't have to make sense for you to be traumatized.

I couldn't stop hearing Kinsley's voice in my head, and it drove me crazy as I stood in the doorway of the school and looked out at the parking lot. The rain was still mostly a drizzle, the parking lot empty except for Kinsley's car in the student area and a small gathering of vehicles that belonged to the few teachers and janitors that were still inside.

I kept rereading his letters in my mind but with his voice now, his low alto voice, soft like a feather, almost exactly how I imagined it was. Except with a male lithe to his voice, instead of a female. I looked at the papers in my hand, the butterfly, the words. I knew why he did it. It was the fastest and easiest proof. His drawing technique, he knew I would recognize it. I lifted the butterfly higher and studied the intricate swirls and the pristine shapes. I was - for a moment - fascinated. How he had managed to make something so beautiful, so intricate, in such a small amount of time and so flawlessly, was beyond me.

It was so small and simple but so beautiful all the same. Even now as I ran my finger over the beautiful swirls, I felt a tug in my chest. My heart beat faster, confused, as my soul recognized his. "His," I whispered as I pressed my hand against my chest. "Not hers. He's a boy, you can't do that for a boy," I whispered angrily.

It was one of the main reasons I had told Kinsley no when he asked to be friends. I had gotten so close to him through the letters, opened up so much to him, and gotten so close to feeling like I was starting to have feelings for the person I was writing to. Those feelings were inside me. They slowly grew over time, and I now had to shove them back and destroy them. I took a deep breath and looked at the note.

Another fast easy way to prove it. His handwriting I would recognize more than any others. The number of times I ran my finger over his words late at night as I read and reread his letters to try and block out the noise. The slanted curve of his wannabe cursive writing, the few times he went extra and did a small swirl to the end of his words almost by accident, there was no other handwriting like Kinsley's. He had written a small little note to show me his handwriting. Of course, I would recognize it with a moment's glance, the handwriting that was embedded in my mind.

His words, however. I pulled a notebook out of my bag, gently put the drawing and the note inside it, and then shoved it back into my bag. They didn't mean anything, not like that. Simply as a friend, as he had requested, even though I had turned it down. Why was I saving it? I wasn't sure what I was doing or why, and it burned. Everything burned. My father's voice in my mind, my mother's blank stares, and my brother's furious yelling as he acted out again and again. Burning, everything was burning. The screams of the storm rose and fell like an endless symphony of pain.

I realized that the longer I stood there the more likely Kinsley was going to see me. He would come out eventually and if I still stood there, what then? I moved to the side of the school and hid behind the bushes, glad that the lip of the roof kept the drizzle off of me. I knew it would be better for him to leave first, otherwise, he'd drive past me. Someone like Kinsley, someone kind and sweet like Kinsley, would stop and offer me a ride even after I told him I wanted nothing to do with him. A shiver ran through me as the cold wind thick with the oncoming rain moved against my body, and I felt a dull throb in my chest at my own thoughts. The fact that I knew that about him.

I had never known Kinsley before, only in passing or rumors spread around the school. Either he was dating that one girl he was always with, or he was gay, I hadn't ever really been sure before and I never really cared. But I knew him now. So many letters, so much talking back and forth between us, and I knew it. *Soulmates,* Kinsley had said. *A lifeline,* I had said. Dating, but not.

Confusion swirled around inside me as I pressed my back against the wall and tried to figure out what all of this meant. I was straight, I wasn't gay, I wasn't what my father called me. We hadn't really been dating, we only just talked. It didn't mean anything, because neither of us expected the other to be a boy. He understood it was the end because he figured out I was a guy, and maybe he had expected us to stay talking but that wouldn't work, I couldn't do it. We might not have been dating for real, but even what we were doing was something we shouldn't have, something I wouldn't have if I had known from the start he was a boy. We had just talked, but it wasn't just talking at the same time. *Just falling in lov-*

I sucked in a deep breath, my eyes blinked rapidly as I watched Kinsley appear. He didn't look around, he didn't run, he didn't care. His hood covered his face as he moved slowly towards his car, his bag underneath his hoodie, most likely to protect artwork from the rain. That was why I had recognized him. Always huddled down low, always hidden under his large hoodie, always hidden from view and tried to be invisible. He wasn't the only one who wore all black, but he was the only one who didn't hang out with the others.

The rain started to get slightly heavier, not too bad, but I would probably be soaked by the time I got to work. Suddenly Kinsley slipped, he barely tried to catch himself. He was inches from his car, his head slumped down and his arms across his stomach, and I sucked in a deep breath as he just sat there. He leaned forward and pressed his forehead against his car door. I didn't know how long he sat there, or how long I sat here, but all I could do was watch and wait, unsure of where to go from there.

We'd always been two entities before. Two beings that existed in a sea of fakes, but for a small moment in time, we had been two of the same, pieced together. How to go back to being different? How to go back to not caring? I knew him, from a distance, for most of my life. One of the rich kids, one of the kids on the other side of town. One of those who lived in the fancy houses inside the large fenced-in community. I'd been there before, a few times, because of Bobby and my first ex-girlfriend, Lana. I could probably name all of the kids who lived in those houses.

Out of all of the football players, Bobby was the only one whose parents were rich enough to live there. It was why he was one of the only ones who had a vehicle. Of course, that didn't mean all of the football players were poor, most of us lived with parents who made a decent amount. Even my parents made a decent amount, but most of the money went to replace everything that was always broken or little gifts my father gave my mother when he tried to manipulate her.

Kinsley stood out from the rich kids' group only because he wasn't exactly rich boy material. He had the rich boy title I guess, but he dressed like an emo kid and he hid from sight. The others who lived in that fenced-in development were all sporty kids, their parents proud of them, they all stood out in their own ways and they flaunted the money they had. They grouped together and talked about their elegant parties and their rich snobby parents as if they expected all of us to care for and worship them. I had never really cared before. About him, or anyone else.

I couldn't help but wonder, as Kinsley finally stood up and unlocked his car, what was going to happen now? How could I go without the letters? I had been so tired of existing before Kinsley started to write to me, and while I had known the whole time it wasn't healthy to rely on them, I couldn't stop myself either. I had forced myself to wake every morning by telling myself there would be a letter waiting. I had gone to sleep at night with Sparrow's words rolling around and around in my mind, mixed with the songs of the bands he had given me. At this point, I probably had playlists filled with his music more than mine. His words were a part of me, his songs everything to me, so how was I supposed to go back?

As Kinsley drove off, I slowly followed and ignored the rain as it slid down my body. For an hour, I walked, my head lost in thoughts, and even as my boss scolded me for being late, I silently tried to figure out what to do. How to keep going, how to keep existing, and why. For a brief period of time, I was important to Sparrow. For a brief period of time, I meant something to someone. But I realized something. It was all a mistake, from the very beginning.

My locker was next to Tony's, one of the guys on my team. My locker was also next to Peyton's, that one girl on the swim team. He had said he was forced to get with someone to appease his family, and while I didn't care much back then that I wasn't his first choice, maybe I should have. Because in the end, even if it wasn't the right gender, even if it was a mistake, it just proved what I had known all along. What my father had yelled at me all along. I was never going to be someone's first choice. I was never going to be good enough.

I went home covered in grease and sweat, the house was filled with screams. I walked through the house like a shadow. Shawn was in the middle of the living room screaming and my mother stood there, staring with wide eyes. My father was furious as he slammed papers down on the coffee table. It looked like a new table, but I doubted it was going to be there for much longer. I walked up the stairs and closed my bedroom door. I heard the tell-tale shattered sound of the glass, the screams of my mother echoed while my brother and father yelled at each other.

Sometimes I was jealous of Shawn because he was stronger than me. His spirit was stronger, he was able to stand up for himself, and no matter how hard I tried I was always either invisible or just told I wasn't good enough. We only had one bathroom, and as I stepped into the shower I realized the shampoo Shawn and I used was out. I'd have to pick up more, but for now, all I could use was Mom's, since if I tried to touch Dad's he'd kill me.

As I stepped out of the bathroom, a towel wrapped around my waist, I was shoved back into the bathroom. I nearly fell into the sink as I stared up at my father with wide eyes. "Faggot," he spat, his eyes wide and staring as I flinched. "You smell like a woman."

I knew I shouldn't speak, but there was something about the fact that I was already at my lowest that made me realize there was nothing else I could do but struggle to keep going. Struggle to push and shove, struggle to be brave. Brave like Kinsley. "I was covered in grease, Shawn and I have no more shampoo," I tried to explain.

The crack of his fist against my side made me fall back onto the ground, my head inches from hitting the toilet. "Real men would wear their grease proudly," he spat at me, his eyes filled with disgust. I watched as he turned around, and walked out of the bathroom and down the hall. "I'm going out! I can't be around all of these girls!" He yelled, moments before the front door slammed behind him.

As my mother's screams filled the air -most likely cursing out the closed door because she'd never open it and embarrass herself with the neighbors- I sat there and stared at the empty hall and tried to ignore the throbbing in my side. "But you don't even work on cars, you wear a suit and go sit behind a desk all day," I mumbled quietly, my little act of rebellion. As if I could ever say it loudly, as if I could ever speak up when it mattered most. I curled my knees to my chest and pressed my head against the tops of them. Forced myself to inhale, to exhale, and repeat. There was nothing brave about me.

For dinner, I made us mac and cheese. If Dad was here he'd throw a fit all over again that it was one of us instead of Mom cooking. But Mom hadn't moved from the couch where she stared at the wall with an endless stream of tears that fell down her cheeks. I had sat next to her for a while, tried to put some mac and cheese in her mouth and she swallowed a few bites before she started to gag. I decided to leave her alone and left her bowl in her lap in hopes she'd feed herself even though I knew she wouldn't. I wasn't surprised when Dad came back home with a new coffee table in the box ready to be put together. His eyes narrowed as he looked at Shawn and me. "Mom cooked us mac and cheese," I said before he could say anything. It was a lie, but he believed it as he gave a sharp nod and went to the living room.

After a few seconds, we could hear Mom's soft sobs as he apologized to her. "I'm sorry. I'll do better, I'll be better," he lied. "I promise, Sweetheart." Empty promises to a broken woman who was desperate for happiness. *He knew just what to say,* I thought to myself as I heard the sounds of them kissing through her shuddered sobs. I stabbed my fork into my food and wondered if anyone ever even realized that promises without change were just a form of manipulation.

We both went to our rooms without cleaning since Mom was in a happy mood right now. She cleaned everything with a smile on her face and a soft kiss on our cheeks, her eyes wide and bright as Dad twirled her around the kitchen. I kicked off my clothes and lay in my bed curled up under my blankets, too emotionally drained to care about homework. Normally I'd be reading Sparrow's letters, my headphones in my ears as I listened to either SYML or something louder depending on if my parents were screaming or not.

Finally, as I curled up under my blankets, my door locked and my hand hung from the side of the bed, I let the tears that threatened to spill over release. I grabbed my pillow, pressed it against my chest, and hugged it tightly to me as broken sobs ripped through me. I realized that no matter how hard I tried to fight it, no matter how hard I tried to escape it, my hand that hung over the side of the bed had grabbed my bag, almost by reflex by now to find a letter, any letter, and pulled it out. *'Don't do it,'* I whispered to myself as I gently opened the letter. *'Don't make it worse,'*

My hand and my eyes moved on their own as the letter was opened, and the only words I could see through my tears were enough to break me. The sobs broke through once more; spilled through me, drowned me. The screams of a new fight from downstairs started to echo around the house, mixed with the sound of my quiet strangled sobs. At least for tonight, nothing was louder than Kinsley's voice. Those words screamed in my mind, those words from his letter.

'I wish I could be the one you call at night when you can't stop crying.'

"Even if it's four in the morning?" I whispered into the empty room.

'Even if it's four in the morning, Green.'

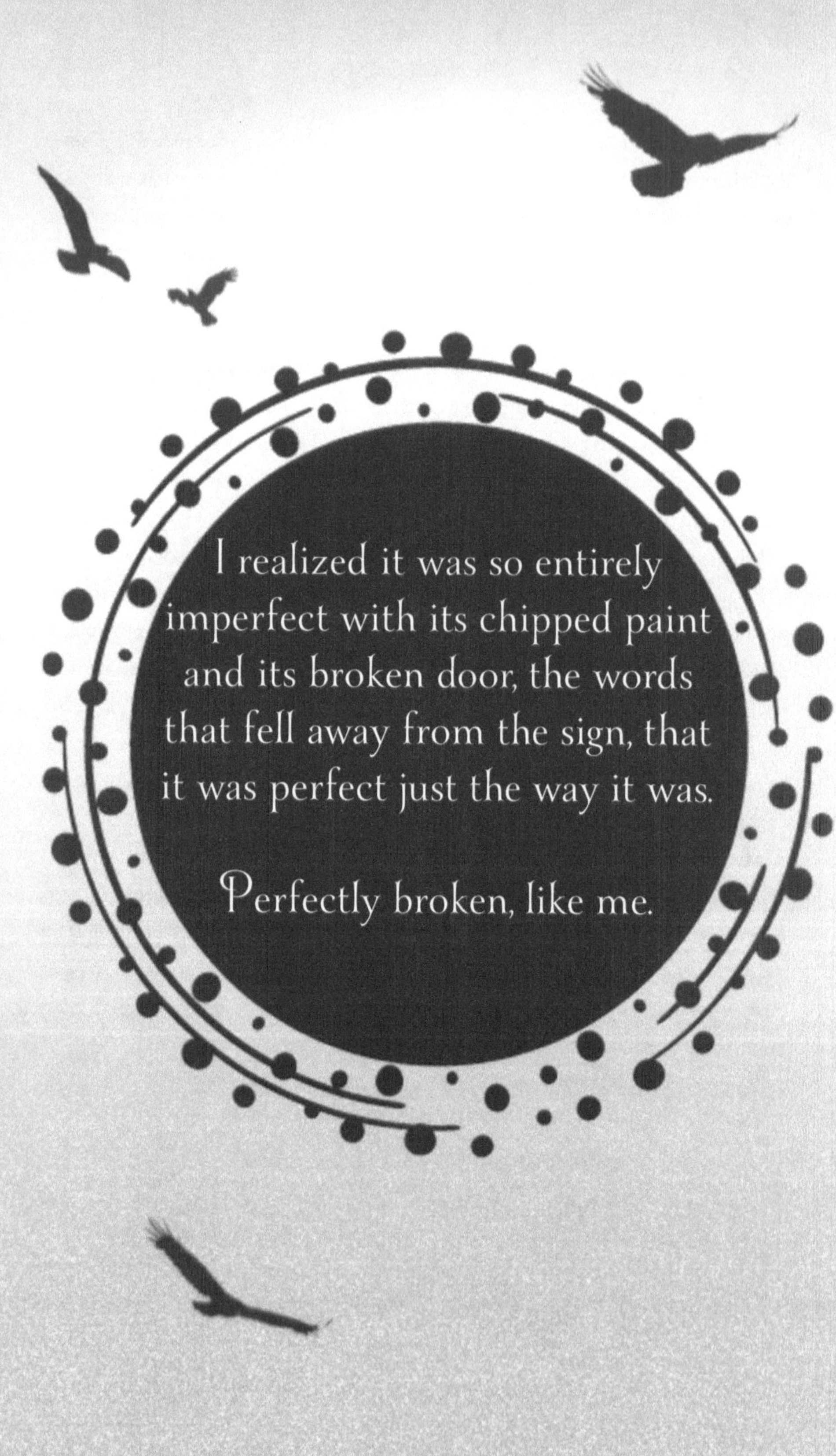

I realized it was so entirely imperfect with its chipped paint and its broken door, the words that fell away from the sign, that it was perfect just the way it was.

Perfectly broken, like me.

Chapter 27
Luke

I skipped school the next day and the day after that until I stopped going for the whole week. My boss was happy. I wasn't sure how to walk the halls and see the smiles. I wasn't sure how to high-five the guys and hear them mock me when there wasn't a letter in my hands anymore. *Heartbreaker,* they'd call me, and expect me to laugh back with them. They'd think I finally turned the girl down. None of them would have expected me to have been talking to a guy the whole time. None of them would have expected me to have been talking to Kinsley Bryant.

Honestly, I was fairly sure the hardest part of all of this was knowing when I walked into the doors, the first thing I would want to do was open my locker. I'd rush up the stairs, my mind would try to tell my body to stop, and my heart would race as some fucked up version of hope spilled through me. Hope for something I should never have had from the start. Then I'd open the locker, and despite how many times I'd tell myself it was supposed to be like this from the start, I'd break all over again.

I'd see nothing but my mess, papers scattered everywhere, a dried piece of gum I shoved into the top corner and never bothered to get out. Textbooks jammed so badly some of the pages were ripped and folded. Broken pens and pencil lead snapped off of pencils, a mess made in my haste to go from class to class all year long. My mind only cared about one thing this whole time, the one thing that I'd never see again - A letter from Sparrow.

I had told Bobby to tell the coach I wasn't feeling well, and instead of him taking me to school, he'd drop me off at the shop every morning. It was on the way to school anyway, and as long as I got up and dressed, grabbed my backpack, and pretended everything was okay, my parents never noticed. Dad was barely home the past few days, Mom stared absently if she even came out of her room, and Shawn was always gone early. A few houses down his best friend lived, and his mother gave Shawn a ride to middle school and home again afterward since it was on her way.

I wondered sometimes if she knew what went on in our house, but then again, I doubted it. She was a really nice lady, and I had no doubt if she knew about our lifestyle, she would've already called child services. Dad would go to jail from all the obvious physical abuse, the holes in the walls, and the broken glass still randomly brushed aside. Mom's dried bloody footprints lingered in a few places showing she had stepped on the glass and didn't bother to notice it or clean it, she had let the wound dry up and scab over on its own. Mom would go to a psych ward for evaluation since she was clearly getting worse again. I was curious how her job hadn't noticed by now, but she was a great actress when she wanted to be. It was only at home she gave up.

Bobby would bring me homework at the shop, and I'd stay my normal after-school hours like usual and go home covered in grease and sweat. No one noticed. Well, no one in my home noticed. None of my team asked questions, they didn't really care about me. The cheerleaders pouted their lips and whined that they missed me at school and on the field, but no one really ASKED.

I would stare at them as they drove, their easy banter as they spoke about rumors and events at school I didn't care about. *'Why are you skipping school?', 'What's going on at home?', 'Why do you have a black eye today?', 'Is that a bloody lip?', 'How are you really doing?'* None of the important questions, the questions that Kinsley would have asked if he was here. Why couldn't one of the straight guys on my team be my friend? Why couldn't they care about something other than what party was going on this weekend, what girl they were going to bang, or who was dating whom? Why was everyone so transparent?

Then again, this was how life was supposed to be, right? Happy, carefree, and in the prime of their lives. To live every day with a smile on their face, great parents who embarrassed them when they gave them the sex talk or handed them condoms in front of their friends to tease them. Parents who made home-cooked meals every day and whined because they felt like they were too old to receive homemade lunches. That was what childhood was supposed to be like, right? No one was meant to live in a storm.

I wanted to get Bobby to open my locker, to check it, but I never had. I knew there wouldn't be a letter there, but what if there was? Kinsley wasn't the type to strike me as stubborn. I didn't think he'd ignore my wishes and try to contact me anyway. However, I didn't ask. If by chance Kinsley did put a letter there, I didn't trust Bobby not to open it.

So I simply smirked at the cheerleaders, slipped them one of the football players' numbers, and begged them to let me borrow whatever textbook Bobby gave me homework for. They didn't care who they ended up texting, as long as they got the attention in the end that they were looking for. I didn't want to call anyone out as being easy, but you'd think that after a full week of none of them getting my actual phone number they'd have noticed, but none of them said otherwise.

My boss had been mad at me that day that I came an hour late, soaked and distant, my mind blank and my hands fumbled everything I was given to do. I made it up to him when I told him I'd pull double shifts the rest of the week. A small break from school. He was my parents' age, he didn't have any kids, and he didn't know or care about the school schedule.

"Did you hear about what went down this week?" It was Friday after school, and I felt numb. I had woken up all week long with cold chills and sweat dried on my skin, my heart raced, and my hand searched for my phone. I struggled to sleep unless I stared at the picture I took of Kinsley's drawing. The dark charcoal lines, the swirls, and those bright cerulean eyes pierced through me. Maybe I should keep skipping, maybe I should drop out. Grab Shawn and move somewhere, anywhere, start over.

Neither of us really needed school, right? Was it really worth it in the end? We only lived once, why waste at least twenty years of your life sitting at a desk trapped behind four walls and listening to teachers drone on about things that we mostly didn't need in life? History class was worthless. Why should I care about wars that were long done or people that were long dead?

I understood the concept of course. They wanted us to make sure we didn't make the same mistakes, they wanted those people to be honored or hated depending on the topic. Honestly, they should have made us learn laws instead. I always felt like history should be replaced by laws, that would have made so much more sense if we studied something that actually pertained to our everyday life instead of what had long passed.

I looked over at Tony, the three of us leaned against the wall at my job as I drank from a can of soda and wiped the sweat from my forehead. I had been about halfway through my break when they pulled up. Bobby and Tony instantly came over to me with their cigarettes already dangled from their lips, their lighters fished out of their pockets as the girls in the truck scrunched up their noses and gagged. Small little ews could be heard from them as I reached over and grabbed the cigarette from Bobby's mouth, pressed it against my lips, and took a small puff of it.

I wasn't addicted like they were, but you don't get raised the way I was in the neighborhood I lived in and not get used to the feel of the stick in between your fingers or the burn that flooded your lungs. So much stress, so much going on, I couldn't help but inhale once more. Bobby frowned as he grabbed another cigarette and lit it up since I stole his. "How would I know what went down when I haven't even been there?" I wondered.

Tony chuckled as he shook his head at me. "You're right, I didn't think about that," Tony wasn't the brightest one. For five minutes I listened dully as Tony rambled on about some girl on the swim team who got into a hair-pulling fight with someone who was on the yearbook staff. Took pictures without permission. Something about a bra being exposed and the yearbook girl refused to delete the photo.

"You should have seen it, bro! They were tearing each other's shirts off!" He said. I nodded, gave a smile, and let out a disappointed sound as they chuckled at me because that was what was expected. I should have been disappointed I didn't see the girl's boobs, right? For some reason, I just felt numb. Broken, I was broken. "Roan beat the crap out of that little fag boy, what's his name? Doesn't really matter I guess. That was pretty sick, not gonna lie," he added with a grimace.

I turned my head toward him fast, the cigarette hung in between my finger and my thumb as my heart started to beat painfully, my eyes wide. "What? Why?" I asked. I tried to calm myself down. They looked at me like I was crazy and I couldn't blame them. How many times had I heard about Roan beating someone up and I ignored it? How many times had it been Kinsley? Why was he always picking on him anyway? Then again, Kinsley told me he wasn't straight. Roan was a massive homophobe, that was probably why. Not that it made it okay. It didn't make any of this okay.

Tony looked at Bobby, giving him a slight shrug. I yelped and dropped the cigarette on the ground as it burned my finger. I cursed under my breath and pressed my finger against my shirt, trying to stop the slight throbbing feeling. "Um," Tony said, clearly thrown. My mouth tasted disgusting now that the cigarette was gone and I took another sip of my soda, swished the liquid in my mouth, and spit it out on the ground. Another chorus of ews from the girls could be heard, but the small squeals about how hot we were blended in. Girls were so freaking complicated, they never made sense.

"I don't know, he just beats them up, you know? Roan is Roan, it's how he does," he said with a shrug. I mean, as much as it frustrated me, I simply shrugged and nodded, because that was what I was expected to do. That was what I would have done before. Why did it matter to me now? Because it was Kinsley. Because he was Sparrow, because he mattered. I shook away my thoughts as I looked at them. "Oh, something about being paired up in photography? Photosynthesis? Whatever that class is called,"

I scoffed as I rolled my eyes while Bobby laughed and shoved his shoulder into Tony's. "Psychology, you dummy. How the hell do you even know what photosynthesis is? That word is way too big for your vocabulary,"

"Your mom is too big for my vocabulary," Tony mocked. He ducked with a gasp as Bobby's fist went flying towards his face, a chuckle coming from Tony as he danced away. He was a moron most of the time but he was fast, I had to give him that.

I grinned as I watched them banter with each other for a few minutes, while inside I couldn't stop thinking about school. Roan was partnered up with Kinsley? That was a horrible combination. The teachers knew they couldn't do much to Roan because of who he was related to, but they did seem to try and steer him away from those he bullied to try and make it easier. They'd never paired Roan up with someone he bullied before, they usually chose hot girls for him to keep him preoccupied. Why did it freaking matter to me? Roan was going to kill him, bring him back to life, make him do the project, and then kill him all over again.

"Your break has been over for a while, Luke. I'm not paying you to stand out here braiding your hair with the boys," my boss said as all three of us jumped. He glared at us, his face covered in oil as he smeared a dirty rag around, just making it worse.

I wanted to roll my eyes at him, to tell him I'd worked overtime that whole week and should have been given a reprieve for being a few minutes past my time. Instead, I nodded and held up the papers Bobby had given me. "Sorry, boss. I was getting schoolwork from them," I nearly cursed myself, realizing I had told him all week I wasn't in school right then. Instead of calling me out on it, he didn't even seem to care.

He gave a sharp nod. I said goodbye to the boys and walked inside, ignoring the chorus of noise that came from the girls as they called out to me. I needed to stop ignoring them. I had been single for a while now; I probably should fix that. I just didn't want to. I didn't think I could love, to be honest. Broken, I assumed I was just broken. How could someone raised like me and who came from my lifestyle be anything other than broken?

That was another reason why I had said no to Kinsley. How could I possibly have talked to him when I felt things, the start of things that I had never thought I could feel? How could I have talked to him when those feelings were so confusing, so unacceptable? I mean, they would have faded away, of course. He was a boy. *'Faggot,'* my father's voice sounded in my head all through the rest of the shift at work. It was like a drum, echoing over and over again. Attacking me, threatening me, and tearing me down over and over again. No, I couldn't have talked to Kinsley again.

When I got home, I was immediately shoved through the doorway and into the living room. A fist crashed into my side and threw me off guard as I fell against the side of the couch. I sucked in a deep breath, forced my tears to suck back into my eye sockets as I peered up at my angry father's face. He looked more like me than my mom did, something that bothered me more than anything. To see his light green eyes and his dark brown hair always bothered me. To know that maybe this was how I would be when I was older.

To stand there, a vein pulsing from my forehead, my eyes darkening in anger as I beat the shit out of my wife and kids. I would never get married, I'd never have kids, worried I'd end up like this. My brother and my mother were more alike with their black hair and brown eyes. I had my mom's curls, but that was mostly it. I felt a kick to my side and forced myself not to flinch, I knew if I did he'd call me that name again and tell me real men could take hits. He never hit my face, not intentionally.

He wasn't stupid in his hits unless he was piss poor drunk. He would go for my sides or my stomach, something I could brush off as football damage. My black eye that week was from when I cracked my face into the coffee table, and my lip into the doorknob when I fell. I took it all, and stood in front of my mother, in front of Shawn, willing to take the pain if it meant they would be okay.

Emotionally, I couldn't do much. I could stand there and take a hit, at least I could do that. To stare into my dad's eyes had always been difficult for me, especially when they were red from drinking. I refused to touch a sip, scared one day I'd end up hovering over someone with red eyes and anger pulsing through me that I couldn't control. No matter how much I tried to tell myself I'd never end up like him, I wondered if that would ever be true. We were one and the same, cut from the same cloth, and the same blood pulsed through our veins. Was it even possible to be different from him? I wondered if, in the end, we all simply became our parents after a while. If I ever became my father I'd kill myself.

"Where have you been all week!?" He yelled, his hands curled into fists as he glared down at me. I could see Shawn grab my mother's wrist, pulling her away, and couldn't help but let out a sigh of relief. "The school called, and your stupid mother had ignored the calls all week," he turned to glare where she had stood a few seconds ago.

I didn't try to stand. I knew he wasn't done as I took a deep breath and tried to figure out how to get out of this mess. I couldn't say it was my boss's fault; he'd tell me to quit. I couldn't say I had difficulties at school; he'd call me that name again, tell me to handle them. I knew no matter what I did or said I'd end up hurt, so I stuck to the simpler answer, the easier one. "I didn't feel like it," I muttered under my breath.

What else was I supposed to say, I couldn't help but wonder as his fists started to rain down on my stomach. Was I supposed to tell him I had found, for the shortest period of time, the calm to the raging storm? That I had had someone to talk to, someone who cared about me, and it ended up being a boy? How was I supposed to tell him that I was breaking inside, my mind missed the pictures, the words, the safety, the lifeline. How could I tell him I couldn't sleep, could barely eat, that I couldn't get past the aching pain that came from telling Kinsley no?

He'd kill me, I knew that for a fact. If I were to ever even tell him I was friends with someone who wasn't straight, he'd kill me. If I were to ever be anything but straight myself, he'd kill me. I heard a crack and chomped down on my tongue so hard I felt blood pool in my mouth and tried not to whimper. It wasn't the first time my ribs had been broken, and I knew if I made a sound he'd never stop. "Why am I surrounded by a household of girls!?" He screamed. When he moved away from me I tried to regain my breathing. My vision had started to go in and out as he picked up books and magazines Mother had sat neatly in a holder. She always tried her best to make the house lovely despite all of the destruction. With sad eyes and a wounded soul, Mom would sit there on her hands and knees and clean and organize repeatedly the same things, to scrub the blood away, and hope that maybe it was the last time it would be broken. It was never the last time.

As the metal from the holder crashed into the wall I managed to stand. I walked as fast as I could towards my room and shut the door. My breathing was ragged, and I could barely shove my shoes off of me as I held onto my dresser. I dropped my school bag on the ground with disdain and glared at it as if it were the principal, but I knew I couldn't get mad at them for calling. It was my own fault, my own weakness, and I should have gone from the beginning. I smelled like sweat and oil, and I knew I'd regret this the moment I woke up and had to spend time changing my bedding, but for now, I didn't care.

I whimpered, tears slid down my cheeks as I managed to shake off my pants and threw my phone on my bed. I didn't even attempt to lift my arms high to take my shirt off. I walked slowly to my bed and as gently as I could, I laid down on it. I never knew laying down on my bed could be so painful and so great at the same time. I grabbed the ibuprofen I had on my nightstand, grabbed a few pills, and swallowed them with the bottle of old and warm water that sat there.

I grimaced at the taste, but it was better than nothing. My face felt disgusting as I wiped at the tears, smeared the oil, and burned my eyes, but I couldn't stop crying. With another whimper, I rolled onto my good side and grabbed my phone where it had been thrown. I gasped in pain as I tried to find the charger cord. I plugged it in, my hands shook as I started it up and waited, impatiently waiting. Finally, the screen turned on and I sighed in relief.

I opened the photos on my phone and found the ones that meant the most to me. The picture of the angel and the picture of his blue eyes, his bright cerulean blue eyes. I felt myself relax as I stared, the screams and the booms of the storm filled my ears from downstairs. But up here in my locked bedroom staring at those eyes, I felt warm, I felt safe, I felt like I was home.

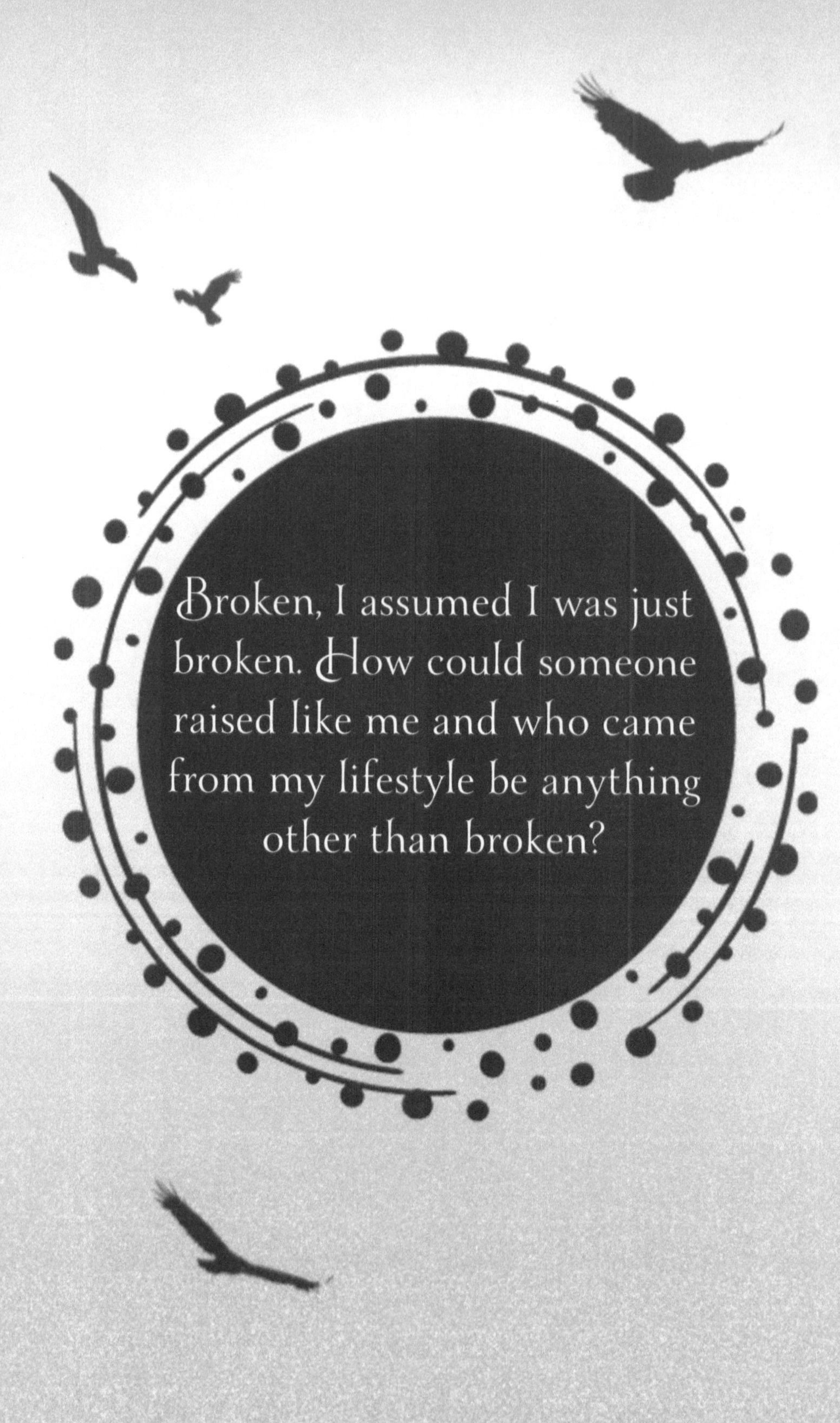
Broken, I assumed I was just broken. How could someone raised like me and who came from my lifestyle be anything other than broken?

Chapter 28
Kinsley

I woke up to bright luminescent lights. Immediately, I squeezed my eyes closed tightly from the brightness. I listened and tried to remember why I was there. I could hear the soft buzz coming from the lights, the small beeps of my heart echoing through a machine. I could hear a small buzz that resulted in the squeeze of my upper bicep. It tightened and held itself firmly on me before it let the pressure go with a soft beep. The top of my hand ached, and my body felt like I had gotten run over by a truck.

I didn't need to feel or hear any more than that to know where I was and why. Despite that, I waited a little longer, my lips pressed tightly together, unable to stop the images that poured through my mind. Roan's tantrum that I had been assigned to be his partner. He had purposely hurt me for the rest of the day, targeting just me instead of the others he tended to bully.

After school, instead of going to practice, he chased me down in the parking lot and beat the shit out of me. I didn't really understand why. It wasn't like I assigned him to be my partner, but he was furious and took it out on me. I didn't understand why I was assigned to him to begin with, since the teachers seemed to try and separate those Roan bullied from him. They knew they couldn't do much with his connections but tried to help as much as they could. I heard the door open and close, and the sound of a clipboard being jostled. "Has he woken up yet?" A woman asked softly. A nurse, most likely.

I realized I didn't really need to be asleep anymore, there was no point. I expected to see my parents when I opened my eyes, unsure how long I'd been there. I had blacked out in the parking lot, I remembered that. Isabella had already left, it was Friday and her mother came and got her for work on Fridays. I had been all alone when I passed out, surrounded by a crowd of kids who laughed and cheered, egged Roan on as he beat the shit out of the *'Fag'*. I let out a soft groan as I opened my eyes and tried to ignore the pain in my hand and my body as I slowly sat up. My head was swimming and I laid back down. Hands rushed to touch me as my eyes closed once more.

A soft hand, slightly cool, a female hand. For a moment my heart sped up, and I almost believed that it could be hers. That my mother actually cared. Had it been a few days? They would have needed a few days to get back from Italy, and I doubted I could be released without them. But as I opened my eyes I was both happy and sad at the same time.

Sad because, of course, it wasn't my mother, it wasn't my parents. They wouldn't touch me so gently, they wouldn't be looking at me with concern in their eyes. But I was happy, because I knew her, and she was someone almost just as important to me as Isabella was, her mother. *"Como te sientes, Mijo?"* She asked, her hand gently sliding against my forehead, my cheeks, and my neck. I gave her a puzzled look and she shook her head at me as she thought for a moment. Her accent was thick when she finally spoke, trying to find the English words for me. "How do you feel, Son?"

I allowed her to help me sit up again, slower this time as Isabella put a pillow behind me. She grabbed another one to put behind my head to help me stay in a sitting position. I could see the nurse clearly now. She had long curly black hair and brown eyes, a woman I'd never seen before, but she looked familiar to me. "My name is Mrs. Wilson, and I'll be your nurse for the evening, Kinsley. I'm sure you have questions, but I'd like to ask a few of my own first if you don't mind. Can you tell me what day it is? What month, what year?"

I answered every question she had and learned a few of my own in return because Isabella's mother bit at her every time she asked a question she thought was irrelevant. Mrs. Wilson asked the date, and Mami would tell her it was a stupid question and to get on with it. She'd ask about the year and Mami would ask her if she thought I would think I was an alien. She didn't give Mrs. Wilson even an inch of room to breathe, glaring daggers into her as she radiated fury, and the number of times I saw her twitch her fingers worried me since I wasn't sure I could handle the slap of her shoe right now.

However, I did learn the questions were meant to be asked because I got hit in the head, and I couldn't help but sigh as I wondered just how awful I must look right now. A few times she'd make Isabella translate a word or a sentence for her and give her a sharp smack if she didn't say it the right way. The two of them had a soft fight for a few minutes more than once in Spanish as Mrs. Wilson stood there and awkwardly waited for them to finish.

"I'd like to talk to you, Kinsley, about your condition. Do you have any family present that can hear what I have to say? I also need your parents to sign forms; we had to do a few scans on you, and stitches, and all of those procedures are usually signed off beforehand. We will go ahead if there's no parent or guardian here and the patient is unconscious, however. We treat first and ask questions later, it's our policy."

"Do I look like a fish? Can't you see he's my son? *Dios mío*, just say what you have to say, I'm waiting," Isabella's mother said, she glared at Mrs. Wilson as she stood up tall.

Mrs. Wilson gulped visibly, her hands clutching the chart tighter as she took a step back, and I gave her a sharp nod to let her know it was okay. I doubted anyone could have stopped Isabella's mother when she was that angry, and the vein in her neck throbbed so much, that I worried it would pop out of her skin. Mrs. Wilson nodded, looked down at the chart, and flipped through a few pages. It was then that I realized that, although she looked nothing like him, she had the same last name as Luke.

I shook my head and tried not to throw up as the sudden movement pulled at my stomach, and a queasy feeling spread throughout me. They didn't look much alike at all, Wilson wasn't an uncommon surname. Besides, it wouldn't matter anyway. Even if she was his mother, did I expect her to have him trailing around behind her? He wouldn't be there, so it didn't matter one way or another. She seemed nice though, but I couldn't help but notice a small bruise that showed on top of her wrist before she pulled down the white long-sleeved shirt she wore underneath her scrubs.

"You have two broken ribs, Kinsley. They're your two lower ribs on your right side. They broke cleanly, so you won't require surgery for them as long as you bind them daily. It's almost impossible to help how you move when you sleep, but you should try to sleep on your left side for now. It takes about three to six weeks for ribs to heal, and your discharge papers will show what number and what office you need to call to have your follow-up appointment for your ribs."

From the way Mami's eyes were glazed over in anger, and the soft whispers from Isabella as she quickly translated everything for her, I had no doubt in my mind that she'd get that discharge paper and would call all of the doctors on the list for me, to make sure I went to each appointment.

Mrs. Wilson continued to flip through the papers, and I knew she wasn't finished since there was a mention of stitches. It was hard for me to tell all of what was wrong with me when I ached all over and could barely move. "It seems like your car window was busted when you were hit, and you fell on the glass. You had a few large gashes in your back and we had to get the glass out and stitch the wounds. Your left wrist was fractured as well, and you hit your head so hard you have a concussion," she added as she lifted her eyes to look at me once more. She had a soft pitied look in her eyes and I didn't like it. I didn't need her pity, it wasn't like it was her fault Roan was an asshole.

"Where are the police? I called them the moment I came here, but they never arrived. What about the person who did this to Kinsley?" Mami talked slowly as she made sure to say each word carefully. A few words she had to repeat for Mrs. Wilson, who wasn't able to fully understand her accent. I had known Isabella and her mother for years now and it didn't bother me, but I guessed those who hadn't heard the rich and beautiful accent before had trouble understanding some of it.

Mrs. Wilson looked uncomfortable, her fingers shook as she put the chart back. "They won't be coming, I believe. The incident at the school was reported by a student who was there. Everyone claimed to not know who did it, and without evidence, there isn't a case. The police contacted the doctor in charge of Kinsley, but when he informed them he had a concussion, they assumed he wouldn't remember either. The kid who is being protected is very popular in this town and has a lot of higher-up influencers, and while we all know who did it, there's nothing we can do about it.

"He's related to the principal, and his mother is the chief of police. Unless that boy killed someone, I don't think they'd do anything to him," Isabella's mother tensed and Mrs. Wilson took a step back, her hands lifted to her face as she cowered. Almost instantly Mami relaxed, a confused look on her face as Mrs. Wilson took a step back. "I know it's not the answer you want, I'm sorry, I'm not the person to complain to about that," she said softly. I nodded, my head felt slow and painful as I looked at the clock that hung on the wall.

"Can I go to school on Monday?" I asked slowly. I didn't want to stay home since my parents would most likely come back. The thought of my mother hiring someone to come take care of me while my father went on and on about how weak I was wasn't something I looked forward to.

Mrs. Wilson walked around the opposite side of the bed and adjusted the pain medication. "The discharge papers you're going to get when your parents arrive will suggest you make an appointment with the orthopedic doctor you're going to be assigned to for your ribs and your wrist. The ribs and the wrist won't make you unable to go to school, as long as you don't do any sports, and you'll get a note for that. However, your head suggests you should stay home for a week, to contact your pediatrician, and schedule an appointment with them before going back to school. They'll want to make sure you're alright as well."

I winced, I definitely didn't like that she said a whole freaking week, especially since next week was spring break. I'd get two weeks off in a row. Maybe that would make some kids happy, but that meant two weeks for me home with my family. If they even bothered to come home. "Can you leave that part out of the discharge papers?" I muttered with a weak smile. She shook her head at me, and I didn't need to hear her as she said no.

I leaned back on the pillows as she left, informing me that someone would send dinner to me since I had missed dinner already. "Did you see her flinch? She was scared I'd hit her," Isabella's mother said slowly, her eyebrows knitted together as she stared at the closed door.

Isabella handed me a cup of ice-cold water as I started to cough. I lifted my right hand, immensely glad I was right-handed, and grabbed the cup. The relief of my throat from the icy cold water was heaven, and I felt ten times better just from that. I wondered if I could convince everyone that I was better because of the miracle of water so I wouldn't need to stay home from school.

It was silent for a while, and I noticed my phone sitting on the table near Mami. No doubt she had gone through it to call my parents, and probably handed the phone to Isabella to have her talk to them. They disliked Isabella, but they disliked her mother even more. They didn't like people they couldn't understand and were convinced she was constantly cursing them out in Spanish. Though, to be fair, I knew for a fact that she was. "So when are they coming?" I asked. My voice was harsh, my throat ached as I coughed.

Isabella's mother instantly looked at me, her eyes filled with worry. "They should be here in the morning, *Mijo*. I told them what I could, Isabella told them about the Roan boy, but they said there was no need to press charges if there was no evidence. I'm so furious. If you were my son, *Mijo*, I'd do so much. If it was Isabella I wouldn't care if his mother owned the country I'd burn it down to the ground for her,"

I took a deep breath as I tried to calm the flood of tears I felt at her words. How many times I wished she was my mother if only it could be possible. "Okay, that's pretty illegal, just saying," I winced as she smacked my arm lightly.

"Don't think just because you're lying here that I won't spank you, *Mijo*. Don't test me," she warned. "They don't know what they're doing here. This hospital isn't doing enough, these blankets are too thin, and you'll catch a cold. *Mija*, you stay here, I'm going to go get the good pillow, and the warm throw blanket that your Abuela sent me for Christmas," she kissed me on my cheek, pinched it for a second before patting it, turned her back on me, and walked out the door. I chuckled under my breath as she muttered something about horrible doctors in this town under her breath as she shut the door.

I looked at Isabella, a frown on my face. "Can we trade lives for a week?" I asked as I batted my eyelashes at her.

She snorted as she made a shoo motion with her fingers to make me scoot over so she could sit down on the bed next to me. "I don't think you'll do well with Spanish class for a week, and they'll notice the difference. Unless you let me dye your hair," she added with a hopeful smile.

I shook my head at her with a laugh as the doors opened to a different nurse and a large tray of food. "Ma'am, he's injured, you can't sit in the bed with him," the nurse said stiffly.

Isabella glared at her, her eyebrow raised. "He needs me near him, it's for support. I'm his emotional support person," she said firmly. I snorted as the nurse shook her head at us and moved the table to float over my legs and set the tray down. "There better be something good in here, or else I'll let Mami know. She'll probably bring you back tamales anyway," she muttered under her breath.

I felt my stomach groan in anticipation and batted my eyelashes at her for a second before she huffed and pulled out her phone. "Mami, our Pretty Boy requests tamales," she said. I snickered as her mother's voice was heard on the other end. Isabella scrunched up her nose as she pulled the booming angry Spanish yelling away from her ear. *"Sí, Mami,"* she said as she quickly hung up on her.

"She said how dare I assume she wasn't going to bring you food," she said as I laughed at her. We were quiet for a while as Isabella picked through the food they brought me. It wasn't too bad, but it tasted dry. The bread of the burger was too stale and I left it alone, instead tearing off pieces of meat and chewing on it while Isabella lathered each fry in ketchup before she popped them into her mouth. "She was his mother, or his aunt, right? She doesn't look like him, but she's got the same last name," Isabella said softly.

I flinched, then groaned softly as I placed my hand against my ribs and sucked in a deep breath. My back didn't really hurt all that much even though I leaned on it, but I had a feeling it was because of the pain medication that had gone through the IV that was in my hand. "Please, Izzy," I mumbled as I grabbed the tomatoes, sprinkled salt on them, and popped them into my mouth. I pretty much ate all of the burger without the bun, at least the tomatoes and the lettuce were fresh.

Luke was a sore spot for me and she knew that. The whole rest of the week she'd tried her best to stick by me and remind me constantly she was there if I needed her. I didn't give her every single detail, just a small bit. I told her I had told him I wasn't gay, but I wasn't straight either. I told her he had said he was straight, and he didn't want to be friends with me. She was furious, I knew she'd be furious, but I had told her it wasn't his fault.

I didn't want her to be mad at him when all of this was my fault, to begin with. I had walked through the halls in a daze the past week. I couldn't smile, I hadn't drawn all week, I just felt empty. Heartbreak sucked ass, that was for sure. "He doesn't deserve you anyway, Kins. You're too good for him." She instantly defended me. She snapped her fingers as she nodded her head. "You're too much of a bad bitch for him, pretty Boy."

I snickered at her. "It's fine, Izzy. He's not a bad guy, just because he didn't feel comfortable being friends with someone who isn't straight. This town was full of ho-mophobes, at least I was accidentally writing a letter to a nice one. He didn't beat me up, so that's something, right?" I asked as I pointed toward my body. The fact that Roan beat me up even though he didn't know for sure whether or not I was gay kind of scared me. If I ever did get a boyfriend Roan would probably kill me.

"I'm just not good enough, I guess. I'm a guy and Luke wants a girl. I'll never be good enough for him, and it's not his fault that he's not interested in me. It's probably for the best anyway, you know? Who would want me anyway, right? I'm... me. I'm just invisible me," Isabella sat up fast, her eyes filled with anger as she slammed her hand down on the table. I sputtered and quickly grabbed the bowl of ketchup before it fell onto the blanket. I stared at her like she was crazy as she slapped the table again and again, the loud smacks echoed through the empty room. "What the hell, Izzy?" I asked, my eyes wide with alarm.

She pointed at me, and I swear from how red the bottom of her hand was, it was probably throbbing. "I can't beat you, Kins, because you're already slightly broken right now. But I assure you that what I did to the table was you in my mind," she said with a glare. "Kinsley Daniel Bryant, repeat after me," her hands pressed flat against my cheeks as I groaned. "I, Kinsley Daniel Bryant, am the most amazing, the most beautiful boy in the whole entire world!"

"I, Kinsley Daniel Bryant, Suck ass -Ow!" I snapped. I giggled softly as I rubbed where she pinched my cheek. "Am the most beautiful boy in the whole entire world," I repeated in a monotone voice as she raised her eyebrow at me.

Isabella stood up on the bed, kicked her shoes off, and squeezed the blanket with her toes. She raised her finger into the air, and I just knew she was going to get worse. "I'm the most baddest bitch in this whole town, and all them motherfuckers don't stand a chance with me!" She shouted.

"I'm not freaking repeating that, I swear to God, Izzy," I muttered as she glared at me. I huffed as I rolled my eyes, but I couldn't help but smile at her, my cheeks red as I shouted after her. "I'm the most baddest bitch in this whole town, and all them motherfuckers don't stand a chance with me!" I shouted as the door slid open.

Of course, right then, Isabella's mother came in. Her eyebrow raised as she stared at us, and a smirk fluttered on her lips. She had a blanket rolled up under her arm, a container of the best-smelling food ever in her hand as she flung the pillow in her other hand to the end of the bed. She lifted her fingers into the air and snapped to the left, to the right, and swished her hand back down to the left again. "Ain't that the truth, *Mijo*," she said with a nod at me.

I felt my face flush because I was caught acting like a fool, but a second later her shoe flew at Isabella as she yelled at her for standing on the bed and I laughed as hard as I could, even though my ribs hurt like a bitch, because for the first time in a while, I was happy. At least tonight, right there with the two people who meant the most to me, I was happy. But not long after they left, my stomach full and the silent room filled with the echo of the machines, I felt the sadness wrap around me again as I lay awkwardly on my side. I lay there and held my phone in my hand. I stared at pictures I took of the letters, my eyes watered as I read the words over and over again until I closed my eyes. I thought about Luke and the words he wrote to me.

'Soulmates,' Luke's deep voice filled my mind. Tears slid down my cheeks and fell against my pillow. *'You're the calm to my storm, Sparrow.'*

"Am I still your calm? Or are you lying there crying at four in the morning, trapped in the storm?" I whispered into the darkness.

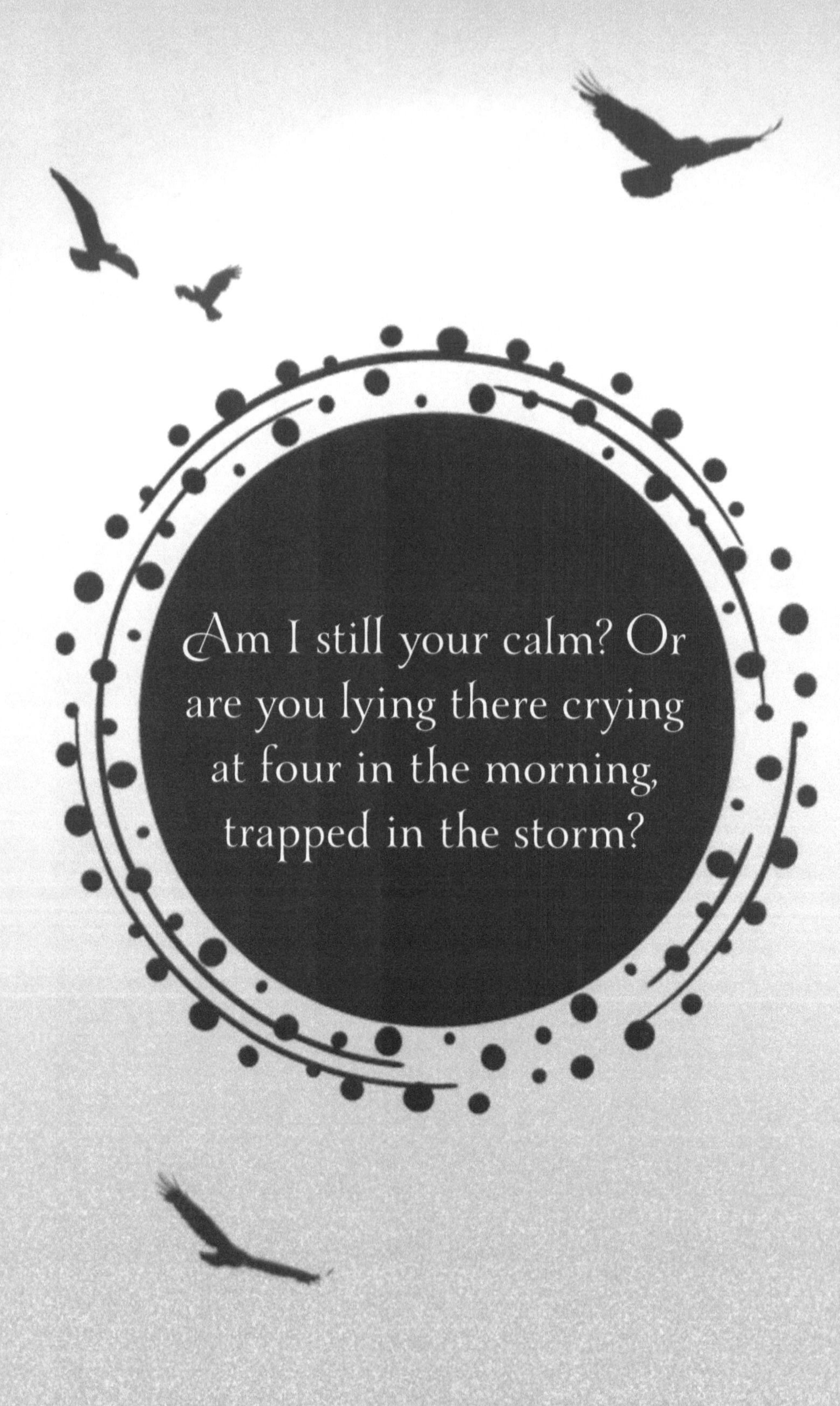

Am I still your calm? Or are you lying there crying at four in the morning, trapped in the storm?

Chapter 29
Luke

My body ached as I walked into the garage on Sunday morning. I remembered Saturday morning as I walked to the break room, grabbed my overalls, and slipped them on slowly. My mother had woken me up Saturday morning with a soft knock on my door, a sad hesitant look on her face, and I knew the ritual. She was a nurse; she knew how to take care of us when we got hurt. I followed her into the hallway and stood there in the bathroom stiffly as she took a pair of scissors to my shirt and quickly pulled the cut garment from my body with a soft gasp from both of us.

I could see myself in the mirror, my body dirty and caked with dry grease. My hair was everywhere, my curls greasy and stringy down my face. I knew Dad must have been gone for her to take care of me like this. If Dad was here, she wouldn't have left her room after last night. "He doesn't mean it," she lied as her fingers poked at the large bruises that decorated my skin. I ignored her words, her useless words, and stared at myself in the mirror. "He loves us, he's going through so much."

Did parents really think we believed their lies? I wondered sometimes as she poked at me, her fingers expertly assessing my body, if the lies were really meant to calm us or if they were meant for them. The more you told a lie, the more you believed it, after all.

"It's your fault for not going to school, you should have known better! If only I had just answered the phone!" She said with a furious sigh. Always our fault, my mom's, my brother's, mine. Never his, apparently. I wondered if she even saw at this point just how toxic it all was, or if she was so far buried inside her protective bubble of lies that all she could see was him.

"What's the damage?" I turned around and tried to hide the wince as I rolled my shirt down over the bandage where it had risen when I pulled up the overalls.

My boss stood there with his eyebrows raised as he held out a cigarette to me as if he thought a little bit of a cancer stick was going to help me. "Got pummeled in football, it's all good. Ma said it's not broken, just bruised." I said to him.

He nodded as I put the cigarette behind my ear and dipped my feet into my boots. Dad hadn't come home yesterday so Mom made me stay home, even called my boss to let him know I was hurt. He had a little bit of a crush on her from when they were younger, but she never saw anyone except my abusive asshole dad. They all went to high school together, apparently. It was how I got my job since he knew my mom. He talked about her constantly when he didn't pay attention. More than once I tried to tell him to just take her away but he'd always laugh and shake his head at me. He'd tell me Mom chose the better man. I wonder if he realized just how untrue all of that really was.

Saturday was the strangest day, to be honest. Mom made me soup, changed my bedding when I showered, and brought me books to read so I wasn't bored. It was like, for a short while at least, my mom was a mom again. Before I could even enjoy it, Dad came home from work that night, and the storm erupted all over again.

"Got a new car in on Friday, the Mazda back there. The window was busted, so I had to replace it yesterday. Would have liked your help but I managed, slacker," he said with a wink. "Customer wants the oil changed, a full assessment of the car. I told her to come by this afternoon to get it, you should get it done by then. I'm going home to check on my youngin, she's been tearing up my plants the past few days and crapping all over the house," I nodded at him as I grabbed my gloves and held them in one hand while he handed me the shop's keys. His youngin was his little poodle, he loved that thing despite all the crap he complained about her doing.

I wondered sometimes what it would be like to have a dog, a cat, or any animal, but I never thought to bring it up at home. What would happen? We'd fall in love with it, and then Dad would kill it. Another thing he'd have to throw or step on, but it would be a small fragile animal instead of us. No, there was no way I'd ask for an animal. Maybe when I got older and moved out, I'd get a cat or something.

I went to the lifts, my gloves tucked under my arm as I tied a bandana around my forehead to push back my curls. When I saw the car my boss talked about, I dropped my gloves on the ground. My eyes were wide as my hands fell to my sides. Of course, of fucking course. It just had to be Kinsley's car. I leaned down with a wince and grabbed the gloves off of the ground, then looked back up at his car once more. "No, it might not be," I tried to tell myself.

I mean, it really might be just anyone's. Kinsley was strange like that. Being one of the rich kids, he wasn't the same as the others. They'd drive around in Porsches and Lamborghinis, but Kinsley decided to have a simple family car, a Mazda Millenia. It was a good car, fairly middle class. It was great on gas and it had four doors, so honestly, it could be the car of anyone with two or fewer kids. The boss said it was a she, so it couldn't be Kinsley. However, I couldn't help but see the color of the car, the slick black color, and think about him.

It was the same car model, the same color, so it was a possibility. I looked inside the windows and tried to see if there was anything there that would scream out Kinsley to me, but it was immaculate. I shook my head as I moved to my toolbox and put my gloves on. I wasn't looking forward to doing an oil change because my ribs hurt, but they weren't broken so I'd live. I had popped some ibuprofen before I came to work just in case. I did a full evaluation of the car first, and checked the brakes and the wipers, the turn signals, and the liquids. I wrote down each thing I had to change or fill, just another normal day in the shop.

"It's not his car," I muttered over and over again at random. I stopped for lunch but didn't get to eat for long since an older couple came in for a brake change. I knew I needed to do the Mazda -I refused to call it Kinsley's car- but I stopped for this couple. I was fairly sure I'd get the Mazda done before whoever she was, and this couple said they only had today to do this. I tried to hurry though just in case she came and I got in trouble with my boss. Once they were gone I lifted the car up. I had been working on the underneath of the car, my wrench turned the dial as I held the pan against my chest and lined it up just right, as I heard her. I cursed under my breath at the sound of boots that slapped against the cement, since I couldn't move right now. "Just a minute!" I called out as the oil started to gush into the pan.

If she replied to me, I didn't hear it over the pour of the liquid and I grimaced when some of it splashed against my face. Once I was done emptying it I moved it gently off of my chest and pushed it towards where my legs were so I could easily pull it out when I was out myself. I didn't lift the car up that high, it would be too hard to get the oil changed. This garage wasn't like the newer ones that had a pit built in underneath, another reason I had told myself this wasn't Kinsley's car. Well, I was telling myself that, until I saw her.

I recognized her instantly, because of who she was. I didn't really know her name, but everyone knew her as the scary Latina girl who was best friends with Kinsley. I cursed under my breath as I stared up at her from where I sat beside the car. I grabbed the rag out of my pocket and started to wipe at the oil on my face, peering up at her through my eyelashes.

"Luke," she said. It wasn't a question and I winced because I knew she knew. Kinsley had talked in the letters about his best friend knowing. "My name is Isabella," she said thickly, her arms crossed over her chest as she glared down at me. "Since I doubt someone like you knows my name."

"I- I know your name," I stammered as she raised her eyebrow at me. I leaned over to pull the oil and my toolbox out from under the car. "So this is Kinsley's car then?" I asked with a monotone voice. "Why are you doing all this? Why this shop? He could go to better ones," I was frustrated with myself, why did I sound like a douche? It was like I was annoyed, but why? Because he didn't come to get his car himself? Because he sent her? Why didn't he just get it himself? I clenched my jaw and tried to push away the thoughts before my father's voice started to fill my head.

I stood slowly and tried not to show I was slightly in pain as I lifted the oil pan carefully. "You're behind, it was supposed to be ready." She answered, her tone clipped like she was angry. I immediately bristled, because why the hell was she mad at me? She cursed, called me an asshole in Spanish and I smirked, glad I had decided to take Spanish as my elective instead of French or Italian.

"Yes, it's Kinsley's car. He didn't put it in the shop, I did. That's why I chose this garage because it's close to the school and I didn't particularly have a fun time driving with a busted windshield." she snapped at me. I found myself moving faster just to be done with this conversation as I spilled some of the oil on my overalls as I walked faster to the drain than I should have.

"I'm sorry about that, I had an elderly couple come in needing brakes done. I know you seem to hate me but don't hate the elderly. I'd rather them not drive without brakes, okay?" I snapped right back at her. My eyes were wide as I realized what I said, how I said it, and the tone. I flinched as I turned away from her as guilt billowed through me. I think I shocked her because she was silent. While she was silent I finished emptying the pan.

I tried to blink as much as I could to stop the tears because all I could do was stand there worried. *'You're not your father,'* I told myself as I held onto the pan tightly. *'You raised your voice, you slightly defended yourself, but you're not your father,'* No matter what I said, however, I still felt horrible. I didn't want to be anything like him.

"So, did you give it the works? I requested the works, I want to make sure our Pretty Boy is covered," she said as I finally turned to look at her. She didn't look at me as she spoke, she was bent down to look underneath the car as if it were a mystery. She looked at the pipes and the screws as something she could draw, examined with her artist's eye. I thought about what she said, puzzled over it, and repeated it over and over again. *Pretty Boy,* she had said. Kinsley? I mean, he was, I guess. She said ours, as in mine and hers, but he wasn't mine. He wasn't going to be mine. "Speak, woman!" She snapped and I jumped, my face flushed as her eyes peered into mine.

"I-I'm a male!" I nearly yelled, my eyes wide as all of my guilt and worry faded away.

She waved her hand at me, and a small smile brushed over her lips as she stood. "I don't care, answer the question," she said absently as I rolled my eyes at her.

Well, at least she helped distract me from my thoughts, there was that. She wasn't too bad, I could see why Kinsley was friends with her. "Yes, I just need to put new oil in," I moved past her to the lever, grabbed my toolbox, and started to lower the car back down. I made sure to take off my greasy gloves, threw them in the bin, and grabbed another pair. I took the keys off of the hook and unlocked the car to open the hood. She watched me quietly, and I wondered what she saw.

I never noticed the artist's eye before Sparrow, before Kinsley. I could see it though, the way her dark brown eyes fluttered over everything. The color of the walls, and the shape of the tools, automatically stored it all in memory in case she needed it for later. "Can I..." I shook my head and propped the hood up to open the valve. She looked at me, urged me to keep going and I sighed in frustration. "Can I ask if he's okay? Bobby told me he got hurt, why was his car hurt? Why didn't he drive it himself? I guess there's a lot I missed."

As I moved to the shelf to get some pints of oil, I could see her tap her foot on the ground, almost like she was thinking about whether or not she should tell me. I guess I understood that. I didn't deserve to know, not really. Not after everything. I turned him down, I didn't want to be his friend. But I guess I didn't realize I'd miss him like a person who struggled to breathe underwater and missed the air.

"I wasn't there for the fight. On Thursdays and Fridays, we don't have an art club because I get picked up by Mami for work. Roan cornered him at his car and he was all alone. I heard from rumors that a few stood there and egged the fight on like savages and that Kinsley was surprised. Roan came up behind him and slammed his head into the window. He has a concussion. Roan slammed Kinsley down on the ground, his back on the shattered glass. He has stitches now, there will be scars on my Pretty Boy's back," she growled in anger. HER pretty Boy, she said. I don't know why, but I didn't like the sound of that.

I squeezed the pint too tightly, spilled some of the oil, and grabbed another one with a sigh. "They said he kept kicking him and punching him. He has two broken ribs now and his left wrist is wrapped. No one called the cops, what's the point when Roan's mother owned them? No one told the principal, what's the point when Roan is there too? When Roan was done and Kinsley was unconscious, Roan walked off bored, and went back to his basketball practice so he had a lame-ass alibi." Every word was accented in anger, and my hands shook in my own anger as I listened. I was sick and tired of all of it, so fucking unnecessary.

"His parents? Did they call the police anyway? Did he get in trouble? Where's Kinsley?" I asked her as I dropped the empty pint on the ground and turned to look at her.

At that point, I expected her to throw something at me and tell me I didn't deserve to know any of that, and I wouldn't have blamed her. Why did I deserve to ask questions? How many times had I walked past Roan as he beat up a kid without stopping it? How many times was it Kinsley? I faintly remembered standing in front of a person the other day when Roan was glaring at them, and handing them an ice pack, but I never even glanced at them. What if that was Kinsley? But I didn't know him then, I wouldn't have done anything.

In a way, was I really better than my father if I ignored it? I might not have been the one doing the screaming, the yelling, the hitting, but did it really make me better if I ignored those who were? "His mom is the chief, they went to the school and did a bogus investigation. Nothing was found, no evidence. Everyone knows who did it but they're just saying they didn't see anything. She made a show to Kinsley's parents and said they were going to get cameras installed outside the school but that was about it. I doubt they'll even do that much," she said, rolling her eyes.

"And his parents came back from Italy to sign his release papers. He's been at the hospital since Friday after school. They should be releasing him now, actually. I was hoping to have his car at his house for him so I didn't have to see them, but it's too late now. I'll just pick him up for school on Monday, they won't notice."

I nodded, slightly confused. "Why were they in Italy? They don't live here?" I leaned down and got the empty pint, gathered up the others I used, and threw them all in a large trash can. I remember he told me they didn't really care about him, they were never around, but I didn't know as much as I thought I did. I guess even though we had talked back and forth with letters, there was so much about us that neither of us knew.

"He's half Italian, his grandma was sick and they went to visit her, something like that," she said with a wave of her hand. "They're all irrelevant," she added. I mean, she wasn't wrong from what I'd read in the letters.

"Will he be at school on Monday?" I asked softly as I closed the hood and turned to look at her.

She handed me a debit card that had Kinsley's name on it, and I had no doubt it was unlimited. If my boss were here he'd give her crap for giving him a card without her name on it but I simply grabbed the paper and added how much oil I used and moved to the computer to add it all up. "Why? So you can be his hero and swoop in and give him big kisses and hugs, run off into the sunset with him?" she asked with a snort.

I rolled my eyes with a frown, but I was silent for a while. Why did I want to know? Why did I care? I found it harder and harder to go back to how it was before. Before the letters, before Sparrow and Green. Before we were two beings who didn't notice each other, didn't talk, and didn't cross paths. Then we became everything, one heartbeat, one being. I found it hard to go back to the before, and more than ever I found myself wondering about the after.

Before the letters, there was nothing but the storm, nothing but the pain. I found it hard to move into an after. How could I go back to the storm when for the first time in my life, I had found the calm? "I'm straight, Isabella," I said sharply as I took a deep breath and typed everything in. I could hear my father's voice echo through me and wanted to rip the computer off of the table and fling it against the wall. "But I-I care."

I did, and I was tired of trying to convince myself I didn't. I cared that Kinsley was hurt by that asshole. I cared that he had to lay there with broken ribs and a back full of stitches. I could see his cerulean eyes filled with pain, and I knew that pain because I did it too. He had just wanted to stay as friends. He hadn't asked for more, and I hurt him just like everyone else. Just because of my father. As I swiped the card and handed it back to Isabella she gave me a soft smile, a gentle look on her face as she patted my back.

I noticed absently that while Kinsley always seemed to be covered in lead and charcoal, she was covered in paint. Different mediums, it seemed, but the same passion. It made sense why they were friends. I felt my heart constrict at her touch, her soft gaze, and I wasn't sure why she looked at me like that. It felt weird. Was this a friend thing? I wasn't used to friend things.

I realized maybe there was another out there, another besides me and Kinsley, another that wasn't fake. Maybe she was real too. "He didn't say it out loud, but I could see it. He noticed you weren't there and he was searching. He kept searching for you, kept looking. Trust me, he cares too," she said.

Without a word, I handed her the keys and watched her as she got into his car and drove off. I was silent, lost in my thoughts as my boss finally came back and started to go over the sales and what I'd done since he was gone. He talked to me about his dog, and I'd shake my head or nod. I gave him the answers he wanted, but really I was somewhere else, trapped in my thoughts. Thoughts about Kinsley and Luke, thoughts about Sparrow and Green, and how even though they were two different names, all in all, they were the same people deep down inside.

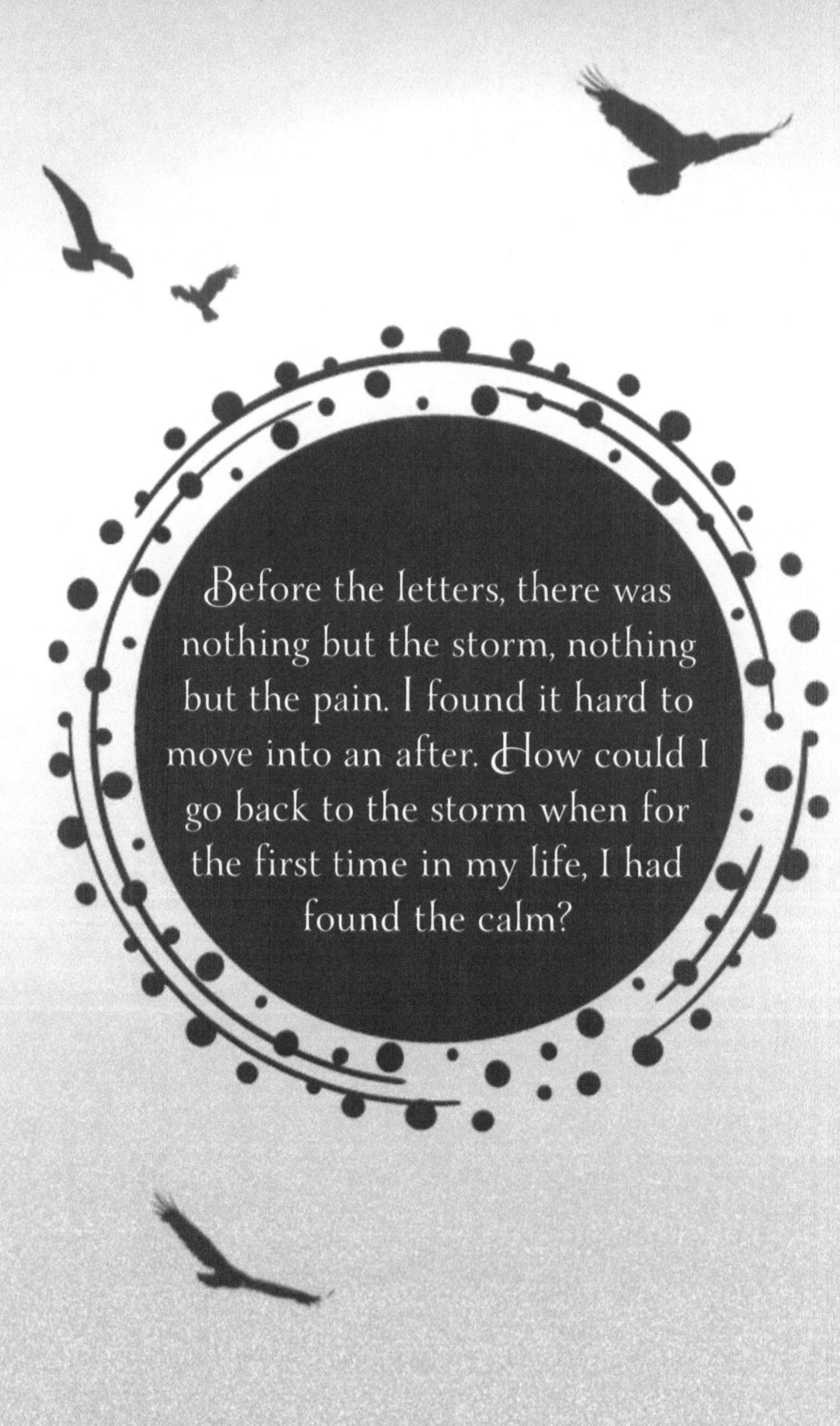

Before the letters, there was nothing but the storm, nothing but the pain. I found it hard to move into an after. How could I go back to the storm when for the first time in my life, I had found the calm?

Chapter 30
Kinsley

Isabella raised her eyebrow at me as I climbed slowly into the passenger seat of my car. I couldn't help but wince as my ribs throbbed, the bandage wrapped tightly around my ribs. I had to sit where my back didn't touch the seat and Isabella handed me some white bags. "Mami got you your meds, here's your debit card back." I thanked her with a smile, accepted the water bottle she had handed me as well as I read over the bags and took the proper amounts of pills for each.

I had worried my parents would force me to stay home, but when the time came for the discharge papers they didn't even pick them up. The doctor left it on the table and my parents left the room so I could change into my clothes. When I was finished and gathered everything in the duffle bag they had brought me, I simply stuffed the discharge papers in it as well and told them I was ready. They never asked what medicines I'd need, they never asked if I needed to stay home. No, they talked the whole way home about how upset my dad was that the person he had assigned to run his business here had messed up the payroll. They dropped me off outside of the house and said they'd be back after they fixed the problem, and I hadn't seen them since.

Honestly, I didn't care one bit, but Isabella was furious. She had driven by after I told her I was home and my parents were gone. She took the list of medications I needed and the list of doctors I needed to make appointments for at Mami's request. Mami promised to have it all handled for me. It was funny, the fact that my parents seemed to think I could handle all of this by myself since there was a charge on my account for work done on my car. They thought if I could get my car fixed and paid for despite being in the hospital, then I could take care of myself too. I didn't even have the heart to tell them Isabella handled that for me. "They're not even home, Kins. You shouldn't be going to school," Isabella scolded me.

I gave her a soft shrug as I tried to pretend it didn't hurt to do that much. "I don't want to be there in that large cage with no company and nothing to do but lay there and stare at the wall and wish I was better already," I muttered as I scratched against the wrap on my left wrist. It was freaking itchy, and I hated it more than I hated the stitches.

"Mami got the medicine for you last night before things closed, but she said she'd call appointments for you later today on her break. She'll text you the places and the times you need to be there. I can drive you if you'd like." Isabella didn't have her license. She had a driver's permit so she was allowed to drive with her mother or an adult who had their license for a while, but she was a careful driver so thankfully she hadn't been pulled over. Isabella clearly didn't care about punishment since almost every other night she was off tagging a building somewhere, but I worried about her. I didn't want her to get in trouble, to have something on her record that made it hard for her to go to college. She was amazing, and she'd do great things one day.

I smiled at her as I moved my feet and my right hand easily. "I'm good to drive, I got both my feet, and my right hand works. I don't need two hands to hold the steering wheel," I said with a laugh. Because of my parents' influence, I was able to get my permit when I was fifteen, so I just got my license a few months ago.

"I'm just worried, you're already broken Kins. Roan might just end up putting you back in the hospital." She said as she parked in front of the school. It was a closer spot than I usually parked in, but it didn't really matter. I always tried to be as far away from Roan as I could, but Isabella was here and while Roan still picked on me with Isabella around, I knew she'd make such a fuss that he'd end up saying it wasn't worth his time and walk off. Seeming to realize I wasn't going to reply to that, she changed the subject with a sigh. "Mami said that my Abuela is coming for a few days to visit. I'm excited, she hasn't been here before." She said with a smile.

I grinned, happy at this particular subject change. I had met Isabella's Abuela a few times before. More than once I'd gone with them for a spring break or summer visit to their hometown. It was how I got my tattoo. Isabella's cousin was a tattoo artist, and when Isabella and I were fifteen we both got tattoos. Mine was the songbird trapped in the cage, and she had gotten a really pretty piece of her art done on the middle of her back, a dandelion. The stem went down her spine and the pappus was spread around as if someone had blown it around her left shoulder blade and up her shoulder.

Mami didn't know about it, and neither did my parents either. We promised her cousin we'd keep it quiet since we were underage. I could still remember the sting of the needle, the smell of the green soap, and the whirl of the machine. It didn't hurt too bad, especially since we had both gotten fairly drunk during it, and once the tattoo healed I was in love with it. I didn't think I'd end up being the kind of guy who had tattoos everywhere, but I wouldn't mind a few more one day. Meaningful ones, maybe even quotes from a favorite book or something. I always loved how word tattoos looked on people.

"I can't wait to see her again," I said as we slowly walked inside. The first bell had already rung, and we tried to stay to the side of the walls to keep out of everyone's way. Isabella glared at everyone who came too close to me, and I was thankful for it since it was just then that the meds had started to kick in. Technically, I should have gone to the office and registered them, but I had left them in the car anyway, so I would just run out there and get them when I needed them again. To register them with the office meant my parents would have to do it, and they'd never take time out of their busy schedules for that.

I could hear the whispers of those who were in the halls as they brushed past us, the whispers of people as they looked at me, wondering if I was a ghost or if I was invincible. So many people had seen what Roan had done to me, and since my hoodie covered so much of me, it was hard to really tell I was injured. The bruises on my face and my body were awful shades of healing green, blue, and orange, but covered under my hoodie.

The hood pulled up made it hard for anyone to see much of my face unless I lowered it or they peered into it, and no one was allowed to get that close to me with Isabella glaring daggers at them. My back, chest, and stomach were the worst, but no one would ever see those areas. I wasn't the type of guy to walk around shirtless, even around my house unless I was playing basketball when no one was around or swimming in the pool.

I nearly punched myself as my stomach fluttered and stood at my locker with a disheartened sigh. To stand here, to stare at it, I hated this. All last week, this was what I had done, and even the first two days, I refused to open it, I had made Isabella do it. But I needed to move past this, I needed to accept this was my life now. For a brief moment in time, I was happy, I was wanted. I was loved, just a little bit. Though life was filled with road bumps, and even though for a small amount of time my road was straight and beautiful, eventually a pothole came and everything got bumpy all over again.

I watched distantly as Isabella opened my locker, not even bothering to care about trying. She grabbed our books for the first three periods and refused to let me carry anything, even though my right hand was fine. I didn't want to look in there and see what I knew wouldn't be there. I was mad at myself for that tiny sliver of hope, hope that just died away over and over again as it had been since I told Luke who I was. I didn't realize I started to cry until Isabella turned to look at me and dropped all of our books on the ground.

The hallway was filled with only a few students as she pressed her hands against my cheeks and gently stroked my bruised skin as she sighed. Her warm chocolate brown eyes were filled with sadness as she peered up at me and, ignoring the few children who were there with the ever-immature oohs and whistles at us, I wrapped my arms around her and awkwardly hugged her. Her hands held onto the material of my sleeves at the top of my arms to avoid my wounds as I buried my face in her neck. She started to softly hum, and neither of us cared that we would be late or that we'd probably get in trouble. She was simply there for me, knew everything I thought and felt, and gave me time to cry.

The bell rang, and everyone ran to their classes and left us alone in the hallway. Just two people who held each other, one of them in tears as books and papers were scattered all around us like a maze of numbers and words. Sometimes I wished I could get lost in those mazes and never come out, buried alive in the twists and turns of the past and future. I knew that no matter how sad I was now, there would always be someone who had it worse, at some point.

But did that mean I wasn't allowed to be sad, just because I didn't have it as bad as others? Was it unfair to cry over the loss of something as simple as letters when some were crying over the loss of food or water? I felt bad when I thought about it like that. Then I realized that in the end, we're all human. Just because we were hurt in different ways didn't mean we weren't allowed to feel our own hurt. To cry for our own sadness, and to try desperately to get past it ourselves.

"Why?" I breathed out against her skin. "Why can't I make it go away?" I whimpered as I clutched onto her tightly.

I felt a wetness in my hair and knew that although she wasn't hurt from this, she was hurt simply because I was hurt, and I wondered once more, why? Why couldn't I have just loved her? Why couldn't it have been Izzy and Kinsley? Why couldn't we have fallen in love and gotten married and had a normal straight family with babies and possibly some sort of sports to appease my family? Why was it that the one person who was the kindest to me, the most understanding, wasn't the one I ended up with? Why couldn't I just be straight?

Isabella shushed me softly as she rocked me gently back and forth. I knew she didn't have the answers to my questions, and I was glad she hadn't tried to give me some bullshit answer about it getting better, or that there were other fish in the sea. I wasn't five, I knew first loves rarely stayed forever. I knew there could be others in the future somewhere down the line. I knew that even though I felt like I shattered into a million pieces every time I opened my locker and found nothing there, I'd get over this eventually.

Right now, however, I couldn't breathe. I was glad that despite rambling about all the stupid things she could try to comfort me with, she was just quietly there for me. Sometimes, the silence was better than anything else, when you're with the right person. But that thought didn't seem to help me at all because, despite everything, I couldn't stop thinking about Luke. About my Green. At least I had Isabella when I needed to fall apart, but who did he have? Who was there for him?

I wasted the whole first period crying, and we went to the nurse's office to hand her my notes. I showed her that I was injured, and Isabella helped me. We had her think we were late to school because of me, and she marked us both as being here and gave us notes as she tried to tell me to take it easy. She read the papers, the paper that said I was supposed to stay out of school because of a concussion, but when I told her my parents were in Italy visiting my grandmother and there was no one to watch me during the day, she nodded and told me she'd keep an eye on me. I hoped that meant she'd watch Roan around me, but seeing as he was now my partner in psychology class, I wasn't really sure how likely that was.

We all had seen the marks on Roan when he'd randomly changed his shirt in the middle of the hallway or in gym class over the years, the old and new marks of a belt smacked into his skin. To have parents of such authority but constantly push their influence must get him in some sort of trouble at home, but he never seemed to learn his lesson. Honestly, maybe some would feel sorry for Roan, to get beat with belts at home for the things he did at school. But some of the things he'd done would have put him in juvie by now if it wasn't for his parents and other relatives, so I wasn't entirely sorry for him. Maybe that made me a bad person, but I didn't have the time or the energy to care for a bully.

The second period was nice. I got to sit in the back with the window open, the breeze was warm but gentle, and it felt good against my face. My body ached, my head throbbed, and I probably should have gotten some ibuprofen from the nurse. Though leave it to Isabella to always know, and when Mrs. Masters went out to the hallway to talk to the principal for a moment, she rolled a bottle of ibuprofen and a bottle of water back down the aisle for me.

I honestly didn't know what I'd ever do without Isabella. Maybe when we were older and we moved to New York, when we eventually found partners and got married, we could get one of those joint houses where we could be neighbors for the rest of our lives. I could just see it, me and Isabella seated side by side in a nursing home. She'd be the one to yell at people and smack them with her cane, and I'd just be beside her existing, laughing. She was right about one thing, what she had said in the hospital to the nurse. Isabella was my emotional support person, and I probably wouldn't be where I am today without her by my side.

I drifted off to sleep during the third period. I wasn't too worried because the nurse explained to all of my teachers what happened to me and what I was going through. I wasn't the best student, but I was good enough that they didn't have problems with me, and they figured if I needed to rest for a class period, they were fine with it, as long as I did the classwork for homework. Isabella copied my notes down for me, her beautiful swirly handwriting flowed and danced against the papers, the small drawings she couldn't do without littered the margins.

I fell asleep to the soft scritch of her pencil against the paper and the murmurs of the teacher as they wrote notes on the board. I Imagined Isabella as a dance in my dream, her body moved to the soft scritch of her writing against the paper. The way she wrote and the way she drew was like a dance, and I wondered if she would take up dancing if she didn't get into art school for drawing. I woke with a soft groan to the bell ringing for lunch, my head spun as I tried to reorient myself.

For a moment, I saw everything in sparkles as I rubbed my eyes, but when my vision cleared, I watched Isabella put both her books and my books into our bags. I smiled warmly at her as she slipped in the notes and the homework I'd have to do later tonight. I grabbed my bag with my right hand and slipped it past the wrap on my left hand and pulled the strap over my shoulder. I couldn't wrap it over my head like I usually did. I had a feeling if Roan noticed, he'd bug me about it, saying I wore it like a purse. "Where are we going for lunch? Or would you rather wait in the art room and I get it for you?" Isabella asked softly. I stopped in the hallway, since we were on the third floor, and frowned.

The idea of walking down the stairs and getting into the car wasn't too appealing, but I did need to get my medicine and for some reason, I just didn't want to be in the club room today. I guess it was a dissociation, the thought of drawing, and I wasn't sure if I could even hold a pencil or try to draw. To be honest, the last time I drew anything was the day I saw Luke, the day I drew him the butterfly.

The hope I felt as I pushed it towards him, the spark I felt in my fingertips as he touched my hand; only to have it thrown aside when he told me he wanted nothing to do with me. I couldn't think about drawing when that was still fresh in my mind. It scared me, the thought that maybe, just maybe; I wouldn't be able to draw again. "Let's go to the cafe. He keeps it nice and quiet and barely lets any of the jocks in." I said softly.

She nodded, a soft smile on her face as she laced her fingers with my right hand and pulled me gently down the hall. I couldn't help but glance at the art room, a look of sadness fluttered over my face. I felt haunted by the charcoal painting that I had ruined, by the sad memories that lingered with the awful smell. The memories of Luke's bright green eyes, his soft dark brown curls, and the way for a brief moment he had smiled before I had pulled down my hood and everything crashed down around us.

Lunch was peaceful, but I was slowly starting to feel scared, knowing what was next. Psychology was my fourth-period class, the one I'd be in with Roan, and I wasn't looking forward to it. I didn't voice any of this to Isabella because she'd call up her mother and tell her I needed to skip and she needed to be with me. As hardcore as her mother was, she knew what I was going through right now and she wouldn't stop Isabella from cutting if it meant she was doing it for me and my safety. But I didn't want to do that. If I ran away from Roan now, I'd run from him for the rest of my high school life, and I didn't want to give him that power.

I didn't want him to laugh and call me a child for hiding from him. Eventually, I'd have to go, so I might as well rip off the bandaid and do it now. Maybe it was stupid, maybe it was crazy, but it was what I was going to do regardless. I felt calmer and my head didn't spin anymore after I took some more pills and ate my lunch. My hand still ached and twitched for a pencil that would just rest there without any motivation, and I wasn't sure what to do about it. Isabella would tell me to draw until the feeling passed but I didn't want to force it like that.

I was scared I'd never want to draw again, and that was a fear I wasn't entirely sure how to speak out loud. I felt stupid for being so affected by this, over something that some would describe as simply letters, but they weren't just letters to me. They were Luke's soul, they were my soul, and for a moment, they were one, even if it was all simply a mistake. "Are you ready to head back to school, pretty Boy?" Isabella asked as she threw away our trash.

I grimaced on the inside because no, I wasn't ready. I was honestly ready to fly to a foreign country. To pick up the art of shrimp boating or something that I could do without needing to tell anyone my name or age or have an ID. To start over the rest of my life that way. Instead, I smiled softly at her and stood, followed her outside, and slid gently into the driver's seat. "Yeah, let's go," I said as she slipped in beside me.

She patted my knee with her fingers and left her hand there as I awkwardly placed my left hand on my other knee and started to shift from reverse to drive with my right hand. "It's going to be okay, Kinsley. We'll get out of here, and we'll be famous artists one day," She said with a huff. I smiled, nodding my head at her as I drove because I wasn't entirely sure what my future would hold. As long as she was in it, it was good enough for me.

Sometimes, the silence was better than anything else, when you're with the right person.

Chapter 31
Luke

Father was there breathing down my neck when I walked to the kitchen. His angry glare, his hands curled into fists. It made me want to run backward, to retreat to the safety of my bedroom. Maybe if I ran fast enough he wouldn't be able to catch me. Was he faster than me? Despite all of his talk about being a real man who did this and that, my father wasn't really the sporty type. He did play soccer for a few years in high school, so he might have been faster than I realized. He went to the gym often, and it was evident in his large muscles, his body flexed and poised as he walked around without a shirt on.

It was strange to see him out of uniform for his job on a Monday, but every once in a while, the lesser employees had Mondays off for corporate meetings at the office for the higher-ups, and I assumed that day was one of those days. He hovered as I flinched and tried to slowly move past him. I felt cornered, my breath faltered, but I had to pretend it didn't matter. I had to pretend I wasn't scared, otherwise, he would hurt me. *'To man me up,'* he used to tell me.

He used to wrestle with me and Shawn when we were little boys, but when he started to go too far and break bones, he stopped when a child services worker came to check on us. Too many broken bones, too many hospital visits, and it drew questions. "You're going to school today, right?" He asked. No, it wasn't like a question, it was more a barking command. His eyes were slitted into daggers as he glared at me. I wanted to ask him if it was manly enough for me to be a bad kid who cut school, but apparently what he thought was manly was something I had to guess at day by day.

Just like his pack of cigarettes on the table. If I went to grab one, nine times out of ten he would nod his head at me in respect, but sometimes he'd get pissed off and beat the shit out of me. I wondered sometimes if he was bipolar, but of course, I could never actually ask him that. I hoped not because that would be just another mental disease I'd have to look out for to make sure I hadn't inherited it.

I nodded my head but knew that wouldn't be good enough. "Yes, Sir. I got my backpack and all my homework done, Bobby will be waiting at the end of the sidewalk so I better start heading out," I said as I tried to slip by him.

Dad banged his hand on the table with a glare. "I'll take you," he said with a growl. I nodded quickly, even though the idea of being stuck in the car with him, in such a tiny area, scared me. At least he had the kind of setup in his car where his laptop rested in the passenger seat, so I could sit in the back.

"I'm going to talk with Bobby's mom, letting him pick you up but him just dropping you off random places without care. He's enabling you from learning. You want to end up worthless at home like your mother!? You need to get good grades, go to college, and make something of yourself!" He shouted.

I nodded absently, I knew there wasn't any point in arguing. He controlled everything. Mom was a nurse, she was not stuck at home or worthless, but he didn't like her making more money than him and he forced her to limit her hours. The weekends, sometimes during the week too, but that was it. He constantly accused her of cheating on him when she was gone every day for twelve to fifteen-hour shifts. He'd call her a whore and say she would get her money from a pimp. I wouldn't be surprised if he tracked her location now as well, while he went off and cheated on her constantly.

"Yes, Sir," I mumbled. I winced inside because that would probably be the last I'd get rides from Bobby. Dad would aggravate Bobby's mom, she already hated him for how he tried to hit on her constantly. I will need to let my boss know I will most likely be late from now on since I'll have to walk after school instead of having a ride.

Shawn leaned over and kissed Mom gently on the cheek, then stuck his hand out and shook Dad's hand like a grown man. It was stupid, ridiculous. I've seen middle schoolers kiss their dads on the cheek, but not my Dad. It wasn't manly, it wasn't allowed. I was jealous of my little brother as he darted out of the house and ran to his best friend's car, I wished I didn't have to ride with Dad either. If he took the whole week off just to make sure I went to school I was probably going to end up hyperventilating by the end of the week. "When is your next game?" Dad asked.

I cringed because that meant he'd be there most likely. He and Mom and Shawn, bright smiles pasted on their faces as they held up signs and pretended to be happy. Pretended to be a family. Probably the only time I'd ever heard my father say he was proud of me was the day I told him I was the quarterback, the captain of the team. I guess being proud didn't last very long, not with him.

"This weekend, it's the first game. It's an away game though," I tried not to show how happy I was. Away games usually meant in the next town over, and Dad hated those. He'd have to move his laptop for mom to sit next to him and they'd have to drive a few hours to see the game.

He groaned, a frown on his face. "They should have made the first game a home game," he mumbled, clearly annoyed. In a sense, it was a home game for the people we were playing against. Someone had to be away, for the other to be home. "I'll talk to your coach about that," I frowned, hoping desperately he didn't. The last time he talked to Coach, I had to run suicides for an extra half an hour while he glared at me as if whatever my father said was my fault.

"Yes, sir," I spoke softly as I finished my breakfast. I left the plate; I knew if I tried to clean it myself, Dad would snap. The idea of being forced to be in a car with him after he was already angry wasn't something I looked forward to. "I'll be waiting at the car if that's okay," I said as I stood.

He nodded, shaking his newspaper as he straightened it. When he looked at the paper, I grabbed a couple of his cigarettes and slipped one behind my ear as I walked out the door. I leaned against the car with the stick between my lips and made sure to stand upwind so the smoke wouldn't cling to me. A short text to Bobby let him know I already had a ride, and by the time I finished smoking, Dad came out. I pulled a mint out of my pocket and popped it into my mouth, then climbed into the backseat as he approached.

I was glad he was silent the whole ride, besides his phone call. Honestly, he probably would have said something to me if it wasn't for the distraction. I felt bad about whoever it was that he screamed at, but at least it wasn't me. Morning practice wasn't too bad. The coach was late this morning, and I was in charge. I got to take a break from my own practice as I ordered the others around. I was glad to have the morning off since my ribs still hurt, but at least they weren't broken.

I wrote down the notes of what I thought the players needed to work on more and stuck the paper in his office before I slowly headed with the other stragglers to get to our lockers before class started. "No more love letters, Lukey?" Tony asked me with a wag of his eyebrows as I opened my locker. I ignored him; I didn't want to answer him.

The moment I opened my locker, my heart raced, my stupid traitorous heart. I tried to tell it to quit its shit, but it struggled to remember that this whole time, Sparrow was a boy. This whole time, Sparrow was Kinsley. "Biology. Why is there a biology textbook here? Crap. I forgot I was taking that," Tony mumbled.

Leave it to Tony to change the subject for me before I even had time to get upset about it. "How can you forget what classes you're taking? Where have you been going all year?" I wondered as I tried to hide the humor from my voice. My eyes automatically searched my locker, and I knew exactly what it was I was searching for. I closed my locker with a small shudder, then cursed myself as I went to open it again, realizing I forgot the damn books for my class.

I sighed; I wanted to shove all of this shit out of my locker and climb inside it. Better yet, pretended I was sick and stayed in the nurse's office all day. Maybe I could sleep in the art room; no one goes in there until after school. But then Kinsley would be there. "I thought I had two free periods," Tony said with a soft sigh.

I laughed at him as I shut my locker once more with a shake of my head. "No one ever has two free periods, you moron," I mumbled.

My eyes automatically scanned the hall, and I wanted to bang my face into my locker. "I thought I was special. I was even winking at the principal, trying to thank him for the extra free period," he grumbled.

I found him. I felt my heart throb just from the sight of him. He seemed fine. I could see a brace on his left wrist that poked out from under his hoodie, but otherwise, he seemed fine. Though I wasn't going to doubt Isabella, she was adamant he wasn't. Two broken ribs, and stitches on his back. He hadn't walked like he was in pain, but then again, he probably was on pain medication. I watched as he looked around, his eyes never quite came over here, as if he tried his best not to really see me.

"You're right," I said quietly, my eyes unable to pull away from the back of Kinsley's head. "You are special." As Tony laughed, he rammed his shoulder into mine. I frowned because at that point, I wasn't sure if I was talking to Tony or Kinsley, and that thought scared me more than anything else.

Classes went like normal. The talk of the upcoming game was all everyone wanted to talk about. The teachers all smacked my shoulder and told me how proud they were that I led the team, my second year as captain, and how successful our winning streak was last year. I would nod, smile, and fist-pump everyone who held out their fists, but nothing stopped my thoughts from trailing.

I knew it was coming soon, and when the bell rang for lunch, I shuddered. After lunch, it was psychology. Normally I didn't give a shit about that class. It was an elective, and I was usually partnered up with a girl who would bat her eyes at me and tell me how much she knew I was busy and would do all of the assignments for both of us. I ignored my texts from Bobby and went up to the art club room. I found that the more I tried to avoid it, the more I felt drawn there.

I remembered the time Kinsley had drawn me the angel picture. Now that I thought about it, the angel was a girl because he thought I was a girl. The blond hair, Peyton, and the green eyes, because I said my eyes were green. It didn't matter, because it was still saved in my room, next to the picture of the field, and the one of the butterfly. I didn't know why I kept them, just like I didn't know why I walked up the stairs to the art room, but I couldn't shake the feeling that there was something I needed to see.

As the halls emptied I turned the knob slowly and pushed the door open as I glanced inside. I wasn't sure if I was frustrated or relieved that Kinsley wasn't in there. It was empty of people, the goo smelled strong from the whole weekend without the windows open and I wondered just where the damn goo was that it stunk up the room so much. The corner with crappy drawings smelled thick like weed and I screwed up my nose, not really liking the smell of it at all. Cigarettes were one thing for me, but I never did anything else.

Then I saw it, as I scanned the room, and I knew without a doubt that this was what called me. My heart dropped and my breath came out slowly as I moved slowly to the picture. On the stand was Kinsley's charcoal picture, and it was absolutely destroyed. The blue eyes were barely visible under the angry streaks of the charcoal, the large angry strokes pressed down so hard it was torn in a few places.

In the middle of the picture where what should have been a mouth were two dried wet marks. The charcoal was distorted from the marks, and I knew it was him crying. I wasn't sure how I knew, but I did. I felt horrible at the fact that I left him seated there in this room at that table all alone for him to do this. I thought he didn't care. I thought I didn't care. I was starting to realize we both cared a lot more than I thought we would.

I stepped on pieces of charcoal as I moved closer to it, my fingers slid down the black lines and stained my skin. When I pulled my fingers away they were covered in it. I rubbed my thumb against my fingers, I felt my own tears well up in my eyes, unsure what emotions moved through me. *Why me?* I wondered as I turned my back on the picture. Why my locker? Why did this have to happen to me? Why couldn't I make this, whatever this was, fade away?

I wasn't sure how long I stood there and tried to calm the storm that raged around inside me, but as the bell rang for lunch to end I stayed there for a few minutes and stared at the sun. "They're waiting for me," I muttered as I forced myself to move. I wiped my fingers against my pants and tried to center myself. "It'll be alright, just go," I tried to tell myself. It worked, to a degree. I felt like a robot as I moved out of the room and to my locker. I switched my books fast and I headed to the psychology room. For a moment I wasn't sure if I had seen Kinsley or not, a black smear walked into the room ahead of me, but I certainly did see Roan.

He was with a group of his friends and talked loudly outside the room. I snuck past him and into the room. I could see Kinsley was already there, and I tried not to stare at him. He looked scared but determined. His hands clenched together into fists as he looked down at his desk. *Brave,* I wanted to tell him. Brave like Kinsley. I could be brave if he could. The teacher looked at me and pointed to a group of seats that was mine and my partner's. I cringed, the teacher had paired me up with Alison Miller, my second ex-girlfriend I had just broken up with at the beginning of the school year. Alison gave me a flirtatious wave, and as Roan walked into the room I wrapped my arm around his shoulder and stopped him. *Be brave,* I told myself. *Brave like Kinsley.* "I need your help," I muttered to Roan. Damn, I wanted nothing more than to punch him in the face.

He raised his eyebrow at me, but so far we'd never had problems with each other so he was fairly carefree as he waited to see what I was going to say. Despite being captains on different sports teams, we had always kept to ourselves and stayed out of each other's way. "What is it, Luke?" he wondered as his eyes swept over the room. He glared at Kinsley and I shuffled uncomfortably next to him as I tried to keep up my pretense.

I dropped my shoulder and tilted my head to the side. I knew most of the class was looking at us now. Even the teacher looked at us with a curious look, but because the class hadn't started yet, we were left alone. As I pulled him towards the corner, I sighed dramatically and wondered if I could even get away with this. "I was paired up with my fucking ex, bro," I mumbled with a loud exaggerated sigh. He looked at where Alison sat. She watched us with her eyebrow raised and blew a bubble with her gum.

"I know she has a crush on you, and I don't want to deal with her, you know? We just broke up a little bit ago," I wasn't sure if she liked him or not, to be honest, but Roan was known for sleeping around and I doubted my throwing her at him would do much. "Can we switch? I don't know who you got, I don't care, just take her, please," I begged.

Roan raised his eyebrow at me before a sly smile lit up his face. He thought this was the better deal like he was about to give me a piece of trash for a piece of gold. I thought it was funny just how wrong he was with that thought process. "Sure, I can take her off your hands, if you're that desperate. I hadn't gotten laid in like two weeks anyway, bro, thanks. My partner is at seat ten A, so have fun. No changing your mind, right? We're good?" He asked as he lifted his fist to bump into mine.

I wanted to roll my eyes because honestly, I was definitely getting the better deal out of this. He'd have to deal with her, and I didn't know what I was thinking. "We're good, I promise. No matter who it was, I didn't care. As long as I'm not paired with her," I mumbled as I banged my fist against his. I wanted to punch him in the face to seal the deal but I guessed this was better than nothing.

Roan moved to talk to the teacher as I stood there and stared at Kinsley. He had his head on his arms, his eyes down as he waited for the inevitable. Trying to make himself smaller, to avoid what was coming. I wondered what I had been thinking, as I walked past my ex and went to sit down next to him. I ignored the startled voices, the ones who laughed at me and whispered to each other that I hadn't realized how bad of a trade I made.

Alison was annoyed, but when Roan sat next to her she shut up pretty fast. Kinsley stiffened as I sat down next to him. I sighed, my hands opened and closed beside my body. We were both stiff for a moment, before I placed my book down on the table, and turned to look at him. I was met with those eyes, those startling cerulean blue eyes, and a shudder ran through me as I saw just how bruised his face was underneath that hood.

"That's not your seat," Kinsley said softly. His right hand clenched tightly around his pencil as his left hand floated out of his brace next to him.

I shrugged as I looked up at the board and opened the book to the right page. "It is now," I mumbled. His voice, it was so strange to hear his voice. "This is all I knew how to do. I couldn't let him sit here,"

He was quiet for a while and I jotted down the notes as the bell rang. I wasn't sure if he was going to yell at me or stand up and act like a drama queen and stomp out. He had every right to be mad at me, and why the hell did I try to protect him anyway? I told him

I wanted nothing to do with him, and that I was doing a really awful job of staying away. "Thanks, Luke," he whispered. It was barely anything, really. Two words, two unnecessary words, but it was enough. I clenched my desk tightly, annoyed with myself. What was I doing?

Class ended fairly fast, and then we went our separate ways, but it was stuck in my mind. His voice, his words, so simple, but so familiar, all at the same time. My body shook as I walked out of the room to watch Roan shove Kinsley into a locker. The hallway erupted into a stream of cheers and boos as Kinsley crumpled, his body gasped for breath as he stayed down.

Two broken ribs, I whispered in my head as Roan high-fived someone behind him. *A sprained wrist, stitches.* Kinsley tried to stand now, his body shook as Roan kicked him in the stomach, and I ran before I realized it. *Be brave like Kinsley,* I chanted into my head as I ran. *Be brave for Kinsley.*

I don't remember how my fist went into Roan's cheek, but I felt his jaw crack. I felt his skin against my fist. It was something I didn't ever want to feel again. The shock in his eyes as he looked at me and held his cheek. I gripped his shirt and slammed him backward into the opposite lockers. I wasn't sure what to feel about it. I liked his fear, I liked that he knew I was stronger than him. I liked how he held his hands up and tried to stop me.

"Don't touch him, ever again," I growled in his face. The blood drained from his cheeks as he nodded. He stood there, his hands up as I turned around and glared at everyone around us. Kinsley lay there unconscious and his books were scattered around the floor. I shook in anger, in fear, because I liked how it felt to scare him.

'I'm not my father,' I mumbled as I leaned down and scooped Kinsley into my arms. I ordered some freshmen on my football team to grab Kinsley's stuff and to follow me as I carried him up to the nurse's office. *'I'm not my father,'* I repeated. I felt mad at myself for what had just happened. It was worth it, though, no matter how angry I was with myself. *'Thank you, Luke,'* Kinsley's voice floated into my mind as I gently laid him on the bed and left him there for the nurse to flutter over.

"How to prove I'm not my father?" I wondered as I stared at the closed nurse's office door. Then I figured it out. I walked to Kinsley's locker, a frown on my face, as I stared at it. I pulled out Kinsley's last letter to me and stuck it into my textbook for safekeeping as I pulled out a new piece of paper. I ignored the throb in my hand and I wrote a small note.

A simple note, no words, because for this, no words were needed. I folded it up, and before I could change my mind, I stuck it into the envelope and slid it through the holes of his locker. "I'm not going to ever be my father," I said with a defiant glare at the locker. I took a deep breath and walked slowly to my next class. I was sure I'd be met with a note telling me to go to the principal's office when I got there. "And I'm not going to let him dictate me anymore."

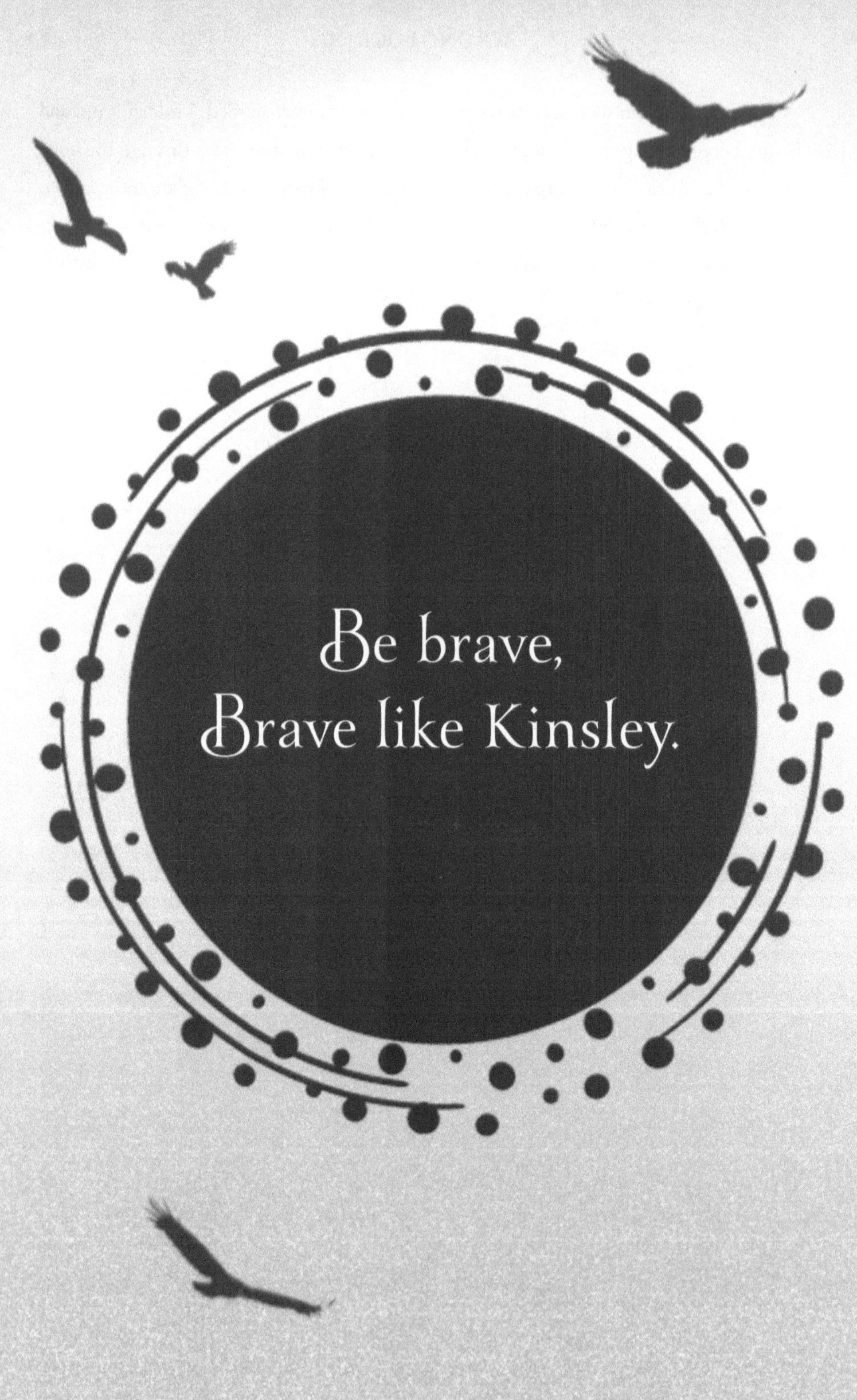
Be brave,
Brave like Kinsley.

Chapter 32
Kinsley

I woke up to the sound of arguing. "Trust me, he doesn't want you to call his parents," Isabella snapped. I groaned softly as I opened my eyes for a second only, before I shut them tightly as pain and dizziness moved like a wave back and forth through me. For a moment, my mind went blank and all I could see was the sea foam, how light blue the bubbles were as they settled on the sand. The soft swish of it moved back and forth with the motion of the water, the ripples danced from the fish as they moved around under its surface.

I tried to focus on that soft swish, I tried to smell the sweet briny smell of the salt in the air, but then the nurse's voice cut into my mind and made everything fade away. "Young lady, you need to get out of my way! He comes in here unconscious, his wrist is in a brace, and his body is covered in bruises! I had to rewrap his ribs which are broken, and clean his stitches! Where is his medications? None of it is on file, and I have no doubt in my mind that he has some for those kinds of wounds. I need to speak to his parents to know what he's taking so I don't mix anything!"

I didn't need to open my eyes to know Isabella stood in front of the phone and blocked her from touching it. However, I did need to open my eyes, I needed to get up and move so that I could stop this before Isabella got in trouble. "If you touch that phone, I'm calling my mother, and I swear if you try and call his parents Mami will come in here raising Hell, her Chanclas ready to go-" Isabella shouted before I cut her off.

Getting out of bed was hard, but I found it was easier to breathe than it had been all day. Probably because I had wrapped my ribs myself after I took a shower last night, and the nurse had rewrapped them the right way while I was unconscious. I didn't even bother to search for my shirt, I stood up shakily as I gripped the sheet that covered my bed and pulled it open. I tried as hard as I could to pretend I wasn't about to black out from the sudden movement, my head ached fiercely, and my stomach ached in an entirely new place thanks to Roan.

"Wait," I said as I cut Isabella off. I blinked a few times and held tightly onto the white sheet as I studied the scene in front of me. Of course, it couldn't be something simple. Maybe a normal person would have simply stood in the way of the nurse or even touched her shoulder to try to keep her attention away from the phone. Not Isabella, though. My wild Isabella had climbed on top of the table and held the landline phone high in the air, her arms lifted above her head, an angry look on her face as she tried to blow her blue strands out of her face.

The nurse didn't touch her but leaned over the desk on her tippy toes, her hand stretched as high as she could to try to reach the phone that was way too far out of her reach. "Please," I added with a deep breath as they both paused and turned to look at me. "My parents are in Italy," I lied. The nurse nodded, reminding me that I had lied about this earlier to her when I had first got to school today. Plus, they had been in Italy before they were called to come home. I kind of hoped they'd go back, but I guess whatever problem was at the office was enough to keep them here.

"They're taking care of my sick grandmother. I don't want them to have anything else to worry about. I didn't register my medications because I don't need to take them during the day, just in the morning and at night. I was fine, okay? I don't know how I got here, or much of what happened, but I'm fine. Where's my shirt?" I wondered as I glanced back behind me again.

The nurse muttered something that sounded like we were exasperating her under her breath as Izzy gasped softly, getting a good look at my back. I didn't need to see her to know she had gotten down from the desk and come over to me. She was close enough to touch me, but she didn't and I stood still, my head lowered in defeat as she examined my back. "Not so pretty anymore, huh?" I asked softly, feeling bad about myself.

I knew it wasn't my fault. I knew these wounds, these scars, they weren't my fault. But when you got a scar, when you lost a limb, when you were deformed in some way or another, depression and self-consciousness didn't care whether it was your fault or not. You were worried that you weren't the same as you were before, that someone would see you and be disgusted at the way you were different than you were supposed to be. To eventually find someone, to love them with every part of you, only to have them look at you with disgust in their eyes for the thing that made you different than expected; it was terrifying.

"You're always going to be my Pretty boy, Kinsley, no matter how many scars are on your body," she said softly. I turned to look at her and felt a wave of sadness spill through me.

For a moment, my mouth opened, then closed as I tried to figure out how to form the words to explain the sadness in my mind. "But what will whoever I end up with in the future think?" I wondered.

Her eyes glazed over and a wave of anger lit up inside her as she crossed her arms over her chest. "If they have something bad to say, in any shape or form, no matter what gender they are, they'll feel my wrath. One of those dramatic *'Hold my purse and my earrings'* moments, Kins, because I'll be pulling some hair that day," she promised.

"Here's your shirt. Mr. McCormick helped me get it off and remained in the room with me while I rebandaged everything and cleaned the blood off of you," the nurse said with a stern look on her face. An unconscious child, at all costs, should not be left alone half-naked with an adult of the opposite gender, a school policy. I personally trusted the nurse; I had known her enough over the past few years I had come here because of Roan's beatings, but I did not say anything. I knew there was a policy to follow. "There's some blood on it, so I'd suggest you use a different one if you have one. It's also the end of the school day though, if you don't have an extra."

The nurse handed me my shirt and my hoodie, both folded neatly in that way that I assumed was a superpower that was unlocked once someone became an adult. Maybe it was because I had a maid who did everything, but whenever I tried to pull out shirts and then fold them and put them back, they never looked perfect. Not like when my mother would hold up clothes from boxes and then fold them back into the box to hand to us after she showed off what she had purchased. Not like the pile of folded and washed clothes the maid would place in my drawers when I was in school. I had just assumed folding clothes was an adult superpower, like magically being able to cook. Those were things I would worry about when I turned eighteen and moved out and got an apartment with Izzy in New York.

I smiled at her because I could see she was still annoyed. I wanted to ask her how I got there, but I did not want to stray. The longer I stayed, the more she would wonder about me and the more likely she would want to call my parents. They would make a big deal if they showed up and were forced to pretend they cared, just for me to have to listen to them scold me for getting hurt and wasting their time, again.

I could still remember how annoyed my father was, the way he told me he was embarrassed by me. Embarrassed that the old star quarterback from back in his day had raised such a weak son. He had ranted on about how the basketball kids would never have stood a chance against a football player back when he was younger. If only I had tried harder, if only I had trained more, if only I had used the gym then I would have been able to stand up for myself.

"Thank you for taking care of me, and it's fine. If it's the end of the school day, I'll just head home and change there. A little dry blood isn't going to hurt me," I said with a grin. She glared at me but gave a tight nod as I started to pull on my shirt. I did not have gym clothes, not this year. Our high school required three years of gym class, and normally people waited to have their senior year free, but I did not want to deal with it this year. I knew Isabella was in it, which kind of sucked, it meant I was not going to have her with me next year.

Trying to get my shirt on hurt like a bitch, to be honest, but I managed to get it on without too much difficulty as I grabbed my hoodie. Sometimes I wished I owned some large coats that zipped, for times like this when it was difficult to pull hoodies over my head. I considered going without the hoodie, but with my parents around I could not risk them seeing my tattoo. Knowing them, they would pay for me to get it removed with that laser technique that sounded painful, and I did not want it removed.

As I gathered my things and put my clothes on, the nurse moved toward her desk and gave us privacy as I talked to Isabella. "Do you know what happened to me? I remember being in psychology class," I started to say before I paused. A small blush rose to my cheeks as I remembered Luke. How he had switched partners with Roan, so I would not have to be paired up with him. I could still feel it, his presence next to me as he sat beside me.

I could still feel how close he was to me. His deep voice, those light green eyes as he looked at me. Looking into his eyes was something I did not think I would ever get tired of. Green like a blade of grass, but filled with small slivers of gold that lit up when the light hit them just right. I wondered how beautiful his eyes would look if I was ever allowed to stand close to him outside under the bright light from the sun without walls or clouds to hide under. His hair was darker that day, the dark brown had only a few hints of dirty blond, but I suspected it was because it was cloudy that day.

The more the sun shone, the more his hair lightened, like a flower that slowly needed sunlight to grow and sparkle the way it was meant to shine. I could still smell him, a cologne that I did not recognize, not too strong but it matched him perfectly. I grabbed a small handful of my hoodie on my right shoulder, since that was the side Luke had sat on, and pressed it gently against my nose to try and see if it smelled like him.

I felt my blush grow even stronger when I realized his cologne wasn't just on my shoulder but all over my hoodie. I wasn't sure why. It was like he had hugged me, or something. Isabella cleared her throat, a confused look on her face as she snapped me back into the present and I remembered I had been in the middle of asking her a question before I had gotten distracted.

I told Isabella briefly what happened in Psychology class. The nurse didn't seem to care that we sat there on top of the bed gossiping, she even came over with a small paper cup of ibuprofen and a bottle of water. She made me tell her the names of the meds I was on to make sure it was okay to take more pills. I was glad for the ibuprofen, my head throbbed just a little less after it started to kick in while I explained to Isabella how Luke had switched with Roan.

"That's probably my fault. Now before you get mad at me, I'd like to point out that I didn't know he worked there when I first went there on Friday," she said as she held her hands up and stared at me. My eyebrows rose in confusion as she sighed with a shake of her head. "When I took your car to a garage, I didn't care about what garage or where. It was the closest one to the school, and I didn't know it was where Luke worked until I went to pick it up on Sunday. I told him about you being in the hospital, and what Roan did to you. He wanted to know, okay? I wasn't just randomly telling him for the heck of it."

My heart throbbed gently in my chest at her words. *Stop it*, I told myself. *Stop beating like that, stop thinking things you shouldn't think. It doesn't mean anything.* "Why?" I wondered. I knew I probably should have said more and explained more, but I also knew she'd know exactly what it was I wanted to know.

She shrugged as she scratched at the back of her neck. "Honestly, I asked him that too, and he said it's because he cares. He said he's straight, but he still cares. I'm not surprised, to be honest. The amount of back and forth you guys did was so important to both of you, he'd have to be a machine or something not to at least care a little bit about you." I nodded as I tried not to focus on those words. Straight, he'd said. Over and over again.

I wanted to write the word down in big bold print and shove it inside me, wrap it around my heart so maybe then it would stop beating so painfully if it was pressed against reality. "But as for what happened, and how you got here, I think you'll find that information interesting," Isabella added with a grin.

I closed my eyes as I tried to remember while I absently crunched and uncrunched the half-full water bottle in my good hand. The sound of the plastic crinkled and the soft scratch of the nurse writing something down was all I could hear for a moment as I thought. I remembered how awkward it was in the classroom next to Luke. I was happy he was there, but confused at the same time. Wasn't sure what it meant, if it even meant anything at all, and I ended up practically running out of the door. It didn't help that as I sprinted down the hallway, I accidentally tripped on someone's textbook that lay on the floor and fell into Roan.

I remembered how he had got pissed off, then the evil smile that fluttered over his face as he started to hurt me. The shove against the lockers, the pain that spread throughout my body, and then the kick to my stomach that made every part of me feel like I was burning from the inside out as my broken ribs shook from the impact. Then nothing. I remember darkness, and that was the last of it. I had fainted in front of him, again.

"It was Luke, Kinsley. I wasn't there, but the rumors were everywhere. Luke had run at Roan and punched him in the face. Roan had blood pouring out of his mouth, he was scared, and Luke shoved him into a locker and told him not to touch you ever again. I don't know how much of this is true, there's also that strange group of girls who were talking about how their ideal ship of the school was Roan and Luke, two captains of different teams, and something about them kissing against the lockers," she said with a frown, her nose scrunched up as we both shuddered in disgust at the image that gave us in our minds.

"He carried you up here, from the second floor and had another football player carry your things. He protected you, Kins. I don't know if that means anything, and I don't want you to start swooning because he's said it constantly, and I don't want you to get your feelings hurt. He's straight, but he cares. Maybe he's changed his mind about being friends. Or maybe he just didn't want to watch you getting bullied anymore. Maybe he felt like it was time someone stood up to Roan. There's also a rumor about Luke and Roan fighting over Luke's ex Alison, so that could be a thing too," she said with a shrug.

All of these possibilities, and I had trouble trying to shove the one I wanted out of my mind. I had to literally take the idea of him liking me and bury it deep down inside me, so deep that hopefully, it would stay there forever. She was right. Luke had said more than once that he was straight, and I needed to respect his sexuality. Maybe he started to warm up to the idea of being friends. Logically it made sense because we were a lot closer because of the letters. They were a mistake from the beginning, a wrong locker that led to two very confused and hurt boys, but I was glad to know he had trouble getting past it just like I was.

I was glad to know he had trouble forgetting about me, even if I had been an accident from the start. *'Someone real,'* he had called me. *'In a sea of fakes, it was nice to know there was someone here that was real.'* I wondered faintly if he still felt that way. After all, I had never once lied to him about anything. I told Green from the start what I wanted and what my parents wanted, and when I found out it was the wrong locker, I told him. Every step of the way, I told him, and I had never deceived him. Maybe, just maybe, he missed me as much as I missed him.

"This is for you. I've already talked to the principal, so you can't go against it," the nurse said as she handed me a piece of paper.

I looked down at it and grimaced. I went to try and argue with the nurse, but the look on her face as she stood by the door, the knob tight in her hand as she held it open for us, was enough for me to know there was no argument with this. Isabella and I both shuffled out the door and instead of answering Izzy about what the note said, I simply handed it to her. "You have to stay out of school for the rest of the week? But then it's spring break!" Izzy exclaimed, her eyes wide.

"Unfortunately. Are you doing anything for spring break this year?" I asked hopefully.

She shook her head, no, and I felt my hope dwindle into nothing. "Mami couldn't afford it, that's why Abuela came here to visit. Can we go to your locker? I want to get my paint out of it," I nodded, my right hand holding the strap of my bag. Izzy carried the books I had with me when I had passed out in the hallway, so I guess I'd need to drop those off as well. Most kids would be excited about weeks off of school, but all I felt was dread.

"Can you tell my Psychology teacher tomorrow? And Luke? I guess he's my partner now on the project. It was due at the end of the week but now I won't be able to finish it," I said with a sigh. He had tried so hard to help me, and in the end, I left him with everything.

Izzy shook her head. "I'll tell the teacher, but there's no need to tell Luke. He was suspended for the rest of the week because he punched Roan's precious face. He won't be allowed to play in the first game, either. He's probably sad about it," she said absently.

I was lost in my thoughts as I followed Isabella down the hallway. Something about that upset me and made me worried. Luke said in the letters he wasn't like the others on his team, but he enjoyed it all the same. I remembered that, and I knew he was sad he had to miss out on his first game. What if he regretted it? What if he was at home right now angry, regretting helping me altogether? Regretting our letters? Then another thought popped into my head, another worry I couldn't quite push down.

There was something there, something deep and dark that he never talked about, but there was a hint, such a big hint. *'What if I'm simply a nobody, someone who goes home each night and curls up in a ball under my blankets to block out the noises, someone who presses my hands against my ears wishing I had someone to talk to, someone to call when I can't stop crying? Would that terrify you?'*

What did that mean? I wanted to ask. The noises, what noises? Did that mean what I thought it meant? What if it was something bad? What if he was in trouble? I shook my head and tried to get the thoughts out of my mind. If the rumors were right and he did terrify Roan like that, then I didn't have to worry, right? He was strong, he was the football captain, and he could handle himself. He wouldn't get hurt like that. Right?

"Kinsley," Isabella's voice cut into my thoughts and pulled me away from the dark spiral I slowly started to slip into. I almost ignored her, it was how worried I was. How worried I made myself think about these things I desperately didn't want to think about. "Kins, there's a letter in here."

For a moment her voice went soft. My heart raced loudly inside my chest as I felt like once more, I was going to pass out. My mouth was dry as I clutched my strap tighter, my head automatically shook no as I took a step back. For a few minutes, I could hear Isabella putting my books into the locker, I could feel her fingers opening my bag and getting the ones in there out and putting those in the locker as well.

She pulled out her paint and I stubbornly stared at my feet and wondered if I could forever just stay here, in this moment. The moment before everything changed once more. I wasn't sure if it was for the better, or for worse, and that was what terrified me the most. What if he hated me now? What if he wrote that after they suspended him, and it's filled with all the ways I ruined his life? "You open it, please," I begged. I licked my lips and tried to wet them. "I can't do it."

I didn't know why I whispered, it was clear there wasn't anyone else out there. The classrooms had small conversations that came from them, teachers gathered together to talk about what happened in their class that day. What students exhausted them, and new methods of grading they had found online. But the students were long gone. Either in their clubs, sports, or at home. Not Luke, I told myself. *He was at home, because of me.* I could hear her open the letter and I took a step back, and another, until I felt the row of lockers on the other side of the hall touch my back. I angled my body automatically to lean against my shoulder as Isabella walked over to me, her eyes steadfast on the little piece of folded paper as she delicately opened it. "Kinsley," she said, her eyebrows pressed together into a frown. "There are no words here,"

I looked at her, and without a word, I held out my hand and tried to ignore the way my heart pounded as she slowly handed it to me. I took a deep breath and counted to ten before I looked down at the small piece of paper that was in my hands. For a moment, I didn't understand what I was looking at until I saw it. The area code, the dash to separate the numbers, a sequence of numbers. "It's a phone number," I said softly as I lifted my eyes to Isabella's. "It's his phone number."

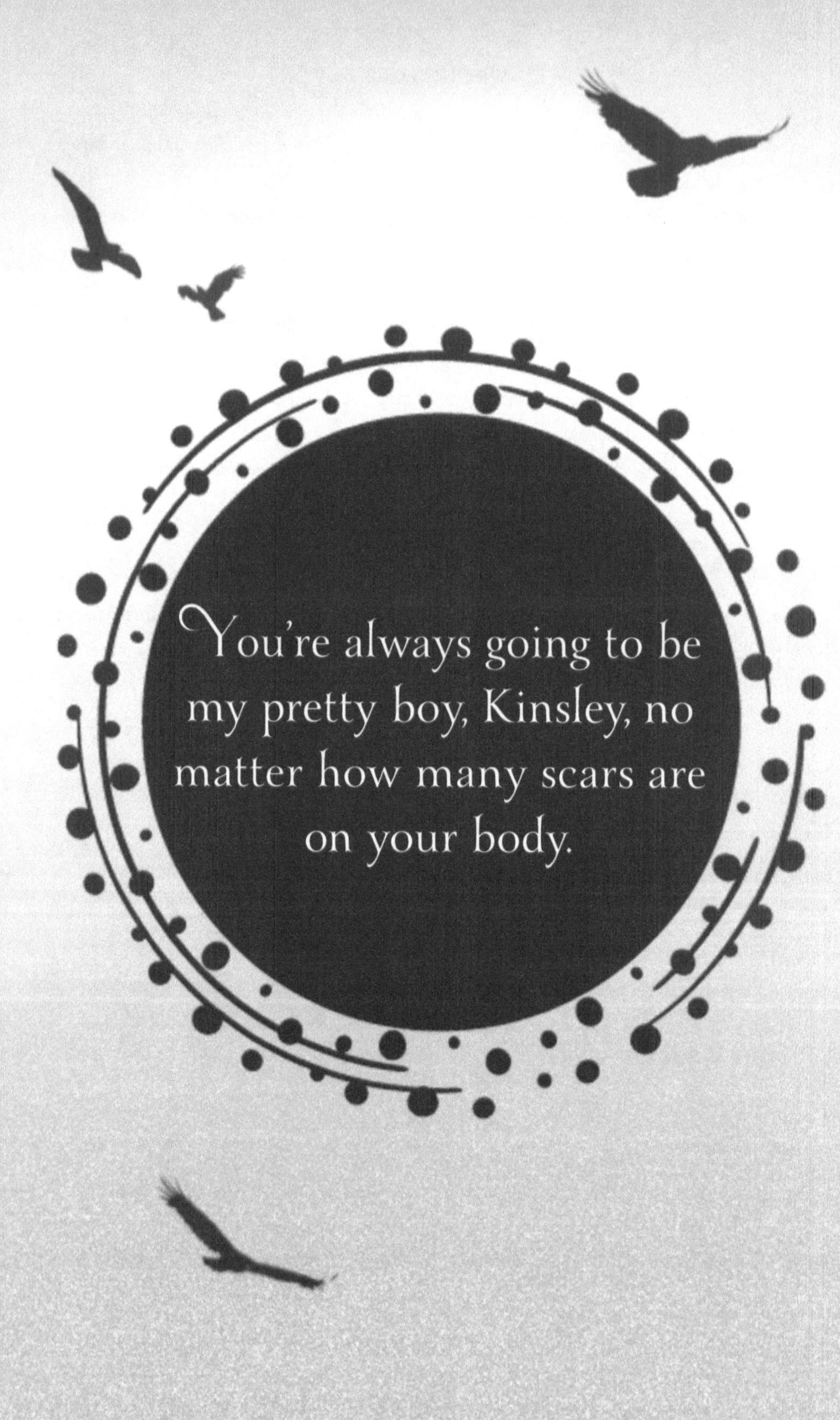

You're always going to be my pretty boy, Kinsley, no matter how many scars are on your body.

Chapter 33
Luke

There were times in my life when I'd walk home from work, and I'd simply stop in the middle and wonder if I should keep going. The walk from work to home wasn't as long as the walk from school to work. I had already been yelled at by my boss for being late. Despite his love for my mom, he still liked me to be on time and when I informed him I wouldn't get a ride from Bobby anymore, he had been cross with me for the rest of the day. It was clear he was unhappy about it, especially when more than once he went over to my car, the one I had purchased from him but left in the shop in the back corner, and started to tinker with it.

I was allowed to leave it there since we were never full. There were always at least one or two free spots in the garage for more customers since this garage wasn't the most popular one in town. Normally, however, he left my car to me to deal with and allowed me to work on it during my break but I hadn't had the money to buy any new parts for it lately and it just sat there. He was so frustrated that I wasn't going to have a ride that he started to mess with it, got frustrated that it needed pretty much everything, and ended up kicking a bucket half full of water across the garage.

I knew he wasn't going to hit me, but the loudness and the violence of the action still made me flinch. Because he didn't understand why I had flinched, it annoyed him even more. People don't realize that even if someone who had been physically abused wasn't around the person who abused them, they'd still be scared on a reflex that it would happen again. It's hard to trust others, especially when someone you had been fundamentally made to trust has shown you that you shouldn't.

By the time it was time to go home, he barely talked to me, and I wasn't surprised about it. I hadn't talked either. I hadn't paid attention to much of anything. I was angry with myself. Angry that I had gone so far, but angry that I hadn't gone far enough. It was fucked up that Kinsley had gotten bullied almost every day by Roan and nothing ever happened to him, but I punched Roan one time and I was suspended for the rest of the week. I already knew my parents knew, my mother had sent me a text as I walked to work before my phone died. Another thing I was angry about. I had finally given Kinsley my number and I had forgotten to charge my phone last night. What if he had texted me or tried to call me after my phone had died? What if he thought I gave him the wrong number, or I was just ignoring him or something?

I wasn't even sure why I had done it. I wasn't in love with him, he was a boy and I was straight. But I realized that to try to live without him was like trying to breathe underwater, and I was tired of the struggle. To need him like I needed to breathe was an understatement. I wasn't sure when I became this reliant on his letters, on his words, on his confidence. Without it, I spiraled, and that little voice was there more than ever. I realized as I stared down at my dead phone, that for the first time in my life, I wanted to ignore that voice. Because of those letters, because of that hope, I wanted to live. My lifeline.

I stood there, my dead phone in my hand, and my eyes on my house in the distance. Halfway there, but not close enough. That feeling inside me spread, the feeling that told me I should turn around and sneak into the garage and sleep on the dusty old couch that my boss had in his office. That I should never go back. I was scared to take another step forward, to walk to that house that looked so peaceful and so clean on the outside, but was filled with destruction on the inside.

I wondered if people really took time to look out their windows when they drove along, those houses they would drive past in those nice and safe neighborhoods. They'd ooh and aww, tell others how pretty the house was. In their mind, they thought about the family. Was the mother a nice and sweet woman? Was the man serious and helpful? Were the kids well-behaved?

They'd see a house with a beautiful garden outside and expensive toys organized on the porch. They'd see a lawn that was meticulously cut and a house that was bright and cheery. Decorations of fancy wind chimes and soft curtains hung in the windows. Tree houses that were propped in trees, rope ladders for the children's amusement.

They'd drive past and they'd think: *How beautiful this family is. How lovely this is, I'm jealous of this, I wished my house was like this.* I wondered how many of those beautiful houses were filled with angry parents, with holes in their walls, broken glass, and screams. I wondered how many of those tree houses were meant for the children to run and hide to try and escape the wrath of a drunken father or mother. How many beautiful houses held secret storms?

My house was no different. Outside was well taken care of, the grass was cut nearly every weekend, the flowers taken care of by mother, and the paint on the house bright and cheerful. Wind chimes softly chimed in tune with the screams that echoed through the house. The furniture smashed against the walls, and the glass shattered over and over again. How many beautiful houses were homes, and how many were actually prisons? Did anyone ever wonder? Did they even care?

I stood there and bounced from my toes to the heel of my feet, one hand clutching my phone and the other the greasy material of my pants. As I stared at the bright outside porch light turned on to show they waited for me, the soft glow lit up the flowers and most of the porch from here, I was torn. Should I turn around and go back to the garage, or walk the rest of the way home? I was scared.

When did a house stop being a home? When did it start? I looked down at my phone and realized if I didn't go home I wouldn't be able to charge it. I wouldn't be able to see if Kinsley tried to talk to me. If I didn't go home, Shawn might end up hurt instead of me, or Mom. A part of me felt stronger because I had stuck up for Kinsley and punched Roan. Because I had shown him I was stronger than him, and I felt stronger. But another part of me desperately wanted to shove that strength down, to hide it away. I wanted no part of the strength that came when I beat up someone else, even if they deserved it.

A part of me wondered if I deserved it, every time my father hurt me. Maybe I did deserve it, after all, he told me constantly I was nothing. Maybe the rules were different for those who were already broken.

In the end, the need to charge my phone, to protect my brother and my mother was stronger than my fear. I knew I wouldn't be able to sleep without charging my phone to see if Kinsley talked to me. I wouldn't be able to sleep unless I looked at the pictures I took of his drawings, of those bright cerulean blue eyes. I wanted to ask him why he destroyed that picture, but at the same time, I was scared to know that it was because of me. I was scared that because I was broken, all I could do was break everyone and everything around me. Maybe it would have been better if I turned around and ran as far as I could. Ran far away, and started over somewhere else. Maybe it would be better for everyone if I simply disappeared.

I shoved my phone into my school bag and wrapped one of my shirts around it. I had taken my extra clothes home since I was suspended, and I was glad for the extra padding in case my father tried to hurt me again. I knew it was coming, as I stood on the front step and stared at the closed door. It was like I could feel him on the other side, like a large muscular angry animal pacing. No matter how much I worked out, no matter how good I was on the field, I was nothing compared to my father.

He was always going to be bigger than me, stronger than me, and there would always be that part of me that wanted to just wrap my arms around him and beg him to love me the way he was supposed to. The part of me that wanted to make him proud of me. To hear him tell people that I was his boy and that he was proud of me just the way I was. I opened the door and managed to make my way inside and dropped my school bag gently on the ground before I was slammed against the front door. The feel of his weight against me, the tight grip on my throat as I gasped for breath. This was probably the first time I had seen my life flash before my eyes and I actually didn't welcome it.

I didn't want to die, not anymore, not now. He pulled me forward by my throat, then slammed me back against the door again with even more force than before. A squeal of pain popped out of my mouth involuntarily as his red-rimmed eyes glared at me, furious. "Fucking faggot," he muttered, his hand pressed down slightly harder. I clenched my hands tightly at my side and hoped he didn't hurt my bag. Hoped he didn't even notice it sitting there. I couldn't make a sound. I had already pissed him off, if I made a sound I was done for. "Your school said you were bullying? Punched someone for no reason? I didn't raise you to be like this!" He screamed as he pushed me even more against the door.

I wanted to tell him that wasn't entirely true. Children usually either ended up being the way their parents were, or they tried to be the opposite because they saw the hate and wanted nothing like that in their future. I had always tried my hardest to be nothing like my father, but as I closed my eyes, I wondered if I deserved this after all.

Maybe it would have been better if I had just pushed Roan out of the way, grabbed Kinsley, and made a break for it. At least this way I terrified Roan for a few days, but to what degree? Now Kinsley was going to be there for the rest of the week without me there to keep Roan away from him. All I did was piss off his bully even more. "All you're good for is your skills, and now you can't even play in the first game! Do you think I'm going to pay for your college? You have another thing coming, Luke!" He screamed.

Dad's spit coated the side of my face as I tried not to lift my hands. Automatically, I wanted to dig my fingers into his hand, to try and force him to let me go. He didn't hold me tight enough to cut off my breathing entirely, but it was tight enough to scare me. Tight enough to make me feel anxious, and I struggled not to gag or throw up in his face. The smell of old alcohol was on his breath and that didn't help either.

"I had been on the phone forever, trying to apologize to that poor boy's parents. They're furious, and did you know his mother is the chief of police? Are you trying to make it so we get kicked out of this town? I swear, if it comes down to it, I'll kick you out instead. I could lose my job because of you, and then what? Do you think your measly little job is enough to pay the bills around here? To pay for your mother's medication and her therapy? I pay for every fucking thing around here, and if I lose my job because you decided it's okay to punch someone for no reason, then you're out of here!"

He dropped me then, and I felt so tiny, so insignificant as I crumpled to the ground and gasped for breath. "It wasn't for no reason," I spat out, unsure where the courage to argue back at him came from.

Look at me, I wanted to say. *Understand me. I'm not the same as you.*

He squatted down until he was at the same level as me, his hand roughly grabbing my hair and yanking it backward. "What was that?" He asked, his voice low and filled with venom. It held a promise that I would regret that I talked back to him, but I couldn't stop now.

I could hear my mother somewhere in the room, crying, but I couldn't hear Shawn. I hoped he wasn't there tonight. I hoped he never came back, for his own sake. My mother begged me to shut up, but I ignored her. If this was the end, then I was going to be brave. Brave like Kinsley. "Roan was beating up my friend, for no reason. My friend had already been injured by him before, and he could have killed him. If I didn't stop him, Kinsley could have died today," I said, my voice strained and weaker than I would have liked from him strangling me.

For a minute, he stared at me, his eyes furrowed together as he thought. Even though we weren't considered rich around here, my father did work for a rich family, and I realized, distantly, that it was Kinsley's father. How ironic it was that all along he had been working for the Bryants. "Kinsley Bryant, my boss's son? That gay kid?" He asked, disgusted. "You're friends with a gay boy?"

Friends, I had said. I wondered if that would aggravate Kinsley, that first I had shoved him away from me and told him I wanted nothing to do with him, but I just pushed myself back into his life and called him my friend without even making sure it was okay. But at the same time, this was Sparrow, my Sparrow. I knew Sparrow would understand. I lifted my head and stared my father in the eyes, startling him. I had never done that before. "Kinsley isn't gay," I said. It was true, after all, Kinsley had told me himself. Even if he was gay, however, it shouldn't matter. His sexuality didn't define him, and it certainly wasn't my father's business. It wasn't anyone's business except for his and whoever his future partner was going to be.

As my father started to punch me in the stomach, I closed my eyes and took it. I felt every blow because, in the end, I was proud of myself. I had defended Kinsley twice today, and I had stood up to my father. But at the same time, I was sad because all I had ever wanted was to make him proud of me. To make him love me again. I didn't think he would ever love me now.

"Stop it!" My mother screamed, both of us surprised by her outburst. Usually, she would just go into another room until it was over, then when my father left, she would come to bandage me, and tell me all the ways I needed to try better so he wasn't angry with me anymore. Tell me we all needed to try harder so he wasn't compelled to hurt us or be angry.

To protect us, she'd say. To keep the peace. I sometimes wondered if she realized the extent to which it really worked. If you had to tip-toe around your spouse to keep them happy, was that really considered a relationship worth fighting for? Father let go of me and for a moment I fell onto my side, my head resting against something sharp but I didn't have the strength to move as it cut into my forehead. "Leave him alone!" She yelled.

I faded away then. Darkness wrapped around me and dragged me under. It wasn't the first time I'd passed out because of my father, and it wouldn't be the last, I was sure. I wondered as I floated in the darkness, if this was what Kinsley felt. I promised myself that no matter what my father did to me, I wouldn't let him feel like this again. Not from Roan, not from anyone.

I woke up and I was still on the ground. It didn't surprise me. Shawn wasn't home and mom wasn't strong enough to do much. Dad wouldn't be kind enough to carry me to bed. I did have a pillow under my head and I could feel tightness on my head and my stomach that told me my mother must have rolled me over and bandaged my wounds for me while I was unconscious. I sat up and looked around at the dimly lit room and tried to ignore my throbbing headache.

Dad was nowhere to be seen and mom was asleep on the couch with a lamp turned on and a book hanging halfway out of her hand. I struggled to sit up and grabbed the blanket and the pillow she gave me and moved to her. Gently, I lifted her head and placed the pillow under it, put her book down for her, and draped the blanket over her body. I had no idea what time it was, but all I cared about was my phone.

I nearly cried in relief as I saw my bag was still there untouched. I hurried to my room and plugged my phone in while I took a quick shower. It was probably the fastest shower I'd ever taken, and that was saying something since I had to work around the bandages and scrub the grease off. I dried off as fast as I could, slipped on a pair of boxers, and walked back to my room, locking the door behind me. I grabbed a bottle of Advil as I laid down on my bed and swirled some warm water from a bottle that was next to my bed as I turned on my phone. For a moment nothing was there and I felt like screaming.

What did I expect? Why would he want to talk to me after everything I had done and said to him? But then my phone finished connecting and suddenly there was a message there, and then another, and then another. I opened them with shaky hands, read through them, and tried to breathe. I didn't realize how much I craved Kinsley's words until they were there again.

'This is Luke, right? I swear to God if you gave me someone else's number I'm going to be angry.' His first text said. I chuckled weakly because that probably would have been funny if I had given him Tony or Bobby's number.

'Are you there? Luke? Oh wait, Izzy said you work after school. I'll be patient.' He texted again. I felt a smile lift the corners of my lips, probably the first time I had smiled all day.

'Look, It's late, and I've been thinking. Your letters, about what you said. You didn't tell me much, but if I'm reading between the lines I can see something that's worrying me. I'm worried about you, and how your parents are taking the suspension. I just need to know you're okay, and then I'll leave you alone, okay? Just tell me if you're okay.' the next text said.

It was the last text he had sent, but it spoke volumes. I don't think anyone has ever asked me if I was okay or not. I don't think anyone has ever worried about me. Even when I stood there screaming, a bandage wrapped tightly around my wrist, no one saw me. I felt the tears build in my eyes, my chest was tight as the emotions bubbled inside me. I ignored the idea of texting and simply hit the call button.

I rolled onto my side as I placed my phone between my ear and the mattress. It rang for a minute, and I wasn't sure if he was even going to answer. I probably should have looked at what time it was, to be honest. I was about to hang up when the ringing stopped, and I was greeted with a yawn. "Damn, I didn't think you'd take the four am offer so seriously," Kinsley said. His voice was deeper than usual, with a sleepy rasp to it that indicated I had woken him up.

I pulled the phone away from my ear for a minute and looked at the time. It read four fifteen in the morning, and I mentally cursed at myself. I took a deep breath as I tried to ignore the tears that slowly slid down my cheeks as I nestled my phone back in between my ear and the mattress. "Sorry, Kins," my voice cracked slightly as I tried to hold back my sobs. "I'll call back later, it's nothing. My phone's been dead all day, and I didn't get a chance to charge it until now."

I don't know if it was the sound of my voice or the obviousness that I was crying despite how hard I was trying to hide it, but after a few seconds of pause, he sounded more alert, more awake. Caring for me. Someone who cared for me. For some reason, that simply made me cry even harder. "It's not nothing. I was just teasing you. What's wrong? I'm here for you, no matter what, Luke. Even at four in the morning," he said softly.

I was quiet, my mouth opened and closed as the tears slid down my face. They soaked the mattress, the pillow, and probably my phone too. I curled my knees up to my chest. I felt like I was a river that had been held back by a dam that was slowly torn apart. Soon the flood would erupt and I'd be unstoppable. My lips quivered as I let out a shaky breath. "No rush, Luke," he said after a few minutes. The phone was closer to his mouth now, and it sounded like his voice was right in my ear, right next to me. "Even if you have nothing to say, I'm here. I'm always going to be here."

I nodded even though he couldn't see me. My eyes were closed as I wrapped my arms around my knees, and simply cried. I couldn't see him, I couldn't feel him, but I could hear his steady breath in my ear and it was enough for me as I let out the soft sobs I'd been holding in. The dam broke, and everything poured out of me.

I had never cried in front of anyone besides my family, as rare as that was, but there was something different about Kinsley. Maybe it was because we already knew each other through the letters, and I started to wonder what the hell I was doing with my life. Even if I didn't want him romantically, I still wanted to be his friend. But at the same time, I was too scared to let him in, to let him see me, even more than he already had. How to have a friend? A real friend. I wasn't sure. So in the end, I didn't say anything. I cried, and he was silent the whole time, just being there.

I didn't realize how much I needed someone to be there until I had it. To realize this just made me cry harder and I felt more scared than I'd ever been before. Scared to have it, scared to lose it; scared of what it could mean.

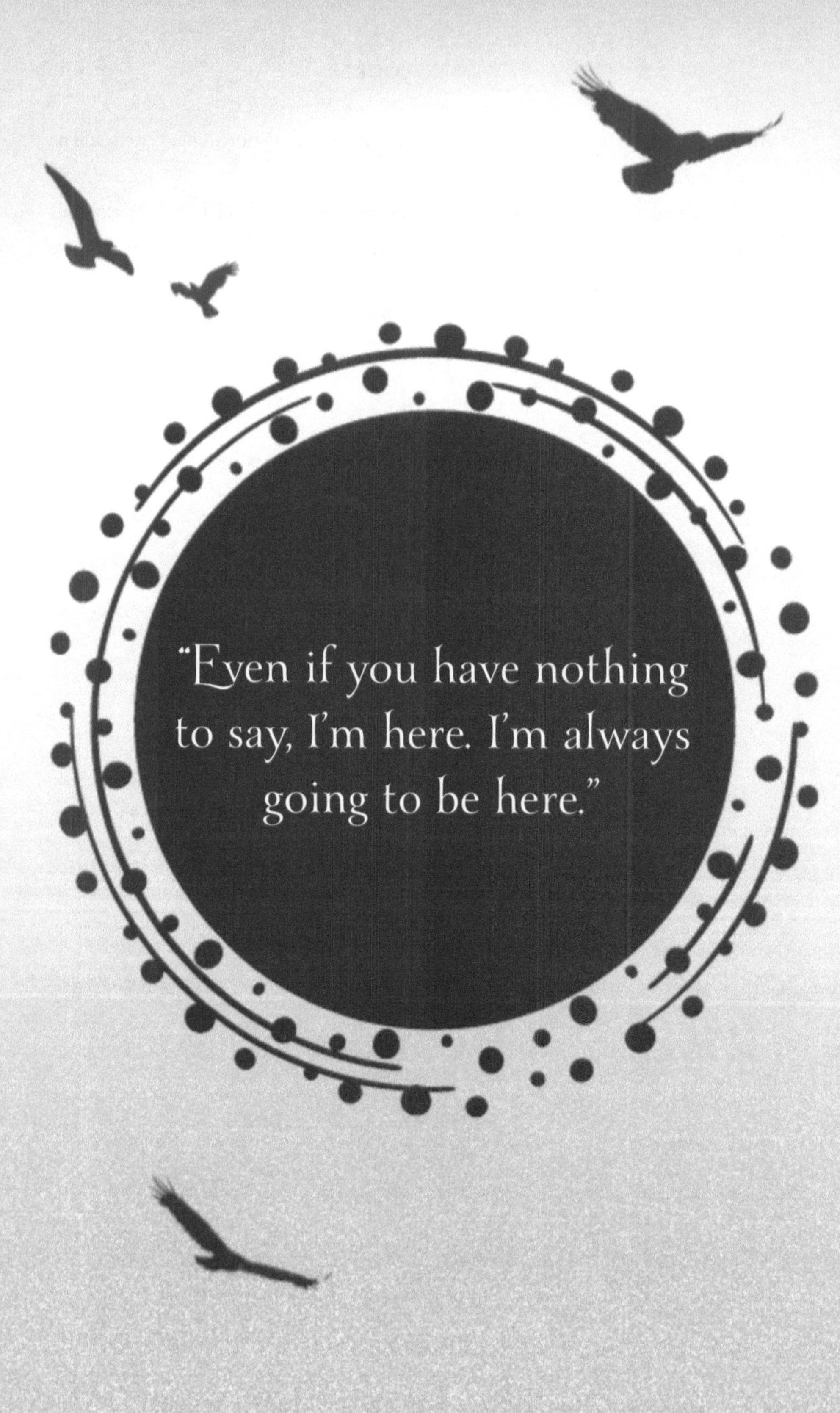
"Even if you have nothing to say, I'm here. I'm always going to be here."

Chapter 34
Kinsley

I woke up to my phone pressed against my ear as the sun slowly rose outside my window. I wasn't sure if it was the shuffling sound or the sun that slowly blinded me and woke me up. The shuffled sound came from the phone I had pressed in between my ear and the pillow. I tried to ignore the sound at first, my eyes squeezed tightly to try and block out the sunlight because my mind was still asleep and couldn't figure out why my body woke up. I was never awake that early and I groaned. Suddenly the shuffled sound stopped and a small gasp sounded from the other end of my phone. It was then that everything started to come back to me.

Last night I had woken up with my phone in my hands, worried that Luke had given me the wrong number. Worried that he was hurt, worried that something bad had happened to him. Then he woke me up with a phone call at four in the morning, and even though not much was said, so much was understood through the silence and the soft sobs. We both must have drifted off to sleep at some point, and judging from the fact that it was only seven in the morning, Luke barely had any sleep. I heard the phone being messed with, the sounds got louder, and as I heard breathing on the other end I decided to speak first. "How the hell are you awake at this ungodly hour?" I groaned.

There was silence for a moment before he laughed. I opened my eyes wide, my face burned as I pulled the blanket over my head to block out the sunlight. Normally I slept on my back but I couldn't with the stitches. I couldn't stop my heart from pounding, I was wide awake now. I was going to be obsessed with his laugh, I could already tell.

"I guess you're not a morning person, huh?" he wondered. He coughed to clear his throat and I had to stifle a groan because his voice was so freaking sexy when it was all raspy from just waking up. It made me wish I wasn't a teenager as I started to shuffle around and tried to ignore how his voice affected me. "Aren't you supposed to be waking up for school anyway?"

"First, I have a car. I don't need to leave at the crack of dawn to get there on time. Even having to pick up Izzy I still made it on time. Second, the nurse told the principal about me. She saw all of the wounds I had and contacted the hospital. They won't let me go back to school until after spring break." I muttered frustratedly. I could hear Kennedy talking on the phone to her boyfriend in the hallway. I cringed because that sweet sappy voice girls did when they liked someone always bugged the crap out of me. Her voice faded away as she walked down the stairs and I sighed in relief that she didn't come to bug me. Occasionally I had to drop her off at middle school before I went to get Isabella if she didn't have a ride.

Luke laughed once more, this time it was a deep chuckle as he started to shuffle around again. When he spoke he was farther away, like he had put me on speakerphone. I wondered distantly what his room looked like but he'd probably be against Facetime. We weren't really friends, right? He stuck up for me and protected me, but he said he didn't want to be friends with me. So I was unsure where we stood now or what this really was.

"Good," he spoke. I frowned, unsure what he meant by that. "I'm glad you're not going back until after spring break. I was worried you'd get hurt because of me, and I'm suspended for the rest of the week too, so now I don't have to worry about that,"

I felt my cheeks lighten up over his words once more. He was worried about me. *Don't be stupid*, I told myself. It meant nothing. He had just protected you, he didn't want to be friends with you. Or maybe he did. Why else did he give me his number? I realized instead of talking to myself and trying to figure him out, I should probably ask him. "Why did you give me your number?" I wondered. My phone vibrated against my ear and I frowned. I put my phone on speakerphone to hear him as I pulled the phone away to check it.

There was a text from Isabella. *'Morning, Pretty Boy! What happened with the number? Did you guys kiss and make up?'*

"I...um." Luke stammered. I paused, my fingers floated over the keys as I listened to him. I wanted to see him if he was going to stammer like that. Was he blushing? What would Luke look like with a blush on his face, I wondered. I tried to smack myself and realized this was stupid. He might want to be my friend, but he was straight. I needed to get over these feelings if I was going to be friends with him. He'd be creeped out by them otherwise. "I'm going to work. I have a break around lunchtime, do you want to come to visit me? I'd rather talk in person,"

I nodded, then cursed myself because obviously, he couldn't see me. "Sure. Izzy told me where you work so I can do that." I took it off of the speakerphone and put it back to my ear. I'll just text her afterward. For some reason I wanted to just press the phone against my ear, to listen to his voice where it was right next to me, almost as if he was here. We were silent, and I noticed he wasn't making noise anymore. I wondered if he just stood there staring at his phone as he tried to figure out what to do or say. I guess this was where we said bye, right? Where we both hung up and went our separate ways. Normal people talked on the phone and hung up constantly. I guess I wasn't a normal person, not with Luke.

To hear his soft sighs, the sound of his breath against the phone as if he was right next to me. I wanted to hear the deep rumble of his voice forever. I realized getting over these feelings I had for him was going to be the hardest thing I'd done yet in my life, and I wasn't quite sure I could do it. I nearly jumped when he started to speak again. I had been so lost in my thoughts about him that I hadn't been paying attention anymore. "What are you going to do today?"

His voice was softer, and I could hear the sound of a door opening and closing. He was moving throughout his house most likely, keeping quiet not to wake anyone. I wondered distantly what his father did since his mother was a nurse. Maybe they both worked a night shift and slept in. I heard a cabinet opening and closing, the sound of an aluminum wrapper of a pop-tart for breakfast before he left. No good mornings from his parents, no breakfast waiting on the table for him.

I thought it was funny how we were two different people on two different sides of a coin, but still the same at the same time. How different this tall, strong, football player was from my shorter, weaker, artistic lifestyle; but at the end of the day, we were the same. The same parents who didn't care, the same family that let us take care of ourselves. Maybe that was why we struggled to stay away from each other. Because, in the end, we understood each other more than anyone else ever could. "Probably go back to sleep. Not all of us can exist on three hours of sleep," I said with a yawn. He chuckled, and I heard the sound of something clicking repeatedly. "What is that?" I wondered. "That clicking sound."

"A lighter," he mumbled. His voice sounded so close to my ear that a shiver went through me.

I was quiet for a minute as I listened to him slide his finger down the little coil, the clicking sound once more. He must have put the phone against his shoulder and his ear to free his hands. I could just see him as he walked down the street, his hands cupped around the lighter to block the wind from taking the flame away. "You smoke?"

He gave a grunt of affirmation and I waited, knowing he wasn't able to talk until he had finished lighting it. "Yeah, sometimes. Does that bother you?"

I shrugged, once again smacking myself over having non-verbal responses. His voice just sounded so close to me that it was hard not to feel like he was next to me. "Not really. Most of the kids in the art club are stoners, so I'm pretty used to being around it." He laughed, and I couldn't help but smile at the sound of it. "Pretty sure they're only in the art club to have a place to smoke, actually. Whenever they draw it looks like something a kindergartener drew. But they have fun and they're kind of cute, like our children or something. Plus it's good for us, the principal would have disbanded our club if there were only two people in it."

He laughed once more, and I found myself planning more things to say, trying to find more funny topics just to hear him laugh. "I don't smoke weed, just cigarettes sometimes. You don't smoke? Being around it constantly?" he wondered.

I caught myself this time before I started to shake my head. I was kind of proud of myself for it. "No way. My dad would kill me," I said with a grin.

"I thought you said in the letters that they don't really pay attention to you. How would he even know?" he wondered.

I ran my fingers through my hair with a wince of discomfort. I was already feeling embarrassed and I hadn't even told him. "It's embarrassing, okay? My dad is delusional. He makes me pee in a cup constantly. He's been talking about me doing drugs for a while now," I mumbled.

And then he was laughing again, and I was smiling. Who knew Luke laughed this much? His laughter was intoxicating, and I found myself wishing I could see it. Did he have dimples like I did? Did his eyes light up? Did the golden specks in his eyes shine when he laughed? Then I realized I was being stupid again. Friends didn't think these types of thoughts about friends. "I have to go now, I'm at work. See you at lunch, right?" he asked hesitantly.

It was a softer tone, a scared tone like he had gotten shy all of a sudden. I smiled and didn't even care that I was nodding even though he couldn't see me. "Yeah, I'll be there. I'll set my alarm for it."

We were quiet for a few minutes, and I closed my eyes as I listened to him inhale, the soft sound of him blowing outwards. "Okay, well... bye, Kins," he said.

I couldn't help but roll the word around in my mind, I remembered he'd called me that before too. It's not the first time someone's called me that, Isabella always does, but coming from him it made my heart flutter in my chest. "Bye, Luke," I replied. We were both quiet for a few seconds, and it seemed we waited for the other to hang up. Finally, I pulled my phone away from my face and hung up. I looked at the phone and noticed with a small smile that it said I had been on the phone for over four hours. I don't think I had ever talked to anyone over four hours on the phone before, not even Isabella when she wanted to complain about the person who tagged over her latest artwork again.

I sent back a quick reply to Isabella while I was still thinking about her. *'Good morning, but I'm not actually awake yet. I'm going back to sleep. I'll talk to you tonight about it, okay? We're still meeting up, right?'*

She sent me back a thumbs up, which told me she was probably stuck in the car with her mom and didn't want her to see our illegal plans. I chuckled, taking a moment to get up and walk to the bathroom, I knew I wouldn't be able to go back to sleep unless I emptied my bladder first. My body felt stiff as I tried to stretch, something the doctors had told me I should do every once in a while to help with the healing process. It hurt like a bitch but I wasn't going to argue with them. They said if my ribs healed wrong I'd have to have surgery and that didn't sound very fun to me.

I was home alone, so I took off my shirt after I finished washing my hands and took a minute to apply the cream to my back the best I could. I struggled to reach most of it before I sloppily rebandaged it. Honestly, it would have been easier if someone had helped me, but there wasn't anyone around except the maid, and I didn't want to bother her, even if I could talk to her. I climbed back into my bed and situated myself. It was hard to go back to sleep in such an uncomfortable position, but the sound of Luke's voice in my ears and the image of him in my mind was enough for me to drift away.

I awoke this time to the sound of my alarm. Normally, I would groan and whine, but I was more alert this time and instantly remembered what I was supposed to do. I had set the alarm to give me enough time to take a quick shower. It was difficult to shower with the stitches on my back, unable to really get wet, but I managed. I went through the motions all over again of applying the cream and bandages, putting the wrap back on, and my wrist brace. I knew I had an appointment tomorrow for my ribs and my wrist, thanks to Mami.

They would probably give me crap over how badly I wrapped them, but when you don't really have a parent that cares, there was only so much you can do by yourself. Well, I guess my parents care to a degree. I get texts from them asking if I'm okay every once in a while, so I guess that counts, right? Maybe if I pretended it counted, it would hurt less. I sighed as I looked around my room. I knew from texts that my parents wouldn't come home today, and Kennedy was sleeping over at her friend's house again.

It was risky to wear short sleeves, but I kind of wanted to. I wanted to wear something other than my hoodie. It was hot out, and I wasn't going to school. My parents wouldn't be around to see the tattoo, so I kind of didn't want to hide under a hoodie. I guess, in a way, I wanted to look nice. I picked a short-sleeved black shirt that had a hood on it. I guess that's progress, right? I wore a pair of black jeans with holes in the knees and slipped on my Converse. I grabbed my wallet and my keys and headed out to my car, looking at the time on my phone to make sure I wasn't late. There was a text message there.

'I'll be going on break in about twenty minutes. Just a warning, sleepyhead.' I grinned, and instant happiness bubbled up inside me.

I unlocked my car and sat in it, texting him back. *'I'll be there in ten unless someone sucked ass at fixing my car.'*

He replied back with a simple *'Ha Ha,'* and I grinned as I pressed the button on my dashboard to open the garage door and backed out. I was glad I had somewhere to go that day and something to do that night, seeing as I'd be home all alone otherwise. Sometimes I could convince Isabella to lie to her mom about having a sleepover with another girl in the art club so I wasn't alone for the night, but it was rare. Mami was really strict and wanted to know the parents and everything, and it wasn't easy to slip anything past her. Plus, Abuela was coming for spring break, so there wouldn't be much leeway most likely.

The car was perfect, with no problems at all as I drove to the garage. I didn't exactly know the location, but Isabella gave me the address and I had it put into my GPS. I found it pretty easily since it was pretty much on the way to school and parked it in one of the few empty spots outside of the shop. It was a fairly small garage, filled with parking spots full of broken-down cars and a few that looked like they actually ran. The one I parked next to was probably the boss's car because there was a sticker on the back window that said *'Like a boss'* with a bunch of poodle decals scattered around it.

I opened the door and cursed under my breath, jumping in surprise as Luke appeared right there out of nowhere. He stood there with a lazy smile on his face, his hair looked more light brown than dark as the sun beat down on it like that. As I stood up, I realized I was close enough to him to see those golden flecks in his eyes. His outfit was a typical mechanic outfit, dirty dark blue overalls. He had a bandana tied around his throat, and I could tell from the crease around his forehead he had been using it a moment ago to hold back his curls. He leaned on the door, his hand held onto the top of the windowsill as he smirked at me. "Looks like your mechanic was awesome," he teased.

I tilted my head to the side, and my hood fell back slightly as I grinned. "Nah, I nearly died twice. The wheels came off, the bumper rolled down the road, and I'm pretty sure I ran over a grandma," I said with a shrug.

He pursed his lips as he took a step back to examine the tires and the bumper that was still obviously there before he let out a soft laugh. Damn, his laugh sounded better in person. "How did the wheels and the bumper come back?" he wondered.

"I welded them on with my magical powers as I was driving at the same time," I replied as I gave him an obvious look. I took a step away from the car and slipped my keys into my pocket as he shut the door for me. "I'm more concerned with your lack of concern for Grandma," I said with a mock disappointed shake of my head at him.

He shrugged as he ran his fingers through his curls and leaned against my car. "I figured if I asked you, I'd become an accomplice."

I shook my head at him with a soft laugh as I leaned against the car beside him. We didn't touch, but we were close enough that if we moved slightly, we would be. I could feel the heat of his body against mine. I wanted to lean over and rest my arm against his so badly. It took everything I had to stop myself. "Why did you give me your number, Luke?" I wondered.

He scoffed as he pulled a cigarette and a lighter out of his pocket. "Just get right to the point, huh?" He wondered. He shook his hair out of his face as he put the cigarette to his lips and started to flick the little ball to light it.

I watched him for a few minutes as he struggled, it was tornado season and the wind was like an angry child that threw tantrums whenever it felt the need, making it difficult for him to get it to light. The wind whipped against his curls as he frowned in frustration. Without a word, I moved to stand in front of him and lifted my hands to his. I cupped mine around his hands. I hadn't touched him, but I was close enough to help him block the wind as it finally lit his cigarette up.

I took a step back as his eyes raked over me, taking me in slowly. I told myself it meant nothing because he was straight. He most likely just noticed I had on something different than usual. His eyes checked out my tattoo but he didn't comment on it. "I guess I'm the type of guy who gets straight to the point," I said with a shrug. Awkwardly I hooked my thumbs against my belt loops, my left hand being ridiculous to work with the brace as he nodded at me.

"I admire that," He spoke after a few minutes. He pulled the cigarette from his lips and turned his head to the side to blow out the smoke so it didn't go into my face. I realized I was still standing in front of him, probably too close, but he hadn't seemed uncomfortable or tried to make me move so I simply stayed there, waiting. "I'm sorry I told you I didn't want to be your friend. I'm not homophobic, I don't care if you're not straight. My father does. This town kind of does, and the world does, well most of it. But I don't. I just care that you're Sparrow, and that's good enough for me."

He looked at his cigarette as he turned it over in his hand and pressed it against his lips once more. I was glad he hadn't looked back at me, because I was ninety-nine percent certain my cheeks were on fire, and he would have been able to notice the moment he looked at me. I tried to calm the beating of my heart as he sighed and gave a soft shrug.

He lifted his eyes to mine and chewed on his lower lip for a second. I realized he had started to rock from his heels to his toes, and thought it was cute that he was so nervous. I wondered if he even realized he was doing it. "Can you give me another chance? To be my friend? I'll probably suck at it. I've never had any that actually really mattered. But I want to try it if you'll let me. I miss you, Kins."

I took a deep breath as I tried to tell myself to calm down. He missed me in a friendly way, it all meant a friend way, nothing more. It wasn't ever going to be anything more.

Distantly I heard a guy call for Luke, and both of us turned to look at him before we looked at each other again. I guessed Luke's breaks weren't very long. I felt bad that I took up his time and couldn't help but wonder if he'd eaten anything besides breakfast. I knew he needed to get back, so instead of standing there taking forever to reply, I smiled at him. It was enough, just to see him breathe out in relief. "I miss you too, Luke," I said with a grin. "What are you doing tonight? Do you want to do something illegal?"

He blinked at me in surprise as he let out a sharp laugh and shook his head. "This is going to be the weirdest friendship ever, but why the hell not? I'll text you. See you later, Kins," He said with a grin as he started to walk away from me. I watched him walk back to the garage and smiled a soft pained smile. I was good enough for him, just the way I was. Even though it meant as a friend, it was good enough for me. It was going to have to be good enough.

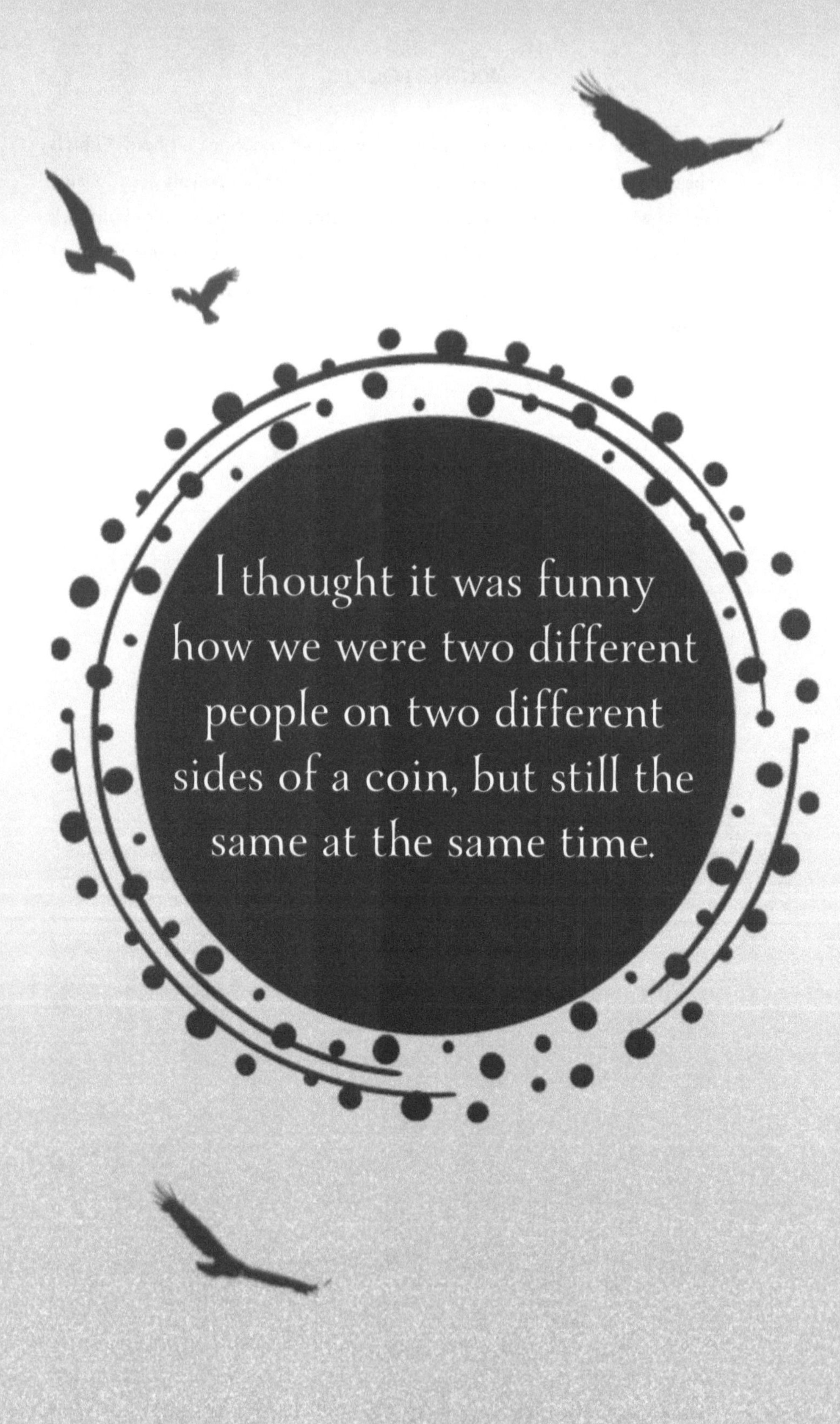
I thought it was funny
how we were two different
people on two different
sides of a coin, but still the
same at the same time.

Chapter 35
Luke

After I got off work, I went straight home to change as I always did. Mom didn't work during the week, so I expected her to be there. There was always a fifty percent chance Shawn would be home, the other fifty percent he was off at his best friend Brett's house. Dad, I wasn't sure what went on with him. He wasn't at work for some reason. He was usually always at work, but he had been home yesterday and today. I was glad that the house was quiet when I got home, and that Dad's car was gone.

Before I took a shower, I had a quick glance around the house, and only Mom was home. She was asleep in her bed, but that didn't surprise me. If he was out of the house drinking, she was in bed asleep or crying. It was their routine, as fucked up as it was. I wondered if one day they would notice how awful it was.

It wasn't until after my shower that I got the text from Kinsley asking for my address. It was strange, the way I gave it to him without a moment's pause. Even Bobby only knew to pick me up on the corner. I never gave out my address, never wanted anyone to come here, because then they'd see all of this. I was glad he texted that he was at my house instead of trying to come inside. "What are you doing here?" I wondered as I looked at Kinsley.

Kinsley had his window rolled down as he looked at me, a sly grin on his face. "I asked you earlier if you wanted to do something illegal," he said matter-of-factly. "Get in, unless you're not allowed to come." There was no judgment there, the way he said it. It made me think of the guys on the team whenever they tried to get me to hang out with them. I probably could have, the number of times my dad barely came home or came home drunk and passed out. He wouldn't have even noticed if I was gone for a day or two. I always used it as an excuse though. I'd tell them my parents wouldn't let me, because I knew how it would play out. We'd be friends, they'd expect me to let them come over and then they'd see my storm. The guys would gripe and whine and say I was a child, they'd tease me for listening to my parents and not trying to go against them, but not Kinsley. He didn't have any sort of judgment on his face, just a shy smile and the healing bruises scattered over his face. I should tell Kinsley no, tell him I wasn't allowed. I should, but I didn't want to.

"I thought you were kidding when you said something illegal," I said instead as I started to walk around the car to the passenger seat. It seemed like when it came to Kinsley, my mouth and my body had a way of doing the complete opposite of what I normally did.

For someone who was injured, he handled it pretty well, then again, the number of times he's been hurt because of Roan and his gang probably made him about as used to being beat up as I was. I sat down and closed the door as I studied him. He had on his large black hoodie again that swallowed up his frame and made him look like a little kid. It was probably the reason why I tended to overlook him before, the fact that he looked so young in that thing. His jeans were the same as before and a soft blush spread over my cheeks as I remembered earlier. I didn't know Kinsley actually looked so different without his hoodie.

I chewed on my lower lip as I shoved the weird strange thoughts out of my mind. Of course he was different, he wore different clothes. I found myself kind of annoyed he was wearing it again, and I didn't really understand why. "I'll never lie to you," he said firmly with a smile at me. It was a simple sentence, but a twinge of unease ran through me as I frowned. It was one my mother used often, and I found myself unable to really believe it.

Lying was what everyone did. My father lied when he told my mother he was sorry, and that he'd try harder. He lied when he told her he wouldn't cheat on her. Shawn and I lied about our lives. My mother lied every time she told me my father loved us. She lied every time she said it would get better. She lied every time she told me she wouldn't lie to me. Or those nights she'd sit there crying as she bandaged yet another wound, and told me she was going to leave him. Those were the nights the lies hurt the worst. Kinsley looked at my house, then at me with a frown. "Don't you have anything darker?"

I looked down at the bright red jacket I had on, my football captain jacket, and shrugged. "I might have a dark green coat somewhere," I mumbled. "Why?"

Kinsley snorted at me as he put the car into park. He unbuckled his seatbelt and leaned over the middle of the seats as he moved things in the backseat around. "Ow, fuck," he mumbled as he searched for whatever he was looking for. The crinkle of grocery bags was loud in the small car and I stared at him in horror as I grabbed his shoulder and forced him to sit back down.

"What the hell are you doing?" I asked as I stared at him with wide eyes. "You're hurt, Kinsley,"

He blinked, his cerulean eyes were so bright in the dark of the car as he studied me. "Trying to find a hoodie," he said as he ignored the second thing I had said. "I know I have an extra somewhere. I have a million of these." That I did not doubt. He was rich, after all. If he was going to wear the same thing every day, at least get a shit ton of the same thing. You'd think the way he moved he didn't feel the pain he was in. He jumped out of the car and went into the back seat to search better, then came back to the front and sat down.

"Here you go, it's really big on me so it should fit you pretty well." He said as he handed me the hoodie. I couldn't help but stare at him. I wondered if he knew he had dimples when he smiled. I looked down at the hoodie he had handed me, then at him, hesitating. A frown slipped onto his lips as he shrugged, a disappointed look on his face as he buckled back up and put the car into drive. "I'm not going to look, Luke. you can take off your jacket." He said with a sigh. We were silent after that, and I wasn't really sure what to say. I hadn't hesitated because I didn't want him to look at me, I had hesitated because I didn't want him to see my wrist.

When we drove down a road that had no street lights on, I tugged off my jacket and pulled on the hoodie. I wasn't sure if he noticed, but he didn't say anything. I guess eventually I'd have to explain, right? For now, I didn't want to. Being friends was exhausting, and I had just started. Maybe I was too broken for this after all.

For someone who listened to music constantly, he hadn't even tried to touch his stereo but I suspected that was because of me. Because we were new at this and didn't know where we stood. I guessed in a way no matter how close we had gotten over the letters, we didn't really know each other after all. I wanted to know more, so much more, and that kind of scared me. He wasn't Sparrow anymore, but at the same time, he was. It was all so confusing. We stopped at a cemetery and I looked at him like he was crazy. The pretty smile was back on his lips again and I nearly sighed in relief to see he wasn't angry. "We're doing something illegal at the cemetery?" I wondered. "Oh God, please tell me we're not robbing graves."

"No," he said with a soft wheeze. "We're getting Izzy. She lives over there, but her mom will kill us all if she sees us here. And it's up to you, but Izzy will probably eat you for sitting in the front. That's your battle,"

I didn't want to fight that battle. She was short and skinny, but I had no doubt in my mind she could have destroyed me very easily if I had aggravated her. I opened the door and got out as he snickered, and came face to face with Isabella. She wore all black as well and eyeballed me, her eyebrow cocked as she frowned. Her blue streaks stuck out from underneath a black beanie as she pulled the bag she had on off her shoulder.

"That's right, this is my seat," she said as she snapped her fingers at me. I smirked as she assumed I'd just hold the door for her as she slipped in. Instead of shutting it for her, I got into the back and tried not to snicker as she had to turn around and shut the door herself. "So, Pretty Boy, were you going to mention the extra addition?" She wondered.

Kinsley had lowered his hood, his fingers ran absently through the blond strands as he focused his bright blue eyes on me. For a moment I was lost in her comment. Pretty Boy, she had said. I didn't think I could really deny that, seeing as I thought he was a girl at first until he lowered his hood. Most people wouldn't have accepted a nickname like that but it seemed like Kinsley took just about everything in stride. "Yeah, about that," he shrugged as he continued to stare at me. For a moment I wasn't really sure what was going on. I couldn't look away from that intense gaze, not until he pulled his eyes away first. "Surprise," he said with a twitch of his lip to Isabella as she huffed at him.

Kinsley started the car again as I bit the inside of my cheek and tried not to laugh at how frustrated she looked. "Fine, he can be your number two, okay?" She glared at Kinsley. "But I'm number one, Pretty Boy, me."

If she hadn't been a human I'd have assumed she was a snake with the way she looked back and forth, crouched weirdly on the seat. I could almost hear her hiss at me and I had to bite my cheek even harder to hold in the laughter, knowing she wouldn't appreciate it right now. "I don't know," He said with a sigh.

I wanted to press my hand against his mouth, with the way he was egging her on. Didn't he see she was going to fuck us all up? She had a freaking shoe in her hand and I had no idea when she had grabbed that. Isabella was like a ninja snake. He started to drive, and even from back here, I could see the smile flutter over his lips. "I kind of like having you guys fighting over me,"

Nearly a second later, he howled in pain as the car nearly went into a tree, and despite how fucking dangerous it all was, I was laughing, and they were laughing, and I wondered if this was what it felt like to have friends. I lifted my eyes to the rearview mirror as we all started to calm down. Kinsley stopped at a red light, and his eyes met mine in the mirror.

For a fleeting moment, it was just us in this little bubble of happiness. Two heartbeats, but for a brief moment, it was one, once more. Then his lips twitched, and the laughter returned. Izzy was confused as Kinsley and I burst out laughing once more. I kind of liked this feeling, whatever it was. I never wanted it to end.

We ended up at the park in a spot that was farthest away from the actual park. It was the spot most of the kids went to hook up since it was close enough to school to get away with it during lunchtime as long as you got back in time. I was disgusted, the number of used condom wrappers scattered around the dimly lit-up space was enough to make me want to gag. At least when I lost my virginity, it was at Alison's house, not in a car in a spot everyone went to.

I opened my mouth, ready to ask what we were doing here, and gasped in surprise. Kinsley had managed to slip in between the seats once more, his hands reached into the bags at my feet as he lifted his cerulean eyes to look at me. I realized I wasn't entirely breathing. His face was closer than I expected it to be, his eyes shined so brightly in the darkness. A soft crimson smear spread over his cheeks as he lowered his eyes and grabbed the bag at my feet before he went back into his chair.

I pressed my hand against my chest and tried to figure out why it felt like birds suddenly took flight in my chest. *Dangerous*, I thought to myself. *But why?* I barely even noticed as he handed me something until they opened the doors and got out. I looked down at my hand and saw a white sturdy-looking mask. I got out of the car to follow them, confused.

"What's going on? Why a mask?" Kinsley and Isabella put their masks on expertly as if they did this nearly every day. Kinsley handed me a pair of clear plastic glasses as he slipped a pair onto his own face in the process, and I wondered if it was strange to tell him they looked good on him. He smiled as he pulled his hood up over his face. I barely knew him, and it was strange the fact that I could tell he was smiling underneath a mask and clear glasses, but I could see it all the same.

There was something addicting about Kinsley's smile. His dimples seemed to draw out the shine in his eyes even more than usual, and it made everything seem so unimportant compared to what was going on. It was like none of my problems mattered, as long as I was near him, as long as he was smiling. *Protect him*, a part of me said. *Protect him at all costs.* I didn't know what part of me was saying that, but as I watched him smile once more, I couldn't help but agree. For some reason, it was all I wanted to do.

"So you don't get sick from the fumes," he answered mysteriously as we crossed over a small barely-used bridge to the bank that was next to the park. I knew this bank because it was the one my parents used. Isabella talked about different hues of colors, her bag swung around and around with large rolled-up pieces of paper and plastic, and I couldn't keep up with most of what they were saying. My heart pounded in my chest as I followed them, unsure of what was going on. I wanted to ask them if we were robbing the bank, but I didn't want them to call me stupid for asking. I realized I really cared what they thought of me.

At the same time, I didn't think they'd do something all that dangerous. Maybe we weren't really doing anything illegal at all, maybe he just said it to tease me, to see my reaction when they led me to something simple like a picnic or to gaze at the stars. I had mostly convinced myself that this was the case until we stopped next to the side of the bank, and Kinsley started to pull out canisters.

Isabella hummed as she pulled her drawings out, large rolled-up papers that had plastic stencil-looking things wrapped inside them. She grabbed a roll of duct tape out of her bag as Kinsley looked at me, that alluring sparkle in his intense gaze, as he handed me a canister. "Do you want to try it?" He asked.

I stared at the canister, then at Kinsley as Isabella obliviously started to duct tape her stencil to the wall. It was large, and beautiful from what I could tell. A girl with a lovely flowing dress ran in a field of flowers as petals danced around her. If it was anyone else but Kinsley, it might have sounded like peer pressure. But he hadn't forced anything, he hadn't taunted me. He didn't wave it around and tease me. He simply stood there and waited with a patient look on his face underneath the cover.

Graffiti, I realized. They were the taggers that put up all that artwork around town. I remember my father complained at one point earlier this month about how useless and annoying he thought it was. I realized as I watched Isabella start to spray paint, that it was far from useless. It was just another form of art, after all. Illegal, yes. But it didn't hurt anyone, not really.

I grabbed the canister from Kinsley and he chuckled softly at me as he grabbed another for himself and twirled it with his fingers. "What next?" I wondered as I watched Kinsley start to freehand what looked to be the start of a tree. He turned to look at me as he started to shake the bottle, the clink sound was loud in the quiet of the night. "Are we going to murder someone next?"

He was grinning again, that grin that I could feel rather than see. It was like a part of me was always going to know him because I had already connected with him before I had even met him. In a way, it was kind of like it was impossible to stay away from him, impossible to be mad at him. A half couldn't stay away from what made it whole. Maybe it was strange to describe it like that because we were both guys, but with Kinsley it just made sense. "We leave our murdering for Tuesdays," he said casually, so very casually that if I didn't feel the smile on his face then I would have thought he was serious.

Isabella started to laugh then, drawing Kinsley and my eyes away from each other. "You two are too similar to be near each other." She said as she shook her head at us. "*Bicho raro,*" she muttered.

I laughed out loud as Kinsley looked at her with a confused look on his face, before looking at me in surprise. "She called us a weirdo," I told him, grinning. "I take Spanish class,"

She smiled the widest smile as she leaned forward and patted the wall next to her picture. "I like you. Come over here, Curly," she said as I laughed at her.

"So I'm Curly, and Kinsley is Pretty Boy?" I wondered as I moved around Kinsley to stand on the other side of Isabella. I was worried I was going to ruin her picture so I did something small and simple, something that mostly looked like shit because I couldn't even draw with a pencil let alone a spray can.

She nodded, her head tilted to the side. "He is pretty though, isn't he?" she asked as she wagged her eyebrows at me. I looked away from her, unsure how to reply to that question as she laughed. "Unless you'd like to be called something else? How about Green?"

I smiled then, I knew she mentioned it because of the letters. Although we hadn't exchanged letters in a while, just the mention of the pen name I used was enough to remind me of the past. For a second, all of Kinsley's words spilled into my mind and rolled lazily around me as I remembered them. On the one hand, I missed the letters, but on the other, I didn't. It was hard to miss them when I had Sparrow right here next to me. I had been so scared to meet Sparrow, so scared of them finding out where I lived, about my life.

I looked at Kinsley and saw him watch me with an unreadable look on his face, I realized none of it mattered. The road was rough, but in the end, it worked out alright for us. Maybe not lovers, but friends, all the same. "I like Green," Kinsley said, his eyes shined for a moment as we stared at each other. Then he looked at the wall again, his hand effortlessly sliding back and forth as a stream of dark brown spilled from his canister to detail the tree he drew, and I was unable to move.

I was unable to turn away, to breathe for a minute, until Isabella's soft singing to a familiar Spanish song tore my eyes away from the side of Kinsley's face. Because he said he liked my name, but at the same time, it could have meant he liked me, too. I shook my head as I went back to my horrible drawing and I tried to clear the thoughts from my mind. *He's a boy*, I told myself. He might be Sparrow, but he was always going to be a boy.

'Protect him', a part of me said. 'Protect him at all costs.'

Chapter 36
Luke

My heart raced, and my breath was louder than it had ever been before. Some might think it was from the running. Maybe in a way, it was. My feet slapped against the pavement as the soft yells of those behind us filled the crisp night air. I was used to running; it was what I did almost every day. Football practice always had us running, and in the mornings when I could force myself to get up early, I went running before school. Running was something I was comfortable with. Maybe my heart raced like the wings of a thousand hummingbirds in my chest because of the pounding sound of multiple pairs of boots that slapped against the pavement behind us. Maybe it was from the sound of hoarse voices that called for us and screamed at us. *That was it*, I told myself. That had to be it. It definitely wasn't because Kinsley's hand was wrapped around my wrist as he pulled me behind him. Isabella ran right behind me with a softly muttered curse that spilled from her lips.

The sound of crinkled paper behind me told me she had tried to run and shove her stencil into her bag at the same time. A few clinks from various spray paint canisters rolled around in her bag as she muttered another curse. Her shoes were probably the loudest of them all since she had decided to wear flip-flops. I wondered who in their right mind would wear flip-flops to spray paint a wall late at night, knowing there was a chance we'd have to run. Then again, I had started to realize just how chaotic these two were. Especially when Kinsley turned back around to look at me, his cerulean eyes looked darker like the ocean in the dark of the dimly lit alley.

I found it hard not to stare at those eyes, to want to anchor myself down in the calm ocean that was Kinsley and stay there for as long as possible. I could feel his grin again, despite the glasses and the mask that covered most of his face, and I wondered just how crazy these two were. Isabella was more concerned about her stencils, and Kinsley grinned as if this was the most amazing thing ever, while behind us were two police officers who chased us down the road. "Stop! Get back here!" One of the police officers yelled.

Kinsley snorted, and I wondered what he was made of. For someone who always looked so tiny, who wasn't on any sports teams, he ran without much difficulty. He wasn't even breathing hard. Neither was I, but I was a football player. "Yeah, do they think we're going to stop and turn around and hold out our hands? Maybe we should stop and do the macarena, give them a show," he said casually.

I did notice he was slightly breathless, so at least he was somewhat human. I had started to wonder about his sanity, but as a soft laugh spilled from my lips unexpectedly, I realized maybe I should worry about mine as well. Suddenly, Isabella winced, a soft whine came from her as she started to breathe heavier. At least one of them had started to act like a normal non-sporty human. Maybe when Kinsley said earlier that he used his magic powers, he wasn't joking.

I pulled my wrist out of Kinsley's hold and turned to look at Isabella as I ran backward for a minute. She threw her hands up in the air as I looked at the police who followed us, and how much they had started to fall behind. If we kept up this pace or even went a little faster, we'd lose them. "Seriously!? Show off," she muttered with a glare at me as she pressed her hand to her chest and closed her eyes tightly.

Her shoes were like a gunshot going off every time they slapped against the ground, and I did the only thing I could think of to both help her and stop the sound that echoed through the alley. I scooped her up into my arms and ignored her startled squeal as I draped her unceremoniously over my shoulder. "Sorry," I muttered, even though I didn't feel all that sorry. "Can you run faster?" I asked Kinsley.

He looked back at me, a grin lit up his eyes as he chuckled at Isabella's angry flaring state. She had started to talk fast, but I believe she was calling me a dumbass in Spanish right now. "Yeah, let's go!" He said as he picked up speed. The clink of the cans in the bags he held and the bag Isabella had on was louder as we ran, and I wondered once more as I followed him what he was made of.

He ran like this was normal and he didn't have two broken ribs. However as we turned a corner and Kinsley grabbed my arm once more to pull me into a small little stairwell that led up to an abandoned apartment building, I started to see just how affected he was. It was narrow here, and I let Isabella slide down me as Kinsley nearly collapsed in my arms. His breathing was irregular as he clutched onto my shirt and Isabella muttered under her breath. She pressed her hand against his mouth as the police ran past us. "Damn," Kinsley breathed as he took deep ragged breaths. "I was doing so well too."

"Pendejo," Isabella spat with a glare at him. "You, carry him this time, not me." She said as she marched out of the stairwell.

I rolled my eyes at her as I looked at Kinsley, who shook his head no and tried to regain himself. "No, it's okay, I'm fine," he said between short pained breaths.

"Shush," I replied as I leaned down and scooped Kinsley into my arms gently. "It's not the first time, and I guess it's probably not going to be the last time I end up carrying you since you guys are fucking crazy. Do you get chased by the police a lot?" I wondered as he let out a soft breathless laugh.

Isabella lit up the walkway back with her phone as if she was looking for something. "Only on Wednesdays," Kinsley said casually.

I shook my head at him as Isabella grabbed her hat off of the ground and smacked it against her leg as she glared at me. I grinned sheepishly at her, I guessed she must have dropped it when I picked her up. "Seems like you kept a pretty busy weekly schedule filled with illegal activities. What's on the agenda for Thursday? Scoring some drugs and blowing up houses?" I wondered.

He laughed again, and I looked down automatically. His hand gripped my hoodie tightly as I pulled him closer to me. It was strange, the way that I had picked Isabella up like a sack of potatoes without a pause but when it came to Kinsley I seemed to be automatically more careful with him. Then again, he was slightly broken right then. "Nah, we save that for Friday. That way if we end up in jail we have the whole weekend for Isabella to flirt us out," he replied.

"I heard that! *Tonto*!" she shouted. I snickered as Kinsley looked up at me with a confused look on his face.

"Dumbass," I said, grinning. "She called you a dumbass."

We made our way back to the car without seeing the police again and were glad to see they hadn't checked the park yet. Though of course that meant we couldn't linger. It wasn't exactly too late for cars to be out to make us look suspicious, but if they saw us driving around there they would probably stop us to see if we were the same kids they had been chasing. "What do we do? I can't take your car home, Kinsley. My Abuela is at the house a few days early. She'll tear me a new one if she sees me driving without a license. But you're not in a good state to drive after running like that,"

I lowered Kinsley to the ground and instantly grabbed his left bicep as he swayed for a second. I already knew he was going to say he was fine, so instead, I took his keys out of his hand and sighed. "I'll drive you home, Isabella, and then I'll make sure he gets home."

"Do you even have your license?" She asked with a glare at me as she made her way to the passenger seat.

I opened the back door for Kinsley as he got in. As usual, he seemed to just go along with it all in stride as we made decisions about his car. "Do you?" I countered. She was silent as she stuck her tongue out at me and I grinned. "I drive cars constantly, I have to. We have to test the cars before we give them to the owners. I would have tested Kinsley's car if you hadn't gotten there so early."

"You were late, I got there on time," she muttered as she flipped me off. What a charming girl she was. Kinsley laughed softly from the backseat as I followed Isabella's instructions back to the graveyard near her house. "Be careful, Pretty Boy. Don't forget to take your meds, and clean your wounds. You need to learn how to wrap it and bandage it better, I told you I could talk to your maid about it. She's very nice, I'm sure she wouldn't mind," Isabella said with a huff as she got out of the car.

Kinsley got out, wrapped his arms around her, and laughed. "It's fine, Izzy. I know you're going to be busy with your Abuela but text me, okay? I'll be bored and lonely at home until the break is over. Love you," he pulled his mask and his glasses off to kiss her on the cheek.

"Love you too," she said as she lowered his hood and ruffled his hair. It was easy to see why the school was so confused about them, half the time I was as well. "Be nice to our Pretty Boy," Isabella said with a glare at me as Kinsley took her spot in the front seat and passed her the bag she had brought with her earlier.

I nodded at her as I rolled the words around and around in my mouth once more. How strange it was that she called him that, although it was true. The more I thought about it, the more I realized he was the prettiest boy I had ever seen. Then again, it's not like I looked at guys like that. *'Faggot,'* my father's voice echoed through my mind as I clenched my teeth tightly. I gripped the steering wheel tighter, and if Kinsley noticed he didn't comment on it.

I had to drive past my house to get to Kinsley's. I didn't know which house in the fancy gated community was his, but I knew he lived there with all the other rich kids. I stopped the car across the street, a churning feeling in my stomach as I looked at my father's car. It hadn't been there before. I was hesitant to come home, later on, to sleep there, knowing he was there. I guess the more I spent with Kinsley, with the calm, the more I realized just how much I hated the storm.

"Stay at my house for the night. I'll sleep on the floor," Kinsley said as he broke the silence. I looked at him, his eyes lit up in the darkness of the car as I chewed on my lower lip. I wondered if it was okay to do things friends did. To sleep over at each other's house was something friends did, but then they'd expect to come over too, and there was no way in hell I wanted Kinsley to come over. I was already embarrassed, if he even stepped foot inside he'd come face to face with the beautifully intricate designs of my father's fist in the wall. "I won't touch you, Luke. I know you're straight, I respect your sexuality," he added after a few minutes of silence.

I could hear the hurt in his voice and wondered how I could fix it. He probably was annoyed that I was so hesitant about everything. He didn't understand, but that wasn't his fault. How could I make him understand this? "I'm not vain, Kins. I don't think that you're attracted to me just because you're not straight. I'm just..." I took a deep breath, unsure what to even say. As I stared at his patient gaze, I realized that it was the same. The same as the letters, except face to face. It was Sparrow, and Green never lied to Sparrow. "I'm worried if I do normal friend things with you, you're going to want to come over to my house and you can't. You just... can't."

He was quiet, and I was scared. It was the closest I'd ever gotten to explaining my life to anyone. I was worried I had fucked all of this up before it had even started. I'd never been this scared to lose something in my life, and that in itself was probably the hardest part of all of this. "I understand, Luke. I won't pressure you to go to your house. But you can come to mine anytime you want. I won't ever make you do something you don't want to do. I promise," he said with a soft smile.

I felt it again, the flutter of wings as they brushed against my chest. I wasn't sure if it was normal, but then again, this was the first time I had a friend. A best friend even. Maybe that's what it meant. Maybe this was normal, for best friends. We might have only talked face to face for a short amount of time, but the number of weeks we spent as we got to know each other by letters was enough to know that he was the most important person to me; a best friend.

"Give me five minutes?" I asked. He nodded as I got out of the car and ran to the house. I stood on the porch and paused, my hand hovered over the doorknob as I took a minute to examine the outside. The flowers were beautifully placed in the planters and the welcome mat was swept, a task my mom forced herself to do daily. All of the outside maintenance was something she forced herself to do so the neighbors didn't notice that no matter how beautiful the house looked outside, it wasn't actually a home inside. I pressed my ear against the door and cringed. I could hear the soft crash of glass and the screams between my parents. I knew from how loud it was they were right there in the living room, and if I opened the door, I'd be caught up in it.

I let go of the doorknob and jogged around the house to my room, grabbed the ladder I used to get the leaves out of the gutters, and started to climb up quietly until I got to my room. I opened the window with a soft groan and slipped into the window with a mild pain that spread through my body from the last beating I had. It didn't take me long to pack a small duffle bag filled with some clothes and grab my charger. I hesitated over the folder I had hidden under the mattress, the folder that held all of the letters and drawings, but I didn't want to leave it here in case my father came up here to search for me.

My mother screamed back again and I was slightly impressed she had started to hold her ground. I realized as I listened to them, that she had defended me last time before I blacked out as well. I wasn't sure what it meant, but if it meant she had started to really see how awful he was, I was all for it. Maybe the next time she promised me she was going to leave him, it wouldn't be a lie.

If Kinsley noticed I had slipped around the side of the house instead of through the front door he didn't say anything as I got into the car and drove to his house. It was like he already knew, and that was what worried me the most. He seemed to know everything about me, without me even needing to say it. Well, not everything. I looked down at my wrist, even though it was hidden under the hoodie, and clenched my jaw.

To say I wasn't slightly excited about this would be a lie. I never expected I'd have a real friend. That I'd have sleepovers and hang out with them, I was excited that I was finally getting the experience. I had expected his house to be a mansion, and I wasn't surprised to find I was mostly right. Of course it wasn't really a mansion, not like the kind that the celebrities spent millions of dollars on just for a handful of people to live there and get a bunch of maids to clean fifty rooms that were never used. It was extravagant, though. His parents had a large fence, one of those gates that opened with a button on the dashboard, and another button to open the garage. So much security even though all of these homes were nestled into a gated community already.

I was amazed by everything I saw, from the fancy cars hidden under coverings to the house that had been meticulously cleaned inside and out. I wondered why Kinsley seemed so uncomfortable about it. At least his house wasn't filled with broken glass and holes. We kicked off our shoes and he led me up the stairs and down the hall towards his room. There was one giant family photo, formal, but the rest of the frames on the walls were filled with artwork. I thought most of them were tacky, to be honest. Kinsley's art was much better, but it wasn't my place to point it out. It was late, and we had both had dinner before we decided to be illegal, so we weren't really hungry. "Do you want to take a shower first, or should I?" Kinsley asked as he grabbed a pill bottle off of his nightstand and popped a few in. I cringed as I noticed he swallowed it dry without anything to drink.

"You should take a shower first, Kins. I'll wait until you're finished," I told him as I shut the bedroom door behind me. He looked exhausted but gave a soft nod as he yawned. I watched him walk into the bathroom, only to stop and turn around with a blush on his face. He grabbed some pajamas out of his drawer almost like an afterthought and then shut the bathroom door behind him, leaving me alone in his room as the sound of water spilled through the door.

I was surprised by how little he had, compared to the rest of the house. He had two dressers, and I was sure the closet was a large walk-in thing and the bathroom was spectacular. Besides the bookshelf, a TV, a small couch, and the large bed with nightstands there wasn't much else. There was an impressive L-shaped desk with a nice gaming computer and a small easel propped on the other side, a large filing cabinet next to it, but that was about it. I had already figured out Kinsley didn't really care about being rich, but I had expected he'd at least try harder than this. For someone who loved to draw and music, I assumed his walls would be covered in artwork and bands, maybe even quotes from books or something artistic like that. Instead, his walls were plain, everything was mostly bare.

The water turned off and I walked to the bookshelf and ran my fingers over the books. They were all various art books, different styles, and techniques, along with his own portfolios. I wanted to look through them, but as my fingers hovered over them, I realized it was wrong to do so without asking first. Suddenly I heard a soft curse and a loud bang come from the bathroom and without thinking I moved to the door and yanked it open. "Are you okay?"

I realized how stupid I was the moment I looked at him. I had startled him, he had turned sideways to face me. My mind didn't connect the way it should have. I simply heard him curse in pain and something loud drop, and I reacted. *We're both guys*, I told myself as my eyes quickly roamed over his half-naked body, before I averted my gaze to the floor. *It isn't weird*, I tried to tell myself.

I saw guys half or fully naked all the time. We got dressed in the locker rooms, and took showers in the open stalls, it wasn't strange to see a naked guy in sports. But this was Kinsley, and for some reason, a knot tightened in my chest as a soft blush floated to my cheeks. I hadn't seen much before I looked away. Black sweatpants that hung low on his hips, the hint of gray boxers. He had the towel in his arms and a tube of something white at his feet told me that had been what he had dropped. The tension between us was as thick as the steam in the bathroom and I refused to look at him, even though I knew he was looking at me. "I'm fine," he said softly, hesitantly. "Just trying to deal with my back."

I instantly felt anger rise inside me because I knew he had those wounds because of Roan. Because no one ever did anything about him, and let him do whatever he wanted. As long as he didn't kill someone, then he'd probably get away with anything in this small town. "Let me help you. My mom is a nurse, and I've gotten used to it-" *Because of my Dad*, I wanted to say, but let the words fall off my tongue.

I looked at him after a moment of silence, his eyes wary as they stared through me. "You'll see my scars," his voice was a soft hesitant whisper. "It doesn't look good."

"It doesn't matter what I think, right? You're still you. You're fine just how you are," I told him. I walked over to him as he turned around slowly, his eyes squeezed tight as I stood behind him. He shook, slightly scared as I stood behind him.

His body was filled with tension as I leaned down and grabbed the cream from where he had dropped it on the ground, and looked at his back again. I applied the cream to all of the places he had stitches and bandaged them appropriately. I noticed the wrap on the counter and I grabbed it without asking and moved closer to him as I started to wrap it around his ribs. He sucked in a deep breath as my fingers ghosted over his skin, goosebumps rose as I moved closer, and I found myself fascinated by them.

I lingered as I stared down at the shape of his neck and his shoulder blades, and forced myself not to touch him. *Pretty Boy*, Isabella called him. He really was pretty after all. Kinsley moved away from me when he realized I was finished. He grabbed his shirt and slipped it on awkwardly. "Thank you," he said as he started to walk out of the bathroom for me to have a turn. Before he shut the door, he turned around to look at me, his fingers fiddled with the bottom of his shirt as his eyes refused to look into mine. "It does matter, by the way," he said as he sucked in a deep breath and let it out slowly. "What you think matters to me," he paused for only a second before he shut the door and left me alone.

I was lost in thoughts as I took a shower and dried off. I put new clothes on from my bag Kinsley must have flung into the bathroom for me while I had been in the shower. I couldn't stop thinking about his words as I brushed my hair in front of the mirror that was partially covered in steam. He cared what I thought. I wondered why. I didn't think anyone had ever cared what I thought before. Maybe my exes, but they left so easily without a fight, it made it seem like they didn't care as much as they had let on, to begin with.

I couldn't understand why he cared. Maybe he was just saying that? But this was Kinsley, and Kinsley didn't just say things without meaning them. I wondered if he was simply confused because I wasn't anything special for anyone to care about. I was a piece of paper that was ripped to shreds over and over again. I tried to tape the pieces together but nothing ever worked. I wondered how many times the pieces would rip until I couldn't find a way to put them together again.

When I got out of the bathroom, Kinsley was already on the bed asleep. I assumed whatever he took was for nighttime, to help him sleep. I locked his bedroom door in case someone came and was freaked out by my presence. Gently I picked Kinsley up, slid him under the covers, and tucked him in. Maybe it was strange, to take care of him so easily when I barely knew him, but I didn't feel like I barely knew him. I felt like I'd known him all my life.

I turned off his light and tugged on the long-sleeved shirt I had on nervously. I stood there and chewed on my lip as I watched him sleep. The Moonlight lit up his blond hair and made his face have a sparkling gleam to it as his lips parted, and his eyelashes danced on his cheeks. I wasn't sure if it was allowed, but I slipped under the covers as well, making sure to be a distance away from him in this large bed. Maybe Kinsley intended for one of us to sleep somewhere else but I was too tired to care right now. I was exhausted by everything that happened today, in a good way. It was so much I normally didn't do, but I didn't regret any of it. Being near Kinsley was calming. It felt natural, and I found myself gravitating toward him without even trying.

I laid there on my side and stared at Kinsley as he slept, lost in my thoughts again. If Kinsley was the calm, then I was the wind. I wondered if it was okay for me to be here. If I was too much for him. I wondered if I should leave before I blew through him and upset his calm with the raging howling storm that was inevitably building inside me.

If I was a good person, I'd leave. I'd stay away, far away from the safety and the calm that was Kinsley. I wouldn't want to burden him, to cause him any more trouble. I sighed as I leaned forward and moved a piece of his hair off of his face. I guessed in the end, I wasn't a good person after all; because I couldn't imagine a tomorrow without Kinsley in it.

Maybe I was the storm after all, I couldn't help but think as tears started to spill down my face and settle silently in the pillow below me. Maybe in the end, I'd always be just like my parents. To wreak havoc and destroy everything in its wake. "You have to be strong enough to handle everything, Kinsley. Because I can't walk away, not again. You have to be strong enough to handle the storm. I'm sorry I'm such a burden."

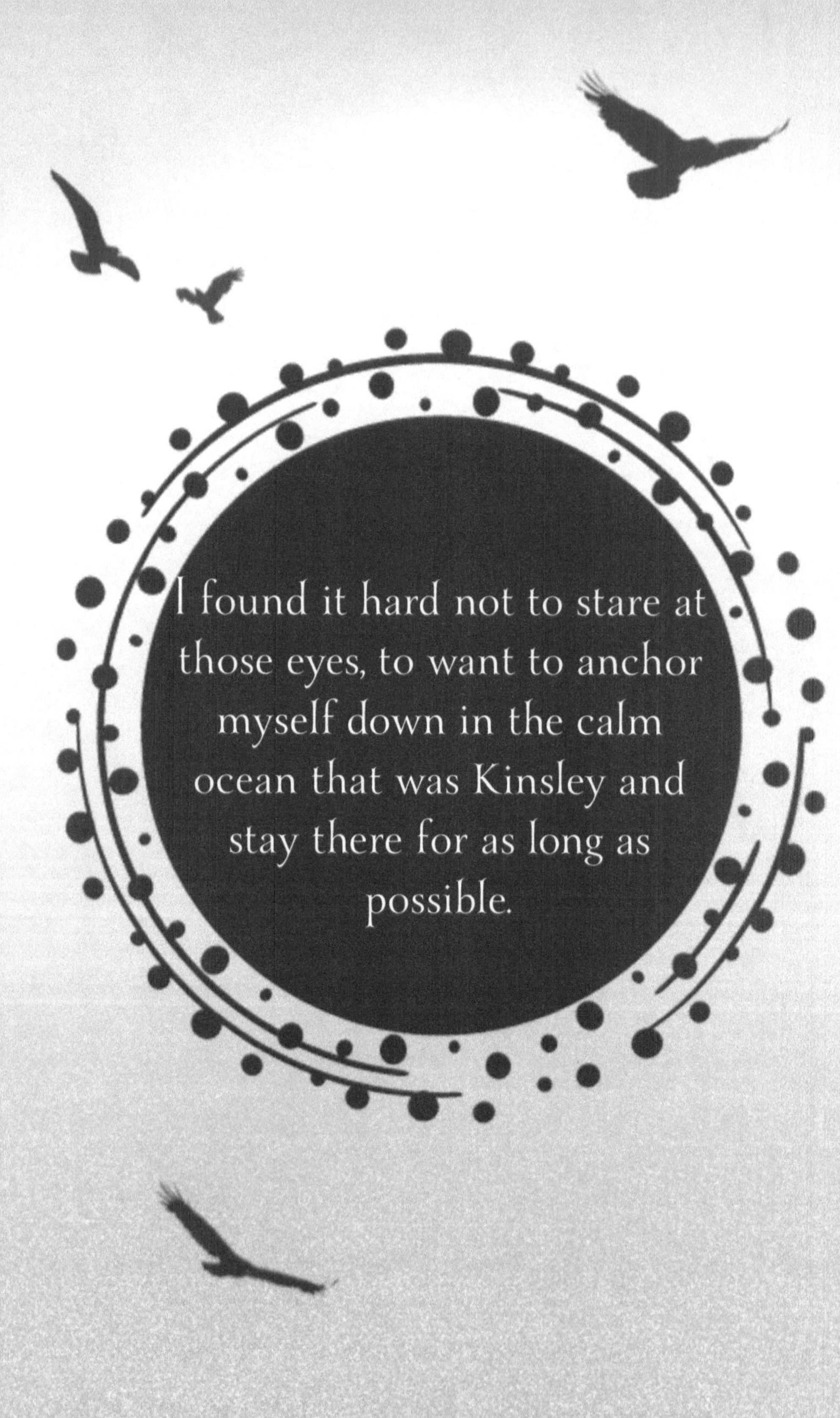
I found it hard not to stare at those eyes, to want to anchor myself down in the calm ocean that was Kinsley and stay there for as long as possible.

Chapter 37
Kinsley

I woke up to the sound of birds chirping outside my window, along with a strange alarm that I had never heard before. As I opened my eyes, I couldn't fully comprehend what I was seeing. The birds had taken refuge on my windowsill about a month ago, and while I hadn't complained initially, now that their eggs had hatched, the noise was becoming unbearable. Isabella had told me to just ignore it, assuring me that the baby birds would eventually leave the nest and I wouldn't have to see or hear them anymore. She said I would miss them, but at this point, I was ready to push the entire nest off the sill.

Of course, I would never actually do that, but that didn't mean I didn't want to. The alarm sounded distant and muffled, and for a moment, I thought it was my sister's phone. She still had to go to school for the rest of the week, but I didn't. I had made sure to turn off my alarm the day before, hoping to sleep in.

I tried to move, but I realized I couldn't. When I opened my eyes to see why, I gasped silently. I was lying on my side, my left side thankfully, since my right side had broken ribs. My left arm was stretched out, and my fingers felt numb and lacked blood flow. It felt strange, and despite blocking the blood flow, I kept squeezing my pinky finger and thumb together to try and regain feeling. There were soft brown curls pressed against my nose and brushed against my lips. I could smell a mixture of my hair wash, body wash, and something else that I never wanted to stop smelling. Something amazing, something Luke.

Luke lay on my left bicep, his forehead pressed against my lips and his nose curved around my throat. His even breaths tickled my collarbone, and my right hand trembled as I fought the urge to move it. I resisted the temptation to run my fingers through his hair or pull him closer to me. His hands were tangled in my shirt, intertwined like vines in a bush, to the point where I couldn't tell where my shirt started and his fingers ended. His stomach pressed against my lower half, and I tilted my hips slightly backward, hoping he wouldn't wake up and feel how excited this made me. My heart pounded, my eyes blinked rapidly, and I was torn between the desire to hold him closer and the need to cry.

We're just friends, I told myself, as my right hand hovered over his messy curls. *Just friends*. A single tear slid down my cheek, and I gently wiped it away, trying not to move or wake him. My hand lingered in the air, my fingertips brushing against the tips of his curls, as I struggled to keep my breathing steady and my chest relaxed. He shifted slightly, and I quickly lowered my hand, closing my eyes tightly to pretend I was still asleep, desperately attempting to even out my breathing. I was afraid he could feel how fast my heart was racing beneath my shirt. He let out another sigh and pulled himself even closer to me. I hissed under my breath as I felt something hard against my thigh before I moved my leg away.

'*It's nothing,*' I told myself. All the boys woke up like that at some point or another. It meant nothing. Another tear rolled down my cheek, and I wiped it away quickly. Once again, my hand lingered over his body. '*Don't do it,*' I warned myself. I sighed as my hand fell to rest on Luke's waist. I was disappointed in myself as I lightly brushed my fingers against a small patch of exposed skin. His long-sleeved shirt had ridden up, revealing a portion of his body.

I forced myself not to look as my fingers slowly traced the curve of his hip and brushed against his abs. I trembled, my body throbbed, and he began to stir. I quickly moved my hand back to rest against my own hip as he shifted again. He held onto me tighter, pressing his body against mine, and I bit my lower lip as hard as I could when I felt him move against my leg. A soft, breathy sound escaped his mouth against my collarbone.

I wanted to curl up in a corner and disappear. I wanted this, I wanted him, but I knew it meant nothing to him. It was just a boy experiencing pleasure in his sleep, nothing more. It wasn't the first time it had happened, and it wouldn't be the last. We couldn't control it. We woke up like this all the time, especially as teenagers, and it meant nothing. We could react and feel pressure while asleep, and it didn't mean anything because we weren't aware of what was happening.

He didn't know what he was doing, and I didn't blame him for any of it. But that didn't stop the tears from flowing. My right hand was against my face again as I tried to stop the tears with the sleeve of my shirt. I tried not to wake him as my body shook slightly from my silent sobs. I adjusted my hips so that my lower half wouldn't touch him, despite how much he continued to move towards me in his sleep. It meant nothing to him, but it meant everything to me.

The alarm sounded again as I wiped my tears. My right arm fell back onto my hip as Luke started to stiffen next to me. I knew he was awake by the way his breathing changed and I forced myself to be still. I forced my breathing to be even, my eyes to close, and to stop crying. He took a second to wake, I could tell by the way his body stiffened, then relaxed, before stiffening again in surprise. His fingers untangled from my shirt, and a soft confused sound came from him as he tried to figure out where he was and what was going on.

"What the heck?" He breathed out with a deep rasp as his fingers slid down my chest. I bit the inside of my cheek as I struggled to keep my breath even. He lazily lifted his hand back up my chest, then gently pushed himself away from me. He still laid on my arm though, just far enough away that he was probably looking at me. I realized the strange alarm was probably his. It stopped going off again as his fingers stayed pressed gently against my chest, and I could feel how red his face was from the way he laid on my arm as he finally pulled his lower half away from my leg. "Fuck," he mumbled under his breath.

Don't panic, I wanted to tell him. *It means nothing to you, I understand. It's fine.* But instead, I stayed quiet. I kept my breathing even, and I pretended to be asleep because I didn't want him to feel embarrassed about this. It wasn't his fault his body reacted the normal way it did for guys. My breath nearly stopped when his fingers slipped into my hair to gently brush the strands from my cheek and my forehead. I tried so hard not to shake, not to cry, as he touched me.

I never wanted him to stop touching me. It was going to be so hard being his friend, knowing that he was straight. Maybe as long as we stayed friends it would be okay. I could hold my feelings in check, and I got to keep him by my side. Eventually, I'd fall in love with someone else, right? Then I wouldn't have to worry anymore. As long as I got to keep him in any way, shape, or form, then it was worth it.

"Kinsley," he called softly. I couldn't quite stop the tremor that rolled through me at the sound of his deep, raspy morning voice. "Kins, wake up," His fingers were pressed against my shoulder now as he shook me carefully. He lifted himself off of my arm and I knew I had to stop pretending.

I forced my body to go through the motions of waking up, my right hand lifted to my eyes to rub them as I blinked my eyes slowly to open them. I nearly had a heart attack.

I didn't expect him to be that close to me and I stared with wide eyes, my heart raced as he chuckled. He leaned on his elbow to hold his body weight off of my arm as I slowly pulled it out from under him and toward my own side. It was doing that annoying prickly tingling thing it does with the blood that was starting to come back but I ignored it, I ignored all of it as I tried desperately to remember how to breathe.

Why was he so handsome? I felt like I was dying inside. "Good morning, Luke," I said softly, slowly. I was cautious, unsure of what was going to happen now. Was he going to yell at me for being so close to him? Was he going to call me a freak because he had accidentally dry-humped me? I wasn't sure how any of this was going to work. How to be friends with a guy I had a crush on? This felt nearly impossible.

Instead of getting angry, he just stared at me for a minute. I figured if he was going to stare at me, it was okay if I stared back. His hair looked slightly brighter where he was half leaning, the sunlight from the blinds spilled through the room and caught against the back of his head. He looked like he was shining, and his cheeks had a soft crimson tint to them. His shirt was pulled slightly from how he was leaning and exposed some of his neck and his shoulder. I tried not to look at the small gathering of freckles that brushed so perfectly against his throat.

I was still trying to make my own little problem go away and found the more I stared at his freckles, the more I wanted to slide my tongue against them. I wished I could take a picture of him so I could draw him, just like this. I wondered if he'd be offended if I asked him. I figured it would be safer not to. "My alarm was going off for waking up for work, but I don't actually have work today." He said after a few minutes. I nodded as I wondered if he could feel it. The way my heart raced. My fingers scratched against the blanket gently, I picked at the soft material as we stared at each other. I tried desperately to stop myself from grabbing his shirt and pulling him back against me.

I knew what a kiss felt like. Isabella and I had actually kissed once before when we were with her family. Her cousin had alcohol and we passed it around as he tattooed us, and we were giggly and tipsy. She tasted like strawberries and neither of us liked it. We both ended up throwing up afterward as we giggled at each other, and it was all we needed to know that there would never be an us. It was like kissing my sister. But as I stared at Luke's lips, I wondered what it would feel like to kiss him. I'd never kissed a boy before, but as he parted his lips and subconsciously licked them I found myself moving ever so slightly closer, before pulling myself back.

Dangerous, I thought to myself. *This boy is going to be dangerous for me.* I had to be careful, otherwise, I could ruin everything. "Why did you set the alarm then?" I tried not to show how uncomfortable I was. He made no move to leave the bed, and I wasn't either. I tried to think about old women, mathematical equations, and things that smelled like trash. I started to count backward as I tried to get the pressure down. I wasn't really sure why he hadn't moved, why he was so comfortable laying there like that next to me, but I didn't question it. Maybe he was trying to make his problem go away too.

"I... " He started to say. I knew there were things he hadn't said yet, so many things. I hoped he realized I wasn't going anywhere, and no matter what he had to say, I'd always accept it. He was the other half of me, even if it was just a platonic friendship for him. "I must have forgotten," he stammered. His left eye twitched, and I wondered if that was a tell. It seemed like he didn't lie very well.

I chose to not call him out on it, knowing this wasn't the time or place. Not when I was trying so desperately to hold myself back from pushing him down and kissing him. "What now then?" I wondered.

It was a simple question, but it meant so much. Probably had different meanings for both of us, unfortunately. To me, it meant what now for us? What happened next? But for him, I was sure it only meant what do you want to do now? Or at least that's what I thought it would mean to him until fear flashed through his eyes. "I don't want to go home." He blurted out. He was the color of coral now, a beautiful color that I wanted to see more of. I quite liked seeing the way he blushed. "I mean, um. You don't have to keep me company all day if you don't want to. I can leave."

It was dangerous, but I lifted my fingers and gently touched his chin for a second before I let them fall back down onto the bed. A strange move, my hand moved on its own, but what surprised me the most was the shudder that ran through him as my fingers slid against his chin. It was slightly prickly, the beginnings of a beard he probably shaved every morning or so. I was trying not to think of how much I wanted to touch it again.

"You don't have to go, it's okay. I'll be here all alone anyway." I sat up slowly and turned to sit on my butt. My knees were lifted under the blanket now, and I pressed my arms against my knees as I took a deep breath and tried to ignore the slight throb in my ribs.

He got out of bed, and I wished he hadn't. His shirt was lifted and showed off his lower back, the hint of dark green boxers peeked out of his sweatpants, and I cursed under my breath once more as I had to look away. "Are you hurting? Do you need any water to take pills?" He asked. I hadn't even replied to him before he was out the bedroom door, wandering my large lonely house as if he owned it himself.

I wasn't sure why I liked the idea of that. I stood up as he was gone and nearly raced into the bathroom to lock the door behind me. I tried to cool myself down and think other thoughts as I washed my face, brushed my teeth, and used the toilet. I ran a brush through my hair, something I normally didn't care to do when I wasn't going anywhere. My feet were cold against the tile and I tried to channel the cold to stay, to keep me calmed down, so I didn't have to worry about any problems again. I walked out of the bathroom and saw Luke digging through his bag with a frown on his face. There was a water bottle placed next to my pills, waiting for me.

"Thank you. What are you looking for?" I wondered as I opened my bottles and took the pills I needed.

His eyebrows were pressed together in determination, and once more I wanted to take a picture, something to draw later on. Instead, I willed myself to memorize the images, to burn them into my retinas. I was fairly sure I wouldn't forget any of this for the rest of my life. He was like art. The way he moved, the curves of his body, the different colors of his eyes, and his voice was like music. I sat next to him on the ground as if I had been pulled to him like the earth revolved around the sun, I was unable to stop myself from gravitating toward him. "A toothbrush. I think I forgot it," he said with a sigh.

I stood up and brushed my hands on my knees as I tilted my head toward the bathroom. "I have extras, they haven't even been opened yet,"

He followed me and I showed him my toothbrush holder. It was one of the fancy machines that hung on the wall, the kind that held the toothbrush and sanitized it after each use. There was one there that had sparkly purple gel paint on the outside, something Isabella had done to show off which one was hers whenever she was able to pretend she was staying at another girl's house. There was a third slot with a toothbrush still in plastic that sat in it, along with a drawer full of unopened toothbrushes to replace the others when I needed to.

"Everything is so fancy here," he mumbled. I shrugged because I knew it was true. It wasn't anything I wanted though, not really. I couldn't care less if my toothbrush sat in a cup on top of the sink like most households. He brushed his teeth as I stood there and watched him. After he rinsed his mouth he put the toothbrush in the third slot, and I wondered what he thought as he stared at it. The act of keeping a toothbrush there, as simple and non-important as it was to some, what did it mean to him?

Luke turned to look at me and noticed I had been watching him, as that coral tint wrapped around his cheeks like a paintbrush slid against his skin. "Turn around," he nearly whispered. I faced the sink once more as he stepped behind me. I felt his fingers against my shirt, touching the hem, and I sucked in a deep breath as he lifted it. Our eyes met in the mirror as he lifted my shirt up to my shoulders and held it there until I lifted my hands to hold it in place. My fingers grazed against his ever so softly as he pulled his hands away, only to slide them against my skin.

He unwrapped my wrap, and my skin burned at every soft touch, every brush of his fingers against my skin. It was like a rough feather slid against me. The callused pads of his fingers scraped ever so slightly against my skin as he wet a rag and cleaned my stitches so carefully, drying them, and putting the cream on each one. He was so careful, so soft and gentle, and I couldn't help but watch his eyelashes dance against his cheeks while he worked on me. My skin throbbed everywhere he touched, and my eyes burned.

"Why is your home so empty?" He wondered softly as he grabbed a fresh wrap and started to slide it around my body. He was so close to me now, the heat of his body against mine, so familiar. It wasn't foreign like it was when the doctors touched me. It wasn't foreign like it was when my parents hugged me, patted my head, or touched my cheek as rare as those little touches were. Even Isabella had a slight foreign feel when she hugged me, the understanding that she was my friend, my sister. But this wasn't foreign, not to me. When he touched me, it felt like something had come together at last; it felt like home.

I realized what he asked wasn't about the useless gadgets or unnecessary decorations, but about the atmosphere of the house altogether. "Because it's a beautiful prison," I replied as I met his eyes in the mirror.

He pressed the tips of his fingers against mine and held them there as we stared at each other for a few seconds that felt like minutes before he finally lowered my shirt back down over my body. "Are you hungry? Can we go raid the kitchen for breakfast?" He wondered.

I felt the mood slowly fade away as he turned his back on me and padded out of the bathroom and towards the door. I nodded, even though he didn't look back at me. "Sure, let's go," I said with a forced smile. I stared at the back of him as he held onto my bedroom door frame and tried to calm myself as I looked at the defined muscles that poked through the back of his tight shirt. "I'm starving."

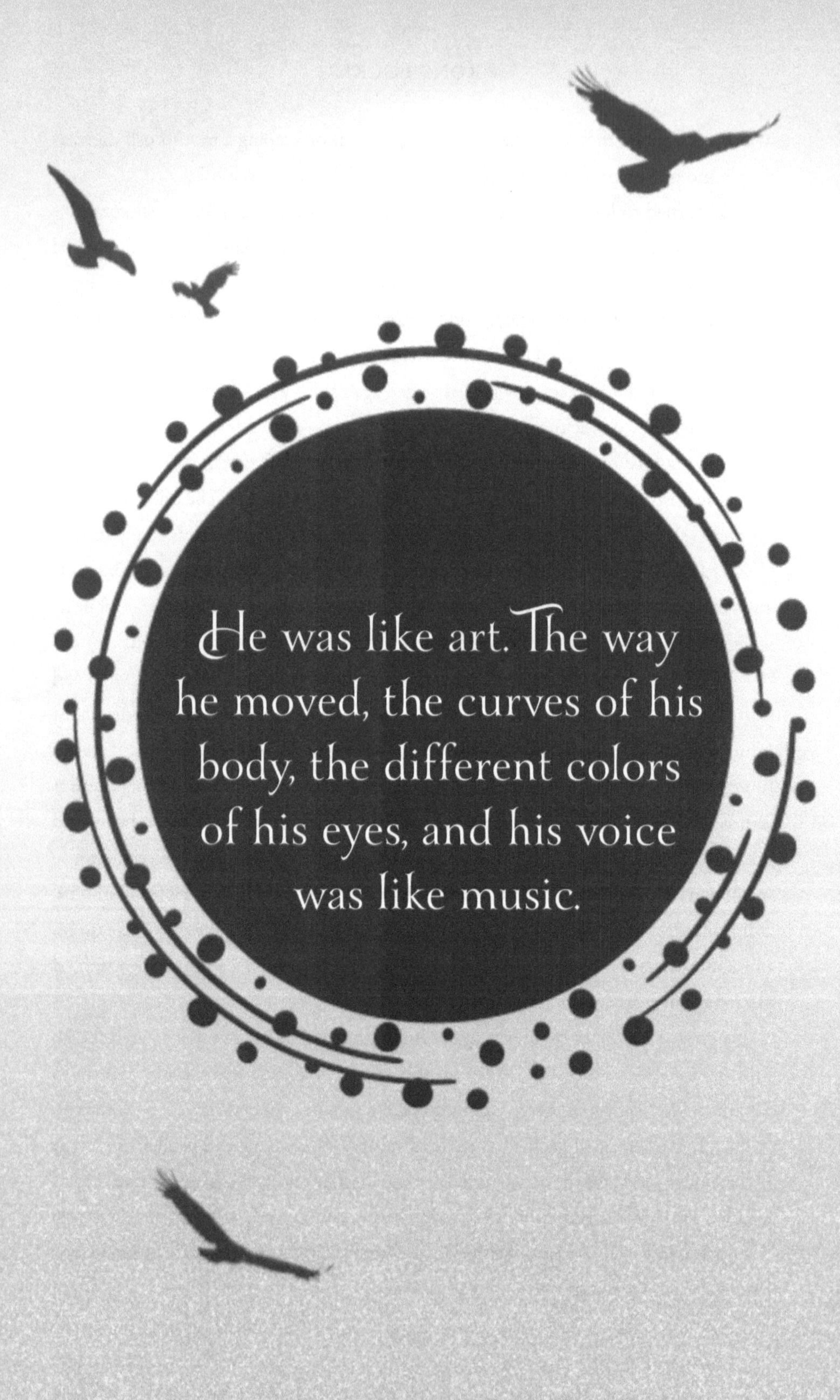

He was like art. The way
he moved, the curves of his
body, the different colors
of his eyes, and his voice
was like music.

Chapter 38
Luke

I tried not to think about how strange I felt, how strange all of it was. Inside, I desperately tried to hide my embarrassment. I knew what I was doing when I woke up, against his body. Somehow I had moved over to him in my sleep, and I was just glad I woke up before him. I felt disgusted with myself, my father's voice boomed over and over again in my head because I had touched Kinsley so easily. I had slept curled up against him, my head rested on his arm, my body pressed against him, and it had felt safe. Should it feel safe? Should I be fine that I felt safe with Kinsley?

I thought it was funny, the fact that he was smaller than me, but stronger all the same. I didn't want to leave this strange house, I didn't want to run away from these empty walls filled with gold and silver, the pristine dust-free sparkling prison that screamed nothing but cold. I didn't want to leave because I didn't want to be separated from Kinsley. I didn't want to go home and deal with my father who probably noticed my absence, his loud screams, and his slurs.

I didn't want to go home to my mother's vacant stares or changing mood. To try to figure out if she was herself, or if she was gone in her mind, or if something or anything I said or did would snap her into her gone place. It was exhausting. I didn't want to go home. I could have lied and told Kinsley I had work. My boss probably would have let me come in anyway if I showed up, but I didn't want to lie to Kinsley, and I didn't want to leave either.

I pulled out my phone as I walked down the halls, my bare feet sunk into the soft plush carpet. Kinsley had moved ahead of me, and I found it hard to stare at him for a long period of time after what happened in the bed. He probably found it weird, the way I had stayed there and stared at him, not getting up to move. Or the way I had nearly bolted out the door to get him water even though I didn't live here and I barely knew my way around. I was worried if I had moved before I could get my problem under control, he'd notice and then he'd be disgusted with me. A part of me figured even if Kinsley did notice what I had done in my sleep he wouldn't give me crap for it.

He was always so calm, so collected. Nothing seemed to bother him and he always seemed to take everything in stride. He wasn't straight, it's not like he'd punch me and call me names, but it would be so awkward especially since it wasn't intentional. All guys got morning wood at some point or another. I felt guilty for it all the same, because there was a very small, strange feeling inside me that tugged on me, and wanted me to pay attention. A small part that wanted me to admit to a feeling I'd never admit to, a feeling of something I'd never felt before. Something I desperately couldn't let exist. Push it down, I told myself. Push it all down and bury it away before Dad saw and accused me of something I'm not. Something I couldn't be.

'Hey, everything okay?' I texted. I slipped my phone into the pocket of my sweatpants as the shock of cold against the soles of my feet nearly made me gasp in surprise. I had blindly followed Kinsley and hadn't realized we were in the kitchen until I felt the cold of the linoleum floor underneath my bare feet. His house was ridiculous and unnecessary, but it wasn't my place to say that. Maybe it was because I was used to living in a fairly modern house with enough space, even if it wasn't overly plentiful. My mom had a small desk in the living room she used for putting together puzzles when she was herself. We had three bedrooms and two bathrooms, and it was enough. I had a feeling this house had an extra room for offices bigger than my bedroom. Heck, Kinsley's bathroom was bigger than my bedroom, I was fairly certain.

I followed Kinsley as he moved around a large island that was a dark blue color, swirls of gold woven into the surface of the counters as if someone had dipped a paintbrush of gold into the blue and slid it around and around. If there was anything about this house that I'd find beautiful, it would probably be these counters. Despite how intricate and overwhelming this house was, these were fairly simple and pretty. Kinsley opened one of two large fridges as I felt my phone vibrate in my pocket. I leaned against the counter as I pulled it out and looked down at it. *'Dad's pissed. You didn't open your bedroom door and he broke it down. You weren't there, so he destroyed your room. I'm cleaning it now, but you might want to come home at some point. Otherwise, you know he'll go to the garage and make a scene.'* Shawn texted.

I grimaced, and my upper lip twitched in frustration. I didn't want to ever go back, but I didn't want to leave Shawn there to deal with it all either. I slipped the phone back into my pocket as I noticed Kinsley watching me. His eyes were always so intense, so bright and I always found it hard to turn away from that stare.

The way he looked at me made me feel like he held me in his hands and turned the pages as if I was a book for him to read and discover with each turn of the page. I realized I was shaking, as he turned away. I wondered if he would turn the pages too fast, and read too quickly. If he wondered if this particular book was worth the effort of turning the next page. One of these days, I had a feeling I wouldn't be able to hold anything back anymore, and I was certain the moment he learned about who I really was, who my family was, he'd close the book for good. Leave me behind on a shelf to collect dust; forgotten and unconcerned.

I wondered if he was going to say or ask anything. There was so much I had hidden so far, so much in the letters that I danced around but never really spoke of. Instead, he surprised me with a soft smile as he turned around to look at me while he held a jug of milk. "I don't really know how to cook, but I can make cereal," Kinsley said. I shouldn't have been surprised, not really. He'd be patient, he wouldn't push me. He would wait for me to explain. I just wasn't sure if I'd ever be ready. Who was ever ready to explain a storm?

"Cereal is fine," I said with a small smile. There was something about his smile that made everything seem brighter. Maybe it was because of his light blond hair, or his cerulean eyes, maybe it was because of his dimples. Whatever it was, he reminded me of sunlight. It made me feel warm and safe around him. "You don't know how to cook?" I wondered as he led me to the largest pantry I had ever seen filled with all kinds of cereals. I noticed most weren't opened, only about two, and those were the two Kinsley held and compared. The only two he liked, maybe? Then what did the others eat? Did they even come home?

He shrugged, an embarrassed look on his face. "I know I should probably learn but I'm a disaster in the kitchen. The last time I tried to cook anything the water got burnt and somehow the kitchen towel ended up inside the burner, the alarm went off and the whole kitchen smelled like a burnt towel. Gloria said if I tried to touch the stove again she'd beat me with a spoon," he said with a chuckle.

There was a warm glow in his eyes as he nodded at one of the boxes, deciding it was the one he wanted, and put the other one back. The way he talked about this woman made her seem like a mother, but you don't normally call your mother by her first name.

"Who's Gloria?" I asked as I tried not to laugh at him. Burnt water? How on earth do you burn water?

Kinsley scratched the back of his head awkwardly with his left hand, his brace slightly poking out from under his long-sleeved black shirt he had on as I grabbed one of the unopened boxes. I figured if no one else was going to eat it, I might as well. "She's the cook. She has been the family cook for as long as I can remember, almost like a mom I guess," he veered off as he said that, and even through the silence I could hear the unspoken words. *'More than my real mother.'*

It was strange, how we were so different but so similar at the same time. "Gloria comes once a week for family dinners, and she comes during the week as well if my parents request her to or during parties. She likes to make a lot of food and stick it in the fridge for leftovers for me. She's really sweet," he said with a soft smile on his face.

I chewed on the inside of my lip as I looked at him and tried to push everything away. There was something soft about the look in his eyes, the sadness that wrapped around him so easily. The vulnerability made me instantly want to hug him. I wanted to protect him, to take care of him, and I wasn't sure why. He moved away from me out of the pantry and I followed at a distance and tried to shove my father's bloodshot eyes out of my mind as his spit sprayed against my face, that word I hated so much repeated like an echo over and over again until I felt like I was going to go crazy.

Kinsley stood on his tippy toes as he tried to reach the bowls and I couldn't help but smile. I put my box down on the counter and stood behind him. He stiffened as my chest pressed against his back and I put my free hand on the counter to hold my weight off of him while I grabbed the bowls with the other. I moved slowly, the tickle of his blond hair against my nose as I took a deep breath and breathed in his scent. There was something about his smell that calmed me, something about him altogether, and I wasn't really sure what was happening to me. He let out a soft shaky breath as I looked down at him, his eyes focused on the bowls as I watched him.

I looked away, startled. This was probably strange. This position, the fact that I was pressed up against his back, but why did it not feel strange? It was an automatic reaction. I saw him struggle and wanted to help him. Maybe I did too much. I handed him the bowls as I took a step back, I felt slightly embarrassed with the rollercoaster of emotions that moved around and around inside me. *Friends,* I told myself.

Friends were weird, friends were strange. I had to figure out what it meant to have friends. Was this even normal? I felt like I should just give up while I was still ahead. But as Kinsley turned around to look at me with a soft smile on his face and his shoulders back, I realized it was okay because it was him. It was always going to be okay. "Who takes care of you?" I wondered as I leaned against the counter.

He had moved away from me to the island with the bowls as he started to pour the different boxes of cereal into them. He was surprised by my question, I could see it, but he kept his eyes down as he poured. "I do,"

I didn't doubt that in the least, since it wasn't much different from me. "Well, maybe it was time someone else started taking care of you," I muttered, unsure where those words even came from.

He flinched, and some of the milk poured onto the island as I grabbed a paper towel from where it hung from a fancy holder under the cabinets. I moved closer to him as he moved away, like a cat and a mouse we chased each other over and over again. He grabbed spoons out of a drawer as I cleaned the spill, and at first, I wasn't sure if he was going to reply to what I had said. As he handed me my spoon, however, he did. "Do you have any suggestions on who?" He wondered with a soft laugh.

The spoon lingered in between us in the air, and I wondered about the silence once more. How thick it was, how unknown, and I realized something. For the first time, the silence didn't bother me, with him.

Yeah, I wanted to say, the words thick on the end of my tongue as I simply shrugged. He grinned as I grabbed the spoon from him, and seemed to take my shrug as the answer as he grabbed his bowl and moved out of the kitchen. *How about me?* Almost the second I thought it, the words faded away to be pushed back far, very far into my mind buried with the feeling I wasn't quite sure I understood.

Instead, I changed the subject as I followed him. It seemed like every conversation was filled with something that caused me to become confused. "You're allowed to eat in your room? This place is meticulous, I'd be scared of ruining the carpet or something."

He looked back at me as he laughed, and I couldn't help but notice the way his nose scrunched, or how his dimples sunk into his cheeks as his full lips curved into a smile. "I don't really give a shit, to be honest," he admitted. I barked out a laugh as an embarrassed blush fluttered over my cheeks because, for someone who looked so angelic, he was certainly the opposite most of the time. "Do you want to go eat outside? It's pretty at the gazebo,"

I nodded, and as I followed him outside I was amazed by what was out there. A basketball court was fairly close to the back door, along with a large swimming pool. There was a long curved slide that brought out the child in me and made me want to tear off my clothes and slide down it. The backyard looked like something out of a magazine. The different flowers, the stone pathway, and the patio furniture that was perfectly placed. "Is this why you're in shape?" I wondered as I followed him down the stone path to the gazebo.

It was beautiful, wrapped in vines and flowers. There was a swing on one side inside the gazebo and a long bench on the other. As we sat down on opposite sides of the bench and turned to look at the backyard I noticed that it was a fairly pretty view, as well. It wasn't too windy, wasn't too hot or too cold, it was perfect. The air was slightly thick with the hint of oncoming rain, peaceful.

The smell of flowers was strong in the gazebo but it wasn't too strong. The roses were stronger than the others, but I could smell the lilies as the wind slowly moved around my forehead, my curls tickled my face as I absently ran my fingers through them. "I don't join sports at school because of Roan, but I will play basketball. I'll swim, and there's a gym next to my room too," he said with a shrug.

I wanted to ask him so many things but wasn't sure if that was okay. Maybe it would be better to learn them slowly, instead of trying to understand everything at once. Maybe if we figured everything out right away we'd get bored, and while I didn't think I'd ever get bored of him, I had a feeling he'd get bored of me. He was stronger than me, mentally. I had a feeling he had handled the slight break between our letters better than I had. At least he had been able to go to school, I stayed home the whole week too scared to look at him. We finished our cereal quietly, the silence was there but it didn't bother me.

I realized that while I was scared of the silence at home, it wasn't the same there. The loudness at home was like a boom of thunder, while the silence was silent and deadly, like a strike of lightning. A storm raged around and around inside me, but here, it was different. There wasn't a storm here, not with Kinsley. I found peace in his silence.

"You can talk to me about anything, you know. I said it before, I'm not going to judge you, and I'm not going to leave." Kinsley said as he stood up and stretched.

His cheeks held a scarlet shade as he looked away from me, his hands lowering down his body with a slight wince that told me he was probably due for more medicine soon if he had started to feel the pain. I stood, my hands sliding down my butt as I straightened my pants. He turned his back on me for a moment as he looked out at the swimming pool. I studied him, unable to really stop myself.

Both of us wore long sleeves, and I wondered if his skin held secrets like mine did. If his skin was scattered in lines like a map that led to nowhere, the same as mine. Just some broken lines on a broken boy. No, his secrets were different from mine, but the same at the same time. How two people who were so different could be so much alike was scary.

"You don't have to hide anything from me," Kinsley said after a few minutes of silence as he turned to look at me once more. "Not from me." He added as if he needed to repeat it to make sure I heard him. Of course, I heard him, I was always going to hear him.

"It's strange. Hearing you speak out loud the words you wrote on paper. To hear the words that are embedded in my mind come alive with this mouth, with this voice. It's surreal," I said softly as I ran the pad of my thumb over his bottom lip. I hadn't even realized I had moved, or that I was touching him. I jerked my hand away, and mentally cursed myself. A blush slid across my cheeks, I burned in embarrassment as my eyes widened. "Sorry, I don't..."

"It's okay," Kinsley interrupted, that pretty smile danced over his lips once more. "I understand." He shrugged nonchalantly. Kinsley turned around and busied himself with the flowers that hung near his face, and all I could do was stare at him.

I was glad he understood because I had no idea what was going on anymore. "It's going to rain," I said, unable to think of anything else to say. It was hard to breathe. My fingers tingled, and my chest felt like it was filled with so many birds that fluttered around inside me that I was vaguely worried I'd end up throwing up feathers all over the floor of the gazebo.

Kinsley looked up at the sky with a chuckle and cleared his throat as he turned to look at me. "I love the rain," he replied, his eyes dancing with happiness.

I love- "I love it too," it was a whisper, my cheeks burned as I looked down at the ground, unsure where my thoughts were even going anymore. *The letters,* I told myself. I was still confused by the letters. The more time I spent with him, the more it would be obvious he was a boy, and the confusion would fade away. At least that was what I tried to tell myself, after all. "Why do you love the rain?"

Kinsley sat down on the rail, his head resting against the post as he looked up at the sky. I moved to stand next to his feet, my hands pressed down on the rail as a soft droplet of rain fell on my skin. I stared at it, and watched it fall slowly as another followed. "Because it's pretty, it's calming. It looks like the sky is crying and painting all at the same time," he replied. He looked at me, then away once more. "Why do you love it?"

But I couldn't answer him, and I was glad he didn't push me. Because I found that the reason I loved the rain so much was the fact that I could stand in it, and no one would be able to tell that I was crying.

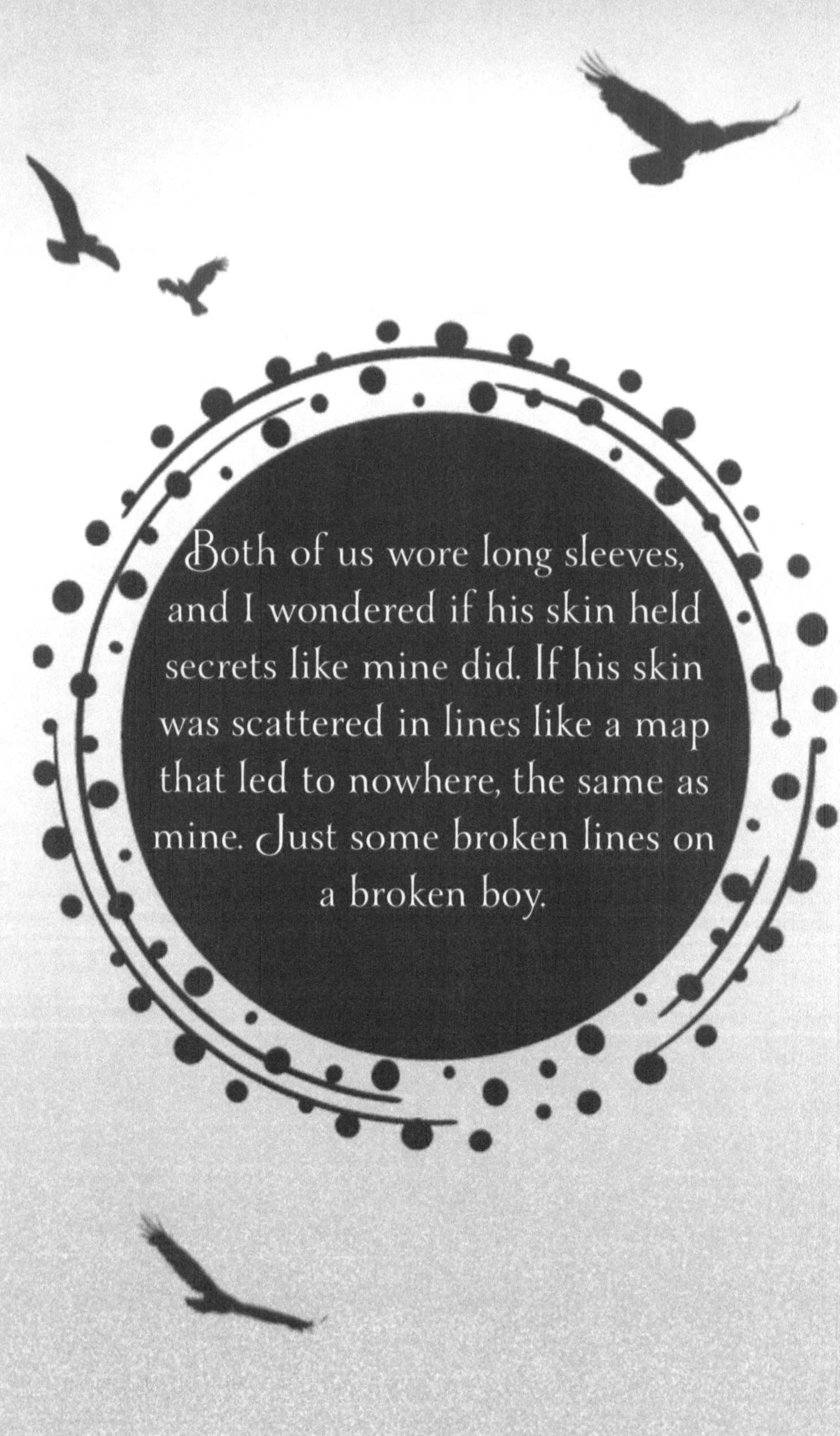
Both of us wore long sleeves, and I wondered if his skin held secrets like mine did. If his skin was scattered in lines like a map that led to nowhere, the same as mine. Just some broken lines on a broken boy.

Chapter 39
Kinsley

I breathed out softly, a slightly pained whine came from my mouth as I squeezed my eyes shut and tried to block out the pain. "I don't think this is a good idea, Kinsley," Luke's voice was deep against my ear, his breath tickled my neck as I let out a ragged breath.

Despite his words, he didn't stop. His hands slid against my back as he backed away slightly and pushed against my back. I was surprised by how gentle he could be, for someone who had rough calluses on his fingertips. I tried to ignore the way his touch made me shiver, to hold in the shaking that tried to come out and prayed he wouldn't look at my neck and notice how he gave me goosebumps. "Push harder," I demanded as he clicked his tongue against the roof of his mouth.

I let out a soft gasp of surprise as I felt pain spread through my chest. Almost instantly Luke stopped pushing and I fell backward against him. I whined in pain as he sighed, his hands gripped my shoulders tightly as he made sure I sat upright. He had his legs spread behind me, and I sat in between them, my own legs straight out in front of me as Luke attempted to help me stretch. I could still feel the distant throb of pain in my ribs, the tiny throbs in my back from where he pushed too hard against my cuts. I was aggravated as I turned around, my legs criss-cross as I stared at him.

"I told you this was a bad idea. You have to stretch slowly, small stretches as it heals. To try to touch your toes is too much for your ribs." He chuckled. I tried my hardest to keep the pout on my face. How dare he look that beautiful when he laughed at me, I was trying to be mad at him, rude. Luke's knees lifted into a bent position around me, one hand leaned behind him to support him against the carpet as the other was tangled into his dark brown curls.

The slight sweaty shine was from when he discovered the home gym a few days ago, and when he refused to let me work out with him earlier I tried to force him to at least let me do stretches. Not that it seemed to work out very well.

"I thought it would be okay," I breathed out as I tried to catch my breath again while the pain slowly faded away. I was tired of being broken. "I've never had broken ribs before."

He sighed, both of his hands now behind him as he leaned back slightly. I tried so hard not to look at the strip of hard sweaty abs that peeked out from his shirt lifted up. How he could work out with a long-sleeved shirt on was beyond me. I had on a long-sleeved shirt as well, but I hadn't really been working out and I had no choice but to keep it on.

It was funny, the fact that I always tried to hide my tattoo, but my parents never tried to come into my room to see me. They never even noticed Luke was here the past week. Of course Luke had left to go to work nearly every day as well, I took him to work and picked him up when he asked if he could stay just one more night, and one more, and one more. He made sure to put a pillow in between us this time, however, so I knew he was embarrassed about what he had done to me by accident that first night.

"I have," Luke said. His voice was distant, his eyes veered to the side as he stared at my bed frame. He had this unreadable expression on his face, closed off, but I could see the small shake of his lower lip, the smallest hint that I should venture slowly. I had started to figure him out, over the past few days he'd stayed here. My parents came and went, and for the most part they never really checked on me.

Kennedy came home once, but for the most part, she seemed to stay at her friend's house this week. Luke didn't tell me much, just that he had gotten a phone call from his little brother that his father left for a business trip, and he decided to just keep staying here. I was pretty sure he was only staying because he was worried about me being alone. He didn't say it, mostly he just griped about how awful I was at bandaging myself, but I was pretty sure it was just him being worried. There wasn't any other reason I could think of that he'd want to stay for this long.

I didn't ask him why his mother was just okay with that, or his father for that matter, because I didn't want to intrude. I could feel it, the secret he had buried deep inside him, and I was scared if I stood there and poked at it, he would never tell me. Eventually, he'd trust me. Eventually, he'd let me protect him. For now, all I could do was wait.

"Football?" I wondered. I started to realize that it probably wasn't from football. An assumption, not one I'd ask without knowing for sure, not one I'd ask period. He'd tell me when he was ready. I had to have faith that he'd tell me eventually. In the meantime, I tried to think of ways to help, to be ready if or when he needed me.

"Yeah... from football." He said quietly. The little twitch of his left eye again, the tell that he had lied. I nodded as if I believed him, because until he told me otherwise this was his truth and it was the only one I was going to absolutely believe. I didn't do rumors or assumptions, I simply listened to him and what he said, when he was ready to say it. The way he looked at me was always the same. There was something about the way we worked together. It was like we had always been this comfortable. There wasn't anything strange with us, no awkward trying to explain anything, we just seemed to know.

If only I was a girl, I told myself wistfully. Then maybe this would be so much more than it was now. I shook my head as I let out a soft sigh. It didn't matter about if only, or what-ifs. This was the way it was meant to be and I tried to accept that. We stared at each other for a few silent minutes and it wasn't strange, it wasn't awkward, it was simply just us. Sometimes when he stared at me it was like I could feel him trying to ask me a question.

Are you okay? Is this okay? Maybe there were deeper questions there. I'd like to believe there were because my questions were always deeper. I looked back at him and silently stared as I asked my own questions. *Are we okay? Will you ever leave? I don't want you to leave.*

He sat up, and I thought he'd scoot away from me now but instead, he scooted closer. The inside of his legs nearly touched my knees as he pressed his hands against the carpet in front of me. This close to him and I could see it again, the golden specks that shone in his iridescent eyes. I loved staring into his eyes, and I was glad he never seemed to have a problem with being close to me.

Maybe others would find it strange, the way we sat, the close proximity as we stared each other in the eyes and asked our own silent questions. I found it peaceful, I found it to be right, to feel like home. He had a look in his eyes that pulled at me and I leaned slightly closer to him. Entranced by the tension, the close proximity, and the feel of his fingertips as they gently slid down my arm and wrapped around my right wrist. Despite the cloth that was in between his fingers and my wrist, I felt every touch and the trail of fire that it left in its wake.

I let out a shaky breath. Both of us heard the sounds of doors open and closed but we ignored them. Luke had figured out by the past almost week of experience that whoever it was, most likely wouldn't remember I existed.

If this was anyone else, a guy who wasn't straight, or a female that made it obvious she was attracted to me, I might have thought maybe this was the moment my life was going to change. I would have let myself have hope. But this was Luke; and while he looked at me in the way I wanted him to look at me forever, touched me in a way I wanted him to touch me forever; I knew this wasn't ever going to be our moment. I knew we'd never have a moment, because Luke was straight. I accepted that. No matter how touchy and clingy he was, and no matter how hard it hurt.

Because he was Luke. I loved him just the way he was, even if the him that he was, wasn't in love with me.

"About that," he started to say. His teeth found his lower lip and chewed on it nervously as a coral smear splattered across his cheeks. His head lowered to look down at me, even if his eyes were trained on the carpet near his foot. His curls hung in his eyes and I was torn between wanting to brush them aside and wanting to pull his lip out of his teeth and tell him to just spit it out already.

About that, he had said. Not about us, never us. I knew that despite the time that had passed, he still thought about his ribs. I wondered if he ever really thought about us at all, but then again, why would he? There was never going to be an us. I needed to stop thinking about what would never be. To move past it, and focus on being his friend, his best friend. Maybe then he'd trust me with what he had been hiding. "I-" He started to say, as the doorknob turned.

We didn't have much warning, but we were fast, and for some reason once again we worked in sync without needing to say a word. His hands wrapped around my ankles as I bent my legs, my arms lifted under my head as I laid back. We pretended we hadn't been sitting here staring at each other, but instead doing exercises. My ribs burned from the sit-up and I clenched my teeth to hide the pain as I turned to the side and looked at my father's shocked expression.

It was weird to see him, it made me realize I hadn't seen him in a while, honestly. The occasional glances when I was downstairs and he ran in and out of the house. The last time I really heard his voice was the day he took me home from the hospital. "What are you doing? Who is he?" He asked, his eyes narrowed as he stared at us.

Honestly, I wasn't sure which question he really wanted the answer to. I was trying to think of something sarcastic. Maybe I could call Luke the president of the United States or tell him we were obviously skydiving when Luke beat me to it. He stood up, his hands leaving my ankles as he walked over to my dad. I could tell by the way Dad looked him up and down, taking in Luke's tall frame, muscular body, and the sweat that was still slightly evident on his skin. It was a good thing Luke had messed around in the gym earlier. It helped make it look like we were actually exercising in here.

Luke held out his hand, and my dad looked at him with a tight nod, his face scrunching in a way that showed he knew the person in front of him was someone he needed to get to know more. Sizing up the competition, Mom would say, even though Dad was too old to play anymore, even if he could. "My name is Luke Wilson, sir. Kinsley is my friend," he said. He turned to look at me then as I pretended that trying to sit up wasn't killing me. A smile fluttered over his lips as he looked at Dad again. "My best friend."

I don't know why, but for some reason, that about killed me and made me happy all at the same time. "You play a sport?" Dad asked.

I rolled my eyes as I stood up and moved toward them. I could smell it now, and it reminded me of what today was. I should have remembered it was Sunday. I should have told Luke no when he asked if he could stay the night once more. His dad was coming back tomorrow, he said. He told me he probably wouldn't be able to stay over tomorrow, and while some might be glad he would finally leave after staying with me for almost a week, I wasn't. I wanted him to stay longer. There was still one more week left, the official spring break, and I wanted him to never leave. It had been nice not having to be alone. "He's the captain of the football team," I said, knowing it would both bug and impress my dad.

He frowned as he seemed to need to eye him up once more. As if he needed to make sure the person who was in his old position was good enough to claim the title. "I'm glad you have gotten yourself a better friend, Kinsley." I opened my mouth, ready to tell him off for talking bad about Isabella, but before I could, he smacked Luke on the back and pulled him out the door, leaving me to follow after. "Join us for dinner, Luke. We have family dinners every Sunday. It's a tradition." I wanted to ask him about the many Sunday nights that was absent as they pretty much abandoned me to go to Italy or when work was just more important, but I kept quiet.

I wasn't really surprised everyone loved him at dinner. Kennedy drooled at him, even though she was apparently planning her and her boyfriend's wedding with Mom. Mom was excited to see someone new while my dad pretty much talked over everyone and asked Luke all of these questions about football and games, numbers, and scores that meant nothing to me. "So how did you two become friends?" Mom asked once Dad finally shut up and started to eat his spaghetti.

I sighed as I twirled the spaghetti and stuck as much in my mouth as I could. I chewed loudly as my mom cringed and Luke tried to stifle a laugh. "We were partners in psychology class," Luke said after a minute.

I mean, it wasn't the way we met whatsoever, but it wasn't really a lie either. We were partners for like five minutes. Kennedy started to talk about her boyfriend, how he was apparently some amazing football player despite being like ten, or however old you are when you're in seventh grade. It was a useless conversation, but it was enough to make my father remember the very thing I desperately wanted my family to forget. "Kinsley, what about that girl?" Dad asked. I groaned as Luke lifted his head in wonder and slurped some spaghetti into his mouth. "Did you ask her out? Did she say yes?"

Luke coughed as he looked down at his plate. He reached out to grab his glass of water, missed it, and tried again to grab it. I wanted to study this look, to ask him what he was thinking about to make it, but I knew that would make it pretty obvious to everyone staring at me that I was in love with him. I desperately wanted to just like him as a friend and not be in love with him, but it seemed like the world loved nothing more than to torture me. "She said no," I mumbled.

I stabbed my fork into my spaghetti, slightly annoyed as Luke flinched beside me. If I wasn't annoyed, I'd have laughed at him because in a way I had just called him a girl. "I'm not surprised," Kennedy said. I looked at her as she stuck her tongue out at me. It was coated in a scarlet carpet of sauce and a little piece of noodle that made me cringe in disgust.

If that had been me, I probably would have been getting yelled at right now, but everyone ignored her as Dad banged his large hand on the table, and a frustrated sound spilled from his lips. "We're Bryants! We don't get told no!" He said, with the largest freaking ego I had ever heard. Was he suggesting I shouldn't have been turned down simply because I was made from his sperm? If anything, that should have given anyone a reason to turn me down. I would have turned myself down, for that matter.

I shook my head as I tried to ignore how ignorant that sounded. "Oops, guess she didn't get the memo. I'll make sure to write Bryant on a label and tape it to my hoodie next time," I said as I nodded seriously at him.

Luke banged his knee into mine slightly, probably to tell me I was being rude or to stop because he was trying not to laugh. Either way, both were probably true. Dad glared at me, his face flaming red, the anger in his eyes almost as obvious as the vein in his forehead that throbbed steadily. "It's because you're on drugs," he spat out in frustration.

I sighed loudly as I rolled my eyes without care. "I'm not on drugs, Dad. You check my pee constantly." I was slightly embarrassed by the fact that Luke was right there, listening to this. Embarrassed that he had to meet any of my family, and I was worried he was going to leave and never want to talk to me again.

I was frustrated that this was my family, these people that were nothing like me. "Maybe I should start watching to make sure it's actually your pee," he growled. I clenched my hand tightly around my fork as Luke's fingers brushed against my knee, almost like he was trying to help me calm down. Either that or he wanted to comfort me, one of the two. Dad turned to look at Luke, fuming. "Are you supplying him with pee?"

It took me a minute to figure out what that even meant, but Luke seemed to understand as he started to sputter, his eyes wide as his fingers left my knee. I found myself unhappy with the coldness his touch left behind. "You want to watch me pee now? Be my guest," I said, wishing this evening was over already. "Sounds kind of gay to me," I added quietly.

Apparently, it wasn't as quiet as I thought it was. "No one is gay in this house!" Dad screamed as he banged his hand on the table once more. He was angry, my mom looked horrified, and Kennedy gagged in disgust. It kind of made me want to go hug them all and then whisper in their ear that I wasn't straight to see if they acted like I had cooties and was going to infect them with the non-straightness. "That's a sin! Disgusting!"

He was busy fuming as my mother did the sign of the cross and I considered giving them a lecture that he shouldn't just assume gay was the only option. I wondered if I should ask him if no one was gay, were we allowed to be something else? There were quite a few other letters in the LGBTQ+. He needed to learn how to specify his homophobia.

"It's okay, darling, calm down," my mom said as she patted my dad's arm. He looked at her with adoration, his eyes shining as he nodded at her. She chuckled as she lifted up the noodle in front of her with her perfectly manicured nails and pinched the noodle like it was a worm. "Besides, everyone in here is as straight as this noodle," she said with a laugh. She held the end of it as it lay straight in front of her.

I wanted to groan at how stupid that was but looked down at my plate and smiled. I leaned closer to Luke and pointed at my noodle that was in a spiraled circle. "I think mine got wet," I whispered as I pointed at the circle. "Doesn't look very straight to me."

Dad was busy laughing loudly at Mom's stupid comment and Luke's eyes went wide in surprise. He turned a strange shade of red and started to cough, his eyes tearing up as I proceeded to smack him gently on the back. Choked laughs spilled from his lips as his face grew even redder, I couldn't help but let out a soft laugh as I handed him his water.

I guess it hadn't been so bad after all, dealing with my parents because I had him by my side. As long as he was okay, as long as he was my friend, it was enough. It had to be enough because it was all I was ever going to have. Right?

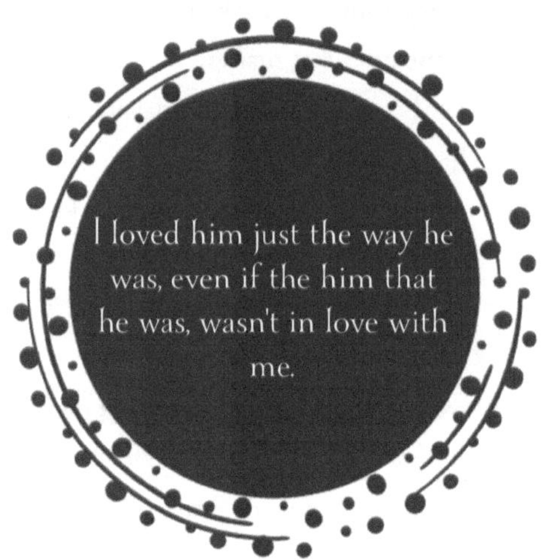

Acknowledgements

Wrong Locker is a book that started off being a small little bud of an idea that grew every step of the way like the unfurling of a flower, uncontrollable and inevitable. What was meant to be one book turned into two, and I promise there are more than two to come for this series. The Wrong series is near and dear to my heart because it tackles problems that are very real and very out there right now for teenagers to deal with. You never know who the quiet hidden kid under the hoodie with the headphones in their ears really are, or what the jock with the easy-going smile on their face really thinks. It's easy to walk past them and to keep going, but underneath the surface, everyone has layers, if only you take the time to stop and find each and every one. This series' characters all have a very big part of my childhood, pieces of myself and my past are in each and every character, and in a way I allowed it to help the characters grow into the amazing characters they are.

I couldn't have done anything without the support of the readers who backed me every step of the way. To the ones who followed me on Patreon and Ream, I want to thank you all immensely for your continuing generosity and support. I'm able to write because of you, and I'm honored you chose to follow me. I want to thank all of my closest friends, the ones who took the time to help me go through the book and edit it, pointed out my mistakes, and helped me get where I am now. Desiree Lynn, Amanda Lilly, Nicole S., and Arielle Lavecchia.

I want to point out two people that had pushed me from day one, standing in my corner. My eldest sister Ashley Douglas, who even when I was a little girl she'd religiously read all of my chapters and all of my ideas even when they probably weren't very good. She encouraged me to keep going, and even now ten plus years later she hasn't grown tired of me shoving more and more at her in search of her unwavering encouragement. I also want to talk about my husband, who I had stood there so shyly as I showed him my very first book and my very first chapter and he looked at me like he was staring at the sun as he told me how amazing I was.

Thank you again for all of my amazing readers, and I hope you stick around because this is just the first of many.

About The Author

Mallory Grant is a mother, a wife, and a cat mom. Born in Ohio, she's lived in North Carolina most of her life until recently she moved to Oklahoma and has been living there for three years now. Mallory used to hide beside her nightlight after lights out with a book in between her hands and an imagination filled to the brim with stories. She grew up knowing from a young age that all she'd ever wanted to be is an author and to share her imagination with the rest of the world.

Other Books By Author

THE CHAINED SERIES
Chained To Fate

THE WRONG SERIES
Wrong Locker

9 798330 288649